BEAUTIFUL
BROKEN PROMISES

ALSO BY KIMBERLY LAUREN

Beautiful Broken Rules
Beautiful Broken Mess

BEAUTIFUL
BROKEN PROMISES

KIMBERLY LAUREN

Montlake
Romance

Text copyright © 2014 Kimberly Lauren

Published by Montlake Romance, Seattle

www.apub.com

Amazon, the Amazon logo, and Montlake are trademarks of Amazon.com, Inc., or its affiliates.

ISBN-13: 9781477828465

ISBN-10: 147782846X

Cover design by Mumtaz Mustafa

Library of Congress Control Number: 2014957336

Printed in the United States of America

To my mom, who is my best friend for life.

Okay, this is where you stop reading, Mom.

- Prologue -

We make promises to the people we love because we want them to feel our loyalty, or maybe it's a way to hold ourselves responsible. We want them to know how much they mean to us; and, even if it seems impossible, we make these sometimes preposterous vows because maybe . . . just maybe . . . we actually believe it's possible to keep them.

When I promised that I would always love you no matter what, and that I would always protect you, I had no intention of breaking those promises. I could never fathom a time in my life when I wouldn't love you. The moment I first laid eyes on you, my soul knew you and smiled as if he had been waiting for you all this time.

And God, had I been waiting. You were the most beautiful person I had ever seen. In that moment, I knew without a shadow of a doubt that I would lay my life down for yours if needed, and that you would always come first. I couldn't see any other possibility. How could life go on if there were no you?

You made me the luckiest man in the world . . . that is, until you were ripped from my hands so brutally. My ability to keep those promises I had sworn by was taken from me, and I was never even able to tell you I was sorry. I never meant for it to be this way. I never wanted to break my promises. *They* forced me to.

And sadly, life does go on without you. It's as if I'm drowning, and every time I'm about to finally fade into the blackness, I'm pulled back up to the shore so I can be reminded of all the happy faces around me, only to be submerged into oblivion again. Sometimes I think it would be easier to just let myself go. Let the depression win out. But then I think of you and your beautiful face. How I hope so damn much that you are out there, just waiting for me to find you. Waiting for me to make those promises again, and keep them.

So, I don't give up and I won't let them win. I *will* find you and I *will* make sure that you know you're my everything . . .

- ONE -

LANE -

Our heavy breathing was loud in the quiet of the sleeping house. Her fingers continued to tug and pull at my shirt until she had it fully removed from my waistband. As soon as it was possible, she frantically slipped my shirt buttons from their holes and, in her frenzy, shoved the shirt from my shoulders, letting it flutter leisurely to the stairs. All I could feel were wild, desperate hands and our hot mouths colliding.

My liquor-filled brain didn't function quite as fast as hers did, but I managed to pin her to the wall with one of my legs on a higher stair, stopping her from moving any closer to the top. From what I could tell through my double vision, she *was* pretty. Long, blond hair. Nice rack. Tight skirt that was about to be on the floor. Shit, that worked for me.

I returned to the arduous task of unbuttoning her shirt. My fumbling fingers weren't cooperating, though, so her blouse ended up being a ripped mess, causing buttons to fly every which way. My mouth had instant access to her bare chest. No bra. But let's be honest: That was one of the reasons she was here right now. Everyone in that bar knew she hadn't been wearing much under her barely-there clothes.

"Ethan . . ." she gasped, as my lips touched her breasts. I suppressed a chuckle as best as I could, because I had forgotten she thought that was my name. Ethan and I were being jackasses and decided to trade for the hell of it. Shit, maybe some girl was calling out my name at Ethan's place tonight.

When my fingers slid up the inside of her thigh, she moaned forcefully. My hand instantly clamped down over her lips to stop the loud noise erupting from between them.

"Shh . . . we need to get to my room before you wake everyone up."

"Who else is here?" she asked, panting breathlessly. I ignored her question and pulled her the rest of the way up the stairs. Her hands continued to paw and bat at me as we staggered down the hall. She walked backward, clinging to my burning skin, until I finally found the right door.

She strutted around topless inside the room while checking out her surroundings and running her fingertips across the edge of the bedspread.

"Huh . . . it's kind of small. I thought with a house this size . . ."

"It's a guest room," I replied. I stalked toward her and attempted to remove my shoes and unbutton my pants in the same beat.

"Do you always take girls to your guest room? Show me your master, gorgeous," she tried to whisper seductively.

Towering over her, I placed my hands on her hips and moved her back onto the bed. My fingers grazed across her flat stomach, and I found the clasp that held her scrap of a skirt together. The fabric released and drifted down her fake-tanned legs, and she kicked it aside.

"I want to . . ." My hand was over her mouth before she could even finish that maddening request.

"You're talking way too damn much, baby girl." I flipped on my back and scooted until I met the headboard. With my pants unbuttoned, I extended my hands out on each side of me in a welcoming gesture. "This is where you get me. Your call."

She smirked and turned fully toward me. Her fingers pulled each of my socks off and tossed them to the floor. She grabbed the hem of my pants and worked them down my legs, and they quickly joined the socks on the hardwood. Her eyes were immediately fixated between my legs, and I knew what her decision would be. With a grin, I put my hands behind my head and rested against the headboard, watching as she crawled up my body.

"You're just going to lie back and let me do all the work?" she asked with a perfectly arched eyebrow.

"Sweetheart, you're the one that went home with a guy who drank half the bar." I could feel my lids beginning to droop, the alcohol swimming wildly through my veins. She shrugged her shoulder casually and bent forward.

Her hot mouth began to go to town and it felt fucking great. In my experience, only the girls who wore see-through clothes or skirts that barely covered their asses could do that kind of work with their mouths.

When I felt more than a hot mouth wrap around my dick, my eyes shot open and I looked up to find her smiling face above me. In a panic, I sat up ramrod straight and thankfully saw she had an empty condom wrapper in her hand. Close call.

What the hell just happened? Two seconds ago she was sucking me off and now she was riding me?

"You were enjoying that," she whispered into my ear.

"Yeah . . ." Although I was pretty sure I had just fallen asleep. Hey, point for me that I kept it up while I took a little nap. At least she didn't catch me.

"You feel so good," she called out excitedly. I didn't like the sound of her voice anymore. It was too loud . . . too nasal. Had it been like that at the bar? Surely Ethan would have told me if it was. Then again, he was probably more concerned with whether she was about to have a wardrobe malfunction—we all were. "Ethan!"

My hands grabbed hold of her ass and I moved her over onto her stomach, entering back in from behind. Much better.

As I pumped into her, I started questioning why guys felt the need to have sex all the time. It felt good, that was obvious. It was fun and it shook up an otherwise boring day. But in that moment, I wondered why I bothered with this girl. It would feel good and then she would go home. *Thank God.* There wouldn't be any lingering feelings for her, and no need to do it again. There would just be . . . nothing.

Shit, I needed to tell Ethan *No more whiskey*. It made me a fucking sap.

I heard her cry out into the pillow and I assumed she had reached her release, so I let myself finish as well. With one last shuddering pulse, I fell to the side and closed my eyes while catching my breath.

The feeling that always came after every time I finished began to creep up on me. I didn't know why I always seemed to forget how it felt—the feeling that I shouldn't have been with yet another random chick. The sex definitely hadn't been worth it, but when I saw a pretty face and whiskey joined the party, I couldn't seem to talk myself out of it.

My phone startled me with a resounding ring. With a foggy brain, I tried to decipher what the hell was going on. The blond chick was lightly snoring next to me. Seriously, whiskey was *not* allowed on my bar menu anymore—it fucked with my head. I thought that I needed something harder tonight, something to help the memories fade, but all it had done was make my brain muddled and confused. The beep of my phone reminded me that I had a message awaiting my attention.

"Hey, wake up," I tried to whisper nicely. She stirred and swatted away my hand that was trying to gently rouse her. "Sugar, it's time to go."

"Stop. I'm trying to sleep, Ethan," her voice grumbled.

I pulled the covers off her naked body and tapped her ass. "Nope, it's time to move it along. I have things to do."

She glared up at me from her pillow and slowly pushed up onto her elbow. "You have things to do at . . ." She grabbed her phone off the nightstand and checked the illuminated screen. "At three-thirty in the morning? No . . . Wake me when it's at least eight."

She searched for the covers again and I kicked them off the bed. I knew my phone was still in my pants, but I had to rack my brain to remember where those could be. Standing, I spotted them across the room, close to the bathroom door. I could see the alert light blinking through the dark fabric.

"Quit playing around!" she screeched.

Once my phone was in my hand, I noticed it was from Charlie and immediately put it up to my ear so I could hear his message. He rarely called in the middle of the night, and I shouldn't have fucking let it go to voice mail. I could hear my late-night visitor huffing and puffing behind me, but her concerns meant nothing to me in that moment.

Charlie's gruff voice whispered in my ear, causing my whole body to lock up with each word spoken. "Tijuana. Tonight at seven. I got you a spot. Meet up with Mateo. Call me back tomorrow."

I had been listening to Charlie's cryptic messages for the past four years, yet I was never prepared for them. I couldn't predict what kind of news he was going to deliver, and every day I felt as if I were waiting for the one that would knock me in the gut so hard

I would never recover. However, this one gave me hope because another day had gone by that he wasn't calling to tell me she was gone . . . forever.

When I knew I had a job to do, it got my blood pumping. The adrenaline shot through my veins, and I could already feel my feet bouncing. This time, however, insecurities began to float in and out of my head. I should have been training harder since moving to Texas. I should have been perfecting my right hook or strengthening my footwork.

But then I remembered that winning didn't matter. My presence *did*. If Charlie got me a spot tonight, that meant *he* would be there. And if *he* was there, then maybe it could lead me to *her*.

"What's your name again?" I pointed at the girl, who was trying hard to look sexy sprawled out naked on my bed. Any other night, I would have gone another round because obviously I was a glutton for punishment, but it was time I hit the road.

"You're joking, right?" she yelled, way too damn loud for three in the morning.

"Hush, will you? I don't need you waking everyone up," I hissed while throwing on my pants.

"Who the hell are these other people, Ethan?" Her voice was getting extremely loud. "Am I really just another notch on your headboard?" I shrugged my shoulders, because what the hell did she think? She went home with a drunken idiot in the middle of the night and I hadn't even *asked* her name. "*Fucking bastard!*" she screeched.

Almost immediately, I heard the loud wail of a baby blasting down the hallway. *Shit* . . . Her face froze and she gave me a glare that could melt all of Antarctica.

"Please, don't tell me you have a family," she growled.

"It's time to go, sweetheart . . ." I started to say when my door slammed open, the hinges barely containing the forceful blow. There stood a drowsy-eyed and extremely pissed-off Jace in my doorway. He was only wearing boxers, and his chest was heaving as if ready for a fight.

I fucked up. "Dude, I'm so—"

He quickly interrupted my apology. "Do you know how long Audrey and I spent getting Jocelyn down? No, of course you don't, because you don't give a fuck!"

"Of course I care; don't say that. How was I supposed to know she would start screaming like a damn five-year-old?" I pointed to the guilty party still sitting on my bed.

Jace glanced over as if he hadn't known there was someone else in the room. I knew the instant he realized she was lounging seductively in her birthday suit because he immediately looked away.

"Seriously! You have about ten seconds before Audrey comes down here and kicks your ass. Get dressed and get her out of here," he growled.

"I think I need to talk to Ethan in private," my obnoxious visitor addressed Jace, even though he wouldn't even look in her direction.

Jace threw his head back and laughed, "Oh, boy! You *have* been an asshole tonight. His name is Lane, by the way," he added, right before he stepped out into the hallway.

I heard her gasp of breath as she scurried off the bed and scooped up her skirt. In a huff, she pulled it up her legs and secured it around her waist.

"Look . . ." I paused, realizing I still didn't know the girl's name. *Shit!*

"Gemma. My name is Gemma and it seems that yours is Lane. I'm glad we finally introduced ourselves." She rolled her eyes in annoyance.

"Look, Gemma, it was a good time." I tried to backtrack. I'd been even more of an asshole than usual.

"You're a riot!" She laughed incredulously and searched for her shirt.

I cleared my throat and hesitantly said, "I think it's on the stairs." Where I had ripped it off of her. "Here, just take my shirt," I tried to say before she walked out the door, but she waved me off and strutted out of my room—topless. *Fucking great.*

"Oh, this must be some kind of joke, Lane Parker!" I heard Audrey shout from the hall. I rushed out and tried to block off a naked Gemma, but she just didn't seem to care who saw her. "You!" Audrey said to me while holding little Jocelyn. "You wake up the baby that we just spent two hours trying to get down, and now you have *her* strutting around naked in front of *my* husband. Jace, so help me God, if I see you even trying to look at her!"

Jace had his back completely facing Gemma now, and he held his hands up in surrender. I could tell Audrey was level-ten pissed off because she never yelled at either of us. Jace's eyes burned into me, threatening pain in the near future.

"Please, leave my house," she said to Gemma without even looking her in the eye.

Gemma descended the staircase and scooped up her shirt. She lazily pulled it over her shoulders and turned to face us. I cringed when I saw that her breasts were still exposed, since I had torn all of her buttons off in my haste.

"Hey, Jace," she called up to him, and instinctively he turned at his name. She licked her lips and winked at him with enough seduction to light the room on fire. Jace groaned in annoyance as she slipped out the front door.

"I'll kill you," Audrey whispered to me menacingly while still trying to bounce an uncomfortable and tired baby.

"I'm so damn sorry, Audrey. Seriously, I didn't mean for any of that to happen." I made my way toward her slowly, hoping that the baby in her arms would protect me from harm.

"I can't do it again tonight, Lane. I just can't. I'm too tired," she said as she started to cry. "I need you to put her back to sleep." She pushed Jocelyn toward me, and Jace jumped forward quickly to stop her.

"Don't! Don't touch her, not when you still have alcohol on your breath." He quickly scooped his daughter into his arms and held her close. With the baby quieting down, he turned to Audrey and swiped a thumb under her wet eyes. "Babe, it's okay. Please don't cry." I flinched as I watched him comfort and kiss her. I knew Audrey was still highly hormonal, but I never wanted to be the one responsible for making her cry. "I'll take her; you go back to bed and rest."

With a kiss, they parted ways. Jace bounced on his toes, trying to get Jocelyn back to sleep, and Audrey trudged down the hall toward their room. I stood there, feeling terrible for interrupting their somewhat peaceful night. Then my feet followed Audrey into the bedroom, hoping she wouldn't kick me out . . . or in the balls.

I heard her sniffles as she climbed into their king-size bed and threw the covers on top of herself.

"I'm coming in behind you, doll," I whispered.

"No, Lane," she replied harshly.

"Too late." I lay down on the bed close to the edge so I wasn't anywhere near Jace's side. That would have been like breaking some kind of man code, even though I was already crawling into *his* bed. I pulled her in close and kissed the back of her head. "I'm sorry; don't hate me." She groaned in frustration, but she didn't swat me away.

For years, Audrey had been the closest thing I had to . . . anything. To family. To friends. I had parents, but I'd pretty much pushed them away. Audrey had helped me wake up every day and continue living.

When I escaped to California four years ago, I was a man on a mission, bound and determined to find the girl I loved. I'd decided to go back to college, so I wasn't being a complete slacker. I'd already earned my bachelor's degree in criminal justice, the one I got immediately after high school, finishing it within three years. But when I moved to California, I switched things up and went for a second bachelor's in accounting. I realized that those two degrees were miles apart, but who says you can't change your mind?

I ran into Audrey in our college community center when she was looking for a roommate. Surprisingly, she was in the same program as I was, and I just happened to have a spare room. She was beyond damaged, and because I wasn't much better off, we were two peas in a pod.

Every day I told myself that I let her move in because she looked so wounded . . . that she needed my comfort. I told myself that I was doing a good deed by helping her. In the end, I realized she was actually helping me. I thought I was protecting her, but she was silently doing the same for me. Together, we took life a day at a time and protected each other from drowning.

Last year I turned twenty-eight, and we walked across the stage together with our master's degrees. I knew I had her to thank for helping me get there as well.

I knew everything about her. I knew that her biggest fear was being alone. I knew that her hair got outrageously frizzy with even a small amount of humidity. I knew that her friends were everything to her because the family she left behind all those years ago meant nothing to her—at least she tried to make me think they meant nothing. I knew that she loved to sneak peanut butter in the middle of the night and that she had to keep two cups of water by her bedside because she always woke up thirsty. And I *knew* she was in love with Jace Riley the very first time she spoke about him, even if it was to tell me how much she hated him.

I could only hope that the next time I fell in love I would know the girl half as well as I knew Audrey. She was my sister, maybe not by blood, but in every way it counted. She was my best friend, and I knew I wouldn't be able to sleep until I'd made amends with her, no matter how small the divide was between us.

Audrey knew me better than anyone, but she didn't know everything. I'd kept some of my biggest secrets from her, and if she were to ever find out, it would kill her. I understood her heart, though. If she knew all of my secrets, she wouldn't rest until everything was resolved. And that was not her job—it wasn't her burden to take on. It was mine. *I* had made those promises, and I was doing everything in my power to make things right.

"Doll, you have to know how sorry I am. I realize how tired you've been lately with a newborn. I'm sorry a thousand times over. Good news is, I'll be out of your hair soon. My landlord said that the house should be done any day now, and I need to head out of town tonight, so you and Jace will be Lane-free in a matter of hours."

"No!" she cried and then shifted so we were facing each other. "You can stay here; please don't leave. I hate when you go out of town . . . you never come back happy." Tears began to well up in her eyes and I had to remind myself that Audrey was on hormone overload—every little thing could bring on the waterworks. *Tread lightly, buddy.*

Audrey was used to my out-of-town trips, as I'd been taking them since she met me. I never came back happy because I never got the result I was hoping for, which was having *her* back in my arms. Going on those trips was the only thing that made me feel as if I were actually getting closer to her.

"Trust me, you could do without me for a few days. I think Jace will like having his girls all to himself again." I teased her. The mention of Jace brought a small smile to her face, but it was fleeting. I had a house in town that I rented, but while my landlord had been fixing a burst pipe, I'd been hopping between three of my buddies' homes.

"I wish you would just stay here."

"Doll, half of my job involves travel, so there will always be times when I have to go. Don't forget that your husband is my boss. It's his orders. Besides, we can't all afford big estates on our own piece of land." I may have omitted that this trip was not on her husband's orders.

She rolled her eyes. "Why would you bring a girl home? You have never, and I mean *never*, done that. And why *her*? Is there something special about her?" she asked, grimacing.

"I just learned her name when Jace barged in the room. Trust me, doll, it wasn't the girl. I messed up. I drank too much and she gave me a ride home. Before I knew it, she was following me up the stairs and . . . well . . ."

"Yeah, I don't need to know the rest," she replied in a flat tone. Then she sighed deeply, and I could sense her heavy thoughts.

"Spit it out . . ." I coaxed.

"I just hate . . ."

"Come on, I won't leave until you tell me, and it might get weird when your husband comes back to bed."

"I hate that Jace saw her body. It was so perfect. Perfect breasts. Perfect ass. Not a stretch mark on her. While I'm . . . well, I can't even talk about it."

My mouth dropped open and I had no words. I knew she wouldn't be happy seeing a trampy bar girl parade around her house, but I never thought she would compare herself. Maybe she forgot that she'd *just* had a baby. Or maybe she forgot how her husband worshipped the ground she walked on. The idea that Jace would give even a second thought to Gemma made me laugh hard.

"Don't laugh! This is serious," she scolded.

"Shit, I'm sorry. I tried to hold it in." I continued to laugh. "Man, I wish Jace had heard you say that."

"I don't," she groaned.

"Too bad, babe. I could have heard that ridiculous comment on the other side of the house," Jace interrupted.

Audrey's body locked up underneath the covers at the sound of her husband's voice. I quickly leaned in so only she could hear. "I saw his face when he first saw her, and if I had seen anything other than annoyance, you know I would have knocked his lights out. Trust me, the way he looks at you, even with bags under your eyes, messy hair, stretch marks, and . . . ouch!" I yelped when she pinched the shit out of my stomach. "You said it first!"

"That doesn't mean you get to list it all!" she whisper-shouted back.

"Fine, fine. But there is no comparison. He looks at you like you're his whole world and his only reason to breathe. A random topless girl is not going to pull his attention. Besides, so what if he looks at naked tits? The day he stops looking at tits is the day you *should* start worrying." She laughed quietly but gave me one more hard pinch under the covers. "Cut that shit out, Audrey!" I chuckled.

"All right, playtime's over. Outta my bed and hands off my girl, Parker," Jace grumbled while climbing in on the opposite side of Audrey. He immediately pulled her across the bed toward him in his typical possessive fashion.

I began to climb out from under the covers and said, "This kind of feels like that one time we almost slept together, doll. Remember during your freshman year?" I could barely contain my cheesy-ass grin because I couldn't help but fuck with Jace on a daily basis.

"Lane, he doesn't fall for your terrible lies anymore. Go to bed," Audrey said, giggling. And that was all I needed to feel better. If she was happy, we were all happy.

Jace glared at me on my way out but didn't say anything. As soon as I hit the hallway, I heard him softly ask her, "That didn't really happen, did it?"

I chuckled, but silently, so I wouldn't wake up the baby again. It never failed with that guy—he was way too easy to rile up. Right before I stepped into my room, Jace jogged down the hall toward me.

"It was a joke, dude. I couldn't resist."

"Nah," he whispered. "I know that. It's just that she told me you're heading out of town again?"

I sobered and told him, "Yeah, I got a call a little while ago. I have to go."

"What about the Nolan job?"

Jace and Jaxon Riley were twin brothers who came into a lot of money when their father passed away. Immediately after they graduated from college in California, they took ownership of his security company, the Riley Group. Their best friend, Cole, had family money as well, so all three of them and their wives built houses on a big plot of land here in Texas, which is where they are originally from.

After graduation, Jace and Jax hired Cole and me to join them in Dallas, and we all left the Golden State behind. It was a hard choice, considering my original reasons for being there in the first place. But I couldn't imagine being away from Audrey, and I knew I would make decent money and be able to make my occasional trips whenever I was called.

My job title was a little more unconventional compared to the others. I oversaw a lot of the financing, because that's what I was good at and because I had recently acquired a Texas CPA license. But I also flew out to meet potential clients who were considering using the Riley Group for security purposes when they came to Dallas. Most of our customers lately had been high-profile, so they expected a face-to-face consultation before they trusted us to safeguard them. I couldn't seem to stay in one place for too long, and didn't have anyone to come home to, so taking on that responsibility just made sense.

"I'll hand the Nolan case off to the rookie," I answered Jace.

"You're going to trust Ethan with a quarter-of-a-million-dollar job?"

"We gotta loosen the reins at some point. I'll be in touch with him throughout the entire deal. Look, I *have* to go. *He's* going to be there." I tried to hide the pleading in my voice.

Jace's type A personality required him to keep a close eye on his employees, and even more so on his family. Audrey was like my sister, so when he married her he gained a brother at the same time. He didn't spy on me, but he started asking all the right questions, and one day I had to break down and spill before I lost my job. He knew everything now. It wasn't something I enjoyed keeping from Audrey, but Jace had agreed with me that she didn't need that stress put upon her, especially now with the baby.

His voice turned stoic and he asked, "You're sure he'll be there?"

"As sure as I can be. Charlie got me a spot in the ring and says he'll be there."

"Where?" he whispered.

"Tijuana. The usual."

"Let me transfer some money over for you," he stated nonchalantly.

"No, seriously, I'm good. I can take care of this myself."

"I'm sure you can. But I also know that these trips come close to wiping you out. You don't want to be broke once you actually get her back, do you?"

I knew that this was why Audrey fell for Jace. He was completely selfless and would help any of his friends or family, even to the point of hurting himself. I could always count on him when I was in a bind, regardless of whether I'd asked for help or not.

"I'll pay you back. With interest," I replied brusquely.

"You just make sure Ethan gets Nolan to sign on the dotted line and that'll be payback enough," he said with a grin. He reached his hand out so I could shake it but then promptly pulled me in, and we swiftly patted backs.

"Thanks, man."

Before he made it to his room, he turned and said, "Bring her back here, okay? I want to meet her."

I nodded but didn't reply. I tried to never go into these trips with my hopes up anymore. Years of returning home empty-handed had taught me that, in order to guard my heart, I always had to expect the worst.

- Two -

As I bounced on my toes, Mateo continued to wrap my hands for me. The basement we were standing in was dark and smelled of piss and mold. A single rusting light fixture dangled above us, allowing Mateo just enough visibility to get his job done.

All I wanted was to get this over with. I hated coming to these things. Training in a well-lit gym where I knew I wouldn't catch hepatitis was fun. Fighting in these sketchy underground matches made my skin crawl and fucking blew.

"Have you seen him yet?" I asked.

"I saw two of his guys. He's here," Mateo responded under his breath.

"I don't think I've been training enough lately. Shit, Teo . . ." I rambled nervously.

"You look pretty fucking cut. More so than the last time I saw you, so you must be doing something right." He nudged my right hand down and pulled up my left to begin wrapping it.

I watched as he slipped the loop around my thumb and wound the red material over my wrist, between each finger, over my knuckles in a dizzying pattern, and finished with a final pull over my wrist.

"How's the support in your thumbs?" he asked.

I shook out my hands and flexed my fingers, feeling everything out. I allowed the blood to flow through each appendage before I cut it off swiftly with a tight fist and then opened them again. Sweat beaded in the small area between my shoulder blades, and I could feel a single drop running down the center of my spine toward the black shorts I was wearing.

"Feels good, man."

"Okay, just remember you're not here for the same reason as these other guys." Mateo began the same speech he'd given to me time and time again. "You don't need to fight to the death. If you're injured, just go down. Winning doesn't matter. You just need to get into the ring once so we can get into the after-party." He took my hands and checked his wrapping job one more time. "But . . . if you win, we do get bottle service, so it wouldn't hurt if you tried a *little* bit," he added, smarting off. I laughed despite the stress and jabbed his shoulder lightly.

I looked forward to the day when I wouldn't have to come to these fights anymore. I enjoyed boxing; don't get me wrong. The sport was exhilarating and the best workout I've come across so far, but I hated these underground fights. I hated the people and all of the dealing and betting that they did on the side of the ring. Conniving bastards. I hated being associated with them for even a night. What's worse, the fights were only a distraction from the real criminal undertakings they had going on.

"Don't try to pull any fancy new techniques. Stick to what you're good at," Mateo continued as we walked down the long, filthy hallway. The tile was cold and the walls were peeling down to the bare wood behind it. The moldy smell was nauseating. "Most of these guys are brawlers, and they lack the finesse you've been trained to show. You gotta lose some of that in the ring or they'll be suspicious. Throw all of your power and energy into your hits. Don't get too caught up in mastering your footwork."

The loud roar of the crowd began to invade our ears, and it became harder and harder to hear Mateo's counsel. Without thought, I commenced bouncing again. My blood was pumping, the crowd starting to hype me up. I was the underdog—the one who popped in and out of these events but never stuck around long enough to take it all. They knew me, but they didn't *know* me. I intrigued them, and they never knew whether to cheer me on or boo me out of the ring.

As we entered the large, open warehouse, women grazed their fingers across my bare skin. Some tried to reach up and grasp my hair, while others just openly winked at me. My stomach churned because these were the absolute last kind of people I wanted to be around.

Business as usual. Mateo continued with his spiel, moving closer to my ear so I could hear him. "You're up against Barrera tonight. Get his defenses down and then throw a right uppercut and finish him with your deadly left hook. He won't be able to withstand it; his chin is too weak."

Mateo knew most of the fighters down here. He studied them at every fight, but just like me, he wasn't here for the shady dealings. He used to be on the Mexican police force, but once he realized the extent of the crime and corruption, he got out. I've always had a feeling he's some kind of undercover agent, but he's assured me that he's only here to help people like me. Regardless, I'd never be able to repay him for everything he's done.

Someone shouted to Mateo in Spanish and he hollered back, "*Sí, estamos listos!*" When he turned back around, he ran a check over me for the thousandth time. "You're ready, yes?" I nodded and he tapped the back of my head toward our corner.

Right before I straddled the ropes to step into the ring, he grabbed my arm and pulled me down to hear his tight, whispered words. "If anything goes down, you meet me at my car. It's parked in the southeast corner of the building. Get there, *mijo*. It won't do *her* any good if you're six feet under." He threw in that last line because he knew it would sink in and hook me.

I was doing it for *her*. I tried so damn hard to picture her in my head for motivation . . . the color of her hair, the deep blue of her eyes, or how her skin shone like porcelain. I pulled out the tattered picture of her that I carried around everywhere I went. The edges were torn, some areas were peeling up, and it was way too small, but it was all I had. Every day I worried that it had been too many years and she wouldn't look anything like the picture anymore. I shoved it back into the pocket of my shorts and let my fingers graze across the slick surface before I had to force myself to let it go.

I knocked my face around to get myself back in the moment. If I started zoning out now, I would never make it two seconds in the ring with Barrera. I quickly remembered what I came here for and began to scan the crowd, looking for the one in the suit—the richest bastard here. He wasn't hard to spot, and I clenched my fist when my eyes found him and his whole crew. He threw his head back and laughed boisterously at something one of his disgusting lackeys said, as if he didn't have a care in the world. *Not this time. You won't get the slip on me this time, Flores.*

I didn't keep up with the ins and outs of the underground world—that was usually Charlie's or Mateo's job, and they just told me where to be and when. Therefore, I was surprised to see Barrera step up to Flores, and the two looked deep in conversation before Flores patted the back of his head and nodded toward the ring. So Barrera belonged to Flores, huh? Well now, the fight just got a little more interesting.

The shuffling of feet began as people started finding their seats. A topless brunette walked down the front aisle, holding a tray. She stopped in front of Flores to hand him a glass with golden liquid sloshing around inside. I could go for that right about now. She tried to stick around and flirt, but I watched Flores slip something into her waistband and shoo her off.

Barrera eyed me as he slithered through the ropes and into the ring. I continued bouncing on my toes, trying not to lose my adrenaline high. I watched his movements and attempted to spot any weak areas, particularly any injuries he could be concealing. He stood up straight and began to bounce as well. He moved from side to side and then began spinning in a full circle, around and around, too busy paying attention to the crowd. The fucker was going to get dizzy, but that could work in my favor.

The commencements of these fights were simple. There was no Mexican version of Michael Buffer shouting, "*Let's get ready to rumble!*" in Spanish. There wasn't a referee explaining that he wants a "good, clean fight" or asking us to touch-bump to begin. There was just a little old man named Santiago, who looked at each of us, probably to make sure we were in the ring. Then he nodded his head while drumming a bell. *Go time.*

Shouts immediately could be heard from all corners of the warehouse, echoing loudly off the aluminum walls. The crowd yelled in English and Spanish, and I even thought I heard some Portuguese out there. I couldn't tell who they were yelling for, although I could vaguely understand they were all calling out different punches to throw or defenses to put up.

But it wasn't the screaming that pulled Barrera's attention away from me; it was the deafening noise that came from outside. I lunged at his distraction. My torso shifted and I swung my right fist upward in a rising arc, connecting with a clean hit to his jaw. Spit flew from his mouth, and I watched the drops land on the mat below our feet. His knees gave and Barrera fell directly to the ground. He wasn't out, so I kept bouncing, ready to give him another when he was fully upright.

"Reyes!" I heard Mateo shout up at me. It took a long second before I remembered that Reyes was our agreed-upon last name for me in the ring. I didn't think anyone was actually going to believe I was Hispanic, but it was better that they didn't discover my real last name. "Rey-es!" he enunciated, louder this time.

I snapped out of my tunnel vision and took in the scene around me. People were scattering quickly to all corners of the building. My stomach dropped and I immediately ran to the ropes to search for Flores, only to find that he was no longer in the front row.

"*Mierda!* This could be a raid. We gotta get out here," Mateo shouted up to me. "I'm not spending the night *en la cárcel* while we wait for Charlie to bail our asses out. My car, *ahora!*" When Mateo was stressed, he began to speak Spanglish, switching back and forth between the two languages. He probably didn't even know he did it.

But despite his warning and demand, I hadn't come all the way out to this nasty hellhole, after not seeing or hearing anything from Flores for over a year, to lose my chance again. I just couldn't go another year. It had to end, and it needed to be tonight.

I spotted Flores's security detail huddled together at the back west corner of the wide-open space. They frowned at one another while tapping their earpieces frantically. If their frequency was catching interference, then it was highly likely that we *were* in the middle of a police raid.

Without a second thought, I launched my legs over the top rope of the ring and jumped to the floor.

"*Lane, don't!*" Mateo shouted in anger from behind me. So much for not using my real name.

I feverishly began ripping the wraps from my hand, knowing I would need the full use of my fingers. The first wrap was hard to get loose, but I continued to remove it while I pushed my way through the shoving bodies. Once my right hand was fully freed, I began working on the left, but the majority of my attention was focused on finding Flores. More loud pops and bangs continued to filter into the warehouse. Women were screaming and the crowd became more frenzied by the moment.

When I reached his entourage, his balding, ugly ass was nowhere to be found. I pushed right through the middle of them and jumped on my toes to peer over their heads. Nothing. My instincts told me to search the open space again, and just before he cleared the doorway, I spotted the tail end of his navy suit jacket dodging around the corner. Hell, if he wanted to separate himself from his own protection and take off solo, that only made my job easier.

With singular focus I sprinted forward. People fell and stumbled around me, but there was no time for apologies. I wasn't sorry anyway.

It didn't take long for me to catch up with him. He was a smart son of a bitch and had been able to elude me for years, but now that I had the opportunity to get my hands on him, there was no denying that he was the weaker opponent. Especially since I still had the fight energy from earlier coursing through my veins.

I reached forward to grab the collar of his jacket. My right hand was free, but I had a long stream of the wrap from my left hand trailing down to the floor. I didn't have time to mess with it before I dragged him backward and flung him onto the ground. He grunted, but other than that, I didn't hear another peep from him.

"Where is she?" I growled, crouching down over his frail body and holding his throat in a tight clench.

"*No hablo inglés,*" he gasped. His tiny smirk lit a fire within me and I squeezed harder.

"You're gonna have to do better than that, Flores." I wanted him to understand that I knew exactly who he was, but there wasn't time for this bullshit. "Where is she?" I roared.

"Who the fuck are you talking about, asshole?" he rasped. His English was good and only carried a hint of his accent.

It hit me then that he had no idea who I was. I couldn't help but throw my head back and laugh in extreme frustration. I could understand that he never recognized me in the ring, but up close and personal like this? He should have fucking known.

"Amateur! You're a fucking amateur," I yelled. "Don't you know to keep your friends close and your enemies closer? Shouldn't you be keeping an eye out for the people whose lives you destroy?"

"That's not my job. I pay people to do that shit for me!"

Just then his eyes lit up as he looked over my shoulder, and I quickly spun to the left. Not fast enough, though, because instantly I felt a piercing, cold pain slice into my shoulder blade. As the moron behind me pulled his knife out swiftly, the sharp, biting pain began to take over the entire right side of my body.

I stumbled against the partition and watched as the guy's body was suddenly slammed into the wall. Mateo landed hard on top of Flores's not-so-little minion and with one quick jab, it was lights out for the lackey. Flores began to laugh wickedly behind me, and I scrambled to grab hold of his shirt before he could even think about escaping.

The moment I got a hand on him, the Mexican Federal Police, dressed in all-black riot gear, surrounded us. I clutched Flores but my right hand couldn't grasp anymore—it felt as if there were needles shooting up my arm. I reached with my left hand and held on to his throat with everything I had left in me.

"Where. Is. She?" I spat out.

"Señor Flores," one of the officers called through his face shield. He grabbed Flores by the arms and pinned them behind his back roughly. I saw a brief look of horror cross Flores's face as he realized the complexity of his situation, but when he turned toward me again, his pure evil smirk was firmly back in place on his ugly mug.

There was a loud ringing in my ears, and the thought crossed my mind that if I had been stabbed, I should probably be feeling more pain than I was right now. Classic symptom of shock. I pushed through because there was no telling if or when I would ever see Flores again. They would hide him away in a Mexican prison, or he would pay his way out and I might never find him.

I stood eye-to-eye with him and pulled the last hope I had out of my pocket. With my left hand shaking, I held the picture up to his face. The officer continued to wrestle Flores backward, but I pressed on. I felt a coldness begin to creep over my skin, and I couldn't seem to catch a long enough breath.

"Where is she?" I tried to shout over the high-pitched drumming in my temples. He satisfied me for a moment by actually glancing at the old, worn photograph in my quaking palm. His lips turned up and my stomach dropped to my feet.

The officer finally tugged Flores to an open doorway, and right before he was jerked outside, Flores uttered, "Check the bottom of the Sea of Cortez."

My vision darkened as if a camera shutter had snapped shut, and the last thing I heard was a string of curse words flying out of Mateo's mouth.

- THREE -

After hitting the cold concrete floor of the grimy warehouse, all I could remember were flashes of moments that happened afterward.

Mateo dragging me out to his car.

A bumpy drive that lasted an ungodly amount of time.

Pain. So much pain.

Stopping to rewrap my shoulder.

Crossing the border without looking suspicious.

Hospitals.

Mateo trying to explain to the doctors why I had a stab wound.

My eyes were groggy and my head felt fuzzy. I tried to put all of the pieces together and remember how I got here, even if I didn't know where *here* was, exactly. The warm sun filtered in through the sheer curtains in what looked like a hotel room, and I guessed it was late morning, but hell if I knew. I pushed to sit up and pain shot from my right shoulder blade up into my neck, radiating down through my toes.

"Agggh!"

Beads of sweat broke out across my forehead, and the intensity of the pain caused me to suck air in and out raggedly. I pushed up with my left hand so I could throw my legs over the side of the bed. I had to get up before my bladder screamed any louder. My right arm was in a sling that I didn't remember putting on. The bedroom door swung open and Mateo walked in carrying a tray.

"Good morning, sunshine. They gave your ass so many drugs, I was wondering if they'd gone ahead and finished you off themselves," he said with a little too much pep in his voice.

"I need more," I rasped out. My throat felt like it had been rubbed raw with sandpaper. "Fuck . . . my throat." I tried to swallow, but it felt as if I had swallowed a handful of gravel.

"Dude, I'll bet it hurts. You were snoring so damn loud, it sounded like there was a chainsaw in the next room." He placed a tray of water, orange juice, and fruit in front of me. "You can have more meds after you call Charlie. He's been blowing up your phone."

I finally shoved off the bed and stumbled toward the bathroom. My feet caught on the bottom of my pants, and I looked down to see pajamas I know I didn't own.

"Did you dress me, Teo?"

"I don't wanna talk about it," he grumbled. I laughed through my aching throat and closed the bathroom door behind me.

When I flipped the light on, I was startled to see my ghostly reflection in the mirror. Besides the pajama pants, I didn't have anything else on except the sling on my right arm. My skin was flushed and pale. I had bruises on my inner arm where I assumed an IV must have been inserted. I leaned over the edge of the counter to get a closer glance at the gauze taped around my shoulder.

The second I leaned forward, the memories of the previous night hit me like a bat to the face. Getting only one hit in the fight against Barrera. Chasing Flores down. Being blindsided with a knife to the back. Police arresting Flores right after he told me . . .

She was dead.

The weight of his words sliced through me sharper than a thousand knives to the back. My knees buckled and I hit the tile floor with a loud thud. I slid my legs out in front of me and let my head hang forward. I didn't care about my screaming shoulder or the fact that I still hadn't pissed in God-knows-how-long. Those were nothing compared to this black, soul-crushing pain. I was too late . . . too fucking late.

How long had I been chasing a ghost? Days? Weeks? Years? All this time I thought I would just *know* if she was gone, as if a piece of my soul went with her. But I'd felt nothing at all. Instead, I had to hear my worst fear from the repulsive mouth of Flores himself.

The door slammed open and a wide-eyed Mateo searched the large bathroom for me. His eyes finally fell toward me on the floor, and I saw the discomfort and pain in his eyes. I tried to straighten up and realized my face was wet. Tears. With the back of my hand, I quickly wiped them all away. I pulled my knees up and wrapped my left arm around them.

"I'm good," I quietly breathed out.

"Call Charlie." He held out my blinking phone. I took it from his hands and laid it on the ground next to me. It was fucking humiliating to have one of the best boxers I've ever known look down at me on the floor with pity in his eyes. I couldn't hold eye contact with him for too long. "I'm sorry, man. I wish there was more I could have done. I should've tried to dig deeper into him," he whispered.

"Don't," I said into my knees. "Don't put any blame on yourself, Teo. I'll never be able to repay you for all your help."

He nodded his head, and I was thankful we weren't going to sit and discuss that right now. "Seriously, though, if he calls my phone one more time, *all* of the phones are going out the fucking window."

"How long was I out?" I asked before he turned to leave.

"It's only been a few hours since we got back from the hospital. Doc said the blade didn't hit anything crucial, but you need to check back with him in a few days. You'll also need to rehab that shoulder."

"Well, that won't work. I'm getting out of here."

"Yeah, I told him that you would. Take the meds. Get it checked." With that, he turned on his heel and headed back out to the living area.

≈

I quickly learned how annoying it was to have to hold my arm against my chest. While taking a shower, I had to bend like a contortionist to prevent the water from hitting my bandage. It was worth it, though, to get all that grime off of me from last night. My shoulder was beyond jacked, but I knew that if I took any more pain meds, I risked being laid out on my ass for another day. I would just have to wait until I got back home.

Where the hell was home, anyway? New York wasn't home anymore. California was never home. Texas was full of my friends and their happy little families, but I didn't know how long I would be able to stick around with this new, empty hole inside of me that made me want to push everyone away. I'd become good at that.

Mateo finished shoving my belongings into my bag for me while I finally scrolled through my phone. I had missed calls from just about everyone in my contact list. There were also numerous texts from Audrey. Even my mom had called, which was weird. I hadn't kept in close contact with my parents over the past few years because it had just become too painful. As much as I knew she wanted to, my poor mom tried to not call me unless she had something important to discuss.

I typed out a quick message to Jace, letting him pass the word on to Audrey that I was heading back. Within a few minutes, I had a reply.

Jace: We'll leave the lights on for you.

Me: I'm staying at a hotel. My place is almost done anyway.

Jace: Did it go that bad?

Me: I should be at work on Monday. Plenty of time before Nolan's arrival.

It was shitty of me to leave him hanging like that, especially after everything he's done for me. But there was no way in hell I was talking about this until I was ready, and I damn sure wasn't going to discuss it over a text message. At any rate, I would have plenty of questions to answer when I walked into work, what with the sling and stab wound and all.

Mateo pulled the zipper closed on my bag and patted it, indicating that it was packed and ready. I didn't have a flight home scheduled yet. I figured I'd buy a ticket when I arrived at the airport, and if I had to sit around and wait—well, who the fuck cared anyway? Mateo gestured that he was taking the bag down, and I nodded in understanding.

The shrill ring of my phone broke up the quiet of the room, and I looked down to see Charlie's name pop up on the bright screen. I might as well get this over with. Plus, he had helped me the most out of anyone, going above and beyond the call of duty.

Charlie and I had been partners when I used to be a cop in New York. We saw each other more than we saw our own families.

I would have taken a bullet for him, and he would have done the same for me. He kept his ear to the ground for me and always let me know if he got a lead on Flores, even though it wasn't his case. All while I quit the force, moved down to San Diego, and tried to find him myself.

"Yeah," I mumbled into the phone.

"Shit, Lane," Charlie's gruff voice whispered into the line. "I thought you were fucking dead."

"I thought I was too."

"What the hell happened? Scratch that, you can tell me in a bit—"

I interrupted his speech and said, "I need you to get Flores extradited to the US. He needs to burn. He'll just pay his way out down there."

"You know I don't have any power to do something like that—"

"Talk to Chief," I interrupted again.

"I tried, man. But seriously, enough with Flores . . ." he whispered again.

"*Enough with him?*" I boomed into the phone. "He fucking killed her, Char. He killed her and he had the goddamn balls to laugh in my face about it. If you guys can't do anything, I'll go down and end him myself."

"Chill out for one damn second! You've got bigger fish to fry," he whisper-shouted into the phone.

"Why the hell are you whispering to me?" I hollered back.

"I have her, Lane. I've been trying to get a hold of you to tell you. I have her."

He may as well have been speaking a different language. I had to replay the words in my head ten times before I could wrap my mind around what he could possibly be saying.

"You . . ."

"Have her," he repeated quietly.

I could hear Flores's words in my brain. *Check the bottom of the Sea of Cortez.* All of a sudden, I was picturing boats and underwater search diving teams. But there was no way they could have found a body that fast. It had only been a few hours since he'd told me she was there. I couldn't figure out what Charlie was saying, and all I could feel right then were the damn tears dripping down my face again.

"Lane? Are you still there?" He must have heard me sniff past the overwhelming grief lodged in my throat because he hurriedly said, "I have Kate . . . alive."

My heart froze in my chest for so long, I began to wonder if I would even continue breathing. "Wha—how? I mean . . . is that possible?!" I exclaimed.

"She's sitting right next to me. Yeah, it's fucking possible, man. We finally did it!"

"Dude, just stop cussing." I inhaled deeply and plopped down on the bed, dropping my head in my hands. Forgetting that one of my arms was in a sling, I let out a string of profanities when I moved it the wrong way. The irony that I had just told Charlie to knock off the sailor mouth was not lost on me. My body shot back up and I began pacing in my hotel room.

"*How* is it possible? Are you sure? Did you check her—"

"Her wrist?" he interrupted the onslaught of questions I was firing his way. "Tiny heart birthmark on the inside of her left wrist. It's there, man. I know that missing persons report backward and forward. It's Kate."

All the air I had unintentionally been holding in flew out of my chest and my head became light. I quickly looked around for a place to sit, but I couldn't make it, so I slid down the side of the wall until my ass hit the ground.

"She's so beautiful. Dude, you'll be blown away. She still has the most stunning blond hair, except it's long now. Almost to the middle of her back."

"Should I . . . I don't know . . . should I say something to her?" My mind was jumping up and down in excitement, pumping its fists in pure joy, but my body was clearly still in shock.

"I don't think that's a good idea. You just need to meet us in New York. Besides, she's sleeping right now. She hasn't heard anything I'm saying to you."

"Where the hell *are* you guys?"

"On a plane back to New York. I picked her up five hours ago in San Diego," he stated.

"San Diego?! I'm in fucking San Diego. You mean she was only a few miles away from me?" My heart plummeted at the thought. Was it possible she was always that close to me while I was *living* in San Diego?

"Before you start thinking what I know you're thinking, she didn't live there. She was south of the border, like we thought. Look . . . it's a long story. Get your ass to New York. I'm buying you the next available ticket right now. We'll talk once you get there."

"Wait, how are you talking to me on a plane?" I questioned.

"Dude, get with the times. The sky is not the limit anymore."

I quietly chuckled but sobered when I thought about Kate sitting right next to him on the other end of this line. Kate. My beautiful Kate. I wanted to keep Charlie on the phone just so I could maintain the only connection I've had with her in years. I was so damn afraid to lose that feeling.

"How does she look?" I whispered.

"Good, man. Really good."

"If she wants anything before I arrive, get it for her. Anything at all. I don't care if it's a fucking chocolate bar dipped in gold, you get it for her."

"I think I've got it covered, Lane." He chuckled.

My sigh of relief was enough of a response for him, and he signed off quickly. I placed the phone in my lap, staring at the tiny little device that managed to turn my world right side up once again.

∽

Me: Change of plans. I won't be in on Monday

Jace: Dude, call Audrey. I can't continue to keep this from her

Me: It's all over, I'll be telling her everything soon enough

Jace: What do you mean it's all over?

Me: On my way to NY to pick up my girl

Jace: Are you serious? HELL YEAH!!!!

- Four -

My hands shook and a familiar smell permeated my nose as I pushed open the same doors I'd been through countless times since I was a kid. My dad was currently an officer, my uncle was an officer, and even my grandfather had been on the force. The 72nd precinct in Brooklyn would always feel like a small piece of home to me.

The place quieted down as I marched in, and heads rose to double-check that they were seeing things correctly. *Yeah, assholes, it's me.*

"Parker?" I heard old Frank's voice question from across the room.

"Yes, sir." I nodded my head in his direction and continued toward the back, where I knew I would find the peeling, tiled stairs. All of the offices and interrogation, or "interview," rooms were located upstairs. I smiled when I saw that the lightbulb directly in front of the ladies' restroom was still burned out. All these years and no one had thought to change that damn thing?

My shoulder hurt like a bitch, and the pills I could hear rattling in my bag were calling my name, but they would have to wait. The taxi ride from JFK had taken about forty-five minutes, and the entire time I battled with myself to not take anything before I saw her. I was pretty sure I smelled like I had been on an airplane all day, but I didn't care. *She* was here. Kate was in the building, and I was only moments away from her.

"No!" I suddenly heard a woman's voice vehemently gasp from above where I was climbing up the stairwell. "We are not prisoners. We *will not* go into your little interrogation chamber so you can all gawk at us through your stupid two-way mirror. Out here is fine, thank you," she stated angrily.

My feet pushed forward up the last two steps and I rounded the corner into a packed hallway. Officers were leaning up against every wall: ones I had worked with before and a few new ones as well. I tried to take in all the faces staring back at me, but I was only looking for one.

I heard a tiny intake of breath and then what sounded like a little boy whispering, "Superman!"

My eyes tried to peer through all of the bodies, but I couldn't see where the pint-sized voice was coming from. There were too many people in such close proximity. I decided to look for Charlie first. He would know where *she* was.

"That's not Superman. That's Daddy!" the sweetest little voice called out.

My body shot ramrod straight and all my attention was focused solely on that voice. My knees buckled and hit the ground with a loud thud, but now directly in my line of sight was the face of an angel. She barreled down the hall and through the crowd, running directly toward me.

Every time I played out this moment in my head, never did I imagine it happening like this. I watched her long blond hair trail behind her and heard her little pink shoes slap the tile loudly. Right before she launched her body at me, she came to an abrupt halt only inches in front of me. We stared at each other. She looked at me with curiosity, and I took in every single inch of her that had changed in the past four years. She was four now. Four years old. Four years that I had missed.

"You *are* my daddy, right?" she whispered for only me to hear, as if it were a secret between just the two of us. Her eyes were the deepest blue I had ever seen. Her hair was the exact same shade as mine, but somehow it looked better on her. Her skin had the light hint of tan . . . same as mine. Her nose sloped down and turned up just a fraction, identical to her mother's. Her ears were the same shape as mine, only a much smaller and daintier version. She was the most beautiful girl I had ever laid eyes on, and I couldn't believe she was already four years old.

I tried to speak but I couldn't get anything to come out, so I just nodded my head like a dumb-ass. Her entire face lit up with joy that could only parallel mine, and she threw her arms around my neck. I stubbornly pulled my arm from the sling and, despite the pain—which felt like absolutely nothing right then—I hugged my precious daughter with everything I had.

In that moment, everything I had done and everything I had been through had all been worth it. I knew that nothing could have ever filled the void in my life like she could. I also knew that I would always fight to the ends of the earth for this little girl in my arms right now.

"Kate." The word bubbled up out of my throat, and I began to sob into her tiny shoulder. "You know who I am?"

She pulled back just enough to flash her brilliant eyes at me and giggled. "Of course, silly. You're my daddy."

With tears coursing down my face for everyone to see, I squeezed her back to me tightly. "I feel like I've been waiting an eternity for you, Kit Kat."

Her eyes popped open wide at the nickname, and she pushed on my injured shoulder to take a look at me. I tried not to cringe at the pain, but it had been a good twenty hours since I'd last taken something for it. Instinctually, she lightly patted her hand over my wound. She couldn't see the bandage under my shirt, but somehow she knew. Her touch was like a feather, and maybe it was all in my head, but it really did lessen the stinging ache.

"You have an ouchie?" she asked innocently.

"It'll be okay. See?" I tenderly pulled back the collar of my shirt. "I have this great big Band-Aid making it all better."

It was amazing to be able to just watch her expressions. I saw myself in so many of them, and I'd never realized what kind of feeling that would give my soul. She was this beautiful part of me—the very *best* part of me.

As she examined my bandage like a trained nurse, she slowly bent forward and kissed the covered area. My heart stopped beating for an entire handful of seconds. I would have thought I was having a heart attack, but there was nothing numb inside me at this moment. I was feeling every emotion, and for once, I couldn't have been happier about it.

"Kisses make ouchies better." Her face lit up with pride.

"They certainly do," I choked out.

I let my bag slip off my opposite shoulder so I could stand while holding her. She wrapped her arms around my neck, but she was cautious of my injury.

I gently wrapped my fingers around her dainty wrist and flipped it over to see the confirmation I absolutely didn't need. There on the inside of her left wrist was a tiny birthmark in the shape of a heart. I noticed it the second she had been all cleaned off after birth. It was such a perfect mark for a perfect little girl. I'd been searching four years for that heart-shaped mark.

"Bubba was right; you are like Superman," Kate said while gazing directly into my eyes.

A look of confusion crossed my face as I tried to figure out what she had just said. "Who is Bubba, little one?"

With one arm wrapped tightly around my neck, as if I would actually try and escape her, she swiveled around and faced the crowd surrounding us. I finally took in all of the faces that were staring at us. The crowd had lessened, but the ones who remained had all been watching our reunion very closely. Women were wiping their faces dry, while the men were clearing their throats and avoiding my glassy eyes as they tried to give me at least the appearance of privacy.

"Braden is Bubba!" she excitedly told me, pointing through the bodies at a little boy who appeared to be about the same age as Kate.

But it wasn't Braden that stopped the blood flow throughout my body once again. It was the woman sitting next to him. She was the one person, besides Flores, who could stir up intense anger inside of me. The one person I had suspected of aiding my daughter's kidnappers. *Raegan Hayes.*

RAEGAN -

We had been sitting in that dark and dingy police station for hours. Not that we had anywhere to go anyway. Braden and Kate's bedtime had long since come and gone, even with the time difference. Where did they expect us to sleep tonight? Because it sure as hell wouldn't be here on the cold floor.

I knew *he* would be coming, but I just didn't know when to expect him. I'd heard Officer Charlie talking with him on the phone while we were flying out to New York, even though he thought I was sleeping along with the others.

When Lane Parker's huge body filled the door of the hallway we were all congregating in, my breath was stolen straight from my chest. Lane had always been every woman's fantasy, but over these last four years he had become, somehow, even more beautiful. Even through his polo shirt I could see the stretch of tight muscles, and everything else on him looked incredibly hard. Four years ago, he hadn't been built like that at all. He had been lean, but I wouldn't have called him muscular. Now I could see that the gym had been his friend.

My eyes welled up with tears when he heard Kate's sweet voice for the first time. His entire face zoned in on her, even if he couldn't see her yet, and when his knees hit the ground, we all felt it shake beneath us. I couldn't have been happier for Kate right then, but the selfish side of me wondered what that meant for us.

No one in the station could look away from the heart-wrenching father-daughter reunion. Kate, true to her boisterous and outgoing nature, ran to the only man she's ever known to be her father—even though she never really knew him. I couldn't begin to keep track of the amount of times over the last four years that she had asked me when she could see him again.

Braden, ever the silent, stoic protector, inched closer just a smidge so he could keep an eye on her at all times. Lane wouldn't get very far with Kate, not without a small four-year-old male tagalong. Braden took a long look at him holding Kate and eyed me nervously, and I knew he was silently wondering if she was about to be taken away from us. I wiped the moisture from my face and averted my gaze from his inaudible questions because I didn't know the answers. And I was too afraid to ask.

My legs ached from sitting all day. I'd sat on a plane for five hours and then came here and alternated between the floor and hard wooden chairs. I couldn't go on for much longer. If I had any money at all, I would have just told them we would be at a hotel, but now I wondered if I had any control over what Kate did. She was technically not mine; well, at least they wouldn't see it that way.

It seemed as though no one around here really knew the protocol for having missing persons return after four years. I guess after a year or so they just assumed you wouldn't be coming back. It made me wonder if anyone had actually been out there looking for us. I had always hoped they were out there at least trying. Then again, could I have really expected them to search for us for four years?

Every time I'd asked Officer Charlie what it was we were waiting for, he told me a different person. First, we were waiting on some sergeant, and then it was an attorney. I had heard him speak of the police chief, and finally he said a psychologist. It was obvious that he had no idea and was giving me the runaround.

"Braden is Bubba!" I heard Kate excitedly tell Lane, whose face had this unease and complete confusion on it. He looked straight to where her finger was pointing and took a second to glance at Braden, but his eyes didn't linger. They quickly found mine, and though I had wondered how seeing each other again would go, never did I imagine the immense anger and even hatred I saw in his eyes.

The heat of his glare made me shrink back, but only for a moment. I grabbed hold of Braden's hand and began to search the crowd for Officer Charlie. It was time to get things moving along so Kate, Braden, and I could get some rest.

I found him at the opposite end of the hall, talking to a man who wore a dark business suit and a scowl on his face. Another officer was trying to ease Charlie away from the conversation, but he wasn't having any of it.

"Charlie Doyle, right?" The man in the suit eyed him, and Officer Charlie nodded his head in frustration. "Doyle, I'm sorry, but this incident has crossed border lines. It's not your case anymore. I'm sure you've done a fine job, but I'll need all of the files and any evidence you have," the disgruntled-looking gentleman requested.

"Oh, *now* you want to do your job? After I hand-deliver it all solved to your desk? You didn't give two shits when I tried to get the FBI involved. Now you fuckers want to step in? Fuck off, Agent Johnson," Officer Charlie bit back.

I quickly jumped to cover Braden's ears, but the look on his face told me that I shouldn't even bother. He had heard it all. Officer Charlie spotted us standing behind him, and he blanched at my glare.

"Shit!" he exclaimed. Then, realizing he had just cursed in front of a four-year-old *again*, he smacked himself in the mouth, creating a loud pop.

"Please, Officer, quit while you're ahead," I drily told him.

"I'm sorry, Raegan," he apologized sheepishly. I was just glad he was finally calling me by my first name and not "ma'am" anymore. I was younger than he was, for God's sake. I watched as he squatted down to speak directly to Braden. "Hey, sport, forgive me. I shouldn't have said any of those words. I really don't want your mama to kill me, so do me a huge favor and don't repeat them, okay?" Braden nodded his head with a small smirk at the corner of his mouth, but that was all he would be giving. "A man of few words. I like you, kid."

When he stood back up, I couldn't hold in the giant yawn that stretched across my entire face. It was less than attractive. "Officer Charlie, please. We're all tired. It's way too late for us to still be sitting around. We need to sleep."

"I know; I'm sorry. This assho—" he started before quickly catching himself. "This man right here is trying to distract me from getting hotel accommodations. Excuse me while I ignore him and take care of you guys." The gentleman behind him rolled his eyes and then followed Officer Charlie into a nearby room.

Braden tugged on my shirt and I looked down to meet his sweet gaze.

"Mama, I have to go potty." Before he could complete his sentence, he began bouncing in an erratic manner. Boys! Why do they insist on waiting until the very last moment?

I shoved through the crowd with Braden holding my hand and found the ladies' restroom at the end of the dark corridor. I directed him into a stall and then leaned over the counter so I could look closely in the mirror. I didn't know how I'd forgotten about the surgical tape that stretched from my forehead down my temple and stopped just before my right ear.

It was the source of so much incredible pain for so long, but it was worth it. I'd endure it again and again to know I'd be here . . . instead of there. I wasn't sure where we would be tomorrow, let alone a month from now, but at least we could finally have a life. Braden and Kate could go to school, meet friends, and live a life children should be allowed to live.

Thoughts of Kate brought a feeling of melancholy, and I just wanted to scoop her up and hide her away from everyone. My eyes were unfocused in the mirror as I stared at my blurry image. My thoughts were a million miles away, but I slowly faded back in. I soon realized that Braden had been in there for a while. He was still new at using a stall, so I knew he hadn't locked it. Slowly, I pushed the metal door open and peered inside.

"Braden, sweetie . . ." I found him sitting fully clothed on top of the closed toilet lid, and his thoughts seemed to be a million miles away as well. My sweet introvert. He had been a worrier for as long as I could remember. "Did you use the potty yet?" He nodded his head and I crouched down in front of him. "What's going on, bub?"

"Will we ever see Kate?" he asked softly. My heart lurched and I scrambled to find the right words that could bring him even an ounce of comfort.

"Of course we'll see her. They won't be able to keep us away from her. Don't you think Kate would be very sad if she didn't see us?"

"I think she would cry."

"I agree, and no one wants her to cry, right?" Hesitantly, he shook his head. "Look, I'm not going to lie. Things will be different.

Kate has her family again, but now they'll have to realize we're her family too. I'll do everything in my power to make sure we still get to see her as much as possible." And I would. If we had to follow the Parkers to the ends of the earth just so we could be in her life, we would. She and Braden were both my children. I would never be able to say that out loud, but in my heart it was true.

"Okay, let's put that worry away and go find her. It's time the three of us get in a nice comfy bed and sleep until next week!"

"Mama, we can't sleep that long. Our bellies would be so hungry!" He giggled and I melted.

"Oh, darn. I am really tired, though, so maybe you guys could sleep in just a little bit tomorrow." I winked at him.

"I'm tired. Kate's tired too," he stated confidently.

Braden hopped up on the sink so he could wash his hands. I looked in the mirror and ran my finger across my bandage one more time. When it grazed over a particularly sensitive area, I stopped and pressed a little harder. I pressed hard enough that it made me wince, and I relished the feeling. The pain meant I wasn't dreaming . . . that I wasn't going to wake up soon and still be in *that* room. Still trapped.

I pressed harder and tears welled up in my eyes from the stinging, but I couldn't seem to stop. I needed to know we were really here. Out of the corner of my eye I caught Braden watching me in the mirror, and I immediately dropped my hand. With a smile, I reassured him that everything was okay, and he gave me a tentative grin in return. This kid was too wise for his years.

We held hands and pushed the creaky white door open that would lead us back to our girl. The crowds of people were still a bit overwhelming, and for the hundredth time today I wondered why the hell everyone was assembling in the hallway. And didn't these people have other jobs to do or families to go home to? I felt like a zoo animal being closely observed, and I'd had enough of that over these last four years.

I looked down at Braden, who was trying to peer between everyone's legs. I heard words like *FBI*, *kidnapping*, *Mexico*, and *hospitals* being flung around, and I just wanted to shout for everyone to shut up—we were right here! At least have the decency to talk about us behind closed doors.

"Braden, sweetheart, do you see Kate or Mr. Parker anywhere?" He shook his head back and forth and I began to push through people, becoming a little panicky. I wasn't comfortable with the three of us being separated. I tried to allow Mr. Parker his time alone with her, but now I didn't like that I couldn't see her.

Braced against one of the door frames was a gentleman who had helped us get some food earlier. "Excuse me, Officer . . ."

"Bradley," he finished for me.

"Yes, Officer Bradley. Have you seen Kate? Or Mr. Parker?"

He looked a bit confused when he asked, "Mr. Parker? Oh! You mean Lane? That's hilarious. Umm, no, I haven't seen him. He was carrying his little girl around, but maybe he took her home so she could get some sleep." He stated it nonchalantly, as if taking the little girl who had become half of my world away from me without even telling me was no big deal.

My heart hammered painfully in my chest, and I pulled Braden down the hall faster. "Kate! Where is she?" I began to yell. I had no shame. Especially when it came to my children. "Kate!"

- FIVE -

LANE -

When a case like the one I was involved in cracked wide open, it was a big fucking deal. Our precinct mainly dealt with vandalism, theft, and burglary, and didn't get as much excitement as some of the others, like the 75th. Sure, there was the occasional armed robbery, arson, or shooting to shake things up, but cases like mine didn't happen often . . . especially to an officer.

I cringed when I thought about the many headlines splashed across *The Brooklyn Paper* and *The Brooklyn Daily Eagle*. I even saw my picture in the *Post* once. *Brooklyn police say the daughter of one of their own is the victim of a kidnapping. Officer Parker of Brooklyn PD searches for missing daughter. Cops hunt man after officer's daughter abducted.*

All I saw when reading those words was *Useless father can't even protect his own daughter.* That was what they might as well have said because that was exactly what I felt every day when Kate's mother looked at me.

I squeezed my little girl tighter. We'd been out in all the chaos of the hallway, but I needed answers from Charlie, and I needed them yesterday. He was running around like a chicken with his head cut off, so I told him to meet me in the conference room.

When I turned toward the door, I realized that Kate had slumped down in my arms and fallen asleep with her head on my shoulder. Her soft breath blew across my neck. Now I was glad I'd told Charlie to meet me in the room, because it was much quieter than out there. When I found a chair that looked semi-comfortable, I slouched down in it so that Kate could rest her head on my chest.

How was it possible she could be this relaxed with me? I never once imagined that could happen. As each year slipped by, I had become more distraught at the idea that she wouldn't know who I was when I found her. Technically, I didn't think she really knew me. She just understood that I was her father, but even that I was grateful for at this point. She seemed to be an outgoing little thing, though, never letting a pause linger in our conversation all the way up until she fell asleep.

Charlie strode in the door with his hands weighted down by stacks of papers that I recognized as case files. He plopped them down loudly on the big wooden conference table in front of me, and I growled at him.

"Dammit! Sorry. Fuck, I'm not good with kids," he explained.

"You don't say . . ."

"Yeah, I cussed in front of that other one too." He waved his hand dismissively, and I chuckled at his obvious uneasiness at being around children.

"How much do you know, Charlie? How the he—" I caught myself and then continued, "How in the world does she know who I am? I haven't seen her since she was a baby! And what is that nanny doing out there . . . Shouldn't she be in handcuffs or something?"

The more the words came flying out of my mouth, the more heated I felt. I had always thought the next time I saw Raegan Hayes, I would have my hands tightly clutching her throat. Having

Kate back in my arms seemed to cool my need for immediate vengeance, but that didn't mean I wanted her getting off easily.

Charlie sighed loudly and ran his hands roughly down over his eyes. "Lane . . . I know it's always been easy for you to blame her, but you need to stop. What is Raegan going to think when she hears you say that?"

"I trusted her to take care of my daughter!" I blurted out a little too loudly. As the last word came out, I spotted two little eyes watching me from the doorway.

Before I could say anything else, I heard a commotion out in the hall. A female voice yelled, "Where is she?!" and I instinctively pulled Kate in a little closer.

"Shit, Lane! Did you not tell her you were taking Kate in here?" Charlie scrambled out of the room. Why the hell did I have to tell *anyone* where I took *my* daughter?

Braden was still standing in the doorway, and I swear that little guy was glaring at me! How did a four-year-old know how to cast off a glare that hard?

"That's my sister," he stated while slowly entering the room. I ignored his words because I didn't have the heart to tell the little guy how wrong he was. "You can't take her away from me."

Suddenly, a flushed and panting Raegan flew in through the doorway, her long, dark brown hair swinging wildly behind her. When she spotted Kate sleeping soundly in my arms and then looked to Braden sitting in a chair by the door, she visibly relaxed. Her ample chest rose and fell dramatically, and I couldn't help thinking what lay beneath that white button-down shirt. Kate shifted under my arm, and I snapped out of my ridiculous gawking.

"You can't do that!" Raegan yelled at me from across the room. A cry escaped her clenched teeth, and she furiously swiped at her eyes. When I'd seen her earlier, I hadn't noticed the bandage on the side of her face, but now that she was closer, I could see that whatever was under the white tape was nothing to sneeze at. So many questions, I didn't even know where to begin.

"I can't take *my* daughter into a quiet room to sleep?" I tried to reply nonchalantly.

"You can't just take her out of my sight. I'm not ready for that," she whispered.

"Guys, let's calm down a bit. We're all tired. Chief is on his way up here and when he clears it, I'll take you to a hotel," he said, looking at Raegan while talking. "But you'll have to come back tomorrow morning."

"Joy," she stated sardonically.

"I can take my daughter anywhere I like. *I* have the freedom to do that, because she's *my* daughter. Don't forget that." My words came out harsh and cruel, exactly how I had meant them. If my mom were here, she would definitely be swatting me on the back of the head for talking to a woman like that, but sometimes anger consumed my manners—and this was one of those times.

Raegan began taking in deep, calming breaths while she ran her fingers through Braden's hair. He had passed out too, and his little body somehow managed to stretch across three chairs. This gang was exhausted.

I watched as Raegan slowly sat down at the table and then rubbed her hand over the bandage above her eye. I was pretty sure I spotted her pressing down roughly, and when she winced, she took a few more breaths. What I wasn't sure about was what the hell was going on and whether or not I should be bracing myself for an impending storm.

"Why do I get the feeling you're placing some kind of blame on me?" she asked.

"Well, you *were* hired to *take care* of my child, and well . . . here I am four years later, meeting her again. *Take care*, not *take*. There's a difference."

"Lane! Cut that shit out," Charlie scolded.

She physically recoiled from my words, and as much as I hated doing that to anyone, I just couldn't help it. This was my daughter we were talking about, and I'd missed *years* of her life, thanks in part to the woman seated in front of me.

"Mr. Parker, you think . . ." She paused and popped her knuckles fretfully. "You're telling me that you never stopped for one moment to think that maybe, just maybe, Braden and I were abducted too? All this time you thought I had something to do with this . . ." She waved her hands erratically, indicating the kids, the police station . . . the entire situation. "Are you out of your mind?!"

"I didn't think you were involved at first. And I never would have accused you until I found video footage of you talking to Camilla Flores. You were speaking to her on a park bench the day *before* the kidnapping," I ground out.

She visibly flinched when I said Mrs. Flores's name, but then she caught herself and said, "Mr. Parker, where is Ash? She's much easier to talk to. Why isn't she here?" She looked at Kate in my arms when she spoke of her mother.

Charlie shifted nervously on his feet and turned his back toward us to "read" paperwork. *Coward.* I would have loved to have avoided this awful conversation at all costs, but I had to tell her at some point.

"Ash passed away last year."

She must have been expecting me to say something like that. She had to have. That was the only way I could explain the almost instant sob that ripped through her chest. Her misery almost brought me back to that time. I almost allowed her to bring me down with her, but I quickly locked down my defenses and kept the emotions at bay.

"How?" she squeaked.

"Car accident. She and her boyfriend were intoxicated. They were both ejected from the car." I spoke to her as if I were reading the police report. For a moment I could almost feel the papers shaking in my hands again.

Her eyes cleared for an instant and she glared at me, probably because of my cold manner. "Ash had a . . . boyfriend?"

"We got divorced, Raegan. We could barely look at each other after . . ." I glanced down at the beauty in my arms and was struck by an overwhelming sadness that Ash couldn't see her right now. She would have groaned about Kate getting her nose, but I had always thought her nose was adorable. She would have loved that Kate still had my hair color. And she would have laughed at how outgoing Kate was—we'd always wondered what her personality would be like.

"So, no, Ash won't be joining us. It's just Kate and me now. I'm not a cop anymore either, so I think my new job will allow me to be at home more often with her." I was rambling and I quickly zipped my lips. She didn't need to know anything about me.

I brought my arm up to brush some stray hairs out of my daughter's face, but my shoulder pulled painfully. For the first time since Kate had kissed it, I remembered the wound. The pain had been nonexistent, or more likely I had been too wrapped up in her to notice.

Speaking of pain, I wanted to get back to what had caused all of this in the first place, but based on Raegan's reaction, my theory now seemed less and less solid. There was only one way to find out. "Were you and Mrs. Flores friends? Did you have this planned out for a while?"

"You know what, Mr. Parker? I'm glad you're not a cop anymore because you sure as hell are a terrible one!" she snapped, seething.

"Terrible? I'm the one that found the camera footage! We would have never known where to even begin searching for you guys. I think that's the sign of a pretty damn good cop."

"Yes, but blaming me because of some park camera recording is not! I'll bet that footage didn't even have sound!" When my eyes shifted away from her for only a moment, she jumped on it. "I'm right, aren't I?"

"There wasn't any audio, but I know what I saw."

"You saw *nothing!*" she yelled.

"I saw enough to lead me to Flores."

"Lead you to him?!" Her voice had reached an almost frightening level, and I was impressed that both kids were still sound asleep. "If you knew where he was, where the hell were you? *Where the hell were you?* Where were you when I had to beg for Kate's life because they wanted to toss her?" I flinched at her words. "Yeah, toss her like she was trash, because they didn't want a girl. Where were you when I had to rock two crying babies all by myself, night after night? Where were you when I had to get slashes because I wouldn't let the men take Kate wherever the hell they wanted to take her?"

"Stop!" I shouted and then sank back, berating myself for raising my voice, especially with Kate in my arms. "I'm not ready to hear all of this right now," I said, forcing a calm I didn't feel into my voice.

"I wasn't ready to live it either," she responded quietly. "You," she pointed at me, then over to Charlie and out the door, presumably at the other officers. She rose out of her chair and continued, "Did nothing. *I* took care of them. *I* took the punishments for them. *I* got us out of there. Don't talk to me about this being my fault."

Charlie and I stared openmouthed at the five-foot-five, painfully beautiful woman who stood across the table from us. I wasn't sure what to say, and I had a feeling Charlie was just as dumbfounded. Whatever I was expecting to fly out of that saucy little mouth, *that* had not been it—none of it.

"I'd like to go to that hotel now, Officer Charlie," she stated while slowly sitting back down again with her hands splayed across the wooden table.

Charlie looked at her, but he couldn't quite seem to snap out of his stupor. Finally, he cleared his throat and tried to resemble a professional. "Uh, yeah. I'm just waiting on Chief to get here first."

"*No*," she began just as Chief marched in the door, looking as if he'd been woken from a deep sleep.

"Chief, I'm glad you could make it," Charlie stated professionally.

"Chief." I nodded my head toward the gruff older man who stood in the doorway.

"Knock it off, Lane, and call me Dad. You don't work for me anymore, son," my dad barked at me.

I hadn't seen my parents since Ash's funeral. I knew how bad it was of me to cut them out, but they just reminded me too much of Kate. Of pain and loneliness and all that I had lost. I left New York mainly so that I could look for Kate on the West Coast, but I also left to escape the memories and the pitying looks from everyone I knew.

When my dad finally got a good look at me, I saw the instant he realized what—or rather, *who*—I had in my hands. His face visibly softened and he quietly walked toward us. I swiveled in my chair away from the table and faced him as he knelt down in front of his granddaughter.

"Your mother needs to be here," he whispered, hovering over her. He looked as if he didn't know where or how to touch her.

"Ma can see her tomorrow. They've been here all night, Dad. I think it's time they slept in a bed."

"She's so beautiful . . ." he said, sighing reverently.

"She is, isn't she?"

He pulled out the chair next to me and sat down without moving any farther away from her. His hair was much grayer than the last time I'd seen him, and his face seemed to wrinkle more as he got older. But he was still my dad, the same one who threw baseballs to me for hours every evening after school and used to constantly drill me so I could be successful in the police academy. As much as I knew he loved me, I think that he loved Kate on a whole other level. It killed my parents when she went missing.

"Look, son. I don't know what I just walked in on, but Doyle has caught me up to speed on everything Raegan told him on the trip out here."

I quickly looked over at Charlie, who had a smug look on his face. "You knew everything she was going to say?" I asked, and he nodded his head. I grumbled, "And you just let me lay into her like that?"

"You deserved what you got back," he stated casually.

I looked over at Raegan, who had moved back to the chairs where Braden was sleeping. She wouldn't look at me while she ran her fingers through his hair, and I began to let my mind consider the fact that maybe I had been wrong all these years. I mean, could she truly be guilty of such a crime when she seemed genuinely crushed that Ash had passed away?

Dad lowered his voice so only I could hear. "Son, this little girl only knows those two people over there," he said, pointing toward Raegan and Braden.

I interrupted, "No, Dad, somehow she knows me. She lets me hold her, and she talks to me as if we've known each other all along."

"I see that she appears quite comfortable with you, and I couldn't be happier. But that's not going to comfort her all the time. Raegan has raised her, kept her safe, and loved her. Don't force that separation too quickly."

"You don't think Raegan had anything to do with all of this?" I tried to keep my voice as quiet as possible.

"Son, look at her. I mean, actually look at her. Do you honestly feel like she would be capable of something like that?"

I stared at her hunched figure and watched her eyes droop slightly from exhaustion. She'd never once looked frantically around the room or sneered at police like the criminals I had seen in the past. She only seemed to care about the kids and their well-being.

I sighed loudly and looked down at Kate in my arms and then over to Raegan, who was still concentrating on her son. Could I be enough for Kate alone? Parenthood was supposed to be a learn-as-they-grow type of thing, not a jump-into-it-four-years-later type of thing.

"I have no idea what I'm doing . . . Ash used to tell me what to do."

"Let Raegan teach you," he offered softly. "Remember the girl that used to help you and Ash tremendously? The one who used to get up with Kate in the middle of the night while she was trying to care for her own son, just so you two could sleep. If she didn't stay the night with you guys, she was there bright and early every morning, ready to handle two babies . . . all to help *you*."

"Dad, we were paying her," I smarted.

"Oh, yeah, below minimum wage. Trust me, she wasn't living a profligate lifestyle, by any means. Quit making her the bad guy, son."

I leaned my head forward over Kate and squeezed my temples firmly. I just couldn't seem to get the idea out of my head that Raegan had something to do with it. Maybe it was just the parent in me that needed answers. But how could she have had a conversation with Flores's wife one day, and the next day Flores stole my baby right out of my own home?

"Look . . ." Dad patted my shoulder and I winced at the treacherous blow. At least that was what my shoulder thought of it. "What the hell happened? You know what—you're here, you're alive. Just tell me tomorrow. I'm tired." He spoke louder so that everyone could hear now. "I got you guys adjoining rooms at the Marriott close to the bridge. You can work out your sleeping arrangements between the four of you."

Raegan smiled weakly and stood on feeble and tired legs. "Thank you, Mr. Parker."

Dad made his way for the door and looked back at me, saying, "Oh, and son? This hotel ain't cheap. Work out your situation and find a more permanent location. You know you still have your apartment. Your mother's been dusting it every week since you left it."

"Got it, Dad," I said, quickly shutting down *that* conversation.

"Raegan, dear," my dad said, looking across the room at her. "I'm not sure how all of this will be handled. I know we'll need to do psych evals on all three of you, probably even Lane. There will be a lot of annoying questions. Just be patient, please, and I'll try my damnedest to rush the process along. From there, we can help you find a place to live."

She swallowed harshly and nodded her head while looking away. I swore I saw a wet gleam in her eyes before she could completely turn from my sight. I stood with Kate wilting over my shoulder, still lightly snoozing. Raegan scooped up a backpack, but before she could link her arms through the straps, I reached out and grabbed it from her. She whipped her head around quickly, and I found myself on the receiving end of a death glare from two beautiful, bright green eyes.

"I'll carry your things," I said lightly. "You've got your hands full with him." She slowly released the straps of the bag and I draped it over my forearm. "Is this it?" She nodded her head and I laughed. "Between the three of you, there's only one little backpack?"

She bent over and struggled to pick up Braden without waking him. Raegan was petite, and it looked like Braden would be taller than she was before she knew it. When he was finally snuggled in close to her neck, she straightened and headed for the door.

"Yes, that's our only bag. Next time I plan an escape, I'll remember to pack more."

Although normally I would have smiled at her saucy mouth, her words sliced through me like a rusty, jagged knife. I began to wonder what she meant by *escape* and was once again reminded how little I actually knew about what brought us to this moment.

I caught up to her right before she headed down the stairs and scooped up my bag along the way. Before I could say a word, she immediately held her hand up, halting me. "Not now. I'm too tired. I can imagine your questions, but just . . . not now, please."

"Okay . . . I can do that. As long as you promise to answer all my questions tomorrow."

She stepped out into the warm night air and looked back at me. "As long as you stop accusing me of kidnapping."

I kept quiet because I couldn't get the image out of my head of her laughing on that park bench with Mrs. Flores. The longer I looked at her, though, the harder it was to imagine her stealing a child or even aiding someone who did. I watched as she stroked Braden's back lovingly and looked back to check on Kate's sleeping form. She cared about them, that much was obvious.

Raegen stood at the curb, looking at me expectantly. I then realized it was the middle of the night and I didn't have a car to take us to the hotel. And there was no way in hell my child was getting in a disgusting patrol car tonight.

"Uh . . . I'll go to the corner and see if there are any cabs," I told her. She nervously looked around her at the darkened streets. Just then, another officer stepped out of the creaky old front door. I recognized him from my training days. "Sergeant Williams, can you do me a favor?" He inclined his head my way but didn't respond. "Can you keep an eye on her for a second? I need to run down and catch a cab."

I began stepping away when Raegan hurried to my side and said, "I can come with you. No need for a babysitter."

"Don't worry about it. I know you're tired and you don't need to walk all the way down there. Just wait here." When I tried to step away again, she latched onto my forearm and gave Sergeant Williams a frightened look. She didn't seem very trusting of others. Except me, the guy who had called her a kidnapper . . . she trusted.

"All right then . . . never mind, man. Thanks, though." I waved off the sergeant, who seemed less than pleased that I had just wasted two measly seconds of his life.

I used to be like that. Always go, go, go. No wasting time. No looking at anyone when you were shoving your way down the street. No time for dawdling. That was my New York life. But then I moved and realized that there were more important things along the way, and sometimes it was okay to actually look up and smile at the people around you.

I'd always assumed once I got Kate back we would settle back into our old apartment and try to go back to normal. Now, I just didn't know what I was going to do. Could I move back to New York? Could I really leave Audrey and all of my closest friends in Texas, living fifteen hundred miles away from them? They were my family now. I just didn't know if that was possible.

The cab to the hotel took no longer than fifteen minutes, but everyone in the car except for the driver and me was asleep within five. Raegan slumped against the window, breathing softly, while Braden clung to her neck. As we pulled up under the brightly lit hotel drive, I swiped my card in the slot to pay our tab. Raegan shook awake when she heard the beep.

We scooted across the seat silently, each of us carrying a sleeping child. When I stepped out, I held my hand out to help

Raegan. She couldn't seem to get a firm hold on Braden in her sleepiness, so I reached down and scooped him up right next to Kate. Raegan easily slid out and smiled at me in what appeared to be gratitude.

"I can take him back now," she quietly stated.

"I've got them; it's no trouble, really," I told her, and turned to walk toward the entrance. She quickly caught up to me and slid my bag and their backpack off my forearm.

"I can help," she told me, trying her best to lift my heavy bag. I smiled and allowed her to struggle. If she wanted to help so badly . . .

Dad had given me the key cards to our room before we left the station, so I knew our rooms were on the twelfth floor. The elevator ride up was silent, except for the sound of the kids breathing softly against my chest. I found our side-by-side rooms and handed Raegan her key card while I walked past her to my room.

She froze and cleared her throat at me. Still holding the two kids, I turned to see her glaring at me.

I chuckled and said, "Go in. Open the adjoining door and we'll figure this out."

She was in her room in a flash, and before I could fully step inside mine, I could already hear her unlocking her connected door. I had to shift Kate around so I could use my hand to twist the lock on mine. When it finally clicked to unlock, Raegan immediately pushed the door open.

"Don't trust me?" I asked with a smile. I laughed to myself when she didn't reply. Apparently, I was in a snarky mood all of a sudden.

When I slid Braden down my side onto the bed, Raegan quickly pulled the covers out from underneath him. He curled up on a pillow without even opening his eyes. The movement caused Kate to stir, and her little blond eyelashes began to flutter.

"Where do you think she'll want to sleep?" I quietly asked. My voice trembled because I hated the idea of having to ask someone else about my own daughter, but that was what I had to deal with. I needed to just be thankful I had her. Evidently, if I was given an inch, I wanted a mile. My mom used to tell me that all the time when I was a kid.

"With Braden and me," she replied while pulling the sheets back on the opposite side of the bed.

I began to protest, but Kate's soft whimper startled me. She began to squirm and moan in my arms, so I squeezed her tighter and attempted to gently shush her. Raegan flew around the bed and tried to take her from my arms.

"I can do this," I spat out.

Kate thrashed suddenly and Raegan pleaded, "Just give her to me; I can help her. Please . . ." I ignored her and continued to try and calm down a restless Kate in my arms.

"Shh . . . you're okay. It's okay . . ."

"*Mama!*" Kate's voice wailed in the quiet room. My heart hammered erratically in my chest and I began to panic. "Mama, Mama, Mama!" she continued, all while it appeared as if she were still sleeping.

Raegan looked at me with wide eyes and I asked, "What do I do?" *Of course.* If Kate knew about me, then she must know about Ash as well. There was no way I could tell her where her mom was right now. This was not the time.

With my mind fully distracted, Raegan managed to weasel Kate out of my arms and quickly began to whisper in her ear. I couldn't hear what she was saying, but it seemed to comfort Kate instantly.

Kate's hand came up and rubbed across Raegan's cheek and jawline. "Mama . . ." she sighed contentedly.

"Wait a second . . ." I caught myself speaking too loud. The wheels in my head were spinning at full speed, and I was having a hard time comprehending what had just happened. "Did she call you . . . does she think . . ." I couldn't make myself say it.

Raegan turned and gently laid Kate down on the bed, She left a wide space between her and Braden, and I assumed it was so she could sleep in the middle. Kate began to stir again and then I saw her eyes finally open. She mumbled, "I need Daddy-bear, Mama."

"I'll get him, baby," Raegan replied, and I watched in confusion as she slid past me without making eye contact. She crouched down by her backpack and dug a teddy bear out from the bottom. My heart jumped into my throat when I recognized the bear. *I* had gotten that bear for her when Kate was a baby, and now I suddenly understood how she knew who I was.

I had been a rookie in the force and I'd thankfully gotten partnered with Charlie Doyle, an old family friend. Charlie was only a few years older than I was, but he'd already been on the force for six years by then. I was a spoiled shit and had a hook because my dad was already the chief of the 72nd precinct. Therefore, I knew where I was headed before I even graduated from the academy.

We ended up catching a long break one day and decided to take advantage of it by getting something decent to eat across the bridge. We were still in uniform because we had to get back on our beat after lunch. Charlie and I had an ongoing search to find the best subs, and while Brooklyn hands-down had the best delis, we'd heard about this place south of Central Park that cured their meats in-house and we wanted to check it out. It sounded a bit too touristy for me, but hey, a good submarine sandwich can tempt me almost anywhere.

We grabbed our lunch at the counter and decided to sit on the steps surrounding the Pulitzer fountain on Fifth Avenue. I was right about it being touristy, but the sub smelled amazing. Just as I was chomping down on my first bite, we heard a big commotion across Fifth at the hugely popular FAO Schwarz toy store.

We sorrowfully tossed our subs and high-tailed it across the way. *Fucking oath of being a law enforcement officer twenty-four hours a day, seven days a week.* I was fucking hungry. We entered the colossal toy store and immediately spotted the problem. Two grown-ass women were throwing punches and grabbing each other's hair. One of them clung tightly to a toy that looked like a damn robot dog.

Hell, I thought that shit only happened during Christmastime, not in the middle of the year. Charlie split them up and ordered them to leave the store, and no one ended up getting that damn toy. As we were walking toward the door, I nudged Charlie toward the glass escalator.

"Hey, we're already here. Let's see if I can afford to buy Kate something," I told him.

He chuckled and followed behind me. "She's a baby, dude. All she wants right now is tit." I whacked him across the chest with the back of my hand as we ascended the stairs.

At the top floor, we found a shop where kids were building teddy bears. They could be personalized with sound bites, clothing, and even pictures. I chose a small bear that could hold a photo in the little pocket of his shirt, and I even made a sound bite that she would be able to hear when she was old enough to squeeze his foot. Charlie mocked me the entire way back to Brooklyn for that.

That night, Ash had stuck a photograph of me in a little plastic sleeve on the bear's shirt, and we sat it on Kate's dresser in her room without much thought. When Kate had gone missing, neither of us noticed that the bear had disappeared as well.

Seeing Kate snuggle that bear tightly caused an aggravating tear to slip from my eye, but I quickly batted it away.

"Daddy?" Kate whispered. I hurriedly moved to her bedside and knelt next to her on the ground.

"Yeah, Kit Kat?"

"You aren't going to leave, are you?" she asked innocently.

"Never."

"Cross your heart?" A huge yawn broke out with her last word.

"Cross my heart and hope to die, stick a needle in my eye," I recited the old saying.

Her tired giggle made me smile. "Ew, Daddy. Don't stick a needle in your eye."

"Sleep, baby. I'll be right here when you wake up." I pulled her covers over her little body and kissed her forehead. The moment was surreal—I couldn't believe I was actually tucking my daughter into bed tonight.

- Six -

RAEGAN -

Lane sat on the floor and leaned up against the nightstand as Kate fell asleep holding his hand. I had to admit he was quite good with her. While he stared at her lovingly, I dug through my backpack on the dresser and lined up four different pill bottles. I really didn't care what he thought about those, since he had already seen the huge bandage across my temple. The doctors had given me antibiotics, steroids, medication for my low blood pressure due to my injury, and also some pain meds that I hadn't tried yet. I didn't know if it was my injury that had made me lethargic all day or those medications, but I was ready to feel like a human again and not some walking slug.

I swallowed down the first three doses and stared longingly at the fourth. I twisted the top open, then decided against it and closed the bottle quickly. I had a burning ache on my forehead and was sure those little white pain pills would put me out of my misery. But I didn't know how they would affect me, and I thought I needed to be on top of my game. Nothing could hinder me from taking care of Braden and Kate.

"Pain meds?" I heard Lane whisper. I nodded my head, but decided not to give him anything else. "If you need it, you should take them."

"I'll be fine." I sat on the edge of the bed, unlaced and removed my shoes, and then stripped off my socks. I hated that I had to sleep in my jeans tonight, but I didn't have any other clothes. If Lane was sticking around, there was no way in hell I was walking around in my panties.

"How does she have the bear?"

"They grabbed it with a few other nonessentials," I whispered.

"Why does she call you Mama?" he asked. I knew it was coming, but that didn't mean I wanted to answer.

"She heard Braden call me that," I answered simply.

"Did you try—" he started to ask.

"Of course. I tried for a very long time to get her to call me Raegan. When she finally did, then Braden started calling me by my first name. I couldn't have my own son not call me Mama. So I just let her. Years went by and it didn't seem so bad. Now I realize . . ."

"I understand." I wondered if he actually did, but at least he was letting the matter slide for now.

Lane stood up and pushed one arm above his head—his uninjured arm, I noticed. His entire body stretched out, and I caught a glimpse of a very alluring line of muscles that extended below his waistband. He really was huge. Even when we were at the police station, Lane stood out among all of the officers. He was probably six feet tall, but it wasn't his height that made him stand out. It was his body. Holy hell—his body had been sculpted into this gigantic masterpiece. I quickly turned from the tantalizing view.

When he walked away from the bed and scooped up his bag, I rushed to say, "Don't make me stick a needle in your eye."

He let out a deep chuckle that was way too sexy for *my* own good. Then I watched as he searched through his bag before setting some pill bottles of his own on top of the dresser close to mine.

"Trust me, I'm not going anywhere." He popped the top of his first bottle and let a few slide into his mouth. I watched the muscles in his throat bob up and down as he swallowed. He stared at the second bottle just like I had at my pain pills, but he ignored it as well.

"Pain meds?" I asked mockingly. He grunted in response, and I smirked at the fact that we both didn't seem to trust too easily. I knew I was too afraid of not being of sound mind around him, and I wondered if he felt the same way.

He pulled a few supplies out of his bag and then, to my chagrin, he tugged the back collar of his shirt over his head. My mouth hung open and there was no hope of it closing anytime soon. His body was unreal. It had to have been some kind of illusion, something straight out of my creative imagination.

The muscles in his back moved with a raw elegance that I had never thought possible for someone his size. They bulged and flexed with the movement of his good arm. The graceful line of his spine created the perfect symmetry for each side of his well-defined back. The line was a tease that disappeared into his shorts, and I let my mind wander with thoughts of what his butt looked like. Probably perfect.

His skin was smooth and a blank canvas, all except for a little bit of script low on the back of his neck. I couldn't make it out, but it seemed to fit perfectly, just resting above his shoulder blades.

He leaned toward the mirror over the chest of drawers and examined the area on top of his shoulder that was covered in white surgical tape and gauze. He began pulling back the tape, and I watched the creases in his eyes as he winced. He moved to the other side and tried to pull the tape from there, but I could tell the movement from one arm pulled too much on the other, causing him a significant amount of pain.

I sighed and walked toward him. Scooping up all of his materials, I made my way to the adjoining room. If I was going to do it, I needed light, and I didn't want to disturb Kate and Braden. He stood there frozen, still leaning toward the mirror and watching me through it. I crossed through the double doors, and a few beats later he followed me.

I pointed to the chair near the window and went to the bathroom to wash my hands. When I returned, I watched him effortlessly drag the chair in front of the mirror. He seated himself facing the glass, probably so he could watch me in the reflection.

"Don't trust me?" I asked, repeating yet another one of his lines back to him.

"*Should* I trust you?" he asked gruffly.

If I could have, I would have dug my fingers so far into his shoulder he wouldn't even consider saying something like that to me again. Instead, I kept it short and sweet. "I kept your daughter alive for four years. If that's not trustworthy, I don't know what is."

A harsh breath rushed past his teeth and he closed his eyes, not willing to look at me any longer. Fine, I could deal with that. I grabbed the edges of the tape on his shoulder and quickly yanked it back. I was mindful of his injury, but I really couldn't care less if the skin around it became a little sore.

"Agggh!" he yelled, covering his mouth with his good arm to muffle his cries. "Okay—shit, I deserved that!"

"Please, stop insinuating that I'm a kidnapper," I whispered. "I would never . . ." My eyes became glassy and I stifled the sob in my chest. "I would never put those children in danger. Never." My last word came out as a harsh bite.

"Fine . . ." he grumbled, like a child who had just been reprimanded.

"Mr. Parker—"

"Please stop calling me that. I don't pay you anymore, and it's just weird. Too formal. Besides, you're not that much younger than me."

"How old are you?" I asked.

"Twenty-eight. And you're what . . . twenty-four?" he returned.

I nodded and said, "Okay . . . Lane . . ." I took a deep breath and thought about the best way to approach this without having to drag it into a prolonged conversation. I really would like to catch *some* sleep before the morning. "She tricked me. Mrs. Flores. She used my naïveté against me and she did it well. I just assumed she was some overly curious old lady who wanted to talk about a young girl's life at the park." I used some of the hand sanitizer he had on the dresser and began to take a good look at his shoulder. "I was an idiot."

He hung his head down low for a few long minutes, but I knew he was listening intently. I couldn't see his facial expression, or tell what he was thinking, so I took the opportunity to get the bandage change out of the way. I let my eyes roam for a moment and noticed the tattoo on his neck again. It simply said *Kate*. It was written in a feminine handwriting that should have looked strange on his masculine body, but it didn't. It was perfect.

"You shouldn't have been carrying Kate around. You've already pulled a stitch out." The cut on his shoulder looked angry and red, but it wasn't any longer than about two inches. It was slender like . . . a knife. Had he been stabbed?

"If holding her causes all of them to pull out, I won't care. Won't stop me," he whispered sullenly down into his chest.

"I didn't think it would. I'm pretty sure I can hold it together with two pieces of tape anyway."

He shrugged his shoulders, indicating he really could not care less.

"Is this a stab wound?" I asked curiously, because I couldn't ever seem to keep anything in for too long.

"Yep."

"Should I be worried that you get yourself into situations that cause you to get stabbed?" I asked, trying to get him to elaborate.

"Worried about me or worried about Kate?"

"Just worried." I didn't care to clarify.

"It won't happen again. I used to enter these underground fighting matches a couple times a year because I knew that Flores would be there. He was a hardcore gambler, and it was the only way I could figure out how to get close to him. So I learned to fight and showed up. This last one got a little messy."

"Did *he* do it?" I whispered.

"Might as well have. He told me Kate was dead that night." The break in his voice caused me to tremble. "That was worse than anything a knife could do."

"Oh, Lane . . ."

I couldn't imagine hearing something like that. My heart hurt for him and the man he must have been after that kind of news. His emotions had been tossed about just as much as ours had been lately. I needed to give him a little slack, just as he should have been giving some to me.

After wiping down the injured area with antiseptic and some of the clear ointment, I covered it back up with clean pieces of gauze. I couldn't help letting my fingers linger for a few seconds longer than necessary on his warm skin. I told myself that I was just making sure the tape had properly adhered, but if I was being honest, I just wanted to touch him.

I had been so starved for touch from anyone older than a child for so long that his beautiful, honed body seemed to be singing to the blood that rushed through my veins. The first time I'd met Lane, for my job interview, I'd been attracted to him. It would have been impossible not to be. Even before he was built like a brick house, he was gorgeous. His sandy blond hair looked striking against his lightly tanned skin. His hazel eyes sometimes hinted at being green, which only caused me to want to look a moment too long.

Of course, I never acted on those lustful feelings. Ash had been my friend, and I was eternally grateful to her for allowing me to work for her family. I was in a tough bind, being a young, single mom with a baby. Yes, Lane was nice to look at, but that was all he had ever been to me. Eye candy. *Delicious, mouth-watering* eye candy.

The object of my frustrating attraction stood up in front of me, causing the proximity of our bodies to be too close. He ushered me into the chair he had just vacated and I looked up at him, confused. He didn't say anything but instead just walked away, and I soon heard the water running in the bathroom. He returned a moment later, wiping his hands off on a towel and then tossing it onto the bed.

"Your turn." He tapped the side of his temple, indicating my injury.

I immediately sprang up. "No, no," I rushed to say. "I can take care of it on my own." The last thing I wanted was him anywhere near my face.

"It's only fair," he replied while rubbing the sanitizer gel on his hands. He already had his fingers gently peeling back the tape when he said, "Besides, you're bleeding through . . . you need to have it changed."

My eyes welled up at the idea of him seeing what was underneath all that dirty tape and gauze. Thankfully, it looked a lot better than it had a week ago, but it still wasn't pretty. His harsh string of curse words under his breath let me know he finally had it uncovered. I shot up and tried to walk away.

"Please, I can do it," I implored with tears in my eyes.

"And I can help. It's the least I can do after being an asshole to you." He pushed me back down gently and took a clean swab out of the sterile pack before wiping the area clean. "Why are you crying?" he asked softly. His voice had changed from demanding to calm in a matter of seconds.

"Because it's hideous."

"That's usually how cuts go. I don't think they're supposed to look pretty." I stayed silent in my seat because he had only confirmed my insecurity. He took a deep breath and continued, "The cut is unsightly, not you. Don't worry; you're still as beautiful as ever."

Before my jaw could drop at his words, he quickly rushed on to say, "I can take care of this. Besides, I'm not squeamish, and this has to hurt like a bitch. Am I allowed to ask what happened, or is that rude?" he inquired.

"You can ask, but it's a long story and I really don't want to talk about it yet."

"Fair enough," he responded easily.

I had stitches stretching from above my eyebrow, past my temple, and down to my ear. Where his laceration was cleaned up nice and neat with his stitches, mine still looked jagged and disgusting. I just knew I would have a hell of a scar.

"I wasn't fair to you," he whispered. I almost smarted off at his words because that was a huge understatement, but then decided to just let him continue. "It was always easier for me to blame it on you. I didn't *always* think it was your fault. I had a one-track mind to find Flores, but every once in a while I'd think about that tape of you and his wife and I'd see red. When I saw Kate again and then you, I just . . . I had no idea how to process that. I really am sorry. I never knew how to anticipate this moment."

"I think it's new for everyone," I offered.

"I'm also . . . jealous," he whispered.

"Jealous?" I laughed cynically.

"You've had all these years with her. It's not your fault regardless; I had no room to be an asshole."

I was alarmed when Lane set down yet another soaked piece of gauze in front of me. Should I have been bleeding that much? He gently soothed some of the antibiotic ointment across the side of my face with the lightest of strokes.

"This doesn't look good, Raegan. Shouldn't you be in the hospital or something?" he whispered.

"I've been in the hospital for the past two weeks. That's where Charlie picked me up. They said I should be fine, as long as I continue taking that arsenal of drugs in there."

He started to say something but stopped himself as he stared down into my eyes. For a moment I felt something between us. I sensed so many unspoken words and even a tingling feeling that I was unfamiliar with. He broke the spell first with a slight shake of his head, and then reached out to grab more gauze. I closed my eyes for the remainder of his doctoring, feeling confused.

Once he had me completely fixed up, I stood slowly, trying to catch my bearings. My head began to spin, and I had to close my eyes again and wait for it to pass. Even with my eyes closed, I felt a crushing sense of whirling darkness around me. I reached out for anything that could stabilize this out-of-sorts feeling and was met by two strong arms.

"Hey, hey, you okay?" he asked with genuine worry in his voice.

"Yeah, just dizzy. It's a side effect of one of my meds. It happens a lot, but they said once I stop taking them, it should go away." My eyes slowly opened once the spell began to fade, and I spotted the concern in his. I'd only had a few dark spots in my vision compared to the complete blackness I used to get. That had to be a good sign.

"How long do you have to take them?"

"Until my heart heals and I can regulate my blood pressure without them." I stated word for word what the doctor explained to me just twenty-four hours ago. I regretfully dropped my hands away from his warm skin.

"Your heart?!" he exclaimed, sounding alarmed.

I held up my hand and lethargically said, "Tomorrow, okay? I'm so tired, Lane."

"You're right. I'm sorry. We'll talk tomorrow."

He headed to his bathroom and I reentered the darkened bedroom. I crawled in between the kids, and my head was so thankful for the pillow underneath it that I was out before I even heard Lane turn off the shower in the bathroom.

∿

Soft giggles woke me from my sleep. I hadn't been able to sleep very deeply for the past couple of years. I was always afraid something would happen while I was out, so eventually my body caught up with my mind and learned how to slumber, always in a semialert state.

My back faced the window, and when I opened my eyes, I smiled at the sight of two bright, smiling faces snickering at each other. They were each other's best friends. No matter what kind of situation we had been thrown into, I could never regret the bond that had grown between them. They didn't need TV, video games, or an endless string of toys to occupy themselves. They had each other, and the games they created between the two of them amazed me every day.

Currently, they seemed to be in some kind of staring contest, seeing which one could go without blinking first. Braden could always make Kate giggle, which caused her to blink within seconds. It was the best sound in the world to wake up to.

"Good morning, sweethearts," I said, stretching and wishing I could sleep for a few more hours. I was shocked when I saw that it was already eleven in the morning. Even with eight hours of sleep, I still felt as if I had been run over by a bus. Ever since I'd gotten sick, I hadn't felt like I could ever fully recharge my batteries. I was always running a little low and really hoped that would go away soon. "How long have you guys been up?"

"Shh!" Braden and Kate promptly admonished me. Their index fingers covered their mouths in a highly dramatic fashion.

"Daddy's sleeping!" Kate whispered. "He didn't leave." She smiled brilliantly as if she couldn't believe he had really stayed.

"Duh, Kate. He crossed his heart, remember?" Hmm, he was supposed to have been sleeping when Lane said that. *Sneaky boy.*

I rolled over in the huge king-size bed and looked at where they had pointed moments ago. A cough sputtered out of my throat at the sight of Lane. Last night he had pulled the couch across the room and pushed it flush against the side of the bed Kate slept on.

His large body could barely fit across the length of it. An average human being would have made that piece of furniture look like a normal, full-length couch, but a man built like a Greek god made the poor thing look like an armchair. One of his legs was draped over the low backside and his feet were hanging off the end. His undamaged arm was slung above his head, dangling over the end. He had the sling back on, and his injured arm was cradled against his chest. He didn't look even a little bit comfortable, and I felt bad that we had all stretched out in that magnificent bed while he squashed himself onto that plastic-covered furniture.

"He has a lot of muscles," I heard Braden whisper. I had to agree with him there. He told me that he didn't work for the police department anymore, but I wasn't sure what he did now. Regardless, all of that fighting he had been doing to try to catch Flores really had kept his body in outstanding shape.

"That's because he's a superhero," Kate informed Braden.

"I'm gonna have muscles like that too," he told her.

"I'm sure you'll be just as strong, buddy," I chuckled. "Just remember you have to eat all of your vegetables. I bet Lane always eats his spinach."

The crease in Braden's nose crinkled and I could tell he was deep in thought. I had a feeling he was weighing the odds of leafy greens actually causing muscles in his head, which made me laugh to myself.

"Let's let him sleep in a bit more. We can go play in the other room until he wakes up."

"But . . ." Kate hesitated. "I think he would be sad if we were gone."

"We'll be super quiet, Mama," Braden added with an exaggerated whisper.

"All right. Well, I'm going to take a shower, but I'm serious, you two—do not wake him up." I dumped out books from the backpack and even some crayons and coloring pages for them to share.

"Thank you, Mama," Kate murmured. My heart clenched at her words. How much longer did I get to be her "Mama"? I just couldn't stand the idea of it being any different, but I knew things would unquestionably change sometime soon.

LANE -

Sleeping on the floor probably would have been a better choice than that tiny-ass couch. My legs were hanging off the arm of one side, and my feet were asleep from the blood loss. That annoying pins-and-needles feeling poked from the inside out. I slowly twisted my feet in a circular motion and turned my head toward the tiny whispers that came from the bed.

Kate and Braden were leaning toward each other, deep in conversation.

"That's a really good job, sissy," Braden said.

"Thanks. I'm making it for you, and you can add it to the other pictures I made you," she replied.

"I don't think we're going to get to go back and get all of our things from home," he stated solemnly.

She shrugged and told him, "It's okay. I like it here better. Daddy's here."

"He's your daddy, not mine," Braden expressed sadly.

"Maybe he can be your daddy too." She looked up at him with so much hope in her eyes, I almost wanted to be the kid's dad just so that look would always stay there on her sweet face.

"No, I got Mama, and you got your daddy."

"But I want Mama too," she said, panicking.

"Don't worry, Kate. I'm your big brother, and brothers have to take care of their sisters." I swore that little guy puffed out his chest with those words. Kate leaned over and kissed him loudly on the cheek, and he giggled while swiping his hands across his face. "Eww, Kate!" he protested while continuing to laugh.

I decided to take that moment and sit up. The laughter immediately died from both of their faces, and I felt kind of bad for surprising them.

"Morning," I said with a rasp.

"Braden! Mama said we couldn't wake him up. He needs sleep," Kate said in an accusatory tone.

"Sorry." Braden looked up at me and spoke quietly.

"You guys are fine. It was about time I woke up anyway." I glanced at the clock and groaned when I saw that it was close to noon. Charlie would be calling soon, wondering why the hell we hadn't come back to the station yet. "I bet you two are starving, huh?"

They both stood up and flew into excited balls of energy, telling me how their stomachs had been growling all morning. The theatrics of it all made me chuckle. The silly noises caused each other to laugh as well, and they fell back down onto the bed in hysterics.

I made a request down to room service and ordered practically the entire menu—twice. I had no idea what they liked, but what they didn't eat, I would finish off. I had never gone that long without eating. Usually I was stuffing my face every hour, and now my stomach was cramping in pain from the lack of nourishment.

I heard Raegan moving around in the bathroom, so I got up to go speak with her, away from little ears. On my way over, I leaned down and kissed Kate on the top of her head. She wrapped her arms around my neck before I could lift away, and planted one right on my cheek. I still didn't understand all of it, but hell, I would take all the love she had to give. She released my neck and let me continue toward the bathroom.

The bathroom door clicked open and I pushed my way inside before Raegan could make her way out.

"What the . . ." she grunted at my unexpected intrusion. "Rude!"

"Hey, I wanted to talk . . ." Crap . . . I hadn't planned my invasion very well. Raegan was about six inches shorter than I was, so I hadn't noticed at first because her head only came up to my chest, but . . . she was only wearing a towel, and her heavy breasts created a magnificent swell, poking out from the top.

She hiked her towel up higher, but it didn't help one bit. It only caused them to jiggle and made the scenario even more difficult for me. I shifted, in case I needed to hide a growing problem.

"Lane . . . stop!" she breathed out.

"I'm sorry," I said, chuckling. "I swear I'm not usually this juvenile." She quirked an eyebrow up at me in apparent disbelief. "Okay, I've got it under control," I said. Fuck, she was hot. I so did *not* have it under control. I forced my eyes to her face. When I quickly looked over at the cut on her head, I immediately sobered.

"Shit, Raegan, your head." I searched frantically for something I could use to clean up her cut, which was bleeding down the side of her face. What the hell were these stitches doing if she kept bleeding out of them? I applied a gentle pressure with a wad of tissues. She sucked in air and I jumped to apologize. "I'm sorry. I just need to get the bleeding to stop."

She moved to grab the tissue but then realized that she needed both of her hands on the towel, so she relented and mumbled, "Thank you."

"How are you feeling?"

"Still dizzy and tired, but I think that's normal."

"Can I ask what happened now?" I requested softly, as if I were approaching a wounded animal.

"Can I answer when I have my clothes on?" She looked up at me through long eyelashes and I was gutted by those green eyes.

"I prefer you like this . . . but I guess for the kids' sake, it's more appropriate." I tried giving her my sexiest smirk and slowly retreated out of the bathroom.

"Oh, don't even try that playboy smile on me. It won't work, mister."

I clutched my chest. "Playboy smile? I'm offended!" I exclaimed teasingly.

She shrugged her shoulders in a knowing fashion, the action causing her breasts to rise and fall heavily. I wanted to pounce on her.

I started to speak, and she held up a finger to stop me. "You're probably about to defend yourself, but I don't need you to. Guys who look like you are playboys. I knew guys like you before . . ." She paused and seemed to consider her words carefully. "I just knew guys like you." Her sexy smile told me she was messing with me, but I could tell she still believed her words.

"I'm sure you didn't know anyone like me," I had to add.

"Oh, yeah? Tell me this, Lane, when was the last time you had sex?"

I cringed instantly. I knew I had just given myself away, but I still didn't want to answer. I couldn't tell her that I had actually been in bed with a girl when I got the call to go to Mexico.

"Wow, that recent, huh?" She chuckled at my unease and, after grabbing her clothes from the dresser, she gently pushed me out of the bathroom so she could finish up.

With the door quietly closed in my face, I had to think hard about why I didn't like her knowing that I had been with another woman not so long ago. She didn't know me. Hell, I didn't know her. I shouldn't even care. I had Kate to worry about right now.

A knock on the hotel room door pushed my battling thoughts into the back of my mind. I greeted the gentleman and allowed him to push the full-service cart through the doorway. He lifted up the tablecloth to show me that there was more underneath. We both laughed at my overeagerness as he backed his way out of the room.

I had the kids set up at the table with all of their choices and glasses of milk before I decided to take two more plates into the other room.

"Raegan and I are going to be in the other room eating. Is that okay?" I asked the two of them.

"Yep!" they simultaneously responded with chipmunk-cheek smiles. They really were hungry. I shouldn't have let them go that long without something to eat.

I heard Raegan turn on the blow dryer as I made my way into the connecting room. I figured I had a few moments to myself since her hair was so long and decided to use that time to finally call Audrey back, even though I was dying to shovel food in my mouth. I had gone long enough not talking to her. I knew she would be pissed at me, and my stomach churned at the idea. I hated when people were upset with me, but Audrey . . . I just couldn't let it go any longer.

I picked up the phone receiver next to the bed and dialed Audrey's number, which I had memorized long ago. She wouldn't recognize the number, but I hoped she would still answer.

After three rings, I heard Jace's brusque voice ask, "Hello?"

"Quit being so damn overprotective and hand her the phone," I laughed.

"You wouldn't want me to be any other way." He had a point. I could sleep easier when I left knowing that Jace would protect Audrey better than I could. But that was only because he slept with her. "You may not want me to hand the phone over to her right now . . ." he warned with humor in his voice.

"Who is that, Jace?" I heard Audrey's familiar voice call. Jace didn't answer, so I knew he had to have been giving her a telling look. "Give me that phone right now," she practically growled.

Yeah, I had some explaining to do, and she wasn't going to let me off easy.

"What would you have done if I'd refused to answer your calls or texts for days?" She bit into the line.

"Doll, I need to tell you something very important right now," I said soothingly.

"*What would you have done, Lane?*"

I sighed heavily, knowing what she was doing. "I would have tracked you down and counseled you on the danger of being out of touch. I would have been out of my mind with worry."

"Don't you ever do that to me again. And no, I don't care that you sent Jace a text. *I* needed to hear from you."

"Doll, I need to tell you why I always disappear." My words sobered her rampage and she fell silent. "First, I want to tell you I'm sorry. I'm sorry for the past couple of days, and I'm even more sorry for not telling you where I've been going for the past couple of years."

"Are you a drug dealer?" she whispered.

"What?! No. God, Audrey. That's what you thought?" In the background, I heard Jace hoot with laughter.

"Lane Parker . . ." Shit, I didn't like it when she took that tone. "Does Jace know where you go?" Well, that halted Jace's cackling in a hurry. Good, he was in trouble now too.

"Yes."

"Tell me," she growled.

"I have a daughter."

"What?!" she shouted. "How in the hell? You have a daughter that you've only gone to see a handful of times a year? Lane, I will kill you."

"Audrey, when she was only a baby, she was kidnapped from my apartment in New York."

"Oh my God . . ." I heard her gasp.

"That was over four years ago," I added.

"You've been looking for her, haven't you?"

"Yeah, that's why I moved to California in the first place."

Her words were mixed with tears, and my gut churned. "Let me guess: Her name is Kate?"

"Yeah . . ." I mumbled, knowing that I had once told her my tattoo was a lost love I never wanted to talk about. Which had not been a lie, technically.

"Lane, why?"

"I know you, doll. I know you would have worried just as much as I did every day. That kind of thing eats away at a person. You had enough on your plate already."

"I still would have wanted—"

I jumped to interrupt. "I know, and I love that about you, but it wasn't your burden to bear."

"So, why now? Why are you telling me now?"

"I found her."

"WHAT?!" Then the floodgates were entirely blown away and she was full-on sobbing into the phone. Fortunately, I could hear Jace trying to console her, but I wished I could hug her. I knew I didn't have much more time on the phone with her before Raegan would be done in the bathroom, so I attempted to console my best friend from fifteen hundred miles away, reassuring her that everything was okay now.

- SEVEN -

RAEGAN -

It felt incredible to actually be clean. Not the hospital shower with their sterile-smelling-soap kind of clean, but the really and truly fresh kind. And blow-drying my hair! I hadn't done that in years, and I couldn't believe how light and beautiful it felt. I almost felt spoiled, and then I laughed at myself in the mirror at how ridiculous that sounded.

When I entered the room, Braden and Kate were sitting with their legs crossed at the little dining table. I smiled when I saw how happy they were with their food. We were never given bad food, but it was portioned and all extremely health-conscious. I can't say that I hated the idea of them growing up eating only lean meats and tons of vegetables and fruits, but they never got the opportunity to splurge—ever.

"Mama, Lane said this is a pancake! I think it's my favoritest," Braden said with his mouth full.

"Your favorite," I corrected with a smile.

"Mama, look at this! Have you ever had one?" Kate asked enthusiastically.

I laughed, "Yes, it's called a doughnut. Did Lane only order sugar?"

"No, we ate eggs, bacon, and bananas already," Braden informed me.

"You guys are going to get sick if you don't slow it down." I pointed seriously at them and then gave a little smile before making my way to see where Lane had gone off to.

"So, you don't hate me, doll?" I heard Lane's deep voice asking. I halted in my steps, first wondering why I would hate him and second, why he called me doll.

"I don't know if I'll be able to call every day, but I'll do my best," he continued. I then realized he was on the phone, and since his back was facing me, I slipped out before he even knew I had been there. But before I was out of earshot, I heard, "Love you too, doll. Give the baby a kiss for me."

I heard the phone click back in the receiver and Lane began walking around the room. I didn't know what to think about that conversation. Did Lane have another family? I mean, when he practically implied he had been with another girl recently, I took it as a fling. Now I realized that may have been presumptuous of me. I guess it had felt as if he was flirting with me, and usually guys in relationships didn't do that. I could have been wrong.

I had obviously been out of the game way too long. Hell, even before I was with Braden's dad, I was probably never really "in the game." The question was, did I even care if he was with someone else or not? I *wanted* to say no.

Maybe this was just me worrying about how the situation would affect Kate. When I saw Lane and Kate together, I had really hoped that they would be able to spend plenty of one-on-one time together so they could properly bond. It might be harder for Kate to adjust to another baby or a . . . stepmom. I hated *that* idea instantly.

With my spine stiffened, I walked back into the room and joined Lane. He was now seated at the table, trying to work a fork with his left hand. He was obviously right-handed, but that hand was currently secured in a sling against his body.

"This sucks," he grumbled while practically glaring at his left hand, willing it to do as he demanded.

I sat down across from him and frowned, not knowing exactly how I should approach the matter. I was never the type to silently hold my problems inside. Why let something fester when you could just get it off your chest? He looked up at me and immediately realized my mood.

"I . . . I . . ." he stuttered. "I'm sorry?" he asked with complete confusion in his tone. I wanted to laugh at his ridiculous deer-in-the-headlights look. Typical male, jumping to an apology, although he obviously had no idea what it was for.

"So, how is this going to work? I don't know why I didn't think about it before, but I just don't know how well Kate will adjust. She needs you. Just you. Not a stepmom or a baby. I know that sounds awfully selfish, but I know her . . . and I know she's going to need time. Too many people all at once—"

"Whoa, hold on," he said, interrupting my ramblings, which were quickly becoming incoherent. I was thankful for his disruption because I didn't know what else I could add to prove my point. "I'm confused . . . what . . . what the hell are we talking about here? Stepmom? Baby? You lost me."

"Oh, are you going to ask Kate to call her 'Mom'?" I shrank back in my seat with that last word. *I* was Mom.

"What is going on?!" he whisper-shouted, leaning toward me over the table.

I pointed across the room toward the phone. "The girl . . . that person you were talking to. *Doll?*" I cringed. "Sorry, I overheard." I wrung my hands together under the table and felt guilty for eaves-dropping.

"Ohhh." He laughed. "Audrey is not my wife or girlfriend or anything like that, and her baby is definitely not mine. More like a niece."

"So, Audrey is your sister?" I asked, feeling a bit of relief. For Kate, of course.

"By blood, no. By what matters, yes."

"But you call her *doll*?"

"It's a nickname." He shrugged and sat back in his seat.

"It's a pet name," I informed him.

"Yeah, Jace says the same thing." When I opened up my mouth to ask who Jace was, he answered my silent question. "Jace is her husband."

"She has a husband and he lets you call his wife *doll*?" My mouth must have been wide in shock.

"She was mine first!" he responded defensively.

I raised an eyebrow at him. "Right . . . and you don't see how that would make people question it?"

"Outside of Jace, it's never really been a problem. Look, I met Audrey right after I fled to San Diego to look for Kate. She was just this sad little helpless girl who also happened to be the strongest damn person I had ever met, but she just needed someone to tell her and show her. I, on the other hand, was in so much pain that I couldn't even remember how to breathe. We helped each other. She's my best friend."

I took a deep breath in and out. "That's actually really nice. I had a best friend like that."

"Had?" he asked while shoving a spinach omelet into his mouth, practically whole.

"Well, I haven't exactly seen her in a few years . . ."

"Shit . . . I'm an asshole."

"Don't worry about it. It wasn't just . . . *that*. Braden's dad kind of got most of our friends in the breakup."

"Your friends went with the loser who ditched you with a kid?" He looked at me with extreme confusion.

"I guess I didn't have the best kind of friends after all."

"I'd say so," he mumbled.

"So, you moved to San Diego?" I asked, hoping to change the subject as quickly as possible.

"Yeah, almost immediately after I saw that tape and figured out who Flores was. Ash hated me for not keeping our daughter safe. Hell, I hated me. It hurt to be around each other, and almost a month after you guys disappeared, we knew it was over between us. I think Kate was really the only thing keeping us together anyway. Once she was gone . . . what was the point?"

"That's so sad."

"That's what happens when you get married just because you got a girl pregnant." I sighed heavily. "I sound like a total asshole, especially since . . . she's not even here anymore."

"No, I just think you're being honest," I said, trying to console him. "At least you didn't ditch her."

"I loved Ash, but I wasn't *in* love with her. Corniest fucking line ever, but I think it's appropriate."

I don't know why, but that made me chuckle. It was all so sad, but at the same time he still had this great outlook about himself.

"So, no luck in San Diego," I stated. It wasn't a question because obviously he hadn't found us.

"No luck where it counted, I guess. I did run across Flores a handful of times, but I could never get close enough to pinpoint where he lived."

"I don't think it would have mattered. We were on some kind of weird island. With all of his guys, it would have been impossible to access it." My words must have stunned him because his fork froze midway to his mouth and then he let it clatter to the plate below. I watched as he used one hand to push away from the table and walk out of the room.

"Okay . . ." I said to myself. That was strange.

Lane quickly returned to the room with determination in his eyes. Under his unrestricted arm, he carried a silver laptop.

"Those two are passed out in there. I think they're in some kind of food coma," he said, chuckling under his breath while placing the laptop on a small cleared spot on the table.

I watched as he typed away on the computer in front of him. The lines on his forehead creased with purpose. He looked so stern in that moment that I couldn't help laughing. His face was filled with such severe emotions that it took him a second to wipe it away as he looked up at me questioningly.

"So serious," I grunted, trying to imitate his stern face.

He laughed softly and returned to his typing with less concern etched into his eyes. I stood up and began moving the plates back to the rolling cart. I had taken a few bites of my food, but I just didn't have a very big appetite. Lane pulled the chair I had been sitting in next to him and patted it, indicating that he wanted me to rejoin him.

"Where were you guys?" he questioned.

I looked at his screen and saw that he had pulled up a Google map. Wow, those sure had advanced in the last four years.

"I didn't exactly have a GPS or anyone around who would tell me where we were. Sorry." I felt terrible that I couldn't help, but I didn't really want to focus on where we had been. My only concern was where we would be going now.

I watched the little map as he zoomed in and out of the area around Tijuana. Something hit me as soon as I saw the leg of land that extended south of the United States.

"Oh! Once we reached land off the island, it took us three hours to drive into San Diego." I gave him the only piece of information I could remember that could possibly be valuable.

"Shit, that's extremely helpful, babe." He immediately began clicking things on the computer, but I remained frozen by that last word. *Babe.* Nickname or pet name? It had flowed off of his tongue so easily, but his excitement had added a bit of heat to it. Surely, I was overthinking it. *Babe.*

"I believe you guys might have been on Isla Montague. The distance seems about right, but there are virtually no pictures of this place. Which I guess would make sense . . ." He began rambling, and I figured it was more to himself than me, because once again, I didn't want to talk about where I had been. But something else occurred to me that might be helpful.

"The house was right next to a lighthouse, which definitely didn't work anymore. I saw that thing every night out my window and it never turned on."

He pushed the computer in my direction and pointed to a picture on the screen. "Was this the lighthouse?" I stared at the beat-up old square-shaped building that had always towered over me. I'd daydreamed about climbing up to the top of that thing many times. I had just wanted to know what it would feel like to have the wind blowing in my face from that high up. One time, the thought of what it would feel like to fall to the earth from the top had entered my mind. I'd quickly chased it away with a series of jumping jacks and sit-ups, but that nasty little thought always had a way of getting in my mind when I was feeling the most stir-crazy.

"Yep." I couldn't look at it anymore.

"This place looks like it's just a bunch of sand and dirt. No houses, or at least none that I can find pictures of."

I stood from my chair and walked toward the window. "That picture has to be old. There's a house there now. A very big one. The walls are the color of sand, so maybe it blends in well. I don't know . . ." My voice had begun to take on a panicked tone, and I could feel my chest closing in on my lungs. Seeing that damn lighthouse made me feel as if I were stuck in that room again. "I just . . ." Deep breath in. "Don't see the need to look at those pictures." Deep breath out.

Where had all the air in the room gone? Was I the only one who couldn't seem to find the oxygen? In. Out. In. Out. I glanced back at Lane, who appeared to be breathing just fine. My lungs began to squeeze with an excruciating tightness, and all I could see was that damn lighthouse.

I sprang for the sliding glass door and threw it open. The balcony was small, but it had plenty of fresh air to spare. And no lighthouses in sight. Hopefully, it wasn't lighthouses in general that brought this out in me—just that one. My hands gripped the railing until my knuckles turned a sickly pale color.

Deep breath in.

Deep breath out.

Two hands extended on either side of me and grabbed the railing inches away from my own hands. I felt his heat behind me, but we didn't touch.

"Hey, breathe. You're okay. I'm sorry," he whispered in my ear soothingly, as if I were about to jump over the side. "I'm sorry. That was too early for you. I just got a little eager."

"It's not your fault. I just don't want to ever see that again."

"You won't. I promise."

I wondered at his words. What did he mean? *Promise* was a powerful word. Was he promising to always keep me safe from those people? Surely not. Or was it an empty promise, meaning that I was here now and they wouldn't get me again? God forbid. I wouldn't survive it again.

"Why do you care where we were? We're here *now*."

"Because I intend for them all to pay," he practically growled.

I nodded my head in silence, because what else was there to say? He was mad that they had taken his daughter from him. I didn't think there was any way to talk him out of his need for justice. In a way, I thought we deserved it.

"We should get ready to go to the station. I want to get this over with," I told him, still speaking out to the street and feeling his heat radiate into the skin of my back.

"I'd rather make sure you're okay right now. The station can wait, for all I care. Besides, they're sleeping so peacefully in there." His voice was gentle and his calm demeanor was coming back. I just wanted to melt against him and soak in his tranquility. He didn't seem like the type to ever raise his voice unless someone were to *really* get him heated up. I liked that.

"I'm okay," I responded with what I hoped had been a convincing voice. I pushed off of the railing and a solid stomach met my back. The height difference between us meant that my ass had hit his thighs, and all of the areas in between were melded against me.

I wanted to rejoice in the contact. Real, honest-to-goodness male contact. I craved it. But it wasn't real, was it? This was just an odd situation the both of us had been thrown into, and we were only here because of the kids. I obviously felt the need to overthink every aspect of my life lately.

He finally let his hands fall away from either side of me, and I suddenly realized that his sling was off again. I turned to face him with a reprimand on my lips.

"Why is your sling off? Are you *trying* to pull *all* of your stitches out?" I walked past him back into the room. My hands scooped up the discarded sling off his chair and pushed it toward him. "Leave it on."

"Yes, ma'am," he said with a twinkle in his eye. My eyes couldn't look away as he gently placed his arm back into the canvas fabric of the sling. His body stretched as he pulled the strap up and around his neck. His chest was so wide I could tell the strap was on its last bit of Velcro. When his arm was fully immobilized once again, he looked down at me with a smirk. "Better?"

Maybe when I knew he hadn't damaged himself any further. "Let me check it." I walked forward and reached up to pull his shirt aside, but there was no way with my height that I would be able to see over his shoulder.

I used his good arm to hoist myself up onto the chair next to us and smiled when I got a clear view. I stretched the neck of his navy cotton T-shirt over and very carefully peeled one edge of his bandage aside. Everything looked as if it was still where it should be. I gently pushed the gauze back in place and reminded myself that we both needed to change out our dressings soon.

"You're lucky. It's all still intact." I looked down at his face and nearly gasped at the image below. My breasts had been directly in front of Lane's face, and he'd made no attempt to look anywhere else. "Seriously, Lane?" I pushed his good shoulder and stepped down, trying hard not to trail my fingers down him as I went.

He laughed and shook his head while shrugging his shoulders. "I'm a guy. It's my only excuse." He continued to laugh. "It was all just . . . right there!"

"Perv," I scolded him, but my laugh told him I really wasn't that mad. "Time to wake the kids up."

I walked toward the connecting room, but my sudden descent and quick movements had left me a little light-headed. I continued walking until I was in the next room so I could grab hold of the dresser and control the spinning in my head without Lane's concerned glare. Once my vision cleared and the room stopped whirling, I sighed in relief and began packing up our bag to head out.

LANE -

We caught a cab outside of the hotel. Braden and Raegan climbed into the backseat first, and I realized there wasn't enough room for all four of us to sit side by side. I scooted in next and pulled Kate onto my lap. It's never pleasant to have to ride shotgun with the cabbie, so I was glad that I had found a way to get us all back there.

The ride should have only taken us fifteen minutes, but with traffic coming off the bridge it took a good thirty before I saw the dingy police station. I didn't really mind the drive. Along the way I began pointing out different places to Kate. Even Braden joined in and asked a few quiet questions. Kate was bouncing in my lap, telling me how much she loved riding in cars and airplanes. It took that moment for me to realize she probably hadn't been in either before these past few days.

Another reason I didn't mind the extended stay in the yellow cab—Raegan fell asleep on me. Almost two minutes into the ride, she began to scoot down in her seat. Her head fell lazily onto my shoulder, and I decided I didn't mind the feeling of her using me to catch some rest.

She was really going to need a decent amount of time to catch up on sleep. She tried to be tough, and I knew she was, but I always caught her eyelids fluttering in exhaustion or her head drooping with her immense fatigue.

Last night after my shower, I scanned the labels on her prescription bottles. Even though it had been insanely late, I texted Charlie and asked him to look into what she could be taking those for. I knew the cut on her forehead wasn't pretty; I had seen it twice already. But I didn't understand why she required so many different types of drugs. Surely, they were the main culprit in her weariness and those crazy dizzy spells. Should she really be up and about this much? My guess was she probably didn't know what taking it easy was, though, so I'd have to step in and show her.

We pulled up to the curb of the precinct, and I swiped my card quickly through the cab's card reader. Kate opened the door and slid down onto the concrete. I softly jostled Raegan next to me and felt her sluggishly move, but she didn't bring her head up.

"Hey, Rae, we're here," I delicately crooned. I felt bad for waking her, but I really couldn't let her continue to sleep in a cab. My insistent hands shook her a little more. She moaned and mumbled what sounded like, "I'm coming," but I couldn't be sure because she didn't look like she was going anywhere.

Panic started to hit me when I realized something wasn't right here. This wasn't just normal fatigue. I thought back to our conversation last night when she told me about her heart and her blood pressure.

Quickly, I reached toward her neck and felt for a pulse point. I knew the one in that spot would be stronger than anything I would find in her wrist. I also knew I wouldn't be able to tell what her blood pressure was, but I just felt the need to know that her heart was still pumping.

Lutheran Medical Center would typically only be a five-minute drive, but I didn't know how long it would take in this afternoon traffic.

"Raegan, I'm gonna take you to the hospital, okay?" I told her. Her head bobbed up and down before she finally raised it to look at me.

"No. No more hospitals." Her words were tired, but she seemed to be pulling herself together—clawing her way through the fog was more like it. "I just forgot . . . to take my medicine. Just . . . grab my bag," she said, fading slightly.

I cursed and scooped her up into my arms while trying to slide out of the cab. The driver gave me an exasperated expression. No doubt he was wondering when we planned on vacating his vehicle. *Asshole.* Kate grabbed hold of the backpack, and with all of her might she hoisted it up onto her tiny back. Holding Raegan in my arms, I reached back into the cab and seized my bag from the floorboard. Good thing I had ditched that sling again.

Raegan's body was light and conformed to the front of mine easily. Her head burrowed into the side of my neck, and I almost took that moment to rub my face across hers. It was a little too tempting.

Braden was the last to climb out of the yellow car, and right after he shut the door, the asshole screeched his tires in his retreat. I wished I had the time to catch his license plate number.

"Hey, Braden, you remember where Officer Charlie's office was, right?" He nodded and glanced nervously at his mom in my arms. "I need you to run real fast inside. If anyone tries to stop you, just ignore them. I'll take care of it. Find Charlie and tell him I need a Gatorade right away. Make sure he knows it's super-important."

"I want a Gatorade! What's that?" Kate asked excitedly. It was obvious she was blissfully unaware of the situation, unlike Braden.

"Tell him we need two Gatorades. Now run! Please." I tried to not freak him out, but I needed his little feet to get a move on.

I had scooped Raegan up with my injured arm, and I knew if I tried to transfer her over, I would likely pull something. I walked slowly, trying to not jostle my burning shoulder in the process. When we made it inside, all eyes were immediately focused on us. Braden had likely just run past all of them, and they were curious.

"Hey, what's going on?" April, the desk clerk, asked softly.

"I think she's having a low-blood-pressure episode." My mom used to get spells like this sometimes, which was the only reason I had half a guess. I looked down at her; her eyes were open, but she seemed exhausted.

"Hey, Frank's back there having lunch with his wife!" She perked up with this information but I gave her a look, wondering if I should give Frank a cookie for having a wife or for having one that would actually want to come see him. Why was April wasting my time? Her expression instantly flipped and she said, "Sorry! His wife is an RN. I keep forgetting you don't know what goes on around here anymore."

"Oh, thank God! Grab her and bring her to Chief's office for me." I spoke to her over my shoulder as Kate and I made my way up the stairs. My dad's office was the only one with a couch.

As I turned the corner toward his door, Charlie and Braden came barreling down the hallway with Gatorades in their hands. I knew Charlie kept a ton with him. He was always downing the yellow-colored sports drink. They all followed me into my father's office, and Dad looked up at the sudden intrusion with wide eyes.

"What the hell did you do to her, son?" His words felt incriminating, but his tone told me otherwise.

"I think it's her blood pressure."

"Move, please," a soft elderly voice called out. I looked up as I placed Raegan on the couch and watched a little old lady with white hair part the crowd with authority. She carried a large bag in her arms.

Frank walked in behind her and placed a chair in front of the couch for his wife to sit on. I knelt down in front of Raegan and offered her the Gatorade, and she lazily sipped at it. I heard Charlie behind me explaining to the kids how he had envelopes in his office that they could put stamps on for him. I knew he was just trying to be nice by getting the kids out of the way, but I didn't want Kate out of the way.

"Leave them here, Charlie," I said without turning around.

"She'll be okay; my office is the next door over."

"She's fine here." My voice was final.

"Actually, if we could get the psych evaluations going, it would move this process along for all three of them," my dad said from where he still sat at his desk.

"I don't know . . ." I hesitated. "I think we should wait for Raegan to be fully present."

"The counselor will need to speak with them individually, so it will take a lot of time, son. They'll be okay. Her office is across the hall."

I turned to look at both children standing against the wall with their little hands clasped together. They had already been through so much, but I knew they didn't really understand any of it. I got up, leaving Raegan with the nurse. I looked back at her and then back at the kids. Why was I getting so caught up in all three of them? My sole focus was on Kate, but I wouldn't lie and say Raegan and Braden weren't creeping under my skin as well.

"Hey, guys, remember how Raegan explained that we were all gonna have to talk to a nice lady today? Well, I think it's time to do that while she takes a little nap. I wish one of us could go in with you, but you'll be fine. You can color pictures and she might even have some paint." Both of their faces perked up at the mention of drawing pictures. "We will be right here when you get out, okay? And if you don't want to talk anymore, just come right back here to me."

"I'll go!" Kate excitedly called out.

"No, Kate. I'll go first. Mama needs you to help her get better," Braden said. Kate happily complied and scampered across the room toward Raegan.

I squatted down in front of Braden. "That's awfully brave of you," I told him.

"I need to go first to make sure it's okay for Kate." He shrugged his shoulders casually.

"You're a great brother, Braden." It was hard for me to say that word. I still couldn't call Raegan Kate's mother, but I had to remember this was all they knew. I pushed out my clenched fist in his direction. He stared at it in confusion. "When guys agree on something or they respect each other, they bump their fists together." He reached his closed fist out and lightly tapped mine. "Thank you for protecting her."

I stood up and ushered him through the door. The psychologist was standing in her doorway observing our little talk. She smiled warmly and gestured for him to enter her bright, friendly room. I'd had many victims and their children go in there in the past. The Victims' Service Unit offered crisis counseling and sought to make their occupants feel comfortable enough to divulge information.

"Hey, don't pressure him to talk, okay? He's real quiet." She nodded her head with a smile. In that moment, I wished that I knew more about Braden—something I could contribute to give him an easier time. This is why we should have waited for Raegan. "If he seems at all upset or uncomfortable, I want him to come out. Immediately. I also don't think you'll get much. As far as I can tell, Raegan kept the whole situation from them."

"I would never pressure anyone, Mr. Parker," she responded.

She shut her door, closing her and Braden off from the rest of us, and I felt a pang in my gut. Raegan would want to know her son was in there, and I didn't like him being separated from the rest of us. I'm not sure where this pack mentality of mine had suddenly come from, but I was feeling like pieces of me were scattered when we weren't all together. I liked it better when we were all locked away in the hotel room.

"What happened here?" Frank's wife asked, breaking up my new and scary thoughts. I watched as she pulled a blood pressure cuff and a stethoscope out of her bag.

Quickly, I explained everything I knew and then I had to ask, "You carry all this medical stuff around with you?"

"You'd be surprised how many times I've had to use these outside of the hospital. Besides, I was just on my way to Lutheran Med for my shift, so I like to keep all my belongings with me."

"I'm glad you do," I whispered.

"Can you elevate her legs for me?"

I immediately complied, using my duffel bag to prop her feet up on the couch. It was weird to see someone like this. Raegan was awake, but she wasn't taking in her surroundings, so it was as though she wasn't fully there. I was glad she was at least conscious enough to drink the Gatorade to replenish some of her minerals. I felt Dad and Charlie hovering behind me, trying to glance over my shoulder. Kate leaned up against the wall close to the couch, trying to closely observe everyone helping.

I dug around in Raegan's backpack and pulled out all of the medicine bottles with her name on them. I handed them to the lady next to me, explaining how Raegan had said she missed taking them this morning. As she read the different labels, I didn't miss the distinct *hmmph* sound she made at a certain bottle.

With a quick twist, she had the top off and poured two white tablets into her wrinkled hand. "Get her to take these, please."

I gently ran my fingers down the side of Raegan's face and said, "Hey, babe, open up." I laughed softly under my breath because I usually said stuff like that in much more . . . sensual situations. Her eyes immediately cut to mine, and I swear I saw those beauties roll. "Sorry, not the time for fun." I laughed again.

She opened her mouth and looked me directly in the eyes. When her tongue pushed forward indicating that I should place the tablets inside her mouth, all I could do was stare back at her blazing green gaze. I quickly gave her the medicine and shook my head to break the spell.

"Her blood pressure is very low, but I don't think we need to rush her off to the hospital just yet. Especially if she's already got a prescription. This could just be an instance of not taking her medicine. Just in case, I'm going to call the doctor who prescribed these, and then I'll come back and check out what's under that bandage," Frank's wife explained. Without waiting for my response, she vacated the room.

I took a breath and stood up to talk to the others. When my eyes met the two other men in the room, I froze.

"Why the he— Why are you two gawking like that?" Not cussing in front of Kate was going to be a hard habit to break. At the thought of her, I extended my hand toward her and she skipped to my side. I needed her close to me as much as humanly possible right now.

"Shit . . ." I immediately covered Kate's ears when Charlie started speaking. "It happened a lot faster than we thought," he told my dad.

"Yeah." Dad smiled mischievously.

"What happened?" I glanced down to check on Rae's sleeping form. She had finally slipped into a peaceful rest, and the nurse said it was okay to let her stay that way for a while.

"I thought it would take at least a month. Chief here thought it would take two weeks. Guess we were both wrong . . ." Charlie continued.

"What are you two goons talking about?"

"For you to fall for her," my dad stated simply. "It's written all over your face."

I turned my back on them and faced Kate, who was listening in on the inappropriate conversation but luckily didn't appear to be absorbing any of it. I grabbed my headphones out of my bag and pulled my phone from my pocket.

"Hey, Kit Kat, can I show you something cool?"

"Yup!" She bounced on her toes excitedly.

I quickly scooped her up and sat her in my dad's leather chair. I slipped the headphones over her ears and scrolled through my playlists. Audrey had downloaded a country album on here, and it was the only thing I was sure didn't have any curse words—at least I hoped not anyway. I adjusted the volume to a level low enough for her ears, and when the music began, her face lit up brighter than the California sun.

"This is so cool, Daddy!" she yelled in the little room, not knowing her own volume. I chuckled and then tousled her hair.

I stepped back over to the couch where Raegan snoozed lightly and sat down on the edge near her legs. With a heavy sigh, I faced the two men in front of me.

"Okay, now what in the hell are you talking about? Fall for her? As in you think I fell in love with someone in a little over twenty-four hours? Because if that's what you're yapping about, I think I'm just too tired for this stupid conversation."

"Cranky, much?" Charlie jested.

"Exhausted," I amended.

"Not love . . . at least, not yet. But you care for her," my dad said, pointing to Raegan's prone form.

"Of course, I care. She took care of Kate. She figured out a way to tell Kate about me and I don't know how yet, but she saved Kate. She got her back to me safely, both physically and mentally."

"She made herself sick," Charlie began, "like really fucking sick so they would have to take her to a real hospital. She took a big chance that they could have just offed her, but they took her. When she saw an opening, she called the station and asked for you. You, of course, weren't available, so the next person she knew to ask for was Chief."

My head hit my hands and I contemplated everything this woman had gone through for these kids.

"Look, son, I can see the wheels spinning. You have always admired strength and courage. I can see the way you look at her, and she *is* quite beautiful. But if the feelings do head down that way, make sure they're for the right reasons. Make sure it's because you care about *her*, not what she *did*. Because if you don't, eventually the reasons will fade from your memory and the children are the ones who'll be hurt in the fallout."

"Dad, I think you're taking this a bit too far. I'm grateful for her, but I'm not in love with her. Even I can see the difference."

The two men in front of me exchanged knowing looks, and I glanced down at the girl they were insisting I was "falling" for. She was kind and beautiful and so damn strong, but I didn't even really know her. These two were crazy.

- EIGHT -

RAEGAN -

My head was pounding, and I could tell that I hadn't been drinking enough water lately. That was one of the many things the doctor in San Diego had stressed to me, over and over. I figured every doctor said that, but now I could see his point. Actually taking my medication would probably help as well.

I pushed up to a sitting position and pulled my legs from Lane's duffel bag. His large frame was seated farther down on the couch near where my legs had been, and he stared at me with concern on his face.

"How do you feel?"

"Not dizzy, so that's good," I replied.

"That was scary," he whispered. "You need more rest." He handed me a bottle of water and I gratefully snatched it from his hands and started gulping the cold liquid down. "Why didn't you tell me you had sepsis? A blood infection is a huge deal, Raegan."

"How did you find out?"

"The nurse who helped you called the doctor about your prescription, just to double-check everything."

"I didn't exactly know the right time to tell you about it. It's healing, and it's not as bad as it could have been." I shrugged my shoulders casually, trying to tamp down the seriousness on his face.

"I think an infection that damages your heart is pretty bad."

"And the medicine is healing it. In the meantime, it makes me a bit dizzy." I shrugged again, hoping to downplay the situation.

"It all happened because of that cut on your forehead?" he asked. I nodded in return and looked away, attempting to cut off his line of questioning. "How did you get it?"

"Let's not do this here, okay?" I pleaded. "It's probably not one of those conversations you want to have in front of . . . everyone."

He wasn't happy about that, but he looked satisfied to see me drinking water, and I followed where his gaze had moved. Kate was sitting in a large leather chair with Lane's dad. The two of them each had an earbud in one ear, and they were whispering animatedly about the music that I assume they were listening to. The chief looked beyond joyful, and I wondered if Kate had any idea that she was sitting in her grandfather's lap.

I scanned the room for the other little set of eyes that usually weren't far from Kate. When I came up empty, I immediately shot a look at Lane while trying to push myself more upright.

"Where is he?" I demanded.

"Hey, he's okay," Lane said in a consoling tone. "He's just doing his psych eval. I can see the door from here. I'll know the second he comes out." His soothing words did little to diminish my anger.

"What? How dare you! He's *my* child. I should have been the one to consent to this!"

Lane scooted across the couch and pushed me back down, his hands holding my arms gently. "Rae, you *did* consent. That's why we're here, babe, remember? I'm sorry, I told them we should wait for you, but Dad made a good point. If we want to get this all over with, we need to just get it done. Braden said he would go first. I explained the situation to him and he seemed fine." His words began to penetrate my fiery rage.

"What if she—" I began.

"I gave her very strict instructions not to pressure him," he interrupted. I finally felt a deep sigh leave my chest, and I stared at the closed door. "He should be done soon. Don't worry—I won't let anything happen to him."

I stared at him when those last few words left his mouth and tried to decipher what he meant. I decided it was best just to ignore them for now. There were much more pressing problems at the moment. I laid my head back onto the couch pillow and thought about everything they could be discussing in there.

I had tried my hardest to make our situation appear as normal as possible to Kate and Braden. I never wanted them to know that they had been kidnapped. I didn't want them to know that if we weren't there, they could actually run and play in the sunshine . . . that there was so much more for them outside of those four depressing walls.

"I wasn't sure exactly, but I told her that he probably wouldn't know much," he gently conveyed to me.

I nodded my head. "Thank you."

My eyes had closed, so when I felt his hand lightly squeeze my leg, they snapped open in surprise. "We should head to the apartment tonight so they don't have to keep paying for the hotel."

The fact that he said *the* apartment and not *his* apartment was not lost on me. That was probably the last place I ever wanted to see again besides that house in Mexico. But the apartment I was cruelly taken from years before was a close second on the list. I didn't have much of a choice, though. I didn't even have any identification, let alone money. I would need to figure something out really soon.

"We won't stay there long." His hard tone, indicating that he felt the same as I did about the place, surprised me.

"You must have a nice job now if you can afford to keep a New York apartment you don't even live in anymore." I'm not sure why I said that, but it came out of my mouth all the same.

"Ash's parents kept it. They're loaded, apparently," he ground out.

Ash having money was news to me. As far as I could tell, they were living paycheck-to-paycheck back then. Lane had always been working any overtime shift he could catch just so they could make ends meet and pay a nanny to watch their kid during the day. I liked Ash, and we talked whenever she was home at the same time I was there, but I wouldn't say we were close friends.

"I worked my ass off to keep the lights on and food in the fridge. All that time she had a trust fund with an ungodly amount of money in it. Her parents never liked me, or the fact that she married a rookie cop."

The frustration and hurt in his voice were loud and clear. I couldn't imagine feeling as if your partner had basically betrayed you. I had a hard time believing that she had let him work his tail off, day after day, to take care of his family, when he very well could have cut back some with that trust fund.

"Maybe her parents wouldn't let her have access to it," I suggested, hoping that would help in some way. "If that was the case, she probably didn't mention it because it only would have added stress."

"Maybe," he conceded. "It's all Kate's now, anyway. My mom's been taking care of the apartment, hoping that I'll come back."

"She misses you, I'm sure."

"The Lane they knew and loved was gone. I couldn't stand being here anymore."

All of a sudden, I realized how deep our conversation had become and how he was actually sharing a piece of himself with me.

"I think they love you enough to understand that. No one can fathom what it's like to lose a child until it's happened to them. I used to actually get down on my knees and thank God I was taken as well. I just couldn't imagine being left behind to . . . wonder. Wonder where my child was." I looked up and saw the tears in his eyes, and my heart clenched. "I'm so sorry, I shouldn't have said that."

He swiped at his eyes and looked back at his dad and Kate. Thankfully, they were blissfully ignorant of our conversation. Gently, he scooped up my hand and squeezed.

"Don't ever be sorry." His words were brief, but they meant a lot to me. I'd gone through cycles of grief after the kidnapping. They spread out over the first few years. I was mad at myself. I was mad at Lane and Ash for not waking up to save us. I was ashamed. I even had a period of deep depression that I was all by myself to care for two infants. But his words were correctly aimed at my heart. I shouldn't be sorry.

I accepted his moment of comfort and laced my fingers through his. He squeezed again, and I smiled up at his beautiful hazel eyes, which were more golden than green today.

Charlie chose that moment to enter through the door, and we quickly let go of each other's hands. Lane used his forearm to wipe the remaining signs of sadness from his eyes and then aimlessly dug through his bag. I knew he wasn't really looking for anything; he just didn't want Charlie to see him crying. It was a shame because those hazel eyes sparkled brightly when they had water reflecting in them.

"Uh . . . hey, guys. Should I come back?" Charlie asked.

"Of course not. What do you need . . ." I stopped talking when I looked down and saw what was in his hands. I recognized the bag instantly, the tattered black sides and pink piping expanding every edge. It was the only thing I had owned. That bag carried everything Braden and I needed when we lived here. I jumped up from the couch and snatched it out of his hands.

"How?!" I asked excitedly.

"Well, it was taken to the evidence locker after you were . . . um, well, taken," he said sheepishly. "We usually dump it after a hundred twenty days, but Chief over here can be pretty convincing. I just went and picked it up for you," Charlie stated. I smiled as widely as I could up at him.

"Oh my God!" I hugged the bag tightly to my chest. Besides Braden, it was the only thing I had that reminded me I'd actually had a life before Mexico.

"Wow, I practically saved her life by carrying her up here and made sure she was taken care of, but you"—Lane pointed at Charlie as he spoke—"you bring her an old, fraying bag and you get a smile like that?" Then his eyes landed on me. "A bit unfair, don't you think, babe?" His words were light and playful, which only made me laugh even more.

"I'm so happy right now, I could hug all of you!"

Lane opened his arms wide, and with a bright smile he gestured me in. I took the bait and leaned into him. He squeezed me tightly and repositioned me so we were chest to chest. He tried to subtly rub against me and I laughed, swatting at him as I pushed away.

"Perv," I teased.

"All right, you convinced me," Charlie joked, holding out his arms in the same way Lane just had. The teasing of his tone kept the grin on my face.

"Not a chance," Lane growled, and Charlie roared with laughter.

I heard Charlie's feet retreating from the room, but I was too busy unzipping my bag and searching through all of the items that had once belonged to me. I opened the side pocket first and smiled when I pulled everything out. My American passport, my long-since-expired Colombian passport, my New York ID, and Braden's birth certificate were all in there. I even found four hundred dollars, and I couldn't have been more thankful to the frugal me from four years earlier. I dug further through the clothes and found an old photo album I used to carry with me.

"I've never actually seen one of these," Lane said while handling my burgundy Colombian passport. "Your mom is Colombian, right?"

I nodded my head. "She married an American and convinced him to move there with her." I flipped through the pictures until I found one of my parents. I smiled as I let myself think about them. So deeply in love, yet so naïve as to how to raise or care for a child. They were young, free spirits, who lived only for themselves. Having a child cramped their style.

A thought suddenly occurred to me that I'm sure should have crossed my mind sooner. "Did anyone contact my parents? You know . . . after?"

"They were contacted for information, yes. I remember your father being pretty upset."

"We never really spoke much, but I should call them soon and let them know. If they even remember me."

"Don't be ridiculous, Rae," Lane scolded. He thought I was being overly dramatic, but the truth was that I used to have to remind my parents when it was my birthday. Once I called my mom and she didn't even recognize my voice. Our relationship was distant at best. "When did you move here?" he asked.

"I was about eleven when our neighborhood started having an increase in drug crime. It continued to escalate and my dad demanded we all leave. My mom refused and he wouldn't leave without her, so he sent me to live with his sister in Brooklyn. Aunt Lisa should never have been responsible for a child, but then again, my parents shouldn't have, either."

"If you lived in Colombia for eleven years, I would have thought your accent would be heavier," Lane said, looking through the pictures with me.

"That was Aunt Lisa for you. She was more concerned with having a best friend and teaching me how to catch men. She also berated me for my accent and constantly taught me to speak with more of an American pronunciation. Guess it stuck." I shrugged my shoulders because I really could not have cared less. I've always had kind of a struggle with my heritage. I had no idea what I was. Was I Latina or Caucasian or both? Was I Colombian or American? What was my title? I had dual citizenship, but what did that really say about who I was?

I turned another page and ran my finger over a picture of myself taken when I was nineteen. I remember I had been waitressing in a diner over by the bridge, and my uniform consisted of a white button-up and a little striped skirt. It had been summertime and the other waitresses and I were all out back in the summer heat on a smoke break. I had unbuttoned the bottom half of my shirt and tied it up high so my midsection was revealed.

"How old were you here?" Lane questioned quietly. His fingers grazed the photograph.

"Eighteen," I replied. If I remembered correctly, it wasn't long after that when I met Braden's dad, falling head over heels for his charm. I really should have kept that shirt down.

"God, I am a pervert!" he groaned.

I laughed, "Hey, I was legal."

"Barely, babe."

I backhanded him in the chest and turned the page. This light banter between us felt nice. I was never able to speak to any of the adults at the Floreses' house. Not that I had wanted to anyway. But speaking to someone over the age of five provided almost immediate stress relief. Finally, I could have adult conversations!

Just then, the door across the hall opened and out sauntered a smiling Braden. I was instantly calmed to see that he was cheerful and didn't appear to be distressed by the interaction at all. I stood from my seat and moved quickly toward him. Charlie walked back into the room behind Braden.

"Hi, baby!" I smiled and knelt down to pull him in for a tight hug. "How was it talking to the lady?"

I felt Lane's presence behind me, and then from the corner of my eye, I watched as he squatted down next to me as well. I appreciated his care and concern for Braden more than ever in that moment.

"Hey, bud," he said softly.

"It was so fun, Mama. I painted pictures, built towers out of wood, read a cool book we've never read before, and she even gave me this!" He twirled a blue lollipop in his fingers and I laughed at his easygoing attitude.

Kate skipped over to us and shouted, "My turn, right?!" We all shrank back from the volume of her voice. She had obviously had those earbuds in for too long.

Lane's face dropped slightly, but he picked it back up quickly when he turned to face her. "You're right, Kit Kat. I'll miss you."

Kate brushed her hands down the sides of Lane's strong jaw and spoke sweetly to him. "I'm gonna be right back, okay, Daddy?" I smiled at the way she was trying to console him.

He opened his arms and pulled her into his embrace. She tucked her face in his neck and he began whispering in her ear. She nodded her head and then eventually turned to whisper back in his. It was probably the sweetest thing I had ever witnessed.

He stood up and escorted Kate toward the lady standing in her doorway. "Same goes for her," he said sternly. "If at any time she's uncomfortable, she comes out." There was no arguing with that tone . . . this was the daddy bear in full force. The lady seemed to take it in stride as she nodded her head and quietly closed the door behind them. I was sure she'd experienced her fair share of protective parents.

I wanted to ask Braden everything. I wanted to know what she had asked and how he'd responded. I wanted to know what he'd colored and what he'd built. I wanted to know what the story was called that he'd read. But at the same time, I didn't want to overwhelm him. I knew he would be hungry soon and that I should probably wait to ask all of my questions when I had both of them back.

"You feel better, Mama?" Braden asked as we all settled back on the couch.

"Now that you're here, I feel great."

"Lane carried you like Superman carried that lady in my book." He laughed.

"I don't think it was quite that dramatic," Lane joked from the other side of Braden. At the thought of him holding me, my eyes immediately zoned in on his arm. The arm that was, of course, *not* in a sling.

"Let me check your stitches." I sighed dramatically.

Lane shrank back and noticeably moved his shoulder away from me. "I'm good. I swear it's okay." He spoke too quickly, and for some reason that just made me want to check all the more.

"You helped me; now let me return the favor. You probably injured yourself carrying me up here."

"No, seriously. The nurse who helped you, she looked me over. Said I was perfect." He smiled brightly but still oozed guilt.

I leaned over him and he gave in halfheartedly. I pulled his shirt collar to the side and noticed a new bandage. That was good because we both had needed it. I pulled one little corner back so I could peep without exposing it. I looked underneath and then sealed it back shut against his skin. When I sat back down, he visibly relaxed, obviously thinking he was off the hook.

"That's a lot of blue stitches."

"Yeah, I can't wait to get 'em out. They itch like crazy," he said while looking through my photo album again.

"Interesting how the stitches you had last night were black, though."

"Busted," Charlie boldly sang out from across the room.

- Nine -

LANE -

After what felt like a lifetime, Kate skipped out of the counselor's office with a smile on her face, just as Braden had. Now that all three of them were back with me, I finally felt the tension in my chest release its strangling clutch.

We tried to grab a quick bite to eat, but Kate and Braden were so enamored with the restaurant, it was just too entertaining for Raegan and me to make them leave. They found it fascinating that we could go to a place and order what we wanted and eat around other people eating their meals as well. We stayed late and let them soak it all in.

They charmed the waitresses with their manners and excellent behavior. By the end of the meal, I think they all wanted to keep Braden and Kate for themselves. With a pleased grin on my face, I paid for our meal and walked out holding Kate's hand. I had my arm slung over Raegan's shoulders casually, while she held Braden's hand.

I had no idea what was going on between the four of us, but it was effortless. I didn't plan on questioning it anytime soon, and I hoped Raegan didn't either. She seemed to be soaking in all of the kids' new discoveries, and I could tell that she had wanted this for them for a very long time.

The one thing that could ruin my mood was standing tall in front of us. I looked up at the four-story building that might seem charming to any other New Yorker in Brooklyn, but to me it was ugly and held the worst memories a father could have.

I knew when Raegan realized we had arrived at our unwelcome destination because her body slipped in behind mine. I couldn't even begin to imagine what this would do to her. After seeing her break down on the balcony at the hotel this morning, I realized that while she appeared strong, she still had her own demons. I couldn't make them stay here a minute more than necessary.

"We'll sleep here until we figure out the next step. It won't be long," I whispered to Raegan.

"I have cash now; I can pay for a hotel," Raegan said with a faint voice.

"You only have four hundred dollars, Rae. I won't let you spend that. I can afford a hotel, but let's just try this out first. If it's awful for any of us, I promise we'll leave."

"Braden and I could go . . ." she began. She must have realized where her line of thinking had been going because she abruptly cut herself off.

"Do you want us to separate?" I asked.

"No!" Kate and Braden immediately shouted up at the both of us. They were holding hands tightly, and I scolded myself for having this conversation in front of them.

"I'm sorry, guys. I didn't mean that," Raegan soothed. She squatted down and kissed each of them on the cheek. For a moment, I almost wanted to ask her for one as well—less on my cheek and more toward my mouth, though. Just to soothe my nerves, of course.

I walked up the steps toward the outside vestibule door and unlocked it. Then I let everyone slip in as I unlocked the next door. I used to be grateful for the extra security. Look, two doors to stop possible intruders! What a joke. They both required the same damn key.

I had been a fucking police officer and I couldn't even secure my own building. My neighbors used to thank me, when I came off of my shifts, for moving into the building. They used to gush about how I made them all feel safer.

They never said anything, but the looks I received after my daughter was kidnapped from my own home while I lay asleep in the next room were drastically different. Their gazes were no longer filled with awe and appreciation—rather, shame and disappointment. How could a police officer's child get taken right out from under his nose?

He was a fucking terrible one; that's how.

My feet must have trudged to the second floor by pure muscle memory because I was shaken from my zoned-out state when I felt a warm hand encompassing mine. I had the key hovering over the deadbolt, but my hand was frozen, preventing it from going any farther.

Rae squeezed lightly and guided my hand and the key into the brass lock. I was enjoying the sensation of her warmth, so I let her continue. She turned my hand, which caused the key to turn in the lock. I heard the metal slide out of the latch, and we were finally free to enter. Raegan turned the knob and pushed open the black wooden door.

Kate and Braden rushed in front of us. I knew they would be okay. I had asked my mom to dust the place and fill the fridge for me. I had also asked her to remove all pictures that had Ash in them. I didn't want them thrown away, because I planned on telling Kate about her mother, but there was an appropriate time for something like that, and now was not the time.

Raegan and I remained in the doorway, neither of us moving forward. I couldn't tell who was more uncomfortable with this place. Or maybe she was just standing here to give me the courage to enter.

I glanced down at her slender frame and dark chestnut-brown hair. The strands were shiny and long. The tips were just beginning to graze her ass, and I wanted to wrap her hair around my arm and pull her head back, forcing her to look up into my hungry eyes. Might not be the best idea right now. God, she was hot, though. I'd definitely need to distract my mind from any future thoughts like those.

My eyes took in her movement as she grazed her fingers over a large chip in the paint on the doorframe. This building appeared to have more and more of those chips. It certainly wasn't the finest building, but it was all Ash and I could afford at the time with a baby on the way—or at least that's all I *thought* we could afford. The area Raegan stroked was a larger indentation than normal, and her eyes seemed to be far away, lost in a memory.

"I'm pretty sure this was from my head," she whispered. The words that came out of her mouth were so faint, I wouldn't have heard them if we had been anywhere else besides this silent door-way.

"What do you mean?" I asked with a nervous croak in my voice.

"I was dead asleep when they came in and grabbed me. It took me too long to put together what was happening. They put some-thing resembling a cloth over my eyes and a hand over my mouth." Her fingers grazed across her lips, as she appeared to be remember-ing the violent incident. A tremor ran down my spine. "It wasn't until seeing this doorway that I woke up fully and understood that I was being taken. When we reached about here"—she pointed to the tiled foyer—"I began to panic and started doing everything I could to escape them. I couldn't scream because their hands were too tight, so I started thrashing about. I had no idea someone else was carrying Braden and Kate. I wanted to hit something . . . anything that could wake you guys up. Right as we were stepping through the doorway, I got the blindfold off."

She paused, and suddenly I needed to know everything—every single detail she could give me. Maybe I needed to punish myself in any way possible. I deserved to be tortured by every word that came out of her mouth. I gripped her hand again and pulled it up to my lips. Not exactly a punishment, but Raegan and I appeared to be functioning off of small, reassuring touches. We both seemed to need it, and I liked that I could help her in that way.

She continued when I finally let our hands fall back down. "Once I got the blindfold off, someone slammed my head right here. I don't remember much else until we were in Mexico. When I realized they had . . . taken the babies as well, I was immediately sick at the idea of what had happened while I had been out. But when I finally came to, Mrs. Flores was just rocking and singing to them, like they were her own children. God, I hate that woman."

I instinctively pulled her toward my chest and kissed her forehead, where I assumed that scum had forced her head into the wood. It was ironic that I was kissing the spot right next to her newest forehead injury. I still didn't know what had happened, and every time I brought it up, she shied away from my questioning. I guess I was going to have to give her time. It also seemed brutally ironic that she began and ended this journey almost the same.

"I'm sorry," she whispered.

A lightning bolt shot up my spine and I stiffened like a two-by-four. "What did I tell you about that, Rae? I'm the one who's sorry. God, my stomach drops every time I think about that night. I had just come off working thirty straight hours, and I remember that I'd passed out the second I hit the pillow. It's not an excuse, though. I should have fucking heard *something*."

She spun in my arms and looked up at me, her short stature evident due to our close proximity. She didn't seem to notice that her hands were placed against my chest, but I sure as hell did. Another part of me began to notice her nearness as well. I cursed my libido and tried to remind my brain to stay in the appropriate state of mind.

"It wasn't *your* fault," she said softly.

I ignored her attempt at pacifying my self-disgrace. "You were so strong. You took care of Kate even though . . ." My hand ran down the side of her face and cupped her chin to hold her gaze.

I was battling two major sides of myself. One side wanted to tell her how appreciative I was that she took care of Kate, even when Kate really wasn't her child to care for. She raised her into this beautiful, intelligent little girl, and I couldn't even begin to put into words my extreme gratitude.

But this other side—the side that was quite forceful—wanted to grab her little waist firmly in my hands. I wanted to lift her up so she could wrap her toned legs tightly around me. This side wanted to take hold of her mouth with my own and push her up against the wall. I wanted to show her exactly what I could do to that perfect body— exactly what I think her eyes had been pleading with me to do.

Currently, those beautiful green eyes were boring into mine, and I felt her need in my bones. God, did I want to appease her. And myself.

"Mama, I have to go potty!" Kate's shrill voice cut through our sexual tension like a bucket of ice-cold water, dousing all of the fire running through my veins.

I clutched both sides of Raegan's head and kissed her hair. "I got her," I said, and I retreated toward the hallway with Kate's little hand in mine.

Not long after I showed her where the bathroom was, the doorbell rang. Through the peephole I could see my five-foot-two, grayhaired mother practically bouncing on her toes.

I laughed to myself and opened the door. Her little body slammed into mine before I even had it fully open.

"Hey, Ma." I smiled into her hair and wrapped my arms around her.

"My prayers have truly been answered," she cried into my shirt.

"Well, if you were praying for your son to be a sexy, handsome devil, then yes, Ma, I've come to tell you that you should be satisfied."

She swatted at my stomach. "Oh, you cheeky boy! Still as smug as ever, I see."

"Missed you, Mom," I muttered. "I know I've been a shit son, I just want to—"

"Oh, love, don't you even say it. You followed your instincts and went to find your daughter. I raised you right."

"I didn't protect her when it counted, though." I hadn't really planned on getting into this conversation with her, but there was something about a mother that made you want to spill your deepest sins.

"I dropped you on your head when you were a baby," she replied, shrugging so damn casually. "We can't be perfect, Laney."

"Ma!" I shouted. I didn't know whether I was indignant because of her first comment or her old nickname for me. Both were ridiculous.

"Quit keeping me from my granddaughter. I know all about the hours your dad got with her today. If I have to hear him rub it in my face one more minute, I'll smack him."

"I don't think he was bragging." I laughed.

"That's exactly what he was doing. He's just like you."

I stopped her before she could continue further. "Remember, she doesn't know anything. Let's at least try to keep the tears at bay," I insisted. She huffed past and headed straight toward the living room.

"Hello," I heard Raegan say tentatively.

"Hi!" Kate's voice called out shortly after.

"Hey, guys, this is my mom," I informed them. "Kate, this is your grandma."

"I have a grandma too?!" she shouted. Her little feet carried her quickly across the room until she collided with my leg. She wrapped her arms around it and stared up at my mother.

"You sure do, you precious darling," she cooed. "I've been waiting a long time to see you, but I never expected you to look like a real live princess." My mother gasped dramatically and held her chest in the most playful manner.

Kate giggled and slowly released my leg. "I have pink shoes!" she declared.

"Exactly what I expected a princess to wear," my mom said, nodding her head.

"What's a grandma?" Braden asked, moving to Kate's side.

"A grandma is the most important job in the world, don't you know? A grandma brings surprises." She tapped her large bag mysteriously. "A grandma brings cookies and lets you stay up way past your bedtime. Grandmas are fun!" she exclaimed.

"Wow!" Kate clapped enthusiastically.

Braden's face fell for a moment, but we all caught it and I immediately moved to console him. I couldn't stand that sad look spoiling his adorable face. My mom got there first.

"I can be your grandma too. Well . . ." she started, trying to appear glum, "that's if you'll let me." My mother should have been on Broadway with those acting skills. Had I been so easily charmed as a child?

"You can! You can!" Braden called out excitedly.

"Wow, I *am* a lucky lady." She smiled brightly. "All right, my sweet grandchildren, let's go play with the new toys I've brought you." She pointed down the hall and Kate and Braden happily led the way. "Oh, I also brought you some things, Raegan. I have plenty to talk to you about as well, but I'll save it for a better time. Just know how grateful I am for you, darling girl. I hope you like everything, but if not, it's still a win for me because then we can go shopping together." Mom quickly scooped a speechless Raegan into her arms and dropped a large bag onto the couch near her.

When my mom finally took off down the hall and I could hear her announcing her surprises to the kids, Raegan finally looked in my direction.

"*That's* your mom?" she asked with awe in her voice. I nodded my head, smiling. "Why did you ever move out?"

I shrugged. "You know how it goes. Teenage guy thinking that all he wanted was independence. Besides, I don't think girls really go for the adult-still-living-with-Mommy-and-Daddy type of guy."

"I don't know. She could win over almost anyone." She pointed toward the bag and asked, "What do you think that is?"

"Well, it's obviously for you. Check it out," I said with a grin.

She cautiously opened the large, crinkling plastic bag and dipped her hands inside. Gingerly, she pulled out piles of clothes. I saw T-shirts, blouses, jeans, shorts, and pajamas—all for her and the kids. Shortly after, I saw her take out some bras and underwear, but she quickly shoved those back into the bag awkwardly.

"She bought us clothes?" Her eyes filled with tears and I jumped to sit next to her.

"Don't cry. You needed some, right?"

She nodded and asked, "Did you know she was going to do that?"

"Babe, I knew you guys couldn't continue switching between two outfits like you have been." Her arms were instantly around my neck before I could even finish speaking. I went with it and wrapped mine around her body.

After a long moment of muffled sniffles and us holding each other, she finally spoke. "Should I be concerned she knew my bra size?"

I laughed and pulled away. "I guesstimated. Want me to check and make sure I got it correct?" I mimicked holding her breasts in my hands, and she feigned indignation before laughing hysterically.

She playfully swatted my bicep and cried, "You!" Yep, me. The guy who was starting to enjoy this girl's company a little too much.

When my mom left a few hours later, I was still trying to decide how our sleeping arrangements were going to work out. There were two bedrooms in the tiny apartment: the master, which had a nice big bed in it, and Kate's nursery. It still held her crib and a full-size bed, which Raegan used to sleep on with Braden when she spent the night. So far, neither of us had made any move toward *that* room.

That's where they were all taken.

"You guys go pile in the big bed. I can make do out here on the couch," I called out to Rae, who was getting a glass of water from the kitchen.

"That's silly, I'll just . . ." she started to say, but then thought better of it. I had a feeling she was going to say she could sleep on the full-size bed in the nursery, but we both knew neither of us could stomach that room.

"You'll just sleep in the master," I finished for her.

"Come on, guys. Let's go." She grabbed for their hands, and I watched as they vacated the little living room.

It was fucking hard being back here. I used to rock Kate in the recliner in the corner on the rare night I was home in time to put her down. We used to lay a big quilt on the ground in front of the couch for her to lie on her stomach and have what Ash called "tummy time." This whole place was filled with memories . . . memories I wasn't prepared to dredge up.

I grabbed a blanket out of the hall closet and caught the whiff of fresh detergent. Mom must have rewashed some of the linens because I had definitely been expecting a stale closet odor. I really did need to thank her for being so amazing—I'm sure it hadn't been easy for her to be here either.

I sat down on the creaky old couch and pulled my shirt up over my head. The gym shorts I had put on this morning would have to do for the night. The couch groaned as I tried to find its sweet spot—the spot that would allow me at least *some* comfort. Something jabbed into my back and I reached underneath myself to remove the annoyance. Between the cushions, I pulled out a blue stick of lip balm.

Ash used to have these all over the house and in her purse. She never went anywhere without them. I stared at the small reminder of Kate's mom. My ex-wife. I really wished she could see Kate now. Why did she have to go and get into a car after she had been drinking? I still wanted to berate her for her callousness. Did she just give up all hope of ever finding Kate? And did she really care so little for her own life? I wished she were here so I could yell and give her a piece of my mind!

A tear slipped down my cheek, and I mused at the tornado of emotions I was feeling. I missed Ash. Maybe I hadn't been *in* love with her, but I still wished that she could see the beautiful girl Kate had become. I still cared deeply for her. She was the mother of my child. I would have done *anything* for her.

I guess that wasn't entirely true, though, because I didn't fight for her—I fought for Kate instead. I hoped if she was looking down now that she understood. I would always love her for giving me the very best thing a man could receive . . . my daughter.

I watched the small hand of the clock slowly tick its way past all the numbers and I still couldn't get my mind to calm down. I just couldn't seem to shut down the memories I had of this place. Some good. Some great. Some absolutely terrifying.

I started when Kate tiptoed into the living room, emerging out of the dark hallway. She was holding her teddy bear, and her golden hair was already mussed from lying down.

"Kit Kat, what's wrong?" I asked softly.

"Daddy, why do you have to sleep out here?"

"Well, I don't think I would fit in that bed with all of you. Daddy is much too big."

"I'll just stay out here, okay?" Kate's tired eyes searched the room for a place to rest. When I watched her make her way toward the recliner, I popped up.

"How about I sit with you in the bedroom until you fall asleep?"

"Yeah," she replied sleepily, still clutching her bear tightly.

I lifted her up and walked down the hall, trying to remember where all the creaks and groans were in the wood floors. I missed a few and paused each time, not wanting to wake the others.

The bedroom was dark, but the streetlamp outside cast a yellow glow through the thin curtains. I could just make out Raegan's shape underneath the covers, lying on one side of the bed. Braden was curled up in the middle, his mouth wide open in sleep.

I tried to gently slide Kate onto the bed, but her grip on my arms was unrelenting. She really did not want me to leave her and go sleep in the other room. There was no way all four of us would be able to sleep comfortably in this bed, but I would stay until she fell asleep.

"Okay, Kit Kat, I'll stay for a bit," I whispered.

I sat with my body up against the headboard, and Kate relaxed her head on my chest. I didn't care if I got zero sleep that night. Being able to comfort my daughter was better than any rest I could have gotten alone on that couch. Her fingers made their way up my neck until she had a soft grasp on the edge of my ear. She had done this at the station when she passed out on me the other day. I had no idea what she was doing at the time, but now I guess it was her way of comforting herself.

It didn't take long for me to get caught up in her soft tugs on my ear. If it wasn't calming her mind down, it sure was quieting mine.

~

Something pushed off my chest and I grunted from the pressure. When my eyes slowly peeked open, light from the windows blinded me and I immediately slammed them shut. Kate's body slid off of mine and I heard the thump when her feet hit the ground. She called out Braden's name and I listened as she skipped out of the room.

Damn, it was morning already.

"She got you with the ear tug, huh?" Raegan's voice startled me. I opened my eyes again to see her still tucked under the covers on the opposite side of the bed. The white quilt was pulled high up to her chin, and her eyes looked as if she had just opened them not even moments ago.

"I think she drugged me. I only came in here to lie with her until she fell asleep," I croaked out while stretching my good arm in front of me.

"Yeah, she uses that tug as a weapon now. She used to put herself to sleep doing it, and now she's realized she can put others to sleep." Raegan chuckled lightly and I smiled warmly at her.

I slipped down from my upright position against the headboard, and my back and shoulders protested from the movement. I had been sitting up all night and now my muscles were cramped. I let out a loud groan as I lay flat on my back. I couldn't believe I had slept so hard, all while leaning against the headboard.

"Want me to rub it out?" Raegan asked as she propped herself up. Shocked at her words, my mouth fell open wide. Did she really just say that?

"Okay, get your mind out of the gutter!" She laughed out loud. A light dusting of pink hit her tanned cheeks. She was blushing! How damn adorable was that?

"My mind is *always* in the gutter, babe. Especially when I wake up next to a beautiful girl," I said with a wink.

"You know what I meant . . ."

"I do. And while I would love that, it's probably best you didn't *rub* anything on me at the moment." I tried to keep my tone light, but just the thought of her hands was not boding well for the growing problem in my lap.

"Roll," she snapped. With a twirl of her finger, she gestured for me to do just that. *Great.* Just what every guy wants to do—crush his hard-on beneath his body.

I rolled slowly, trying to keep my arm tucked so I wouldn't pull my shoulder. I also tried to position myself in the most comfortable way I could possibly get in this situation. I closed my eyes and faced away from her. I wouldn't be able to look at her *and* feel her hands on my body.

I felt her legs bump into my side as she scooted closer. Her hands were like ice cubes the instant they touched my body, and I jolted as air whistled past my teeth.

Her hands pulled away immediately and she was silent, as if she was waiting to see what the problem was.

"Cold hands," I rasped.

"Sorry!" she whispered. I heard her rub her hands together vigorously to try and get some blood flow to those frozen appendages.

When they returned, her hands were a fraction warmer but not by much. I held still and tried to let my body heat warm up her hands. It didn't take long, or maybe it was just the amazing feeling of her hands rubbing my muscles. Holding my arm against my body for days on end had really done a number on me. Getting back into the gym would be a real bitch, but I was craving the burn. It had already been way too long.

"What kind of pressure do you like?" she asked quietly.

I turned my face into the pillow and groaned loudly. Was everything she said today going to go straight to my dick? "Hard. I like it hard," I said into the pillow. She pinched my side lightly, letting me know she hadn't missed the double entendre. "Sorry," I said with a chuckle.

Her strokes were slow and firm as she worked around my injury, her thumbs running along my shoulder blades. She found a knot under my left shoulder and slowly worked out the muscle until I felt the knot dissolve under her pressure. Like a heat-seeking missile, she discovered all of the knots in my back, and each time they melted away, I let out a relieved moan.

Her fingers grazed lightly over an area of my neck and I realized she was tracing my tattoo—the only one I had. The only thing I cared enough about to brand myself with.

"The script is cool. Not something I would have expected to see on your skin," she said.

"It's Ash's handwriting," I explained. "Seemed right, at the time. Having Kate's mom write on her dad." I shrugged uncomfortably.

"That's really sweet. Kate will love to hear that someday."

We began to have a safe, nonsexual conversation, and I'll admit it was nice. She asked me what I did now and I explained my job in Texas. She was surprised to hear that I didn't live in California anymore. I told her how I enjoyed boxing and having a beer with friends. I kept it short, though, because I didn't want to rub my good times in her face. To my surprise, she took everything in stride and wanted to hear more.

"We never chatted like this before," I said.

"We never really talked at all. I usually only spoke to Ash," she responded.

"I was afraid of you," I divulged.

"Afraid?" she laughed as if my words were outrageous.

"The guys at work always harped on me about having a hot nanny." I heard her snicker at my words. "I'm serious! I didn't want to cause any confusion for anyone. I knew we paid you like shit, but that was all I could afford. I also knew I was a lucky bastard to have you working for such a small amount. But I couldn't rock the boat in any way. If Ash got any rash ideas or people got suspicious of anything, I would lose the one steady thing Kate had going for her at the moment—you. I kept my distance because once people started constantly talking about you, I was afraid it would only be a matter of time before rumors started flying."

"Wow . . . I had no idea." Her hands continued pressing. "That was actually very courteous of you. I could *not* afford to lose that job. Thank you for never hitting on me then. I worked for a man like that previously; it wasn't pleasant."

"Did he touch you?" I growled. The idea of any man touching her inappropriately made my hackles rise. And I was sure I could still find this so-called man. She soothingly ran her fingers down my spine and told me that he hadn't. I tried to get back to my previous thoughts. "Anyway, I was a married man. It was out of the question."

I swore I heard her whisper the word *was*, but I didn't ask her to repeat herself. Instead, I enjoyed the feel of her fingers and the release of tension that was resulting on my back.

"How the hell do you know how to give a massage like this?" I croaked.

She laughed and said, "It's actually working?"

"Let's just say I've never paid for a massage this good."

"That's nice to hear." She still hadn't answered my question, so I waited patiently, relaxing into her warm touch. Down the hall, I could hear Braden and Kate playing a game enthusiastically, which also calmed the tightness in my muscles. If they were happy, I was happy.

"We were kept in this big room," she began. "It had a lot of stuff for us in it, but we couldn't leave the room—ever. In the room, there was this large bookshelf. It had the most random assortment of books. Like *How to Master Chess*—by the way, I will warn you now never to challenge your daughter in a game." I had to laugh at that tidbit, soaking in every last morsel of information like a thirsty man in the desert. I wanted it all.

My inner cop wanted to question her further; I still needed to know why they were taken. Why Raegan and Braden? Why my daughter? But I realized that getting Raegan to talk had to happen naturally or she would clam up.

Raegan continued, "There were some really nice cookbooks, but we were never able to cook. Food was just brought to us. There was also a *Massage Techniques* book. I liked that one . . . a lot."

Something in her tone piqued my attention. "A lot?"

"It had pictures."

I was still puzzled by her odd reaction to a massage therapy book with pictures, and then it hit me. A woman trapped, kept away from adult interaction, looking at a book that taught how to massage people.

"Rae, are you telling me that you liked looking at the bodies? Male bodies?" I asked in a rough voice.

"Yours is much better than any of those pictures." The sound of desire and wanting in her voice could not be mistaken as her fingers began heating my skin.

The sound of the kids' voices down the hall reminded me that pursuing anything physical with Raegan would be inappropriate at this very moment. But fuck if I didn't want to turn and see that yearning in her eyes. With a strangled groan, I scooted myself off the bed.

"Now I need a cold shower," I grumbled and made my way toward the bathroom, not even looking back. I swore I heard her giggle as I retreated.

That girl was a temptress. I couldn't tell if she was actually trying to lure me in or if she was always this candid. We had never spoken enough before now for me to know. Either way, I was going to fucking need an ice-cold shower.

- Ten -

RAEGAN -

I felt them hovering over my sleeping body and their hands scooping me up out of my slumber. I tried to make sense of my odd surroundings. What had happened to my warm sheets? Why were my feet dangling in the air? A pressure in my ribs became overwhelmingly painful.

A hand pushed into my mouth, while more hands quickly secured a piece of cloth around my eyes. The darkened bedroom was entirely masked and the feeling was suffocating. I distinctly felt a hand slide tightly around my stomach and I jolted, finally realizing that I wasn't in my bed anymore. This wasn't right.

I sucked in a lungful of air so I could let it go in an ear-splitting scream, but then I felt a soft touch brush down the side of my face.

"Rae," I heard a deep voice whisper. "Rae, you're having a nightmare."

I jerked away, but then a warm body slid in behind mine and I recognized that my body was still safely in bed. I wasn't being taken. They weren't back for us. It was just a dream. I had to repeat all of these phrases over and over until my brain believed them to be true.

Lane's body wrapped around me from behind, every inch of my back molded to his front. Our legs entwined, allowing us to be as close as possible. His hand threaded through my hair, and my rapid heartbeats began to slow down.

"Sleep, Rae, I'm right here. I'll never let anyone hurt you again. Sleep, baby. I've got you now," he whispered.

A protest was on my lips. I couldn't help thinking about the children lying next to us, but his warm, comforting arms squelched any thoughts of leaving. So I slept, knowing my body was safe. It was my heart I was beginning to worry about.

~

We had been in the New York apartment for two weeks and we still hadn't spoken about where we were going from here. Or even if we would go together. I knew that neither Lane nor I wanted to stay in this apartment, but it *was* convenient. And I didn't think that either of us wanted to face the real world just yet.

A week into our stay, Lane finally started working again. He logged in remotely from the computer and made phone calls a couple of hours a day. He informed me that his boss, Jace, would be okay with him taking off as much time as he needed, but he hated the idea of not doing his part.

Apparently Jace had really helped him out, and they seemed to have a mutual respect for each other. I assumed Lane valued Jace for being a good husband to his friend Audrey. I couldn't explain my jealousy over a girl I had never met, but it made me feel a smidge better to hear that she was married. Quite happily married, at that. I had to admit, though, that I still wondered about Lane and Audrey, because they spoke on the phone more than any "friends" I had ever been around.

I was beginning to think that I had been the only one feeling the pull between the two of us—that maybe it was just all in my head. Every day it seemed to get a little bit stronger for me. A smile here. A brief touch there. But Lane never made any advances or said anything, so I constantly questioned what I was feeling.

Could it just be that I hadn't had any attention for the past four years and that now even the smallest amount felt like the greatest thing in the world? Could I be imagining the sensations that shot straight between my thighs when he winked at me from across the living room? Or the thrill I felt when I saw that smile he gave me every time we woke up early in the morning.

That was another thing. He was now sleeping in the bed with us every night. Kate wouldn't have it any other way, and I couldn't blame him for falling for those pleading blue eyes. But he also still crawled in behind me late at night, claiming I was having bad dreams. Some nights they were excruciating and I craved his comfort, but there were other nights when I woke and didn't remember having any nightmares. Regardless, before the sun came up the next morning, he would always move back to his side, and it wreaked havoc on my heart to see him sprawled out on his back, so close, yet so far. The morning sun would dance across his blond hair and scream for me to run my fingers through it and beg for him to come back to my side of the bed.

We never spoke of our late-night cuddle sessions. It was as if they were a secret, even to us—something we indulged in only when the nighttime could conceal our desires. I thought it was all in my imagination until last night.

Lane and I had been in the kitchen cleaning up after dinner, and the kids were playing in Kate's old nursery. They certainly had no qualms about that room or playing with toys that were meant for children much younger than they were. It was all new, and that's what they cared about.

After I'd put the last plate on the wooden drying rack, I reached for the dish towel and wiped my hands dry. Lane was washing down the countertops, so I leaned up against the sink to watch his muscles move underneath his cotton shirt. It was a hobby I had picked up lately. He'd gotten his stitches taken out a few days ago and had already started trying to work out again.

Now he tortured me daily with extremely slow pull-ups from a bar that extended across the hallway from one wall to the next. He also made me suffer every time I had to watch him do a zillion sit-ups on the living room floor. And when he did his push-ups and was forced to only use one arm when his shoulder hurt, I wanted to lick all of the sweat off of his heated skin. He never looked at me during his workouts, but I knew he felt my eyes on him, which only heated my skin more.

He probably thought I was the biggest creeper ever, but I just couldn't make myself look anywhere else. I couldn't apologize either; my body had been on fire for two weeks now. Soon the flames would either kill me or I would have to find a way to quench them.

With my hip pressed into the countertop, I watched Lane toss his towel into the laundry room. He turned and looked down at me, and I observed something flicker intensely in his hazel eyes. Before I could blink, he leaned in and slammed his lips against mine.

The approach had been quick and shocking, but the kiss was slow and smooth. He didn't try and force his tongue in or to open my mouth any further, but he did coax me to move against his lips and follow his rhythm. The fire inside of me was a full-on inferno at that point. Just as I started to reach out for his head, he pulled back, breathing harshly against my lips.

"Tell me I didn't just fuck up," he pleaded. "Tell me you wanted me to do that as much as I needed to."

Why were we talking? The flames inside of me were increasing in intensity and burning me from the inside out. I grabbed his neck and pulled him toward me forcefully. I had never been the domi- nant one in my relationships. But when a girl has been starving for affection as long as I have, it looks like she'll do things she never thought herself capable of.

Lane groaned into my mouth when our lips touched again. I gave him back the control but let my hands stay in the hair on the back of his head. The height difference between us was vast, but he leaned forward enough for me to hold on tight. His tongue dashed into my mouth without invitation, and I tangled it with mine. His hands latched onto my hips and I pressed further into his body.

God, I craved the feeling of his bare skin against mine.

We stayed in the kitchen for who knows how long, just exploring each other's mouths, and I prayed he would take me right there. His hard body against mine and nothing in between.

Hours. Minutes. Or maybe it had only been mere seconds later when he pulled back and placed three slow, little kisses on the corners of my lips. Then he turned away and marched out of the kitchen without saying a word.

I would have thought the kisses had been drummed up by my overactive imagination at that point, but I had the swollen lips to prove it. I had felt his body pressed up against mine, and I never even knew a feeling like the one he created within me was possible. I wanted *more*.

LANE -

After breakfast, I settled Kate and Braden on the couch with an extra-thick fleece blanket tucked around them and then finally made my way down the hall. I'd put some comical penguin movie on the television for them, although I could have turned on the news and they would have zoned out just the same. The TV was such a new concept for them that maybe I shouldn't have introduced it—maybe I should have taken advantage of the rare opportunity.

With a shrug, I decided to let them just be little kids who liked to watch cartoons. Plus, a steaming hot shower was calling my name. I needed the kind that would leave me tender and blazing-red afterward, yet calmer. I needed the reassurance that I could do this. I'd wondered for so long if I would even be able to *see* her again and hadn't allowed myself to think about whether or not I could do this dad thing. Doubts were raining heavily on me, and I needed to clear them before I saw Kate's sweet little eyes looking up at me all day—counting on *me* to be the strong one.

Just like my dad had said, Raegan had actually been a tremendous help with the transition. Whenever I was feeling as though taking on this parenting gig solo was a heavy, suffocating fog and I wouldn't be any good at it, she would stroke my arm knowingly. With just that touch, she would reassure me that I was very much capable.

Just to pile more onto my already full plate, I couldn't get the thought of Raegan's lips on mine out of my head. Last night, I had felt her eyes burning into the skin on my back. I'd often caught her staring at me with raw, naked lust, and I knew I could only take it for so much longer. Add that to the fact that she had a knockout chest and toned legs, and she had me at the end of my rope.

I'd been trying to hold back because we had the kids to think about, but fuck, if she kept looking at me like she did last night, I would snap. I had only tasted her mouth, but now that I had sampled the pure honey, I wanted the whole jar.

I pushed the bedroom door open and jolted to a stop when I saw Raegan sitting on the edge of the bed . . . completely topless but with my gray towel wrapped around her little waist. She stared out the window as she brushed her dripping wet hair, the teasing drops sliding down her freshly bathed body. I knew I should have looked away. Every ounce of propriety my mother had taught me was reprimanding me for not being a gentleman and averting my gaze.

Screw the shower; my body was already heating up on its own. The curves of her figure and the porcelain glow of her skin were the stuff angels were made of. My index finger twitched to glide down the line of her back and over the tips of her perfect breasts. This girl was all fucking woman.

I heard a small gasp and then she said, "Lane, I'm so sorry." I silently groaned when she pulled the towel up to cover herself.

Her words finally permeated my stupefied brain, and a small smile cracked my lips. "You're apologizing to *me*?" Wasn't I the one who was intruding on her?

"This is *your* bedroom. I should have gotten ready in the guest bath. I'm sorry."

I smiled at the blush on her cheeks. I seemed my little temptress hadn't woken up yet. The girl who had been seducing me with her eyes for the past two weeks was feeling shy about me seeing her breasts?

My prying gaze still hadn't left her chest, even though it was now covered, much to my regret. I wondered what my face looked like right then. All I wanted to do was place my finger in the space between her tits and gently tug down that oppressive towel.

I forced my feet to begin their reluctant trek toward the bathroom. Luckily, I had to walk right past her on my way, which allowed my eyes a few more moments to try and recreate what I'd witnessed when I first walked in.

"Lane . . ." she breathed out harshly. I immediately looked at her face and spotted the flush creeping up her cheeks again. "Don't act like you haven't seen hundreds of these before." She gestured with a sweeping motion across her chest. My feet immediately halted their forward motion, and I stood towering over her small frame seated on the bed.

"Hundreds? Give me a little more credit than that. I haven't been with *hundreds* of women, babe." I smirked when her breath caught at my endearment. "Let's go ahead and make this real fucking clear right now. No matter how many I *have* seen, I have *never* seen these." I couldn't stop my finger when it touched the dip in her throat and trailed lazily down her heated skin. Seriously, it had a mind of its own. "And *these* are phenomenal."

Infinitesimally, she moved back to lean on her hands that were situated behind her. Opening herself up. To me. *Fuck.* Her chest rose and fell faster as my finger hauled the gray cotton towel down to reveal what I was dying to get my hands on. I knelt down on the ground in between her legs and looked up into her emerald eyes. They darkened and she didn't warn me off. Hell, that was a green light if I had ever seen one.

Still looking up at her, I moved forward until my mouth was a fraction of an inch from her perfectly rounded breasts. I wanted my tongue to be the first thing that touched those, and then my hands could have their turn at the feel of her smooth skin.

She gazed down at me through heavy eyelids. Her breathing picked up in speed, moving her chest even closer to my mouth. My heart pounded loudly in my ears, and besides her breathing, it was the only thing I could hear in this bedroom filled with late-morning light.

In one long, leisurely motion, I ran the flat side of my tongue from the underside of her breast and over her nipple to the top, where I placed a lingering kiss. It almost pained me to lift my mouth away from her skin, but I did it to gauge her reaction.

A quick stream of air departed from her lungs as if she had been holding her breath that whole time. She looked into my eyes as I stared into her scorching green ones. I didn't realize she had moved her arms, but now I recognized the sweet, stinging feeling of her fingernails in my biceps.

"Please . . . please, do it again . . ." she breathlessly whispered. She moved her chest just marginally and directed her opposite, untouched breast closer to my lips.

"God, you're beautiful," I whispered into her skin before my tongue gave it the identical attention as its partner had gotten. My lips finished their prolonged caress on the top swell, and then my eyes peered up to see her head thrown back and her mouth opened in complete bliss. Fuck, I could get that reaction with just a little tongue-play?

A groan ripped up my throat as her name fervently flew out of my mouth. I instantly pushed her back by her shoulders, and when she was flat against my mattress, my lips hungrily claimed her breasts again. I couldn't decide which one to give more attention to, so while my mouth was enjoying one, my hand grasped the heavy weight of the other.

The bulk of my body covered hers and her hands gripped my back, holding me with all of her little might. There was so much more to explore, but I had just been introduced to this area and I wanted to be well acquainted before I had to move on. My tongue flicked across her nipples at a rapid speed, and she began to whimper. Her eyes were squeezed shut and her nails scratched wildly down my shirt-covered back.

Her legs began to quiver, grinding into me in all the right places. My tongue and fingers continued their torment, and soon she lifted her arms and grabbed for the comforter above her head in a clenching grasp. The movement only abetted me by forcing her back to arch, which caused her chest to push closer to my needy mouth.

All of a sudden it had become a relentless pursuit for me, and I was not going to back down until I got what I was after. Her hands twisted and squeezed my white quilt above her head, almost as if she needed to release aggression somewhere else besides my back.

Without removing my mouth, I reached up and laced my fingers through hers, and she moaned shamelessly. Her body shook underneath me and then locked up, rigid as a fucking board.

"Ohmygod . . . Lane . . ." Her words were barely audible. When I looked up at her face, her mouth was gaped open and a silent scream tore from her body.

She finally came down from the high and I growled, "Holy shit, woman. That was the hottest damn thing in the world." My face nestled into her neck while I squeezed her fingers that were still above her head. "Oh, the things I could do to you."

I lifted my body and looked directly down at her beautiful face. My eyes zeroed in on her swollen bottom lip; she must have bitten it while I wasn't looking. I examined every centimeter of her soft, pink lips and imagined what they would feel like on places other than my mouth.

Just then I heard an unfamiliar noise. I lifted up a bit to focus on the sound and it trailed into my bedroom again. The high trill of laughter saturated my lust and caused me to snap back to reality— *our* reality. I realized that Raegan hadn't heard it because, solely focused on me, she was trying to lean in for my lips.

Kate's sweet laugh hit me again, and I quickly comprehended where I was and what I was doing. I jumped backward off the bed and tried not to focus on Raegan spread out like a gift from God.

"Shit, Rae," I groaned while I ran my hands down my face. My hands that now smelled like her. "Shit, what are we doing? What am *I* doing? I'm so fucking sorry . . . I shouldn't have done that. I'm sorry . . ."

Before I could see the look on her face—the disappointment toward me—I stomped into the bathroom and slammed the door behind me. My hands tightened forcefully as my fingers dug into my palms. I needed to punch something. I needed to fucking punch myself. I reared back to pound my fist into the drywall, but I immediately realized what that would sound like to those outside of the bathroom. What if I scared Kate or Braden? So I stood there in the middle of my bathroom, my whole body vibrating with aggression toward myself, breathing in and out unevenly.

What had I been thinking? Here Raegan and I were just trying to help Kate and Braden adjust to a normal life, and I was trying to take advantage of her body. Had it really been that long since I'd had sex? It sure felt like it, but that wasn't a good excuse. I couldn't screw up our friendly relationship, because somehow I would fuck it up and she wouldn't be able to stay. Right now, Kate couldn't handle having Raegan and Braden, the two most important people in her life, taken away. Hell, I couldn't fathom them leaving either.

Turned out I needed that flaming-hot shower after all. My fingers were still tingling from the feel of her soft skin underneath me. When I headed toward the shower stall, I spotted Rae's white cotton bra and matching panties lying on the floor. *Shit.* My throbbing need should have diminished, knowing that my own mother had purchased those for her, but it didn't. It didn't help one fucking bit.

My clothes hit the ground before the boiling spray of the shower had a chance to heat the cold tiles. When I stepped in, I had that first quick instant where my body felt like it was in a tub of ice water, but then my sensory receptors caught up with my brain and I jumped back from the intense heat. The extreme temperatures didn't help my situation at all, though, so I reached down, stroked my length, and thought about a pair of eyes so green the Emerald Isle should be envious.

- Eleven -

RAEGAN -

I lay breathless on the bed after Lane had left me for the bathroom. I realized quickly that the kids laughing in the living room had probably been a huge mood killer for him, but I hated that he had said sorry—not once, but *twice*. I didn't want to hear apologies. I just wanted more of him . . . more of what he had just given me. More mind-blowing tingles that quickly exploded into euphoria through every inch of my body.

Yeah, I needed more.

I wrapped the towel securely under my arms and padded on bare feet out to the living room. Kate and Braden had been so wiped out lately with going to play at the park for hours every day and all of the walks Lane took us on through the city. We'd spent a lot of time inside too, but Lane acted as if he needed to show them everything right now.

I smiled when I saw the two of them fading fast. They'd always taken early naps—I realize, now that they're four years old, that I should just be thankful they still take them at all—but I was also grateful that they always seemed to take them at the same time.

Kate's eyes were drooping as she lay on the arm of the couch. Braden's head was lying on Kate, his eyes already shut. Kate was trying to fight it as she softly giggled, but her efforts were weak.

I checked the lock on the front door for the hundredth time and made sure the alarm that Lane had installed was armed. When I felt that they would be safe in the living room on their own, I shuffled down the hallway, cracked open the bedroom door, and then entered the bathroom without knocking.

I stripped off my towel and let it float to the ground. Lane was already in the shower, and steam had engulfed the room entirely in white. I could barely make out the outline of his body, but I could tell that he had his head leaning against the tile wall, while the water pounded his large back.

I tiptoed closer and then stopped, mesmerized by the movement of his hand. I knew what he was doing, and I shivered at the idea that I had done that to him. Heat crept up from my toes and in between my thighs again, but this time another heat joined it. A furious heat. He had left me on the bed, sprawled out and practically begging him, so he could come pleasure himself alone in the bathroom?

I had never been one to leave a misunderstanding hanging in the air, and even though I could have just sat around and moped about the idea of him not wanting me, I didn't intend to. I tackled those feelings. Hard and fast.

I swung the glass shower door open and his eyes snapped to mine in shock. I felt a tremble rock me when his eyes licked my exposed body from head to toe. His hand hadn't left his erection, but he wasn't moving it anymore.

"Rae . . ." His voice sounded as if he were in true pain.

"I'm mad at you."

"I'm so sorry. I shouldn't have started that." He looked at me again with shame for what he had done, and *then* I was pissed.

"If you apologize for touching me one more time, I will scream."

"I shouldn't have started that with you," he repeated. "We have so much going on . . ." His words trailed off as I stepped into the shower. I knew the water would be scalding. I could feel the heat from here, so I stayed near the edge, out of the spray. He was so surprised by my forward movement that it took him a second to realize he needed to turn down the heat.

"You just left me . . . alone . . . on a bed," I whispered.

When I was happy with the temperature of the water, I stepped underneath the calming flow. My body brushed his—just barely—and he moaned audibly.

"Rae . . ." he started, but I held my hand up to stop him.

"What I don't want is to hear you make excuses for this attraction between us. What I do want is to feel you," I stated firmly.

"I'm trying real hard to control myself, babe. You can't keep saying stuff like that to me." I heard the tension in his voice and noticed his hand squeeze a bit more tightly around himself.

"What are you so afraid of?" I asked. When I extended my hands out to touch him, he quickly stepped out of my reach. I would have felt insecure at yet another rejection, but at the same time I knew how attracted he was to me—even if it was only a fraction of what I felt.

"Sex complicates things when it's between two people who have to maintain a civil relationship. I can't have things get weird between us, Rae. God . . . I want you. I want you so bad, but . . ." His hands moved through the air, mimicking how he would like to run them across my body, and a thrill darted through me. I almost moved closer, but I wasn't that desperate. Not yet.

"No. It's *just* sex and I want it with you. It's been a long, long, *long* time for me, Lane. You have no idea how this feels . . . how much I want." I inched closer and was happy to see that he didn't back away.

"You're fooling yourself if you think this won't obscure lines and confuse feelings," he whispered into the spray of the shower.

"I realize that. But let me handle it. This is *just* sex . . . right here . . . right now." With one hand I reached out and replaced his on his strong erection.

"Damn it, Raegan," he groaned, and I watched as all the fight left his body. I was breaking down the big, tough boxer, one word and touch at a time.

His hand stretched out and pulled the back of my head toward him, our lips colliding in the middle. When he sucked my lower lip into his mouth, I melted. He pushed my back until I was firmly pressed against the glass, and I looked up at his face while his hands ran over my water-slicked breasts.

His eyes were focused past me, almost as if he were looking outside of the shower, and I loved the heat that began to glow in his eyes. I turned to see what had him so turned on. Over my shoulder, I noticed that he could see my body pressed into the glass through the mirror facing us. It was slightly fogged up from the steam, but he could still easily make out the lines of my body in the glass.

Since he seemed to enjoy that, I twirled in his hands and pressed my front against the glass. At that point, even I was mesmerized by our reflection. My breasts weren't small; I could thank a year of breastfeeding Braden for those. They just never went back to my pre-pregnancy size.

But what had my mouth watering was the towering figure behind me. His large frame practically engulfed my much smaller one, and I could feel his giant arms wrapping around my front. The idea that he held back so much of his strength so that he could touch me tenderly had me primed and ready to go instantly. Slowly, he let his hands glide past my navel and into the area I was silently begging for him to stay in.

Through the mirror our eyes met and I said, "You like watching." It wasn't a question because his obvious arousal persistently pressing into my back was my answer.

One of his large fingers dipped into me and my head fell back against his chest. Everything about him was a turn-on to me. The rasping breath in my ear alone could get me off at this point.

"You know damn well that I like it," he said directly into my ear. His lips glided across it lightly, and when he gently bit my earlobe, my hands flew back and I grabbed his rock-hard thighs for support. My fingers clenched into his muscles, but he didn't protest.

"I need to hear you tell me," I pleaded.

In the reflection of the mirror I watched his face shift back toward my ear, but before he could get a word out, his back shot ramrod straight. The flow of the water splashed over his rigid shoulders and I shrieked. The water had lost all of its heat from Lane's blazing-hot shower earlier, and the pounding spray was now straight ice.

I shoved out of the shower door and felt instantly better as the warmth of the bathroom kissed my frozen skin. Lane wasn't far behind me as he lifted me by the waist and sat me on the bathroom sink.

The glacial water must not have discouraged him, because the look he gave me just then could have melted an iceberg. I was glad that the brief interruption hadn't made him come to his senses and try to stop this again. I spread my legs to make room for his wide girth and he promptly filled the void. I looked up at him as he guided himself into me without any words.

He paused when he was fully immersed, and I couldn't have found my breath even if it was served to me on a silver platter. It had been way too long for me, and he was large. Larger than normal, I think. The pain was a good pain, but I still needed a second to adjust. Thankfully, in that moment, he was tuned in to what I needed.

He dipped my head back with his hands, ran his lips over my ear and down my jaw, and then lightly licked my lips until they parted briefly. Just as I was about to squirm beneath him, he moved a fraction of an inch.

His mouth was back at my ear, and his deep, rough voice lit all of my nerves on fire. "Everything about you, I like. Everything about you is a turn-on. So yes, you little temptress, I liked watching you while I brought you to the edge."

His speed had picked up at that point, but I hadn't noticed because his words were just what I needed to relax into the movement. Each drag was heaven, each push was delicious, and every little rough noise that came from his throat was intoxicating.

"Bringing you to the edge is enjoyable, but tipping you over made me crazy. I need to see that face you made again. That complete abandon caused by *my* touches."

"Lane, your voice alone can push me over the edge," I moaned. His rhythm was something of my dreams. A guy this big should have been clumsy and frantic, but he was smooth and confident with each drive of his hips.

He didn't say anything else. Maybe he was too busy concentrating on his own pleasure, or maybe he didn't want his words to bring me to my climax . . . he wanted his body to do that job. I reached up and gripped my fingers through his hair and worked my hips with his rhythm.

The increased friction set us both off in a frenzy to find release, and we didn't last much longer. I crossed the finish line first with my silent cry into the bathroom walls. I didn't care that my head was thrown backward or the absolute rawness of my emotions was clear as day on my face. I was glad that I had enough control not to scream every curse word I have ever known, but I certainly felt like it—the energy that ran through my entire body was like pure electricity.

When I came back around, Lane was staring at me with a strange look on his face. I ran my hands along his collarbone and up the back of his head through his golden hair. I pressed my chest up against his and felt him swell inside of me. His thrusts became jerky and I held him tighter to me, waiting for him to let go. I enjoyed every second of his movements against my highly sensitive flesh.

With a groan, he pulled away and pumped his release onto my stomach, my thighs, and some even made it up to my chest. His eyes flared at the mess he had just left on me. When I saw his lip quirk and a dimple appear on his cheek, I leaned forward and licked it.

He grabbed my face and began devouring my mouth with his own. My fingernails dug into his warm, smooth back as I tried to hold his body against mine.

Finally, we gasped for air and he pulled away from me. My legs had cramped up, so I decided to stay on the sink while I let the blood flow back into each leg. I leaned back until my head hit the mirror behind me, and I waited for my heart rate to slow down. Wow, my doctor should have prescribed *this* for my blood pressure.

"Shit, you're good for my ego, babe. If you keep lying there like I just gave you the world, I swear I'm two seconds away from showing you the moon as well."

I laughed softly at his words. "You can't even imagine how long it's been for me," I whispered.

"I hope it's been a while . . . considering . . ." he replied with a rough undertone.

"Yes, thank God for that, but it goes way further than that. The last time I had sex was when I got pregnant with Braden." His mouth dropped open and I chuckled.

When he seemed to have recovered from his shock, he said, "Well, now I don't feel so mighty anymore. I was basically popping your cherry again. Anything would have made you blissfully happy at that point."

"Trust me, I might not be that experienced, but I can honestly say I've never had anything like *that*," I huffed, still trying to catch my breath. I wanted to hop down, but I still couldn't move my legs. His hands reached around my waist and I felt him turn the water on behind me. It was back off moments later, and I jolted when I felt a cold cloth touch the skin on my stomach.

"Sorry, I used all the hot water, but let me clean you up," he whispered. Lane moved the washcloth lightly over my skin, and as each area was clean to his satisfaction, he kissed it tenderly.

"Why did you . . . ?" I gestured at my thighs, stomach, and chest, hoping he understood.

"I know for damn sure you aren't on birth control, so unless you want Braden and Kate to have a baby brother or sister right now, coming inside you probably wouldn't have been the best idea." He winked at me and grabbed a towel off the bar.

I immediately began shaking my head, surprised I hadn't thought of that myself. "I should get on the pill."

"Already planning round two, are we?" His intoxicating words slid over me as if they were his very hands. I watched as he slipped the towel over every inch of his body; I couldn't make myself look anywhere else.

"I don't want any more children," I whispered while observing his movements.

His hands froze and he swung his eyes in my direction. "Really?" He sounded surprised and almost confused that I would say something like that. I finally hopped down from the sink and grabbed my own towel from earlier.

"Yeah. At least, I'm pretty sure. I don't feel like I'm missing anything by not having another. Braden and . . ." I paused because I didn't know how to approach this considerately. "Braden is enough." I almost physically grimaced from my own words, because my heart wanted to say *Braden and Kate were enough*. But what right did I have to claim his child?

"You can say it, Rae. I think Kate is as much yours as she is mine, at this point," he stated, looking directly at me.

"I just . . . I don't want to insult Ash or tarnish her memory." I looked down at my hands as they fumbled with the towel, which I wrapped tightly under my arms, hoping to find comfort from its imitation of a hug. His feet appeared in front of me, and I felt his fingers pushing my chin up.

"I think Ash would be grateful that, in her absence, Kate has a wonderful mother figure. I'm battling it too. I wish Ash could be here, but . . . she's just not. Kate loves you, and I don't plan on taking that away from her."

There were so many conflicting lines in that statement, but I just didn't have the strength to break it all down and examine his meaning. He leaned down and kissed me until all of the thoughts seeped away.

When he pulled back, he looked at me sternly and asked, "Can I ask where Braden's dad is? I'm not jumping into some guy's territory, am I?"

"What? No! Lane, what kind of person do you think I am?" I shrieked in shock, but my tone was still light enough that he knew I wasn't really pissed.

"Okay, okay!" he said with his hands raised in surrender. "I just didn't feel like kicking anyone's ass . . . well, not today, anyway," he laughed. I swatted at his chest and then my hand didn't leave the warm, tempting skin. He grabbed it and kissed it lightly while looking down at me.

"It was the typical immature-guy response. He bailed at the first positive sign on that little white stick. Couldn't get enough of me one day and the next day—gone."

"Damn, now I *am* going to have to kick someone's ass," he grumbled. This time the words were joking, but his tone was absolutely not.

"Save it for someone who's worth it—trust me."

- Twelve -

LANE -

After Raegan and I finally succumbed to the desires we had been
feeling since almost the first day we met, we escaped the house
for the rest of the day. I needed to get out because if we found ourselves at any moment with privacy, I would have jumped her again.
As it was, I had to pry myself away from her because all I wanted to
do was keep kissing her . . . well, among other things.

Since it was pretty warm out, we took the kids to the Brooklyn
Children's Museum, and the look on Kate and Braden's faces was
worth the hour it took us to walk there. I definitely wasn't accus-
tomed to New York life anymore and having to get around everywhere by your own two feet. We could have taken the subway, but
I had this feeling the last time we took it that Raegan was having a
hard time. I didn't know if it was the screeching of the train on the
tracks or the people bumping into us at every turn, but I realized
then it was best to keep us all aboveground.

I loved watching the differing personalities of Kate and Braden
shine through. They were always attached at the hip and did everything with each other, but at the museum we really got to see them

individually. Kate was all about socializing and talking to the other kids, and I was already cringing at the idea of fighting the boys off my front porch.

Braden, on the other hand, was mesmerized—absolutely captivated—by the greenhouse. He dug right in and covered his hands with dirt, locating all of the worms within the vicinity. Then he convinced Kate to race leaf boats in the pond, and when an employee told him he could actually plant his own flower in the dirt, he looked as if she had just told him Christmas would now be every day.

It made me want to take him back to Texas and plant a garden with him in my backyard. But that kind of thinking was the kind that would get me in trouble. That kind of thinking led to questions that I don't think Rae and I were ready to approach. We were already walking on thin ice, just trying to test out these new parenting waters, and neither of us wanted to step on the other's toes.

That night Kate and Braden barely made it through dinner before they crashed hard on the couch. Raegan laughed as she looked down at their snoring forms. We really had worn them out today. I checked that the alarm was set and then grabbed Rae's hand, pulling her down the hall.

"Lane . . ." she tried to protest, but there was no conviction in her words. My hands were on her waist before we even made it into the bedroom. My mouth immediately zoned in on her neck, and she tilted her head to let me have access.

I pushed her back onto the bed and immediately crawled above her. She giggled at what I assumed was my eagerness, but I couldn't deny that right now *eager* was my middle name. This girl was smoking hot, and I'd had to watch her strut around in front of me all day, now knowing what she had been concealing under those clothes for the past few weeks.

"You sure are excited to go another round, but I think I remember you being the one to warn me off this morning." She laughed.

"What?" I tried to sound innocent. "This is just me trying to get to know you better." I actually had no idea what was coming over me. Raegan had me wagging my tail when she walked in the room and panting like a dog when she even so much as grazed past me.

She moved her mouth and I pulled her lower lip in between my teeth. Her groan confirmed my earlier suspicion that this would be my go-to move to turn her on. With each transfer of our lips, she managed to push her bottom one into my mouth, inviting me to suck and nip on the fleshy area.

I kissed down her neck. Slowly, I moved between her legs and worked my way down her body. Her pants were easy to pull off her toned legs, but I realized if I removed any more clothes this would go a lot faster than I had originally planned.

So I situated myself between her thighs and kissed the tops of them. I rested my cheek against the silky-smooth skin and stared up at her. She had her eyes closed, but when she realized I had stopped, she looked down at me curiously.

"What happened when you talked to Mrs. Flores at the park that day?" I asked gently. Her body locked up, but I kissed her legs again until she relaxed again. "You know I don't blame you anymore, right?" She nodded slowly and I continued, "I was an idiot, but I really do want to know what happened. It kills me to not know, Rae."

"You want to talk about this *now*?"

"I don't see why not. We actually have some time alone," I reasoned.

"And you're just going to stay . . . down there?" she asked, eyeing my precarious position.

"Hey, you gave me the invitation. Don't take all my fun away now. I quite like it down here." I couldn't help myself, so I kissed her lazily through her cotton panties, and she arched her back with a groan. I pulled back and laid my head down on her legs again. That wasn't going to get her to talk—not what she needed to talk about right then, at least.

"Tease," she grumbled. With a deep breath, she situated herself underneath me so she could talk while looking at me. "I used to take Kate and Braden down to the park, just so we could get some fresh air, and I swear they liked hearing the kids play. I know they were just babies and couldn't have actually understood what was going on, but they would always perk up when they listened to the sounds. It was a really peaceful time of the day."

Her pause let me know that it was a peaceful time that was stolen from her. Now it would always be tarnished. I hated the Flores family even more for putting that look on her face. I nuzzled her leg and she gave me a half-smile.

"One day, I was holding Braden in my arms and Kate was asleep in the stroller. An older lady joined me on the park bench and started asking me about the babies. I didn't see the harm. She began the conversation in Spanish and then she was intrigued that I could speak it so fluently. I told her about my family in Colombia. I remember she rolled her eyes and told me that's where I had gotten my ugly accent. I didn't even think much of it because I remembered my mom saying the same thing about people from other Spanish-speaking countries. She asked if I planned on teaching the babies Spanish, and I told her I would try. Definitely Braden would learn, but I didn't really know how long I would get with Kate."

"She seemed nice, just a little nosy. She told me how she never could have children and she was envious of my having the two pretty babies. I didn't know if she understood that I was just Kate's nanny, but I didn't bother to explain myself. Braden started getting hungry and fussy at that point, and she asked me if I breastfed. Then she went on this huge lecture about how it was best for them. I nodded my head and politely excused myself so I could feed him back at your apartment without her advice. That . . ." Her voice cracked and I tensed. My hands gripped her legs, and I lifted up and lightly kissed her stomach.

"She must have followed me. That's the only way she could have known where to find us that night. I was an idiot, Lane."

I finally climbed back up her body and positioned myself above her. "No, babe, you weren't. Even I would have fallen for that. She was a con artist."

"If I would have just kept my big mouth shut, she never would have been so interested. Then we would have never . . ."

"Shhh . . ." I consoled.

"She liked that I spoke Spanish," she continued.

"Do you know how many people speak Spanish in New York City, Rae?" When she didn't answer, I did. "Millions, Rae. Millions. This lady picked you out because she liked you. She wanted what you had, and she just so happened to have an evil bastard of husband to help her."

"I had nothing! My aunt died, so I was on the streets. Braden and I bounced between friends' houses and your house. I don't know why she chose me, but I had nothing."

"You had two of the prettiest babies known to mankind."

"She was sick," she said quietly.

"That she was."

"No, like terminally ill. It wasn't long after we got to Mexico that she passed away. I guess Flores had . . . taken us . . . for his wife. To give her the babies she could never have. I was just the convenient caretaker. They probably planned on killing me once Braden and Kate didn't need me anymore."

"He stole you guys so his wife could have kids?" My temper spiked. "That's the most ridiculous thing I have ever heard! What about adoption?! Legal fucking adoption! What about the fact that one of the babies was mine?!"

I rolled off of her and she followed to face me. I had spent many sleepless nights trying to determine a possible motive. Now that I knew, I felt deflated. How the fuck does someone take someone else's child just because they couldn't have their own?

"I heard one of the guys say that she had been obsessed with me for a long time. I guess . . . she had been watching me." I felt a violent shiver run through her body, and I grabbed her to hold her close—to comfort both of us. "Well, turns out it had all been for nothing. The bitch died and then Flores had no idea what to do with us. So he kept us locked in a room. I guess he hoped that Braden would grow up and work for him."

I took a deep breath, preparing myself to ask a question I needed to ask, even if I wasn't sure I could handle the answer. "You said they tried to get rid of . . . Kate?" I was surprised to hear the weakness that bled from my own voice.

She cleared her throat uncomfortably. "Flores came to me one day, which was rare. He said he had no need for a daughter." I clenched my fist at those words. If I could get ahold of that bastard again, he would die a slow death. He had no right to even use the word *daughter*. Raegan waited for my inner turmoil to cool down.

"He said that only Braden would really be of any benefit to him one day. I clutched Kate to my chest so tightly that they would have to take me to get to her. So that's what they did . . . they took us both. Away from Braden, and I about died right there."

"What? I don't understand . . . you never said you were separated from him . . ." I felt immensely guilty and pulled in a thousand different directions. I was thankful she had held on to Kate, but how could I expect any mother to have to leave her own child?

"They couldn't console Braden . . . no matter what they tried. He was only breastfed, so they couldn't even get him to eat. After what felt like a lifetime, they let me and Kate go back to him. I still hadn't let her go. Then they just kept us there, locked away from everything, hoping that their version of solitary confinement would eventually break me. They came back every couple of months to collect Kate, but I wouldn't let them. So they took to . . . marking me. Each time I refused to give them Kate . . . another mark. I think it was just a fun game to them; they didn't really care about Kate anymore. They just liked fucking with me."

"What do you mean they marked you, Rae?" I managed to get through my clenched teeth.

"Like cuts. On my skin," she whispered.

"What the hell?" I asked a bit louder. I hadn't seen any cuts on her besides the one on her face. Had they done that to her?

She slowly rolled away from me onto her stomach. I sat up on my knees and looked down at her lying there below me. She didn't move, didn't even point to where I should be looking, so I took her in her whole body. It didn't take me long to see what she was talking about, although I wished it had.

There, from mid-calf to her upper thigh, all along the backside of her left leg, were slices in her skin, each about four inches in length. They were all healed but in different phases of scarring and looked like stripes down her leg. Only her left leg, which was strange to me.

"Babe . . ." I stated, at a loss for words.

"It didn't really hurt," she lied.

"Is this why you only wear pants?"

"It didn't seem polite to scare anyone. I know it's not pretty." She turned back over, taking the view of her leg away from me but not the memory of the image.

I pushed between her legs again and raised her left leg in the air. Her breath hitched as I began kissing the skin at the site of the first terrible slash, all the way up to what looked like the newest one, closest to her ass. I hated that one the most. She must have been so scared and humiliated.

"The last one was over a year ago. I think they got bored with that tactic."

Or they were biding their time for something else.

"I never let Braden and Kate see it happen," she added, thankfully interrupting *that* horrific thought. I hadn't even thought about Kate and Braden witnessing it, but I had come to trust Raegan's parenting instincts so fully that the thought had never occurred to me.

"We can get them fixed. I know they have plastic surgeons for all kinds of things. We can have them removed." I tried to tamp down my own hostile feelings toward every guy that had ever worked under Flores. I wanted any sign of their touch gone from her gorgeous body.

"We?" She smiled coyly. I continued kissing her, not addressing what that statement meant. She let it slide and said, "Besides, those are nothing compared to this ugly thing on my face." Her hand brushed past the now healed but puckered scar on her forehead.

She had just gotten the stitches out the day before, and I could tell she was feeling self-conscious about it. The scar was bright pink and it stuck out against her tanned skin, but I still thought that her bright green eyes were the most prominent feature on her beautiful face.

"Tell me what happened," I demanded gently, releasing her leg and kissing along her forehead.

I felt as if Rae and I had gotten to know each other better in these past two weeks, but we were just now talking about the important things. We'd spoken with the kids about their therapy meetings at the precinct, but we hadn't discussed hers. Kate and Braden were cleared after one session because they had been kept in the dark about the whole situation. They never understood the seriousness of their position growing up. Raegan had to endure a few more.

I was starting to know her little quirks. I knew that she hated drinking soda; the carbonation gave her hiccups instantly. I still laugh at her annoyed face after she'd hiccupped for a straight hour after taking a drink of my Sprite. I knew that her long hair was starting to bother her because she was always scooping it up into a bun on top of her head. I knew that she loved a huge slice of greasy pizza from the local pizzeria down the street, even though she always complained about it going to her hips. I could lick those hips all day, so I didn't care where the damn pizza went.

But until now, I had no idea what life was like for them during those years in captivity. If I was being honest, I'd been afraid to know, but it was nice to now fit all the puzzle pieces together.

"I was always trying to think of ways to escape," she explained. "Every other thought for years was about escape. How? When? I ran so many scenarios in my head and none of them seemed to pan out, so I never attempted them. I knew we were on an island. I could see the water from the window, and I pieced it together when the guys outside of our door would talk.

"Running away was out of the question. I mean, how far could I possibly get with two babies under my arms? My guess was not far. Whenever we got sick or had any medical needs, they had a guy come who claimed to be a doctor. I never trusted him, so I only asked in extreme cases. Once I needed some medicine when Braden got a stomach bug, and another time they gave me Tylenol when Kate ran a fever."

I remained close to her face, but I held my body above hers so I wouldn't crush her. I liked the way her words whispered across my cheek and the nearness of her body calmed my agitated nerves.

"I knew my time was running out," she continued. "Braden was getting older, and I knew that Flores wanted to start training him to be . . . one of his guys." She sneered at her words and I had a feeling my face mirrored hers. "So one day, I provoked one of the guys who brought us food. I knew he had a short temper and I sparked it just right. I knew exactly what was about to happen when he swung his arm back, so I braced myself."

"You let him hit you?" I growled murderously.

"All a part of my plan," she informed me. "He hit me *so* hard." My body tensed up but she continued, "My original plan was for his hit to break some skin on its own. I wasn't expecting to be hit so hard that my body flew back and I smacked my face into the corner of a desk. That was the one thing Kate and Braden did see. I spoke with them endlessly about it and assured them that I was okay. They were more worried about my head than scared about anything else." She ran her finger across the scar on her forehead and then followed it down to her ear. "It was more pain than I had prepared myself for, but it still worked."

"I don't understand, and now I'm only more pissed off," I grumbled.

"If I would have cut myself, they would have been suspicious. This way I had someone to blame for the laceration on my head whenever asked. I wish I would have thought of it when they were doing this to my leg," she said, gesturing at the slash marks that marred her otherwise perfect skin. "I spent so much time trying to get those to heal properly, and by the time the idea hit me, they never came back around. So I had to get an injury from them some-how. I took horrible care of the cut on my forehead. Anytime it started to heal and close, I forced the wound back open. It got worse and worse. I expected the wound to get infected, which it did. The blood infection, I wasn't expecting. I ran a fever and finally my lucky streak began.

"Flores was out of town. I guess off to one of those fights you spoke about. The men there had no idea what to do and they could tell I wasn't faring well. I was pale and lethargic. The fake on-call doctor had no idea what to do either. They finally drove me and the kids up to Tijuana, but I begged them to take me to an American hospital. We went to one right across the border, and once I was checked in, they finally got ahold of Flores.

"I could tell by the looks on the guys' faces that he was not happy with their decision. He made them stand guard with me the entire time. I was there a week and a half. The nurses seemed to pick up quickly that something wasn't right, so they never asked why I wouldn't let the children leave my side. I was too afraid of the men hurting Kate or Braden, so when the nurses tried to discreetly ask me if I was okay, I always played the part and said yes.

"I finally caught a break when one of the guys who was supposed to be watching me stepped out of the room during his shift. I lunged for the call button in my room and quickly spit out the situation to one of the nurses. She called the local authorities and they stormed the hospital. Flores's guys must have caught on quick, because they never found them. Right away I was given the number to the New York precinct and was able to talk to your dad, who got the all-clear for me to make the trip back to New York. Apparently, he informed the local police that his guys would be handling the case, but I didn't really understand all the logistics and legalities of it. Plus, I was still highly medicated."

I cleared my throat. "Everyone called me that night, I guess after they had talked to you. I missed all of their calls, though, because I was passed out from this," I pointed to my shoulder. "I was probably only miles away from you that day."

"You're even closer now," she whispered.

"I cannot believe you made yourself sick, almost to the point of death," I said into her neck.

"I got us out. Four years late, but I got us out."

I needed her. I needed her now. I shoved down my shorts and boxers. Her panties weren't difficult as they slipped away with my clothes. Before I could take another breath, I was back at her mouth, taking whatever she would give. I felt her hand reach down between us, and she guided me inside of her.

She was slick but so fucking tight. Besides this morning, I knew she hadn't done this in years, so I clenched my teeth and tried to ease her into this. My mind was running laps around the bed, shouting at me to *go, go, go*! When I felt her little hands on my ass, her fingers clenching the taut skin and forcing me to move, I knew I had the go-ahead.

Our mouths never parted. I wanted our second time to go more slowly, with more exploration, but she'd set my nerves on fire with every detail of her experiences. I needed the comfort, and I needed to give her the same.

Her heat felt so amazing around me, and when her hand cupped over my lips, I realized that my groans were becoming a bit too audible. I nipped at her fingers until they moved and leaned forward for her mouth again.

"Oh god, oh god, god, god . . ." she whispered harshly. Raegan was much better at keeping our activities quiet than I seemed to be. The egotistical side of me wanted to make her scream . . . loud. But the father in me didn't want to push my luck. I'd get her to scream like that someday.

My pace quickened and the headboard began to slap against the wall like thunder. I couldn't stop my movements, so I lunged forward to hold the flimsy wood against the wall. My stretched-out position invited her fingers to run across my chest and stomach, and I savored those touches.

"Yes! Just like that; stay like that," she managed to grind out through her clenched teeth. I had a feeling she wasn't opening her mouth much so she wouldn't let anything louder than her whispers escape.

I watched her tits bounce beneath her shirt, and I mentally slapped myself for not getting that shirt off. Regardless, the feeling of her squeezing around me in her release, the look of pure bliss on her face, and the way her body went absolutely stiff beneath me . . . I couldn't hold back any longer.

Thank God I had the forethought to remember I didn't have a condom on—yet again—so I pulled free. I'm not sure what was wrong with me, because I never went without those rubber guys. The second I pulled out, Rae's hand clutched tightly around my length.

My hands dropped from the headboard and she pumped me forcefully one, two, three times.

"Fuuuuck," I groaned into her neck, while I released all over her stomach. I lifted up and shivered when her hand slid across my now oversensitive skin. I stared down at the area I had once again marked. I had never done this to a girl, and yet with Rae I'd done it twice.

"I think you're forgetting a condom on purpose now," she chuckled.

"I am kind of enjoying the way this looks," I brazenly replied. The comment didn't slide without a good pinch to my side, but nothing could have brought down my high right then.

- THIRTEEN -

LANE -

Now that Raegan and I had broken the proverbial seal, we let loose on each other. Anytime Braden and Kate were down for naps, we jumped all over each other. If they got sucked into playing a game in the nursery, we hid out in the master bathroom, devouring each other's bodies. Since the kids had officially taken over the bed in the nursery, each night was much of the same for us. I couldn't get enough. She couldn't get enough. The past three days have been fucking phenomenal.

One morning I slipped out at breakfast time to catch a quick run. It was time I started doing more than just the exercises I had been doing around the apartment. Kate was just digging into her eggs and bacon when I swore I would return soon.

I decided to run the bridges, considering those would provide more flow of air than in the city, where the hot, muggy air became trapped among the buildings. I ran across the Brooklyn Bridge, up the East River, and cut back down the Manhattan Bridge. It didn't take me long, but I should have been able to do it much faster.

I pushed through the door with my shirt draped over one shoulder. I wasn't going to admit that I had taken it off on my way up the stairs because I liked the way Raegan ogled my body, but . . . it may have been a factor in my actions.

The alarm was still set when I walked in the door, which had made me feel better about leaving them behind for a just a little bit. I knew I couldn't keep Kate in my sight twenty-four/seven, so going for a run today was like ripping off a very painful Band-Aid. But the house was much too quiet for two kids. I sped into the kitchen and sighed in relief when I noticed Raegan's handwriting on a piece of paper.

We're just down at the playground. Come join us!

Her underlining the word *the* meant she was at the playground she had refused to return to. I felt proud of her for making that effort, and I felt better about them being right around the corner instead of eight blocks away.

As soon as I shut off the spray of my shower, my phone started ringing. I knew who it was immediately by the ringtone—Audrey. I rushed to pull on my shorts and snatched up the phone before the last verse blasted through the bathroom.

"Hey, doll."

"I miss you! Are you coming back yet?" she asked, not missing a beat. I smiled when I heard the happiness in her voice.

"I'm about ready. I know we're all tired of being here."

"So . . . *all* of you will be coming?"

"That's my plan."

"How are you getting along with Raegan?"

"Are we playing twenty questions, doll?" I laughed into the phone. "We're all happy, and Raegan and I get along great."

"Oh God, what did you do?" She dropped her voice and said, "Lane . . ."

"What?" I chuckled. "I didn't do anything . . ." Guilty was my middle name.

"You slept with her?!" she shouted. I had to hold the phone away from my ear at her shrill volume. "Oh my God. You better bring that little princess of yours to Texas so I can hug her and spoil her to death. But also bring Raegan! I need to meet her!" The sheer excitement in her voice made me want to backtrack the crazy train this conversation was on.

"You're getting a bit outrageous."

"You didn't deny it! Now why would you put the moves on that poor girl? She must be gorgeous for you to cross that line," she rambled on.

"I didn't cross the line. She did! She came into my shower." As soon as the words left my mouth, I bit into my tongue harshly. Why the fuck did I just say that?

"Ohhh . . . so she's more like Emerson," Audrey concluded, and I could tell she was smiling. Em was our friend back home. During college, she'd had the reputation of being the promiscuous girl on campus, and I'd heard many rumors of how she'd seduced Jaxon. They're married now, but they still talk about her wild days, much to Jaxon's discomfort.

"No! She's not like Emerson." I didn't want her to think Rae was slutty. That wasn't what was going on here, and I felt the urge to defend what was happening between us . . . even though I had no clue.

"Hey! I take offense at that," I heard Emerson shout in the background.

Heat rose up in my cheeks. "Audrey . . ." I growled into the phone. I heard her speaking on the other end of the line, but she must have had the mouthpiece covered because I couldn't make out her words clearly. Finally, she sounded closer than she had before.

"Sorry, Lane! They just wanted to see how things were with you . . . and then . . . the conversation took *that* turn!"

"They?" God, if the guys were there, I would never hear the end of it.

"Just the girls. Em and Quinn. I swear."

"Don't call me on speakerphone anymore," I grumbled.

"I promise, I won't. So you really like Raegan, huh?"

"That seems to be the direction it's going at the moment . . ." I was over this gossip session. I started walking toward the living room to find my shoes so I could join the people I really needed to be with right now.

"Eek! I'm so excited for you! I can't wait to squish little Kate in my arms. You have no idea. I dream about it every night."

"Please, don't squish my daughter." I started to chuckle again.

"I can't help it. I love her so much already, Lane. I seriously can't believe you just said the word 'daughter,'" she said, and I heard the hitch in her words.

"Oh, doll, not the waterworks right now, please," I begged. A girl who's crying is bad. A girl who's crying over the phone is so much worse because you're absolutely powerless to help. I needed to divert her. "Hey, can you start doing me some favors?"

"Of course," she responded.

"Can you start getting my place ready for us to come back? I don't have anything for two four-year-olds. Well, almost five-year-olds now. I'm gonna need your help, but don't go overboard!"

"I'm on it!" I started to hear her name off all of the things Raegan and I would potentially need in the house, but the sound of the key turning in the lock redirected my attention.

My body began to perk up at the idea of seeing all of them. I was ready to hug Kate and get back to our chess game. I was ready to finish reading that comic book with Braden. And I was just ready for Raegan, period. Primed and ready to go for anything she wanted from me.

Raegan slammed the door open, and I watched as she rushed both Kate and Braden through the doorway in front of her. Something wasn't right. She had a death grip on both of their hands and didn't let go as she kicked the door behind them with her foot. Her face was in absolute panic mode.

"Audrey, gotta go." I tossed my phone on the couch as I headed toward them.

With Braden's hand securely clutched in hers, she reached up and turned the lock. Then I watched as she slumped against the closed door with her eyes tightly sealed. Her breath was moving raggedly in and out. Her chest was heaving erratically, and her obvious discomfort had my own heart rate speeding up.

As far as I could tell, they weren't harmed, so I tried to keep the calm by walking quickly but with a pace that wouldn't distress Kate and Braden. I reached over Braden's head and tapped in the code to arm the alarm system.

"Hey, did you two have fun at the park?" I asked with a bright, forced smile.

"Yeah! Then we raced Mommy home!" Kate exclaimed animatedly.

"But Mama cheated because she wouldn't let go of our hands." Braden laughed while still trying to catch his breath.

I couldn't even begin to describe how much I admired Raegan in that moment. Whatever was disturbing her, she never let it filter down to the children, and that made her the greatest mother I had ever known.

"Okay, go wash your hands, get a drink of water, and then can you guys find some books for me to read?" I asked.

Thankfully, Ash and I had built up a pretty good little library for Kate while Ash was still pregnant. We hit up thrift stores and used-book sales every time we saw one, and each time we picked up tons of discounted books. Happily, they agreed and ran off down the hallway.

Raegan's eyes were screwed shut and her body was ever so slightly shaking. She had her fist clenched and braced against the door as if she were blocking out all of the evil on the other side.

"Babe," I whispered, slowly approaching her. "You're worrying me. What happened?"

Her breath shuddered as she tried to speak, but she was too shaken up. I scooped her up into my arms and moved away from the foyer, closer to the front coat closet. At least over here we were out of eyesight of the kids down the hall.

I slid down the wall so I could sit on the floor and hold her. I began to take deep, steadying breaths in and then slowly releasing them. Over the span of about ten minutes, she started to breathe in time with me. I felt her shaking subside, and the racking shudders weren't so violent anymore. Finally, I sensed the clutch of panic leave me as I felt her take a breath that seemed to be more relief and less anxiety.

My hand ran over her hair and down to her back. The continuous motion seemed to bring her heart rate down to a normal pace. Her nose pushed into the side of my neck and I bent down to kiss her temple—right over her scar. The scar that brought my daughter back to me. I didn't care how unpleasant Raegan thought it looked, I'd always love it.

"I'm sorry . . . I'm sorry . . ." she repeated.

"Don't ever be sorry. Please, just tell me what happened."

"I can't stay in New York, Lane. It's suffocating me. The buildings and the noise and the people. I can't breathe . . ." She said the last word as if she were literally grabbing her next lungful of air.

"Then we're out of here," I responded quickly.

"Just like that?" she asked. Her body shifted and she moved her legs so she was straddling my lap while looking up at me.

"Just like that."

Her arms squeezed tightly around my neck, and her lips grazed the skin under my ear. "I ran from an elderly couple," she whispered, almost silently.

"Come again?"

"There was a couple walking around the playground. For some reason, I just felt like it was them. I know she's dead, but I got the crazy sense it was her. I grabbed the kids and ran. I'm such a nutcase now."

"It wasn't her," I offered gently.

"I understand that now, but—"

"You're not a nut case. You're adjusting back to life," I whispered.

"I ran away from two gray-haired, cane-wielding senior citizens." A slight snicker broke through her lips, and I knew she was coming back to me . . . either that or she really was losing it.

"Those old women with canes can be testy," I jested. She pinched at my side and I grabbed her wrist instantly.

"What is it with you and Audrey pinching my sides?!" I laughed.

"Probably because it's the only area on your body that actually gives a little bit."

"Hmm . . . I'll have to work on that."

"You're ridiculous. If you work on this body any more, I'll need my own cane just so I can beat all the women away from you." She laughed.

I grabbed hold of her ass in my lap and pulled her even closer to my body. "You claiming me?" The words were practically a growl, and I realized our lips were now inches apart.

"Are you saying you're claimable?" she murmured.

"Depends on the girl . . ."

"I thought it was *just* sex."

"Those were your words, babe. Not mine."

"I don't want to just be convenient for you, Lane." Her eyes shifted away from me, but she continued to speak. "I'm like a mother to Kate, so I know she'll want me around. Kate and Braden love each other so much, and I hope they can always be in each other's lives. But I feel as if I'm convenient to you, and I don't want to feel that way. So maybe we shouldn't . . ." Her words would have knocked me on my ass if I weren't already there.

I took her face into my hands and looked directly into her blazing emerald eyes. "The only thing convenient about you is that you're a woman. Otherwise, you have a saucy mouth, you never let me get away with anything, you jump on problems immediately, you always take the last chip when we share, you hog the covers in bed, sometimes you snore—"

"I do not!" she interrupted.

"Sometimes you snore. And you always use all the hot water. Not to mention, you're too damn beautiful for your own good."

"Some of those didn't sound like problems to me," she bantered.

"*None* of those are problems. I just wanted you to know you aren't convenient. You aren't easy. I don't like you because you're just around. I want you around because of your saucy mouth and the way you attack problems without letting them fester like most girls. I like that you don't let me get away with anything. I'll always give you the last chip, and you can take all the hot water you want as long as I can be in the shower with you."

"You forgot that you like my snoring." She smiled wide.

"Mmm . . . debatable," I teased. As I should have expected, she pinched my side—hard. It only made me laugh. "Okay, you don't really snore, but you do have this really cute little raspy breathing thing that you start doing sometimes. It's adorable."

She crinkled her nose in apparent aversion. "Girls don't want to be adorable."

I shrugged my shoulders without care. "Adorable doesn't mean I still don't want to fuck you."

"Ah, there's the romantic in you that I adore." She laughed.

Then, without further thought, she leaned in and pressed her lips to mine. I grabbed the back of her head and pulled her in tighter. Her mouth moved and she pushed her lower lips in between mine. I kept moving my lips against hers, knowing what she was asking for, but not willing to give it just yet.

She whimpered and I broke. I sucked her lip forcefully and then bit down gently on the swollen flesh. Her hips rocked forward and I groaned.

"You have to get off my lap, babe . . ." I muttered into her mouth.

"I like it here." As if to show her fondness for her position, she ground into my hardening erection again.

I stood up, and when I was steady, I made sure she was stable on her feet. Her lower lip jutted out and all I wanted to do was bite down on it. Instead, I ran my index finger across it lightly.

"The tiny search party will be out here soon looking for me. I said I would read to them," I whispered.

"Later?" she asked.

"You bet your ass, babe." She smiled, appeased by my words, and I almost moaned at the image of her standing there with a swollen lip and eyes begging me to take her. I stepped back and forced my body to move. I tried to readjust the situation she had given me in my shorts. "No, babe, you are definitely not convenient," I said as I walked toward the hallway.

I felt a lightness overcome me when I heard her breathy laugh. Before I could make it to Kate and Braden, she called out to me, "Hey, Lane . . ." When I turned around, she said, "I think I *will* claim you."

"'Bout time," I called back with a wink.

~

Raegan and I had made an effort every night to spend quality time during the last hour with Kate and Braden before bedtime. No television, no phones, no computers allowed. I didn't care if there were dishes overflowing from the sink or a stack of papers three inches high on my desk. It was just the four of us, usually in their temporary bedroom. We played board games and colored pictures, but mostly we read books. That seemed to be something the four of us could all agree on. This was the time when I learned the most about them.

As I was tucking Kate in next to Braden that night, she smiled up at me. It was the most peaceful, contented smile I had ever seen.

I touched the edges of her lips and said, "I like that smile."

She giggled. "Can we always stay together?"

"Of course. Maybe not here in New York, but we'll always be together." I thought about Raegan's panic attack today and knew that we would be leaving as soon as possible.

"Promise?" she asked innocently.

I stumbled on my thoughts and froze on that word. *Promise.* When she was a baby and I wasn't working, I used to rock her in this very room. I used to whisper promises to keep her safe, happy, and well taken care of. Promises that were broken. Now I knew that promises like that were out of my control, so how could I make an empty guarantee like that again?

"I love you, Kit Kat. Tomorrow, we can go back to that museum you and Braden love, okay?" Thank God four-year-olds were easily distracted.

She smiled widely and turned to look at Braden, who had the same look of excitement on his face.

"Night, guys," I whispered. Raegan leaned over them and gave them each a kiss before following me out of the room.

"Lane, what happened in there?" she asked when we reached the living room.

"You don't want to go to the museum tomorrow? Sorry, that's one of those things where I should have asked you first, huh?"

"You know that's not what I'm talking about. You froze up." She had caught on to that . . . of course she had. Raegan didn't let anything slide.

I let out a sigh. "The last time I made promises, I broke them. Every single one of them. I can't do that to her again. I know she was only a baby, but it meant something to me."

"Lane, none of that was your fault. *You* didn't break those promises. She just wants reassurance that you aren't going anywhere."

"Yes, and I plan on *showing* her that. I don't need to give any false promises, though. I won't lie to her ever again."

Raegan sighed in defeat, although I knew it was only temporary. But for now, it seemed, she would leave me to my demons. She left my side and walked toward the kitchen, while I plopped down on the sofa to think about this new parenting gig and the vast responsibilities that had been given back to me.

- Fourteen -

RAEGAN -

After Kate and Braden had fallen asleep that night in the nursery, I confessed to Lane that I was having panic attacks regularly. Being the great guy that he was, he felt bad for not knowing and wanted to know where it had been happening. He said he had often gotten caught up in playing with Kate and Braden, but he still thought he should have known if I was off in the apartment somewhere falling apart.

I hated that he felt guilty and tried to reassure him that I never wanted to burden him with that. I told him it was just something I had to wait out, and usually it was more comfortable to do it alone. Not surprisingly, he didn't agree with me.

One thing I couldn't get around was that the city didn't give me the same sense of home anymore. Every day we spent here pressed on me like a vise. I was always checking over my shoulder, and I would never be able to set foot in the local playground where I had first met Mrs. Flores—especially not after my ridiculous freak-out today.

When I opened up to him about my feelings, Lane said he knew exactly what I was talking about and added that he felt the same way. The tall buildings he had once loved looking up to now cast ugly shadows on the streets. This place would always be where his child was kidnapped . . . where his marriage fell apart. Maybe one day we would heal and get past this, but we weren't there yet.

Lane told me that every single day we came back to the apartment he wanted to grab all three of us and bolt. He said that he would never be able to live there again, no matter how much he appreciated his mom caring for it. He was even grateful for Ash's parents, who had generously paid the mortgage every month. I didn't weigh in on that topic because it wasn't my place to choose for him.

He confessed that this wasn't where he wanted to raise Kate, and I couldn't agree more in regard to Braden. When I moved to New York at eleven years old, I never traveled outside of it—not unless you counted New Jersey—since my aunt didn't really have any extra money. Then, when I had Braden, any plans on seeing more of the United States went out the window. So even though I basically had never been outside of New York, Lane's house in Texas sounded amazing. He said it was little but that it would fit us just fine.

I knew I should start thinking about getting a job and finding my own place for Braden and me to live. The idea of Lane and me living together after only really knowing each other a few weeks just seemed ludicrous. But for just a little while, I would stay. Separating Kate and Braden like that would have to be approached delicately.

Another reason it would be good to head to Dallas was that Lane really needed to get back to work. He said that Jace would probably start threatening to replace him soon, although based on the way Lane talked about him, I had a feeling Jace would never do that.

So two days after my very public panic in the park, we found ourselves boarding Flight 65 from John F. Kennedy Airport to Dallas/Fort Worth. Thanks to Jace, and much to Lane's discomfort, we boarded as first-class passengers. I was giddy. I hadn't been on many airplanes and definitely nowhere near those first four rows. Kate and Braden sat in seats 3A and 3B, while Lane and I took our seats directly behind them.

The plush leather seats were comfortable, and there was a console in between each seat, allowing everyone plenty of elbow room. There were TVs tucked into the arms of our seats, but I didn't think Kate and Braden had realized that yet.

Lane had grumbled and groaned all morning after he'd finally gotten a look at our tickets. I could tell he didn't like Jace's buying them, let alone upgrading us. His large forearm moved over the middle console, and he grunted as he leaned toward me dramatically.

"See, first class sucks already. I can't lift this huge divider, and now you might as well be sitting across the aisle from me," he complained.

I rolled my eyes at his ridiculousness. Then to appease him, I leaned across the not-so-huge divider and kissed his delicious lips. I realized a few days ago that it would be a long time before I would ever get tired of his lips. They were full and powerful, and I wanted them on me as often as I could have them.

"No, no, don't start pushing that sexy bottom lip on me now," he scolded sullenly.

I pulled back and giggled. I couldn't help it with him. He knew how to push all my buttons just right, and it seemed that my favorite button was the way he sucked my bottom lip in between his teeth.

"Just enjoy this now. You can hash it out with Jace later." I smiled up at him. "Besides, I've never heard of anyone complaining about extra leg room, especially someone of your size." I reached to pinch his side, but snatched up my fingers before they could make contact, which only made me break out into uproarious laughter.

His body instantly moved closer to mine, console be damned. "God, babe . . ." he murmured, his voice husky. "I love that sound."

In front of us, Kate started laughing, and we both peeked through the small space between the seats to see her and Braden playing a made-up game together. "Love that sound—from both my girls," Lane added.

I grabbed his bicep and hugged it tightly. I didn't release it when I was done, deciding to keep my fingers wrapped securely around him and laying my head against his muscles. When the flight attendants came down the aisle offering preflight drinks, he didn't move his arm, instead grabbing both of our cups with his opposite hand.

"Hey, Kit Kat," Lane called quietly to the seats in front of us. Both she and Braden turned to look at us. "Make sure your seat belts are snug, please."

"Braden snapped mine for me, Daddy," she said back.

"Good job looking out for your sister, B," Lane said to my little boy. The moment they turned back around, I instantly buried my face into his arm and sniffled.

"What's up, Rae?" he asked.

I rubbed the side of my face against his arm as if I were a cat vying for attention and whispered, "I've never heard you say that before."

"Well, we haven't been in any cars, so why would I tell them to buckle up?"

"No, not that. You said she was his sister." I squeezed him tighter, and he responded by kissing my forehead. All of this was a learning curve for him. What Kate, Braden, and I had felt for years, he was just now absorbing. I understood that it must be tough. He had expected to get his daughter back . . . not a whole crew. I just hoped that he was fully aware of what that entailed before we traveled down this dangerous path.

About halfway through our flight, Lane dozed off with his head thrown back against the chair and his mouth gaping open. It wasn't often that he looked vulnerable, and I enjoyed the rare moments that I could see him like this.

His strong jaw flexed gently with each breath in and out. His sandy blond hair had grown a little bit longer these past few weeks. His legs were parted and one was stretched out in front of me. While we had extra room in first class, it still wasn't a good fit for someone his size. His arm was extended over the console, gripping my thigh with his large hand. I had tried to move it at one point, but he'd held on tightly, not willing to let me go, even in sleep.

The flight attendant started making another trip down our aisle with her beverage cart. When she stomped on the brake pedal to keep it from rolling away from her, the noise shook Lane awake. I cringed as he started. I tried to rub his arm soothingly, hoping he could fall back asleep.

The flight attendant began asking Kate and Braden what they would like, and they each politely responded that they'd like some water. She told them how well behaved they were, and she appeared to be genuinely impressed with their manners. I watched as she poured their water and began putting together their lunches.

Lane's face began to nuzzle into the side of my neck, and every part of me lit up at the low hum he produced with the movement.

"You did that," he whispered into my ear. I didn't process his words right away, because I was too busy trying to tamp down my heightened sex drive that he seemed to be igniting so much lately. I closed my eyes and enjoyed feeling the scruff from his face rub gently across my skin. "Thankful for you, babe . . ." His voice faded into my muddled brain.

"Huh?" I asked stupidly.

"You. You're amazing. Look how good they are." His head nodded to the two seats in front of us. I could see the flight attendant smiling down at Kate and Braden as she handed them the on-board first-class meal, which was stuffed pasta with roasted sundried tomatoes. Seemed kind of silly for two four-year-olds. "You did that, Rae. You raised them into two of the most perfect children." He kissed my temple, right over my scar, and sat up straight to speak with the approaching flight attendant.

I watched the kids through the seats as they quietly spoke to each other. When Braden needed a napkin, Kate unfolded one for him. When she almost spilled her water, Braden caught it and she thanked him kindly.

I absently noticed that my own food and drink had been placed in front of me. Lane had ordered a cranberry juice for me, which happened to be my favorite beverage at the moment. I watched his arm cross over in front of me as he reached for our silverware and napkins. My thoughts were in the row in front of us as Lane kissed my temple again and thanked the flight attendant.

"You guys are just the sweetest family," she told us. Then she popped the brake and moved back to the front of the airplane. I wanted to respond before she left, but I was still looking at the two "most perfect children."

"What's going on in there, babe?" Lane whispered.

"In where?"

"In that head of yours. I can see the wheels spinning."

"I worry about them," I whispered, so quietly I wondered if he would even be able to hear me over the hum of the plane's engines.

"I just told you that they were perfect and that made you worry?" he asked, completely puzzled.

"They're *too* good, Lane. They *never* misbehave. They never act like normal children. Normal children disobey at least occasionally; they throw fits to show what they feel; they act out and they scream.

I worry that they were too sheltered in that room for so long, kept away from other people."

"Okay . . ." He paused, obviously unsure how to respond.

"You think I'm crazy?"

He quirked his lip and I shoved at his shoulder playfully. "I'm just saying, you're upset that they are *too* good. It's a little . . . crazy." He laughed. "And they do show their feelings. Kate shouts them to the rooftops. I don't think there is any problem there." He smiled fondly. "And Braden always tells me when he likes something."

"What do you mean? I've never heard him say anything like that. He's so quiet."

"That's just it. He doesn't need to *say* it. He bumps my fist."

"Huh?" I asked.

"We fist-bump, babe." When I continued to look at him, he said, "It's a guy thing. Watch." He moved forward and said, "Hey, Braden, this pasta rocks, yeah?"

I laughed when a little fist appeared between the seats and touched Lane's firmly, and then I heard his tiny voice say, "Rocks." So the boys already had a secret language, did they? Why did I find that insanely adorable? Lane had already deduced Braden's quiet personality and yet still found a way to communicate with him.

"It's so good!" Kate spoke with enthusiasm through the seats.

"Listen, babe, I think we need to enjoy *this* now," he said, repeating my earlier words back to me. "They're good kids; I'm not going to complain. I'm sure we'll pay our dues when they're teens. Lord knows I'm going to be meeting Kate's dates at our front door with a shotgun. And Braden will probably break curfew or sneak out of the house just like I did when I was in high school." He sighed dramatically. "Shit . . . I bet they'll really make us pay."

"A shotgun?" I giggled.

"It's Texas; that's what they do." He winked and then reached for his fork so he could actually try this pasta that apparently "rocked."

It would take me a few more minutes until I replayed all of his words in my head. There he went again using words like *we* and *our* and *us*. Future talk.

LANE -

I was nervous as hell. Jace met us at the airport and was now taking us all over to his house so we could pick up my car, which meant I was finally going to introduce my daughter to Audrey. It wasn't just my daughter, though, but also the woman my daughter believes to be her mom and the boy she believes to be her brother. It was as if she was about to meet my . . . family.

Nervous as fucking hell.

I looked in the back at their anxious, smiling faces. Braden and Kate were sitting in little booster-type seats. I hadn't even thought about that.

"Good call on those kids' seats. I didn't know they needed that shit," I said to Jace as he flipped his blinker on.

"Don't thank me; I thought they would be too old. Audrey insisted they needed them, though," he replied, eyes on the road.

Every now and then I noticed Jace glancing at the rearview mirror, and I assumed it wasn't to see out his back window. The trip from the airport to where we all lived was about an hour with traffic. Halfway there, Jace flipped down a little TV from the ceiling and played a movie for the kids. When they began laughing hysterically, Raegan put on a set of headphones too.

"She's a knockout, dude," Jace said lightly. I didn't think that Rae could hear us up here with her headphones, but he still tried to speak only to me.

"Kate? She's beautiful, huh? A little spitfire too. I can't believe how much life and energy she has thrumming through that little body."

"I'm happy for you, man."

I nodded my head but kept quiet. For some reason, I felt my hackles rise, and I had a feeling it was because Jace was gearing up to talk about something I wasn't going to like.

"So . . ." *Here we go*, I thought. "I heard you call Raegan 'babe.' Is that like how you call Audrey 'doll,' or is it . . . something more?"

"Something more," I muttered to the window.

With a deep sigh, he continued, "You really think that's smart? With the kids and all?"

"No." It was the truth, but there was also the fact that I physically wouldn't be able to stop what we had going.

"Just make sure you're smart, man. Take care of your daughter first," Jace whispered.

"What the hell? What do you think I've been doing for four damn years, Jace?" My voice began to rise, and I caught Raegan's movement behind me. I turned and saw her pulling her headphones off, her eyes growing wide. I turned, lay back against the headrest, and closed my eyes, trying to calm myself down. Jace didn't respond, and, thank God, he kept his mouth shut the entire rest of the drive.

We drove down their long gravel drive, passing Jace and Jaxon's mom's beautiful house with its wraparound porch. Audrey loved that porch so much that it was the only thing she had asked for when she and Jace built their house farther down the road.

Jace and Jaxon had been given all of their father's land after he passed away. They each built houses out here, along with their best friend, Cole, and his wife, Quinn. They have become my second family. Even Jace's mom has taken me in as her own. I loved it out here. I loved the pond behind Jaxon and Emerson's house. I loved the quiet and the tranquility of the country.

But right now I was feeling anything but tranquil—I was pissed. And I hated being mad at the people I loved. I was pissed at Jace for thinking that I would put anyone before Kate. He acted like I was a fifteen-year-old who was only thinking with my dick. I clenched my fists and tried to force myself to release the anger. I hated to argue with my family and tried to avoid it at all costs.

So when Jace pulled the SUV to a stop, my hand was already on the door handle. I pushed out before he had the gear in park and leaned up against my closed door. Raegan rounded the back of the car with determination and put her hands gently against my stomach.

"What's wrong?" she asked quietly.

"Nothing."

"Doesn't seem like *nothing* to me." She pressed her body against mine and I looked away. "Okay . . ." She must have deciphered my cold mood because she pushed back, but still kept her hands on me. "I'll let this slide right now because I think that beautiful girl barreling down the stairs is for you."

Her last words struck me because she sounded almost uncomfortable. And when I saw Audrey sprint around the car and crash her body squarely into mine, I swore a grimace crossed Raegan's face. But she hid it well, because in the blink of an eye, she turned and began to help Kate and Braden out of the backseat.

"You're here!" Audrey cried into my chest. She was significantly taller than Raegan, so I didn't have to bend over to pick her up into a bear hug.

"Hey, doll," I said. "Missed ya."

"I'm still so mad at you, but I missed you like crazy!" I had a feeling she would never let me live down that I hadn't told her about Kate. We told each other everything; at least, that's what she'd thought.

"I'm sorry, but we're here now," I consoled.

Rae shut the door and held each of the kids' hands. I looked over Audrey's shoulder to see that Rae had her head fully turned away from Audrey in my arms. Kate and Braden, on the other hand, were staring at us with questions in their eyes.

"Hey, guys," I said, releasing Audrey. "This is my best friend. She's like my *sister*." I tried to overenunciate the last word for Raegan's sake.

"I have a sister." Braden surprised me by being the first to speak up.

"I know! I also hear you're an amazing brother." Audrey took his comment in stride and I smiled. "Braden, right?" He nodded his head and smiled wide.

"And you!" Audrey gasped dramatically at Kate. "You are about the prettiest little girl I have ever seen in my life."

Kate jumped up and down, while still clutching Raegan's hand. "I am? Thank you!" she exclaimed loudly.

"Most definitely. You look just like your daddy."

Kate smiled proudly up at Audrey and then turned to look at me. I opened my arms wide, so she bounded forward and leaped into my grasp. Audrey quickly wiped at her eyes and smiled adoringly at the both of us.

"Oh, I just love this!" she cried. Then she turned her attention to Raegan. "You must be Raegan, who I've been hearing oh-so-much about." *I was going to kill her.*

"Really?" Raegan smiled shyly.

"Oh, yes! He gushes about you. I've been so excited to meet you," she said, walking forward to pull Raegan in for a hug.

Raegan hesitated at first, but then I watched as she finally let the hug happen. She'd better get used to this touchy-feely bunch. "I guess I could say the same about you," Rae replied.

"Okay!" I decided to interrupt this uncomfortable conversation. "We've all met now. Let's just get the keys so we can head back to my place."

"He's embarrassed now." Audrey laughed, giving Rae a wink. I groaned and attempted to pull Rae toward the car. "Oh, no, you don't," Audrey continued. "You've been gone for weeks, I finally get to meet your daughter, and you think you're just going to run off again?"

"I'm hardly running anywhere. I live five minutes away, doll," I chuckled.

She gave me *the look*, the one that told me I wouldn't be leaving anytime soon. I sighed in defeat and pulled Raegan into my chest, because if I was going to endure an Audrey interrogation, I should at least be allowed to hold Rae in the process.

- Fifteen -

RAEGAN -

So Audrey was beautiful. Not like your everyday beautiful—if there was such a thing—but like she-should-be-on-the-cover-of-some-high-fashion-magazine beautiful. Her legs were about as long as my entire body, so I instantly felt squatty standing next to her. I shouldn't have worn flats today. And didn't she just have a baby? Where was the post-pregnancy belly I thought we were all blessed with?

I still didn't understand how she and Lane hadn't ended up together. I had a hard time believing that they lived together for years and yet *nothing* had happened. How is that possible? They were both gorgeous. Gorgeous people migrated to other gorgeous people.

But speaking of gorgeous . . . Audrey's husband, Jace, was out of this world. He was tall—like crazy tall. He had at least three inches on Lane, but he wasn't built the same. I don't think anyone was built like Lane.

I was beginning to feel inferior in comparison to all of these tall, attractive people around me. I hated that feeling, and I used to roll my eyes at girls like that. I needed to straighten my spine and get over it.

Jace moved around the front of the car and grabbed Audrey around the middle. I didn't know if it was intentional, but he moved her away from Lane by a good two feet. Audrey melted into his touch, and the smile she gave him over her shoulder should have removed all doubts about her and Lane from my head. Jace whispered into her ear and she nodded in return, smirking at him.

Just then, a large truck came flying down the dirt road and we all turned to see it approaching the house. I felt Lane pull me in tighter.

"You know I'm not upset with you, right?" I felt his words whispered against my ear.

"I didn't do anything, so you'd better not be mad at me," I replied.

I smiled when I felt him chuckle behind me. "I just want to get us back to the house soon," he continued to whisper.

"Me too."

"You nervous about meeting my friends?" he asked.

"No," I replied quickly. Then I backtracked. "Yes."

The truck that pulled up near Jace's SUV was drenched in mud. Not just little splashes here and there, but full-on covered in filth. I couldn't say what color it actually was if I tried. The windshield was only clean where the wipers had smeared the mud away.

Then Jace got out of the truck. *Huh?* But it wasn't Jace, because he was standing behind us, still holding onto Audrey.

"Whoa . . ." I whispered. Jace had an identical twin. I knew Jace and Jaxon were brothers, but I hadn't heard anything about twins.

"Crazy, huh?" Audrey said from beside me.

"Whoa, what?" Lane growled into my ear. I shivered against him and moved farther into his chest. Kate squirmed down from his arms and reclaimed Braden's hand.

"Umm . . ." I didn't know what to say. I still thought Lane was the most beautiful person I had ever seen, but . . . seeing two of these guys side by side would take me a minute to grasp. They were dreamy.

"Rae . . ." Lane continued, and now he fully held on to me from behind.

He and I had done fairly well at keeping our displays of affection away from the kids. We hadn't kissed or made any advances in front of them. They didn't seem to catch on to his current possessive actions, so I let him continue to hold me.

"Give her a break, Lane. Seeing Jax and Jace for the first time is a lot to take in . . . for *any* girl."

He grasped me a little bit tighter and I went willingly. We all watched as Jaxon, who was covered in as much mud as his truck, ran around the front and opened the passenger-side door. He reached inside and scooped out a girl with long blond hair. This must have been Emerson. She kicked and giggled as he carried her away from the truck. His smile was blinding as he looked at her squirming in his arms. They laughed loudly at each other, probably because they were both caked in dried mud.

Surprise, surprise, she was a knockout too . . . even dirty. "What the hell is in the water here?" I whispered, mostly to myself.

"Why do you say that, babe?" Lane asked.

"It's nothing." Or it wasn't really anything to get worked up over, at least. Maybe in the past four years while I'd been locked away, people just got better-looking for some reason. Although, come to think of it, I didn't remember seeing this many beautiful people in New York.

"Jaxon!" Em gasped. "Put me down!" She managed to escape his arms, and I was happy to see that even though she was gorgeous, she wasn't another long-legged supermodel. She was my height and seemed to have all the same proportions as I did.

"You two are ridiculous." Jace laughed beside us.

"It's her fault!" Jaxon laughed.

"Oh, like you're really going to complain." Em looked at him mischievously and he grabbed her again, pulling her into his body.

"What the hell happened?" Jace asked.

"Dude," I heard Lane growl as he elbowed Jace.

"Sorry, little ears," Jace responded softly.

That caught Jaxon's and Em's attention, and they both looked down at the two kids standing next to us.

"Oh my God!" Emerson cried. "You two are the most adorable little things I have ever seen!"

"Wow, she's like your clone, man," Jaxon added.

"You know, you guys are all pretty overwhelming," Lane said to the crowd around us. He reached down and easily scooped up both Braden and Kate in a protective gesture. They held on to his shoulders to balance themselves. It was quick, but Braden looked down at me with an arresting smile. Lane had just made him feel special in front of everyone. I rubbed his back, excited for him.

"I'm sorry," Emerson cooed up at them.

"No, no. I don't like that tone, beautiful," Jaxon said to Em. "I *just* got you over your last bout of baby fever."

"So, watching Quinn and Cole's baby actually worked?" Jace laughed.

"Chloe doesn't sleep. She's one year old. Shouldn't she be sleeping by now?" Emerson grumbled.

"Some babies are just like that. Braden's almost five and he still gets up in the middle of the night. At least now I can tell him to go back to sleep," I interjected.

Jaxon smiled wide at me. "I like you already."

"Umm . . . thanks," I responded.

"Jaxon's been trying to talk Em out of having a kid since before they were engaged," Lane informed me.

"Not completely. Just not for at least five years . . . or something." Jaxon scooped Em back up into his arms and kissed her quickly. They were really adorable together.

"You could always watch Jocelyn," Audrey added.

"No, thanks," Jaxon quickly replied, setting Em back down.

"Got something against my daughter? *Your* niece, by the way?" Jace questioned his brother.

Em laughed and said, "No, she's just *too* good of a baby. Audrey told us she's already started sleeping through the night. He only lets me watch the more . . . challenging ones."

"You caught that, huh?" Jaxon asked coyly.

"You're not that sneaky, babe." She laughed.

This group was a lot of fun. I didn't know them at all, but the dynamic between them was amazing. They teased each other playfully, but anyone would be able to tell that they truly cared for one another. I couldn't help smiling, just standing around them.

"It's good to see everyone. Now you've all met, so we're gonna head back to my place," Lane announced to the crowd.

"Wait!" We all turned as a pretty little brunette raced across the street, and following behind her was yet another handsome man. Cole and Quinn, I was assuming. Hopefully, this was the end of the welcome wagon. I was surprised I even remembered everyone's names from the late-night talks with Lane back in New York. "Are they here? Is she blond? Did I win the bet?"

"Oh, God, the bet . . ." I heard Em whisper to Audrey. They both looked at me, and when I caught them, they quickly averted their gazes.

"What's going on?" Lane asked.

Quinn ran up to us and scanned the crowd of faces before her eyes finally landed on mine. She visibly deflated, then realized her actions before quickly smiling up at me. "Oh, you're not blond, but dang . . . you *are* gorgeous!"

"Why would I be blond?" I asked.

"What bet?" Lane questioned.

"We were just being silly," Audrey offered. Lane looked over at her and she shrank back into Jace.

"Welcome back, man," Cole said, and held out his hand for Lane. Lane set the kids down, Cole pulled him into a man hug, and they patted each other's backs. Lane quickly moved back to my side before claiming both Braden's and Kate's hands.

I continued to look at Quinn, wondering if she would reply to my question. She finally answered, slowly, "We just . . . thought you'd be . . . blond. It was dumb." She waved her hand, attempting to dismiss the entire thing.

"Shut it, Quinn," Em mumbled, but not quietly enough.

"Mommy, what is blond?" Kate asked.

"Your hair is blond, sweetie," I replied.

I glanced up at Lane and saw him glaring at Audrey. "Do you have a thing for blondes?" I asked. His eyes moved to each of our audience members. "You know I'm a brunette, right?" I smiled.

His hand curled around the length of my hair and gave it a gentle tug so that I was forced to look straight up into his eyes. "Of course I know," he grumbled onto my lips. My heart beat wildly in my chest because this was our first show of affection not only in front of the kids, but in front of his friends as well.

I couldn't hold it in any longer, and I burst out laughing. He looked so uncomfortable with everyone talking about him in front of me; and now, the way he was squirming around, it was hilarious. I just couldn't hold back. The laugh was loud and deep and cleansing. Why did I care whom Lane liked or whom he usually went after? I had never been that kind of girl. So I laughed off the stress that I had placed on myself.

"I like her," Cole said with humor in his voice.

"I do too," Jaxon added.

"Of course you like her," Quinn said. "She's practically the brunette version of Em."

Em and I stared at each other and finally just started laughing together. Yeah, this group was fun.

"Finally, someone I can share clothes with," Em cheered.

"Well, sorry I won't be much fun. The only clothes I own can fit into a small duffel bag." I shrugged.

"We'll fix that!" Quinn announced excitedly.

"Shit," Lane whispered, and I elbowed him for his language.

"Say good-bye to your credit cards now, man," Jace laughed.

I instantly sobered. "Oh, no, I wouldn't use his money."

"All right," Lane interrupted. "This has been fun, but I'm hungry, they're hungry, and we're going home before anyone else shows up."

"Everything's ready for you guys," Audrey said, smiling widely.

"Thanks, doll. We'll see you guys around."

LANE -

"Lane, your house is huge!" Raegan smiled widely at me from the passenger seat.

I laughed because my house wasn't even close to huge. "You're just used to New York City apartments. You saw Jace's, Jaxon's, and Cole's places, right?" I never really cared about how much money I didn't make. It was always enough to do what I wanted and still pay my bills. But when compared to those guys with their families' trust funds, I was sorely lacking.

"Oh, pfft." She waved her hand at me. "Don't get me started on their houses. Beautiful? Yes. Completely unnecessary? Absolutely. They don't need those gigantic things. This house, though— it's perfect."

I'd rented out a small one-story redbrick home with three bedrooms that were definitely excessive; at least they were when I'd put down the deposit. Now they'd be useful. The only reason I chose this one was because it had a big backyard for the dog I hoped to have one day, and it was only five minutes away from everyone else.

I pulled into the driveway, shifted into park, and then glanced back at Kate and Braden in my tiny backseat. Now that I was looking at carting around kids, it was probably stupid of me to buy this car.

"Man, I think I'll need to trade this car back in."

"Why? It's nice," Raegan said, running her hand across the leather seats.

"It seems ridiculous now that they're sitting in the back."

"It's a hot car and they fit." She shrugged her shoulders as if it were as simple as that.

I actually used to drive an old black SUV in California that would have been perfect, but then I moved to Texas and got a new job. I felt as though I needed to splurge a little on my new two-door Challenger; and, hell, I'd be the first to admit that it helped me pick up women . . . fast. But now there were two booster seats latched in the backseat and it just seemed absurd.

"We'll figure it out later. Besides, we have to get you a car too. Everyone drives here," I told her.

"No, no. I can't drive. No car buying for me," she announced nervously.

"Babe, you can't drive?"

"I lived in New York. Why would I need to know how to drive?" she asked.

I smirked at her and replied, "This'll be fun. I'll teach you. Not in this car, though. You can learn on an automatic first."

She rolled her eyes and stepped out, but not before I could check out her tight ass. Even better, she turned around to pull the seat forward so she could help Braden from the back, and I got a full-on show of her tits in that V-neck shirt. My jaw may have dropped, but I would never get enough of those.

"Daddy! I want out too!" Kate bellowed from behind me.

"Yeah, Daddy, get her out of the car," Raegan said cheekily, all while she looked over at me with an intensely burning heat in her eyes. She'd caught me, but she didn't mind. Fuck, I was in deep with this girl.

As I pushed open the front door, I wondered if Audrey had thought to buy more pillows and blankets for us. I had one bed in my house with two sets of sheets and a comforter . . . that was it. That was all I'd needed. I could tell right away that Audrey had come in like a crazy lady and dusted all the surfaces of my living room. There was no way in hell it had sat for weeks and looked like this.

Apparently, she'd done more than that. My beige couch now had a huge, light blue blanket draped over the back and little brightly colored pillows at each end. There was a painting hanging over my fireplace that I had never seen before and a huge tree in the corner. I wasn't going to be able to keep that thing alive, so I hoped Audrey planned on coming back regularly to take care of it.

"This is so nice, Lane," Rae said quietly as she walked in behind me. "It's very homey." As long as Rae approved, the damn tree could stay. I was probably going to toss the annoying little pillows on the couch, though.

"Let's go drop our bags in the room."

"This is your house, Daddy?" Kate called from behind.

"This is your house now too, Kit Kat. Do you like it?" I asked, suddenly feeling nervous.

"Will Mommy and Braden live here too?" Her voice had gone quiet, and I could tell she wasn't feeling sure about her surroundings. I dropped my bags and scooped her up tightly against my chest.

"Of course they'll live here too." The moment the words left my mouth, she instantly brightened, and the Kate I had been falling in love with again wiggled out of my arms.

"Yay! Okay, let's go!" she called out to the house. "Can Braden and I get our own bed? You and Mommy take all the covers."

I laughed uproariously and grabbed my bag from the ground. "Absolutely. You guys should get your *own* beds. There's no need to share anymore."

"Really?" Braden asked with surprise in his voice.

"Yeah, buddy. There's plenty of room for you to have your own," I said, patting his shoulder.

"That. Is. Awesome!" he exclaimed. I smiled at his enthusiasm because I hadn't expected him to be so thrilled about something so simple.

"Whoa!" Kate yelled from down the hall. Rae, Braden, and I turned to see her looking into one of the guest bedrooms, and we quickly followed to see what she was so animated about. I didn't remember there being anything in that room, except maybe a few stray boxes that had never been unpacked.

Raegan gasped as she turned the corner, and when I finally peered inside, I called out, "Holy—" Thankfully, Rae slapped her hand over my mouth before anything else could come out.

Two twin beds with drawers underneath sat against two opposing walls. At the head of each bed sat a bookshelf teeming with books and various personalized items for each child. A giant metal "K" hung on the wall above the pink bed and a coordinating letter "B" hung above the blue bed.

A tall wire basket rested at the end of Braden's bed with basketballs, footballs, baseballs, and more. At the end of Kate's was a smaller shelf that she could sit on if she wanted, but the space below was occupied by dolls and stuffed animals. We had packed up a few items in New York to ship out here, but it looked as if they wouldn't really need anything.

Braden immediately zoned in on a small terrarium on the shelf at the head of his bed. He climbed up and began observing the tiny plants inside with a look of wonder on his face. Thank God I had shared that bit of information with Audrey about him loving the greenhouse at the museum in Brooklyn.

On the shelf at the head of Kate's bed was a small antique birdcage that appeared to have a pretend bird perched on a stick inside. I was relieved to see it wasn't a real bird—I don't do birds.

"How?" Rae whispered.

"Audrey," I replied quietly.

She stepped out of the room and I followed behind. The kids would be occupied with their new things for at least a little bit. Raegan instinctively moved toward the master bedroom, and I reached in front of her to turn the knob. She stepped in first and turned toward me.

"Audrey's just a *friend*, right?" I saw her wince and then she added, "I shouldn't be jealous. I don't have a right, but you guys seem so . . . close." This girl could never let anything go for too long. I fucking loved it.

"We *are* close."

"Close like two people who are *very* familiar with each other . . ." she trailed off.

"We *are* very familiar with each other."

She let out a sigh and I knew I was torturing her, but I wanted this to stick. "I love Audrey like a sister. It's never been anything more or anything less. If we were going to get together, it would have already happened."

"That's all I needed. You won't hear any more from me about it." She'd conceded a little too easily for me.

"That easy?" I asked.

"Would you lie to me?"

"Never." The word slipped out of my mouth before I had time to evaluate it, but it was the absolute truth.

"Then it's that easy, because I believe you."

I moved to set our bags down by the closet, and we both turned to inspect the bedroom. My bed had the same navy blue comforter and the same white pillows, but I noticed a few new little additions.

"More of those damned throw pillows," I grumbled, while fumbling with the small, colorful pillows. "What the hell would we do with all these?"

"They're supposed to be for decoration," she muttered from behind me. I started tossing them off the bed, but then Rae added, "But I'm sure we could get into some pretty good sex positions with them."

I quickly scooped those things back up and tossed them right back on. Well, okay then. The tiny pillows could stay.

Yet another potted plant sat in the corner by the vast window, which looked out to the backyard patio. Two wingback chairs were placed on an opposite wall with a small table in between them.

"I'm pretty damn sure I told her not to go overboard."

"It's nice." She shrugged casually, though it was obvious she was still stressing. Over what I didn't know, but I was about to find out.

I softly nudged the door shut and walked up behind her. My lips found the area below her ear that always gave her goose bumps up her arms. My hands grazed across her hips underneath her T-shirt. Slowly, her body eased back into mine and I pulled her in tighter.

"What's going on, love?" I whispered in between kisses along her jaw.

She shivered, and I liked to assume it was from my new term of endearment. "It's a lot to take in."

"Tell me about it; my house is definitely not how I left it. I have fucking throw pillows on my bed. Trust me, I would have never have made that purchase, and I can't keep a plant alive to save my life."

"No, I mean just being here. And you told Kate that Braden and I would be living here. Now that they have a real bedroom with their own beds and belongings, it'll be even harder to pry Braden away from that."

My body locked up, and I spun her around and tossed her onto the bed. Her eyes were saucers as she glared at me for my actions. I ignored it.

"What are you talking about? Pry him away? Why?" I growled while hovering over her prone body.

"We don't live here."

"Of course you do, Rae."

"You and Kate live here."

"Along with you and Braden," I quickly added.

"We can't live together."

"I don't see why not. You like me, and I sure as hell like you. We get along great. Kate needs you. Braden and Kate need each other. Hell, Braden could use a guy like me. Why rock the boat?"

"It's moving a little fast, don't you think? I mean, a little over two weeks ago, you hated me," she said, looking up at my face.

I flinched from her words and explained, "You know that I never hated you. We've been through this."

"You know what I meant. Regardless, it's only been a few weeks."

"I never hated you," I whispered back. I needed her to understand that right now.

"Okay." She stared into my eyes, but I just didn't understand that word.

"I needed someone to blame. I was a dick. I've told you this, babe. Please, I need you to understand how sorry I am for accusing you like that."

"I'm not trying to rehash that, I promise. I'm just telling you that while Braden and I do need a place to stay right now and we need to be gentle with the two of them, I will eventually find my own place."

"No," I responded quickly.

"No?" She arched an eyebrow above those beautiful green eyes.

"There wouldn't be a point. If you got your own place, Kate and I would be over there every day. Where you sleep, I sleep. Why would we bother paying rent at two separate places?"

She sighed as she thought over my words. I smiled when she didn't have anything to say to that.

"You and me—we work, babe. Simple as that."

"A man of few words," she replied, but her grin told me I was breaking her down.

"I'm taking lessons from Braden," I responded. That pulled a bigger smirk from her, and I moved closer to her body below mine. My hands grazed up her ribs until I had her shirt up over her head. Her bra was held together with one of those made-for-this-moment front clasps, so only a flick was needed to release her perfect breasts.

I crawled away from her body and off the bed before reaching for her ankles and yanking her closer to me. She squeaked as her ass met the edge of the mattress and I stood between her open legs. With two fingers, I flicked the metal button open on her jeans and kissed the skin just above her waistline. Her fingers threaded into my hair while her eyelids fluttered. I slid her jeans down the curve of her hips with ease.

"Lane . . ." she said on a husky breath.

"Right here, babe." My lips nipped up the inside of her right leg, while my fingers ran up the inside of her left.

"Lane . . . you can't seduce me into . . ." A moan slipped from between her lips. "Moving in with you."

"Give me a chance to at least try."

My eyes locked onto the small swath of fabric that barely covered her folds and absolutely none of her tight ass. I growled at the beautiful sight. I had never been more turned on to see a simple little thong.

"I didn't know you had one of these," I groaned against the skin of her thigh. It was true. I thought I had seen all of Raegan's belongings because there hadn't been much. This was the kind of surprise I sure as hell thrived on.

My knees hit the carpet and my face was in prime real estate. Her head hit the bed when I grabbed the triangle of fabric and pulled it up toward her hip. The string down the crease of her ass pulled tight.

My breath skated across the area between her thighs and I could feel her body vibrating with need. My inner caveman was banging the shit out of his chest at the sight of her desire for me. I wanted to breathe her in and memorize her sweet scent. She moaned as she squeezed my hair tighter between her fingers.

I ran my nose up each side of her bare skin, and her hands fell to the sheets as she clenched them in a death grip.

"Lane . . ." she breathed.

"Move in with me," I said into her folds.

My tongue danced lightly across her as her back arched dramatically off the bed. I craved making her body curve like that because it forced her tits high, and I just couldn't resist them. It's as if they were shouting *Me too! Pay attention to me too!* I could never tell them no.

I hooked her legs over my shoulders and dived in mouth-first, while my hands lightly twisted her nipples until they were at their fullest peaks. Her heavy breasts filled my large hands, and I was a king devouring my feast.

My tongue flicked faster over the area where I seemed to get the most moans out of her. Side to side, up and down. Her body was now thrashing beneath my mouth and hands. My fingers dug into her thighs and I wasn't gentle. Once I had tried to be gentle with the scars on the back of her leg, but she handed me my ass for treating her like porcelain. I finally relented once she assured that me they honestly didn't cause her any discomfort.

And who was I to treat her that way? Nothing was more of a turn-on than a woman who was unapologetically comfortable in her skin while tumbling across the sheets with me. A woman like her was rare and beautiful.

"Lane, oh God, Lane, Lane . . ." she chanted. I pulled back and held her hips to the bed. Her eyes flew open and she regarded me as if she were a wild animal that couldn't decide whether to fight or take flight. Her breath came in ragged and harsh, just as her eyes told me everything she was feeling. Lust. Desire. Anger.

We stared hard at each other. She was wondering why I had stopped, and I was wondering why she hadn't answered me.

"Move in with me," I repeated, gripping her thighs again. She held her lips tightly together, as if she didn't trust what would fly out of her mouth. That just meant I was on the right path.

I always tried hard not to gloat, but if there was one thing I had mastered, it was kissing. I could bring Rae to her knees with my lips alone. I used those talents to my advantage when I shifted my mouth back between her legs. I moved my lips and tongue against her as if it were her mouth, and she started to let out a scream, but she slapped her hand over herself to cover the noise. Right as her toes dug into my shoulders, I pulled back again.

"NO!" she shouted. We both froze, waiting to see if we could hear the sound of little feet coming down the hall. After a few silent beats, I smiled up at her.

"Ready to move in with me yet?"

"This isn't fair," she moaned, while trying to move her hips up toward my face.

"I just need a yes," I said into her wet skin. I pushed two fingers inside and hooked them at just the right angle. Her eyes rolled to the top of her head and she fell back against the sheets again. The movements of my fingers were slow and sluggish. She would definitely need more to reach the point she was begging for.

"Raegan, you are beautiful, both inside and out. My only regret is that I didn't find you guys sooner. I need you in my life. Kate and I need you. And if you go, Braden goes too, and I can't handle that. I need all three of you. I don't know how and I don't know why it's all come so fast, but you three are under my skin. Please, don't take that away from me." All of my vulnerability slipped through in that sentence, and I wouldn't have been surprised if she'd laughed in my face.

She scrambled up, causing my fingers to slip from inside her. Before I could comprehend her movements, her mouth was on mine and her hands were in my hair.

"This is crazy. This isn't normal," she frantically whispered against my lips. I had my pants off and a condom on in the next few seconds. She tugged my shirt up over my head and ran her hands down my chest with adoration in her eyes.

Her back hit the bed and my body followed, desperate with want. Everything inside of me was on fire, and I wanted to touch all of her at the same exact time. I needed her skin against my own.

"Hate to break it to you, but nothing about this situation has been *normal*. Let's roll with the punches because I've damn sure never been this happy," I said into the crook of her neck.

When she lifted her hips up to mine, I couldn't stand it any longer. I pushed off the bed a second time and pulled her body across the sheets. She didn't fight the movement or even appear surprised at my actions, and when I flipped her over onto her stomach, I watched a hint of excitement ignite in her eyes. I tugged her thong down over her legs until it hit the floor beneath my feet.

With her stomach on the bed she was too low, so I tapped her knees, indicating for her to get up on them and she instantly complied. I grabbed my erection and slid into her with as much ease as I could, especially since I felt as if I would explode on contact. Her body sagged in relief and she kept her face on the bed with her hands above her head.

She pushed back on me with a speed I didn't think she could possess in her current position, but I got her point—loud and fucking clear. I rocked out of her and slammed back in, my balls tightening in pleasure.

"Oh God!" she moaned into the bed.

My hand came down between her shoulder blades so I could gain more leverage. I brought the opposite hand around to her breast and pinched her nipple while driving into her from behind. Nirvana. Bliss. She was my paradise.

Her walls began to squeeze tightly around me, and I finally let her fall into ecstasy beneath me. What I wasn't expecting was the loud scream that ripped from her mouth. I couldn't stop my thrusts—they were on autopilot now—but I moved my hand over her lips. My dick would never forget the sound of her finally letting go.

The doorknob on the bedroom door began to jiggle. "Shit!" I whispered, while pulling out of Raegan quickly and diving for the opposite side of the bed, away from the door. I heard Raegan scramble for the sheets as she ripped them away from the bed.

"Mommy?" I heard Braden say, once he had the door fully open.

There was absolutely nothing for me to use to cover myself up with except for my own two hands. Thankfully, I was hidden on the ground, but if he decided to come around the bed, he was bound to get an eyeful. My dick screamed for relief and I tried to calm my ragged breathing.

"Braden, sweetie, give Mommy a few minutes . . ." She was still breathing just as heavily as I was.

"Mama, what happened? You screamed . . . loud," he informed her. I tried to stifle a chuckle because she really *had* let loose. And we were apparently idiots for not locking the door with kids in the house. Another parenting lesson learned.

"Oh, I just . . . I'm okay . . . I just stubbed my toe. It hurt so bad, but I'm okay now," she breathed out. I heard the sheets rustle and I could imagine her fidgeting nervously in front of him, while trying to cover her body.

"Mommy, why are you naked? It's not bath time."

"I'm just going to take a shower; it's been a long day. Can you make sure Kate is having fun in your new room?" God, if I wasn't so uncomfortable right now, I would be busting my ass laughing at her obvious discomfort. I guess this is what having a kid was like.

"Mama . . ." he began.

"Braden, please," she interrupted. "Ten minutes and I'll be right out."

"Okay," he replied, and I sighed in relief when I heard the door click closed.

"Oh my God! I think he knows!" I heard her click the lock on the door right before she scrambled across the bed and looked down at me on the floor. Her eyes flared when she saw me lying there, holding my condom-sheathed erection firmly in my hands.

"God, you look so hot down there . . ." The speed at which her tone became sultry caused my dick to throb painfully.

"Get. Your. Ass. Down. Here," I said through clenched teeth.

"So bossy, Mr. Parker," she replied cheekily, while throwing the sheet away from her body and climbing down off the side of the bed. She stood above me as her legs straddled each side of my body. She continued to peruse my flesh, which was locked up in every possible way because I was trying to hold back my impending orgasm. Another shudder ran through me and I ground my molars to ward it off.

When she didn't make a move to lower her sweet body onto mine, I growled. "Raegan, I'm about to fucking explode. Get. Down. Here." I gripped her calves and tried to get her to bend. I didn't care about the hardwood floor under my back. All I needed was for her to be on top of me—now. "Sit down, Rae." My words were stilted because I was a time bomb about to detonate. I could see how wet she was between her legs and I groaned in pain. I couldn't get up because even the air rushing past me would have caused me to come just then. Plus, I didn't want up, I wanted *in*.

Mercifully, she began to seductively lower herself, although it was the slowest I had ever seen her move. My eyes watched the bend of her legs and took in every inch of her breasts as she came closer to home. She didn't make me wait much longer, though, because she lowered herself right onto my throbbing erection.

This wasn't going to take long. I had already been right on the cusp when she found her release earlier. She moaned as I thrust inside her, and I forced my teeth to stay clamped shut.

I grabbed her hand and shoved it between our bodies, right over her sensitive bundle of nerves. Moving her finger in circles, I showed her exactly what I wanted from her.

"I can't come again, Lane," she breathed heavily. "That last one was too much."

"You'll go again. With me," I growled. Call me insane, but half of my pleasure these last few days had been derived from watching her fall to pieces under my touch.

She started to protest, but I grabbed her hips and moved her up so I could rocket in and out of her. Her breasts bounced above me and her inner walls hugged me tightly. Yeah, I definitely needed to feel her explode again before I could go.

"Shit!" she squeaked and I continued relentlessly. "Lane, it's too much, it's too much! Too much," she begged, but her fingers didn't stop circling.

"Fuck, babe, I need you! I'm close." I called up to her as I felt the all-too-familiar rush. My hand circled around the back of her neck and I pulled her down so we were chest to chest, and I pumped into her with both need and force. I couldn't hold back anymore. Not with her. She brought out the beast inside me, and all I wanted to do was pleasure her.

I whispered her name, as if it were a prayer rolling off my tongue, "Raegan."

I felt the sharp bite of her teeth in my shoulder and knew she was shattering on top of me. She muffled her cries into my skin this time.

Dear God, she was amazing. I couldn't ever lose this girl. She meant the world to me at this point, and never had I felt a connection to the very depth of my soul for a woman before. She had buried herself in every fiber of my being.

I thrust my hips once, twice, three more times until I felt a thrill racing up my spine, and then I was coming long and hard inside of her. It was unlike anything I had ever experienced before. There had never been anything better than this. My hands wrapped around her back and I held her body against mine. I let my legs fall and my head rested against the wood floor as we tried to catch our breath, neither of us moving to separate.

"Baby . . . shit . . . damn, that was amazing," I whispered into her hair.

"I don't think I'll be able to get up," she mumbled lazily into my neck. Unfortunately, she did slowly push off my chest and sat back fully on my thighs after I slipped from her body. We both sucked in air at the loss of our connection. Her fingers ran across my chest and down over my stomach, all while her eyes followed the path.

"Lane, you're the sexiest man I've ever seen." Her whisper was almost inaudible, almost as if her words weren't meant for me to hear. "I think this is my new favorite position, by the way."

"Baby, far be it from me to ever stop you from climbing on." I grinned like the Cheshire cat, which made her laugh. I needed to be closer to her. Gently pulling off the condom, I tied the end and tossed it into a nearby trash can. I sat up with her seductive ass still in my lap and pressed my lips against hers in a demanding rhythm. She melted against me as I pulled her lower lip in between my teeth and sucked.

"We live together now," I mumbled against her lips. The cocky grin on my face was forcing its way out.

"You're evil. You know that, right?" She smiled back in defeat.

"I know how to get what I want, baby, and I have a feeling that will always be you." I kissed the scar stretching over her eyebrow and then moved back down to her lips.

- SIXTEEN -

LANE -

I slipped in through the kitchen door by way of the garage and endeavored to sneak down the hallway without Kate seeing I was home yet. I needed to change and get back outside before she knew I was here. As I pushed open the door to my bedroom, I could hear her talking with Braden in their room.

Rae's beautiful face greeted me as she strolled out of our bathroom carrying the suit I planned on wearing tonight. I could already tell she had pressed my shirt and picked out her favorite red tie of mine. Her body jolted when she realized I was standing there watching her.

I chuckled when her hand flew up to her mouth. "Hey, beautiful," I whispered.

"You scared me half to death." She swatted my arm. "Don't ever sneak in like that again."

I hauled her to my chest and breathed in the fresh, sweet scent of her hair. "I'm trying to get out of these old clothes before she knows it's time to go. I want to surprise her at the front door."

"Well, she's ready. She's been practically vibrating with anticipation all day."

"Did she get my flowers?" I asked while slipping my pants off and reaching for the new ones.

Raegan's face melted into a heavenly smile. Before I could get my pants zipped, she grabbed my face and planted her sweet lips firmly against mine. "Lane, that was the sweetest thing. I just wish you could have seen her face." I smiled and kissed her again. "Oh, by the way," she continued, "she said 'yes' to your date proposal."

"Whew." I wiped my hand across my forehead theatrically. "For a second, I thought I was about to be stood up."

She chuckled and began unbuttoning my shirt for me. One thing Rae loved doing was helping me get dressed. Every morning, before it was time to make breakfast, greet the kids, answer their insane amount of questions, drink my coffee, make sure my briefcase was ready, answer more questions, convince Kate that I would once again be home at the same time I returned every day, and then finally slip out the door for work, Rae and I stole a few quiet moments together.

After we showered, she sat on the countertop next to my sink and talked to me while I shaved and brushed my teeth. Then she would help me button my shirt and knot the tie around my neck. If someone had told me a girl would be doing that with me every single morning three months ago, I more than likely would have broken out into a sweat and felt the claws of suffocation around my throat.

But with Raegan, it was comforting. She'd shown me what it really meant to be cared for and wanted. She wasn't solely after my looks or the things I could give her. And I had no doubt that if these moments were taken away from me, I would drown in loneliness.

"This is all just so sweet, Lane," she said as she slipped the last button through its hole. "You're an amazing father."

"Well, I figured if I wanted her to know how she should be treated, I had to teach her. Taking her on dates will show her to never expect anything less or else I'll have to kick her date's ass."

"I have no doubt about that, babe." She lifted up on her toes and kissed my cheek.

With extreme stealth, I snuck back outside and pushed the button to ring the doorbell. I stood on the front porch and heard Raegan call out to Kate. A few moments later, the wooden door slowly slid open and Kate's little blond head peered around.

"Hello, beautiful. Are you still available to go on a date with your dad tonight?"

"Daddy!" she exclaimed. "You sent me flowers. They were pink and purple and red and white!" She stepped away from the door and into the porch light. For the first time, I saw that Raegan had curled her hair in long ringlets that bounced playfully around her face. She wore a soft pink dress that fell past her knees, and she spun around to show me how it billowed out around her.

I felt the damn emotions bubbling up in my throat. There had been a time when I didn't know if I would get these moments with her. I tried to clear my throat before I said, "Wow, you are the most beautiful girl I have ever seen."

"You look handsome, Daddy," she said, giggling.

I took her hand and escorted her to my waiting car. As she crawled into the backseat, an unwelcome thought occurred to me that her dates with me had better be the only times she ever crawls into a backseat. Damn, I really am going to need that shotgun.

When we arrived, I tossed the valet the keys and helped Kate out of the car. At first, we were given strange looks, but as Kate quietly made her way through the entrance with a wide, ecstatic smile gracing her face, they all began to smile with her. We rode the elevator five hundred feet above the ground, and Kate held my hand eagerly the entire journey.

She'd known exactly where we were when I pulled up. Every time we drove past downtown Dallas, she'd asked me about the big building that looked like it had a ball on top. I told her it was called Reunion Tower and that it had a fancy restaurant for adults way up there. That never discouraged her from asking if she could go up there one day.

Out of pure dumb luck, we recently contracted a job with the head chef and owner of that same restaurant. He ended up being this really cool Austrian man who told me he would be more than happy to accommodate Kate and me at the restaurant when he was in town.

So, while everyone here would be savoring their extravagant, seven-course meals, Kate would have chicken nuggets made by a famous chef and I'd be devouring one of his legendary steaks with French fries.

Kate gasped when the elevator doors slid open and she took in her first glance at the view. Floor-to-ceiling windows perfectly displayed a fully illuminated downtown Dallas—it really was spectacular.

When the hostess greeted us, I immediately knew that she had been informed of our arrival. She smiled brightly at Kate and guided us to a small table set up alongside the tall glass windows. Kate pressed her hands and face up against them and took in the vast city surrounding us.

"This is awesome," she stated, her voice filled with wonder. "I think I see our house!"

"It is impressive," I said with a chuckle. Not long after we were served our waters, the food was placed before us. A huge thank-you note would be necessary after this night was done. They were treating my four-year-old perfectly.

"Kit Kat, do you like living in Texas?" I asked before she bit into a piece of chicken.

"It's my favorite. I don't want to move anymore," she stated.

"Would it be all right if one day we moved to a different house but still stayed in Texas?"

"Would I still see Auntie Audrey and Uncle Jace?" she asked.

"Of course."

"What about Uncle Jaxon?" I nodded, and she proceeded to list off the rest of my friends, all of whom she considered family members. I continued nodding, and she finally said, "Yeah, that would be okay."

"I would do anything for you; you know that, right? No matter what, you'll always be my number-one girl."

"Daddy, would you beat up a boy that pulled my hair?" she asked.

"I don't think I'm allowed to beat up little boys, but if there's someone doing something to you, I might need to have a very serious talk with him."

"Bubba punched a boy at the park today." The way she stated it as if it was no big deal almost made me laugh.

"Why would he do that?"

"Because that boy pulled my hair!" Her immediate defense of Braden didn't surprise me. Those two were always on each other's side. "It's not fair. Mama made him sit in time-out and he's not allowed to have dessert tonight! But, Daddy, he said that he's supposed to protect me. I didn't want him to get in trouble, though."

I knew there was a right way to approach this subject, but, damn, I sure wanted to go find that little guy and hug him tightly—and then take him out for a triple scoop of ice cream. "Kit Kat, Mama was right. It's not okay to just hit people, but I will tell Braden that he's doing a good job of watching out for his sister."

"Okay," she replied, only half satisfied with my answer.

I couldn't stop myself from saying, "How about we sneak some dessert back to him?" Raegan was going to kill me.

She lit up like the Fourth of July and practically bounced out of her seat. "Yes! Please, can we?"

"You better not tell your mom." I smirked at her.

"I super love you, Daddy." She went back to her French fries and guzzled down some more water.

"I love you like crazy, little girl."

～

Just as I thought it would be, living with Raegan was as easy as breathing. I told her two weeks ago that she and I just worked, and it was as simple as that. Those words couldn't have been truer, because we seemed to mesh so easily. It didn't hurt that Kate and Braden were as happy as two kids could be.

Although I returned to work—albeit reluctantly—I was shocked to realize how much I looked forward to returning home every afternoon. Raegan made my house a home, and a place I wanted to be as much as I possibly could. Kate greeted me every afternoon as if she hadn't seen me in four years; and it pulled on my heartstrings, not knowing if that was a good or bad thing. I continually tried to make a big deal out of coming home to her so she would know I would never go anywhere. I also had to tell Jace that I couldn't travel anymore, but he seemed to be prepared for that, so we began working toward moving me to a more permanent, finance-only position.

Quinn's mom came into town that week, and tonight she'd asked if she and Jace's mother could watch all the grandkids. Raegan was fluttering around the house nervously when I returned from dropping off Kate and Braden. Those two couldn't have been more excited to hang out with their *cousins*, as they called them. In fact, I'd barely gotten any hugs when I was saying good-bye. They were too preoccupied "helping" with the babies.

The reason I'd taken them solo was that Raegan was supposed to be getting ready for our night out with everyone. When I arrived back at the house, her long hair was curled in loose mahogany waves, which I loved, and she had taken off the T-shirt and cotton shorts she'd worn all day. As I stood in the kitchen, she sauntered in wearing her bra and panties and reached into the cabinet for a glass. I watched her calves flex as she stood up on her tiptoes and then continued staring as she moved toward the dispenser on the refrigerator. When some of the water splashed her stomach, her ass pushed back and I became instantly hard. God, *everything* she did turned me on.

"House is empty," I stated, hoping she would catch on—fast.

"It's weird, isn't it?" she responded, while leaning her bare hip against the counter and sipping her water. "It's too quiet."

"Yeah, but we're all alone. We've *never* been alone. I hear that when you're a parent and you find yourself alone, you should definitely take advantage." I smirked at her.

"Is that what they say, huh?" She smiled coyly and set her glass down. I stalked across the kitchen toward her and grabbed her hips in my hands.

"I don't make the rules," I whispered into her ear and started to nibble slowly.

I growled when her hands ran up the side of my face and into my hair. She knew it drove me crazy when she did that—it made me feel so fucking wanted. Her lips met mine before I could move them farther down her jaw. I pushed her against the counter and pressed my hands to her back soothingly so I could unsnap her bra.

"Right here, in the kitchen?" she said, laughing. "The blinds are open."

"Right here in the kitchen," I hummed against her lips. My fingers tweaked her nipples, and she moaned while pushing them closer to me. I picked her up effortlessly, set her on the edge of the counter, and moved between her thighs.

"Damn, I want you so bad," I couldn't stop myself from admitting.

"Mmm," she let slip from her lips. Her nails grazed my scalp and then she pulled my face closer to hers. "Can we do that new thing from last night?"

Straight to my cock. That's where her words struck me. "Tell me exactly which part was your favorite. I want to hear your saucy mouth," I murmured, moving my hands toward her lace panties.

Before she could respond, three sharp knocks sounded on the front door. I leaned my forehead against her shoulder and pretended that I hadn't heard anything. Her hands began shoving at mine before I could finish my current task.

"Lane, the door!" she whispered, as if whatever asshole was at our door could actually hear us.

"Dammit, who the hell is that?" I groaned. Stepping away from her delectable body, I clenched my fists open and shut.

As I was moving away from her, she reached out to grab my shoulder. I looked up at her in question, and she cleared her throat while pointedly looking down at my crotch. I had a huge situation between my legs that my gym shorts were not concealing. Of course I fucking did! I was seconds away from thrusting inside of my girl. *Sorry, buddy.* I regretfully adjusted myself up into my waistband and concealed the bulge as much as I could with my T-shirt.

"Do *not* get dressed. I'll get rid of whoever this is," I said, seething.

She hopped off the counter as I dragged my feet toward the front door. I took a deep breath and tried to reel in my temper before I bit off our visitor's head. When I opened the door, some guy a few years younger than me stood on my porch, appearing way too damn impatient. As soon as he saw me, he started to peer around my shoulder, trying to look in my house.

"Yeah?" That was as nice I could get. My dick was in the waistband of my shorts, and my girl was probably naked on my bed. This guy had better beat feet.

"Raegan Hayes here?" he asked. At the mention of her name, I immediately started to take him in. Who the hell was this?

"Can I help you?" I spat out.

"Yeah, by getting Raegan for me."

"I'm not your servant. Tell me who you are and I'll think about getting my girl."

"*Your* girl?" He faltered backward, and I immediately locked up.

"You're on my porch, man. I think you can show some respect and let me know who the hell you are."

"Name's Adam," he spouted off, while continuing to look around my body. He had what sounded like a New Jersey accent, or at least an attempt at one. My inner New York cop wanted to come out and interrogate this douchebag. I already didn't like where this was going. "Ree Ree!" he shouted past me.

"Get off my porch, asshole," I growled. From behind me I heard a gasp and the shuffling of feet. I stepped inside and shut the door on my foot, letting it stay open only a crack. Raegan was barreling toward me, and her eyes were as wide as a deer about to be struck by an oncoming eighteen-wheeler.

"Whoa, baby." I held my hands out to stop her. "If you think for one second I'm about to let your fine, *naked* ass out this door, you're sadly mistaken."

She looked down at her body and gasped, apparently only now realizing she was almost completely exposed. She dashed down the hall and returned with a cotton dress thrown haphazardly over her head. I didn't like how quickly she was trying to get out there to see this guy.

"Ree Ree?" I asked her in a hoarse whisper, as she ran on bare feet back toward me.

"You're mad?" she breathed. She lifted her hands up to my chest and I loved the warmth that poured out through my thin shirt.

"Never at you, babe."

"I just need to know why he's here. Please, just let me talk to him. Alone." Her voice was small, but it was also final. There was that word again . . . *alone.* Except this time it didn't include me.

"I don't like this," I admitted. Maybe to anyone else this would seem as if I was being a possessive caveman, but our situation wasn't normal. She had been kidnapped, for Christ's sake. I think my feelings were justified. Now someone from her past life was here—in *Texas*—and all of my protective instincts were lighting up. I wanted to grab Raegan, go get our kids, and keep them all within my sight.

"I don't either, but he's harmless . . ." She waved it off as if she really believed her words.

"I'll be on the other side of this door. That's as alone as I can let you be. Please, don't push it, Rae." I straightened her dress for her, pulled it up higher to cover her cleavage, and looked into her blazing green eyes—the very eyes that I had come to enjoy seeing open every morning and close every night. No one was going to take that away from me.

She moved for the door, and I leaned in to kiss her forehead, right over her scar. I didn't mean to remind her it was there, but to reassure myself that she was actually *here.* She rubbed her fingers over it self-consciously and shut the door behind her.

RAEGAN -

Shit, shit, shit, shit! When Lane and I had been interrupted in the kitchen, the last person I ever imagined would be at our front door was Adam. Adam Murphy, aka Braden's father. Even though he didn't deserve that title.

I could tell that Lane didn't know who he was yet; he just didn't appreciate the attitude Adam was no doubt giving him. Adam had nothing on Lane—literally, nothing. His build was scrawny compared to Lane, and not once had he ever looked at me the way Lane does on a daily basis: as if the sun rose and set on me alone.

There had been a time when I would have followed Adam anywhere. I knew he was an extreme gambler and he set off on trips to Vegas constantly. If at any point he had asked for Braden and me to come with him, we would have. I would have dropped anything for Adam. I was also nineteen and an idiot.

I thought Adam had been just as crazy about me as I had been about him. He was always showering me with gifts and showing up wherever I was to surprise me. I wouldn't hear from him for a week or more, and then he would pull this big romantic gesture and I would melt at his feet. Looking back, it had all been so childish.

Then I found out I was pregnant. I made the mistake of telling him right before we went in to see a movie, but I just couldn't hold it in anymore and he had been off to God-knows-where the previous four days. At first, his reaction seemed totally normal. He was speechless. A tight smile stretched across his face and he grabbed my hand. I knew that he would need time to process the news.

When he excused himself halfway through the movie to go to the restroom, I clearly remembered a sinking feeling in my stomach the second he turned out of my sight. I made myself wait a full five minutes, trying to give him the benefit of the doubt. The restrooms were empty. Yeah, I checked. He ditched me, changed his number, and moved. I had never known someone to be so desperate to disappear.

Of course I would have preferred some help, but I was okay with it being just Braden and me. Adam had come back around at one point wanting to talk, and begrudgingly I'd agreed to meet up with him. Turned out, I didn't make it to that little reunion because

I'd been kidnapped. And then it was just Braden, Kate, and me. Now we had Lane, and I didn't want any newcomers to mess things up. I was happy. Braden was happy. Why was Adam here? And now in Texas, of all places. Guess I was about to find out.

I stepped out onto the porch and looked up into his eyes, cringing when I saw them. I had forgotten how they were an identical match to Braden's. Braden had my naturally tan coloring and brown, almost black hair, but he also had Adam's brilliant golden eyes. Looking at Adam's eyes was like viewing Braden twenty years down the road. My throat choked up at the idea.

Adam looked me over and gasped when he'd finally made a full perusal. "Your head, Ree Ree." His hand moved to gently brush down the side of my face, and I knew he was touching my scar. That damn ugly scar—I would never be able to cover it up. The only reason it was starting to not bother me was that Lane seemed to adore it.

"Don't call me that, Adam. I never liked it," I whispered. His hand made me instantly uncomfortable.

Before I could swat it away, the door swung open and Lane's bulky figure stepped out behind mine. "Hands down if you want to keep them attached to your body." His eerie calm-yet-menacing voice demanded compliance. I turned to see him looking intently at Adam's face and saw the moment the realization hit him. Stepping closer into Lane's body, I hoped to tamp down the emotions bubbling out of him.

"You're Braden's sperm donor?" he growled. I wanted to snicker at that.

"Dad," Adam corrected. "I'm his dad and Ree—" He caught himself from saying my old nickname. "Raegan and I go way back."

"Oh, I've heard. I know *all* about your disappearing act. Where were you when they went missing? You sure as hell weren't looking for them. You sure as hell weren't talking to the police. We didn't know a damn thing about you." Lane tried to step closer to Adam, but I braced myself and tried to hold back as much of his weight as I could manage. "Better yet, where were you when your *son* was born?"

I could tell that had been hard for him to say. Lane would never be able to respect a man who ditched his child. Neither could I.

Adam stared at him for a heated moment, and I watched something similar to confusion cross his face. Surprisingly, he didn't respond to any of Lane's questions, but instead asked, "Have we met before?"

"I've met a lot of deadbeat dads, but I think you're a new one . . ." Lane shrugged. "Maybe I've arrested you before. Ever been handcuffed by a New York cop?" Lane was getting worked up, and Adam shifted on his feet while looking at me again.

I turned to face Lane and looked up into his eyes until he reluctantly pulled his glare away from Adam. His hazel eyes, which had more green in them than usual, slid down to mine and I gave him a small, pleading smile.

"Let me take care of this. Please?" I tried to whisper, but honestly, I didn't care if Adam heard as well. He had been uncharacteristically silent after Lane had torn into him. Probably a survival instinct. Without a word, Lane stepped back inside and closed the door. Adam's eyes turned to the window, and I assumed Lane was glaring at him through the glass.

I was actually surprised Lane hadn't grabbed me and planted his lips on me so hard that there would have been no question as to our relationship. But instead of marking his territory, he had quietly stepped back like I had asked, and now I wished I had let him stay. I needed his strong presence. I guess in a way, Lane didn't need to *bodily* mark his territory. One look and you knew not to cross him.

"Why are you here?" I finally asked Adam.

"For you," he replied. "And Braden, of course," he quickly added, as if it were a hard thing to remember.

"You're about five years too late for me. I *want* to say you're too late for Braden as well . . ."

"Let me take you out, please," he asked softly. "I miss you so much."

"Are you insane? No!" I replied with clear agitation.

"He's my son, Raegan. I have rights and I'll find a way to establish them."

My molars scraped together as I considered his words. "You've never wanted anything to do with him. Why are you even here?"

"I told you, I miss you. You've been gone for years. How would I have ever been able to rectify our situation?"

My hands flew up in the air. "Gone?! We weren't simply gone, you . . . you dumbass! We were kidnapped!"

"And now you're back, so why can't I at least get a shot at making things right again? You're clearly okay," he stated in a frustratingly casual tone.

"Clearly . . ." I grumbled sarcastically. "How did you even find us here?"

"Those bastard cops questioned me. I overheard that you were in Texas with a guy named Lane Parker. He wasn't hard to track down. Seems he doesn't take your safety into consideration." His voice was annoying me and I could feel the beginning of frustrated tears, so I pulled in a deep breath and made myself calm down.

"You'll never have me in any way, shape, or form. And I'll let you know right now I'll fight for Braden. I don't care if this battle takes years in court: I'll fight for him."

"And I'll fight harder, sweetheart. I know you can't afford the legal fees, so unless you're gonna get your juiced-up boyfriend to go into bankruptcy for you, I suggest you and I discuss a few things."

Damn him, he was right. I would never be able to gather enough money to even come close to paying a lawyer, let alone a good one. I couldn't burden Lane with that either. He didn't sign on for all the baggage I was now toting around.

"Face it, babe, he's my son. He shares my DNA, and don't think I won't play the distraught father who has missed his son for four long, agonizing years when we're in court."

"You're a bastard." I was seething.

"All I'm asking is for you to come out with me and discuss this. I'm not asking to take my son home with me."

"You'll never be alone with him," I quickly spat out.

"We'll see. You either come to dinner or I call my lawyer tonight." He tucked his hands into his pockets, waiting for me to respond, and looking as if we were discussing whether or not I wanted chocolate or vanilla ice cream. Not something as serious as *my* son's life.

"We discuss Braden and nothing else." My words were tight, and I hated that he was making me feel helpless.

"Tonight?" he asked. I shook my head and he quickly asked, "Tomorrow night?" I just couldn't. It was too soon.

"I need a week. Next Friday?"

"A week?!" he almost shrieked. "I gotta get back . . ."

"You don't sound like a guy who wants to be in his son's life," I growled at him.

"Fine!" he half-shouted, sounding exasperated and utterly frustrated. "I'll be here Friday. Seven sharp. Be outside: I don't want to have to deal with your guard dog." His chin lifted toward the window and I really hoped Lane hadn't heard that. He started to walk down the path toward the driveway, and I turned to face the door.

"Raegan," I heard him call out, his voice softer than before. I looked over my shoulder at him with my hand on the knob. "You look amazing."

I sneered at the bastard and walked back to the man who was good for me. *Good for Braden.* All Adam was going to do was rock our peaceful boat, although right about now I felt as though he was about to completely capsize it. Why couldn't we just be happy for once? Lane's arms were open wide when I stepped back inside, and I crashed into his warm embrace, burying my nose into the clean scent of his shirt.

"I need a drink," I mumbled into his chest.

"You're still my girl, right?" he asked into my hair. I could tell he had tried to hide his vulnerability, but it was laced into every word he spoke. I reached up and ran my fingers up the sides of his face and roughly into his hair. He closed his eyes on contact.

"Of course, baby."

"Then I'll buy you a drink, and after that, you can tell me what the hell went on out there. But right now, we're taking advantage of our empty fucking house."

I nodded my head because, besides finding Braden and running away to some super-secret hidden location where Adam would never be able to find us, I needed what Lane was offering. So with that, he secured the front door and then pulled me back to our bedroom. I could tell this wasn't going to be slow and loving. No, Lane was feeling a fire raging through his veins, and my body began to vibrate at the anticipation of what he was going to dole out. Oh yes—my man was about to mark his territory.

- Seventeen -

LANE -

B out damn time everyone got together again!" Jaxon bellowed over the music while we watched our girls playing pool. Audrey was schooling all of them, but apparently she'd picked up shit like that when she'd had to drag her drunk-ass dad out of a bar three to four nights a week.

Jaxon was right. We were finally all out on the same night. Cole, Jax, Jace, and all the girls. This time *my* girl was part of that. *My* girl. I had a girl. Actually, I had two girls. I know, I know: I'm a lucky bastard.

Em brought over clothes for Raegan to borrow since they were about the same size, and all Raegan owned right now were T-shirts. I tried to get her to wear this sexy little black dress that showed off her amazing legs, but Raegan was feeling self-conscious about the scars on the back of her leg and wasn't ready just yet for the world to see them. It's a shame because I would have enjoyed watching those stems all night in their full glory.

She was currently leaning over the pool table with jeans that might as well have been painted on, because I could see every damn curve. I also lost the battle on her top, the one that was cut so damn low I didn't even know what the point was in wearing a shirt in the first place. When she leaned over the green felt of the table, her tits were resting on top and I got lost in the valley between—along with every other horny guy within twenty feet of her.

"Lots of eyes on your girl tonight," Jace muttered.

"Yep." It was my only response. I was still feeling the situation out.

"Doesn't bother you?" Cole asked.

"If it did, would it make them stop?" I asked. Cole shook his head and I said, "Raegan's *my* girl. She's not gonna let some jackass touch her."

"She's the only one over there without a ring on her finger. Better fix that," Jaxon smarted off while tipping his beer back.

"Em pregnant yet?" I flung back. I was pleased with his reaction because he spit his beer clear across the damn bar.

"No reason to start playing dirty," he replied. I grabbed the bottle the bartender had placed in front of me and took the first swig. "I'm just saying, if that guy was as close to Emerson as he is to Raegan . . . he'd be missing his balls."

The dick in question was leaning over the table next to Raegan, trying to point out the best shot. He was clearly into her, but he wasn't touching her, so I wasn't going to be hasty. I trusted Raegan's instincts.

"Hey!" Jax called out across the bar. "Two feet, dude. Step back two feet, right now." We all looked over to see that another douche-bag had joined the girls and had apparently stepped too close to Jaxon's wife. Then with his hands, Jax motioned that Emerson belonged to him.

Em turned wide, angry eyes our way and huffed at her husband in annoyance. She straightened her spine and tugged her shirt down a fraction of an inch. Em, like Raegan, had a lot going on for her in the chest department. A wicked smile spread across her face as she marched over to the jukebox near their pool table.

"Shit . . ." Jaxon groaned.

Em grabbed Raegan's hand before leaning over and whispering something to the waitress.

"You did this to yourself, man," Cole laughed boisterously.

"Oh, like you would have let that fucker get close to Quinn," Jax retorted.

"No, you're right, I wouldn't. But I also know my girl. Looks like you haven't learned that Em doesn't like to be put in a bubble where no one may trespass," Cole schooled.

"Sit back, Lane." Jace laughed. "We're about to get a show." He rubbed his hands together in mock anticipation. Jax crossed his arms over his chest and scowled at Em. Quinn looked across the way at Jax and gave him a look, as if asking why he thought he could have gotten away with that.

Whatever was about to happen, it was going to be good. The music commenced, pumping an energetic beat. It felt familiar, but I really had no clue what song was coming.

"She's about to teach you a lesson," Quinn informed Jax as she joined us.

"I know, and it drives me fucking crazy, but I love it so goddamn much at the same time."

"Oh my God! You picked a song I actually know!" Raegan called out, clapping her hands. Did I mention that Raegan was about two drinks too many into her night?

"Why's she gotta bring my girl into this?" I moaned.

"I don't know this song, Quinn," Jax said loudly above the music. "Give me some idea what I just got myself into!"

Quinn giggled and said, "Well, um . . . it's about a promiscuous girl."

I couldn't hold it back because it was all just so damn funny. My head flew back and I let out a sidesplitting laugh.

Jax continued to look at Quinn for more. "It's by Pussycat Dolls," she told him. Then it clicked for me, and I knew exactly where this was going. She continued, "It's about a girl asking a guy to take off her clothes . . ." She waved her hand as if to say, *Catch up, man!* Jax groaned but then leaned forward in his chair to watch the show.

"It's a bad-girl anthem," Audrey added, as she sidled up beside Jace. He kissed the side of her neck and smiled at her, probably happy she wasn't about to unleash *her* inner bad girl.

The beat dropped and so did Em and Raegan, who both crouched down and began to bounce with the tune. The guys around them quickly forgot their games, and it was clear they had found their new entertainment. Two of them stood to make their way toward them, and I caught my girl imperceptibly shake her head over Em's shoulder.

My girl.

God, this girl.

I *loved* this girl.

Still dazed by my new revelation, I watched as she moved her hips to the beat. Her little waist rotated and she could probably give whoever was actually singing this song a run for her money. Em and Raegan moved closer to each other and grabbed at each other's hips, which were still swirling to the rhythm. My heart stopped. Actually, it dropped to the damn floor, along with my jaw.

"Fuuuuck," Jax groaned. Because the only thing that was hotter than your girl dancing provocatively? Your girl dancing provocatively with another girl.

"Yeah. What he said," I mumbled. My eyes were probably the size of golf balls, protruding from their sockets.

The beat was steady and energetic. Em began slowly loosening each button on her navy blue shirt, and, I kid you not, a growl ripped from Jaxon's throat. Raegan grabbed the edge of the pool table and dipped down. Every guy behind her watched her every move, probably trying to catch a glance down her shirt. Jaxon and I both launched to our feet. Em turned her back on us, but I could still see her hands moving in front.

"Emerson . . ." Jaxon said warningly.

When we could all see from behind that her shirt was fully open, our eyes were glued and our feet stayed firmly planted. Jaxon was vibrating, and even Quinn looked shocked. With Em's back facing us, Raegan moved in front of her and smiled. She moved her hands to Em's shoulders. They were up to something, but as long as it wasn't my girl with her shirt off, I didn't mind letting the show continue.

Raegan didn't move her hands from Em's shoulders while they continued dancing, and I could tell the song was winding down. Raegan's hands went under Em's shirt and helped her fling it off. Under her shirt was another sleeveless shirt, and an audible sigh of relief whooshed from Jaxon's chest.

Em spun around and pointed at Jaxon, laughing. Raegan was smiling from ear to ear and looking pretty pleased with herself. The waitress from earlier chose that time to return with a tray full of shot glasses carrying neon-blue liquid.

Rae lined them up along the edge of the pool table and gestured for the guys behind her to take one. Em handed one to Raegan and they all raised them in the air.

"Take this," Em called out loudly, "as an apology from my *husband*. He hates to share and sometimes forgets that his wife isn't a toy!" With a blatant wink back at Jax, she turned back to Raegan as Jaxon let out a bellowing laugh. The two girls wound their arms around each other and flung back the shots.

"I love your girl, dude," I said to Jaxon, after we'd managed to stop laughing our asses off. When his eyebrow rose, I finished, "I love her for doing this with Raegan. She needed to be included. It'll be good for her to have friends that are chicks."

"Yeah, we couldn't all just get to know each other like normal people do. The freight train that is Emerson has to bulldoze straight through to drinking pals," Quinn injected, laughing.

When they finished their shots, a round of shot glasses slammed back onto the table. One of the guys standing close to Rae and Em sucked air through his teeth and asked, "That was too fucking sweet. What was it?"

"It's called 'Blue Balls,' gentleman. Enjoy!" Em called, as she hauled a bouncing Raegan toward us. Cole, Jace, Jax, and I dissolved into laughter as we saw every single one of those dicks' faces drop in astonishment. Em had played that one perfectly.

"All right, all right, you made your point, beautiful." Jaxon laughed and pulled Em into his arms.

"Em, you're married now. Why do you continue these shenanigans?" Quinn chided.

"Quinn, we're married, not dead!"

"God, I love you." Jaxon laughed.

"See, he loves my *shenanigans*!" Em called out drunkenly.

Raegan was out of breath when she reached my side, but that didn't stop me from grabbing her and planting my lips roughly on hers. She tasted like raspberries and vodka. I licked around the inside her mouth, trying to savor her.

"You were moving those hips pretty well," I whispered.

"I can show you more of those moves." Her lips grazed my ear, and I actually shuddered at the amount of lust in her voice.

"We should leave. Now." I grabbed her hand to drag her out, but she pulled back, laughing.

"Not yet! Please. I'm having so much fun." I already couldn't tell her no. She and Kate had me wrapped around their little fingers.

I reached back to the bar and handed her a fresh glass of water. "Okay, you win. But I can't take you when you're passed out drunk."

She chugged down the entire glass, right in front of me. "Well, we can't have *that* now, can we?"

RAEGAN -

Em had broken the ice between us, and I couldn't stop smiling because it had been so long since I'd actually had deep, belly-laughing fun. Even before Mexico, I had been hopping between homes with a newborn baby. There hadn't been time for me to take a break—or anyone around to even allow me to do that. I worked, I took care of Braden—most of those hours were spent with Kate—and sometimes I managed to squeeze in sleep. But anything else, there just wasn't time for.

"I love her!" Em called out to Lane, while hugging me and simultaneously pulling me away from him.

"Yeah, well I loved it when she was over here," he called back, gesturing with his now-empty arms. I smiled brightly at him and followed Em to the pool table, leaving the guys behind to continue talking at the bar.

Quinn brought over drinks for all of us, and we propped up on barstools near the pool table we had claimed for the night. The guys from earlier had cleared out, which was nice because now we had the chance to just hang out without the stress of one of the husbands getting antsy.

"You have no idea how hot your boyfriend is," Quinn said to me.

I laughed at her and took a sip to hide my reddening face. "Oh, I have *every* idea how hot he is."

"Mmm, I'm sure you do," Em added.

"Oh, you guys act like you aren't married to walking dream-boats yourselves," I huffed playfully.

"That doesn't mean we can't fantasize about what he looks like under those clothes," Em started. "Look, I can't think of Cole like that because he's practically my brother . . . it weirds me out. I know what Jace looks like because I sleep with his identical twin every night. Lane's my only mental fantasy." She tapped the side of her head as if the image was there right now.

"Em, if I didn't love you, I'd throttle you right now," Audrey said, laughing. "Don't think about my husband when you're with Jaxon."

"Hey, you're the one who's been with both of them, you lucky bitch!" Quinn yelled, a little too loud. Audrey's face immediately turned as red as her shirt.

"Whoa, what?" I had to ask.

"I was with Jaxon before Jace. It was stupid. I don't like to talk about it." Audrey's words were clipped.

"We need more shots!" I called to our waitress. "This just got good."

"As long as we can talk about something else besides my husband's and Lane's bodies," Audrey begged.

"Aww, why not Lane's?" Quinn fake-pouted.

"Ew, guys, he's practically my brother. I do *not* want to keep talking about him like that," Audrey complained. I smiled because even though Lane had basically said as much, that was exactly what I wanted to hear from her.

Just then Audrey's eyes narrowed in apparent annoyance. The rest of us followed her glare and landed on a tall, beautiful blonde who was walking her hip-swaying self toward Lane. It was obvious she was on a mission, and she was looking at him as if she knew him—in a *personal* way.

"What's up?" I asked Audrey quietly.

"She's a problem."

Em and Quinn looked at each other, and then I saw the light turn on in Em's eyes. "Is that her? The girl from that one night at your house?" she asked.

"Yes," Audrey ground out through her teeth.

"What girl?" I asked again, although they were all zoned in on Miss Way-Too-Short-Skirt that had sidled up next to Lane at the bar. She moved closer, and I watched as he tried to inch away from her. Jax and Cole both scooted farther away, and Jace turned his back on her completely.

"Are you the jealous type?" Audrey asked me.

"I don't . . . think so," I stated uncomfortably. I thought about her question and then asked, "He's slept with her, hasn't he?" She squirmed uncomfortably at my question and then nodded her head. I looked back over to Lane and the blonde. So, I had been right . . . he *was* familiar with her.

The way she moved her hips and pushed out her chest toward him proved she wanted him again, although her boobs were nowhere close to what I was packing and her hair was obviously bottled. She reached seductively across Lane and grabbed his beer bottle. Someone behind me gasped when the blonde took a long pull from his beer and gave it back to him.

"I have to give her credit, she sure is working it," I said, laughing. I looked back at the girls, and they were gaping at me with open mouths. "It's kind of hot, don't you think?"

"Uh . . . hot is the last thing I would call her," Quinn grumbled.

"I'll second that. If she takes one step toward Jace, I'm ripping her extensions out," Audrey huffed.

"Not her," I said, chuckling. "Just the whole situation." I gestured toward the bar, where Lane was tossing the beer bottle into a trash can on the opposite side of the bar as if it were contaminated.

Right on cue, two more scantily clad blondes sauntered over and smiled at him, the same as the first had. Now Lane was the one fidgeting uncomfortably on his bar stool. One of the girls reached out for his bicep, and he politely pulled it from her grasp.

For some insane reason, my body was heating up. The whole situation was ludicrous, because shouldn't I have been wanting to pull out their hair and dig my fingernails into their eyeballs?

"Please elaborate," Em interrupted my thoughts. "Because even *I* would be going all jealous-girlfriend on their asses right now." Jax, Jace, and Cole had fully removed themselves from the groupie party surrounding Lane. Meanwhile, Lane gave each of the guys pleading eyes and they all subtly shook their heads. They wouldn't be going to help him.

"They want him," I stated.

"Yes, I can definitely see that. So shouldn't you be staking your claim?" Em asked.

"He wants me. That's what's so hot about this. They want him, but yet he only wants me." God, I was craving him right then.

In my peripheral vision, I noticed that the waitress had returned with our shots, but mostly my eyes were glued to Lane, watching as he tried to dodge and escape the girls who were clamoring for his attention. With extreme discomfort on his face, he finally braved looking out at me past all the blond hair. At first he gave me a desperate face, as if silently telling me he didn't want their attention. Then, his entire demeanor changed. The lust in my eyes must have been obvious—hell, it was practically written across my entire body.

His eyes narrowed slightly, and he sat up a bit straighter on his stool. The movement made his body appear even larger, and his biceps noticeably flexed under the sleeves of his shirt. He was absolutely delicious and he was looking right at me. I felt my nipples harden under my thin shirt, and I should have looked away from him because I couldn't walk around like that. But I couldn't force myself to look anywhere else. He was too intoxicating and I was too horny.

His hand came up to where I could see through the bodies, and he crooked his finger back and forth at me. I shook my head coyly at him, just to egg him on. He cocked an eyebrow and motioned for me to get over there. *Now.*

I grabbed a shot glass and threw it back. It definitely wasn't another shot of "Blue Balls." This was straight vodka and I hadn't been expecting that. I sucked in air through my teeth and gave myself a moment to stabilize. I was going straight into the lion's den; the liquid encouragement was absolutely necessary.

My feet moved before my brain did. My body was on autopilot as I rounded the pool table, maneuvering my way toward Lane. His eyes were glued to me, and the girls around him had finally turned to see why they had lost his attention. I couldn't wait to break it to them that they never had it.

I made it to the groupie party and Lane parted the way for me with his strong arms. When I didn't move to step in, he reached out and grabbed me. I willingly moved to stand between his legs and looked up into his hazel eyes. Even just by looking at his face one could tell that Lane was in perfect shape. Each cheekbone was chiseled, and I loved to run my lips across his strong jawline.

"Were you and the girls over there laughing at me? I'm obviously really uncomfortable right now," he said, loud enough for everyone around us to hear. Two of the girls huffed and walked away. The first one decided to take her chances and stick around.

"At first," I responded demurely.

"And now . . ." he started, and then he ever so subtly ran the back of his hand across one of my hardened nipples. I closed my eyes at the agonizingly amazing feeling of his stimulation. "You're turned on?"

Because he stated it as a question, I nodded. With the alcohol giving me a bigger voice than I would normally have, I said, "She wants you and she's working damn hard to get what she wants. But what she doesn't understand is that you want me. That. Is. Sexy." My hand cupped his jaw and then moved into his hair.

A rumble shook his chest as he moved his face closer to mine. He looked into my eyes—through my eyes—he looked *into* me, and I saw a change in him. Something was happening between us. Something from which there would be no coming back. If I could bottle up that look forever, I would take it out only when I needed the feeling of being wanted in the most devoted way a man could want a woman. The way Lane looked at me proved the feelings he spoke out loud to me when we were alone in our bed every night.

"Not in a bar," I swore I heard him mumble.

"What?" My voice was raspy and breathless.

"Nothing. It's just that I really need to take you home now."

My drunken Lane-fog was painfully blown away when I heard the blonde's voice directly behind me. "Are you serious?"

"Gemma, why are you still here? Have I shown you any interest?" he questioned through clenched teeth.

I ran my hand up his thighs in a comforting gesture. Damn her for ruining our perfect moment. I didn't care if we were in a bar. We could have been in a barn, for all I cared. I wanted to know what was on his mind just then when he'd looked at me as if he wanted to burn the image of my face into his memory.

"When are we talking about, exactly?" Gemma asked. "Are we talking about the time you were buried so deep—"

"Stop!" he yelled.

I'm not sure why he bothered at that point, because it was pretty clear where she had been going with that. And while the idea of girls lusting over my man was a turn-on, actually hearing the play-by-play of what they obviously once shared seemed to have the opposite effect on my libido.

I turned, and even though I had no intention of leaving, Lane moved quickly to wrap his arms securely around my shoulders. He was still seated on his stool, but he had scooted closer to the edge.

"Don't." The words brushed past my ear in a soft growl.

"I didn't plan on it."

"We had one night, Gemma. If you haven't noticed, I decided not to come back for more. Hell, I gave you a *fake* name!"

Gemma looked down at me from her four-inch heels. I took in her wild blond hair that should have looked like a rumpled mess but seemed to work perfectly, and her tight perky body that had clearly never birthed children. She seemed exactly like the type of girl Lane should be with. But he'd obviously had her and he didn't stick around for more. She sized me up slowly, from my flat shoes to my large breasts, before stopping at my face.

"You'd rather leave with her? You'd rather sleep with *her* instead of *me*?" The ugliness in her voice bled through her entire demeanor, and the beautiful blonde standing in front of us didn't appear so alluring to me anymore. Maybe Lane had seen that side of her as well. "I know you, Lane."

"The hell you do," he interrupted.

She smiled through her bright red lips. "I do. You like pretty faces. Trust me, you'd be distracted all night by that god-awful scar."

Oh, hell no. There remained no more of the warm and fuzzy buzz I had hoped to keep. Damn her again. I didn't even get a chance to react because the instant the word "scar" left her blood-red lips, it seemed as if the bar erupted.

I was suddenly moved to the side with a gentle but demanding force. Lane's large figure stood up so rapidly he was practically a large blur blowing past me. He came to a stop directly in front of Gemma and glared down at her.

"What the *hell* did you just say?" he growled through his teeth. His fists clenched tightly at his sides until they were a pale white color. I put my hand on his back, but it only caused a tremor to rock through his tense muscles. "Don't you ever talk about her like that. I love that scar."

Gemma stood with her mouth agape. "I . . . I . . . I . . ." she stuttered, clearly shocked at his forceful reaction.

Jace moved in quickly and placed his hand on Lane's chest. I could tell he was subtly trying to move him back, but Lane wasn't having that. Audrey dipped under Jace's arm and squeezed in between the two big guys.

"Why am I having to ask you to leave . . . *again*?" Audrey tried to sound nonchalant, but I could hear the anger that she was trying to disguise.

Gemma glanced once again at Lane's face and wisely decided to step away, although I really doubted she felt any remorse for her words. It was that thought that brought the catty side out in me.

"Hate to break it you, but he's been sleeping with me every night for a month. So while you get off in your bed alone over one measly night you had with him, I get the real thing, night after night," I announced. She sneered at me and continued to move away. "And let me tell you, he is *never* distracted." I couldn't help myself, and I swear I'm not usually like that.

After I watched her move through the crowded bar and then out the double doors, I finally let myself turn and face Lane. Jace pounded his back and moved away, while Audrey looked at him with worried eyes. When Jace tugged her along with him, she shot me a nervous look in her retreat. I smiled at her, hoping to reassure her that I could handle this. After all, he was mine to handle.

Lane's hands were still balled up tightly and his eyes were squeezed into thin little slits. A crinkle marred the corners of his beautiful eyes and his plump lips were pursed tightly. I reached up and gently ran my fingers over the signs of stress streaking across his face. I didn't say a word—I wanted him to speak first. I continued to run my hands across his jaw, over his cheeks, and into his hair. Over and over. Finally, I felt the tension begin to subside.

His first words surprised me. "I'm so sorry."

"For what?" I grabbed hold of his shirt and jerked to show my bewilderment.

"I shouldn't have been with girls like her. Why the fuck was I wasting my time with bitches like that?" He seemed to be talking to himself, but I decided to answer anyway.

"So you could save the real stuff for me?" I laughed. It was meant to be a joke to break the heavy tension, something to bring him out of his mood.

He finally looked down at me and took hold of my face. The brown of his eyes glowed into an outer green ring so bright that it was almost hypnotizing.

When I felt his fingers brush lightly across my scar, I closed my eyes. *Why did everything have to go back to that horrid thing?* "She tried to make this ugly." His voice caught, and I could hear the real pain in his words.

"Well, it kind of is."

"Stop."

"I just want to forget that thing is even there."

"I don't." He kissed three times down the length of it. "This scar is *everything*. It's *everything* to me. It brought my daughter back to me. It brought Braden into my life. It brought you. It encompasses *everything* I love about you. Your strength, your determination, your stubbornness. Please, don't let one of my mistakes make you feel worth any less, because I just wouldn't be able to stand it. And if, after all that, you still feel less than beautiful, well then . . . I'll just have to keep finding ways to convince you otherwise."

It was coming—I could feel it in my bones. The moment that would forever change us. The one that would eternally alter the way I looked at the world around me. If, God forbid, we ever parted ways, I would forever chase this moment. I wanted to brand everything about it deeply into my skin. The clinking glasses. The hoots of excitement over a game of pool. Our friends laughing and smiling. But most of all, the look in Lane's eyes when he finally realized that his daughter wasn't the only girl who owned his heart.

My hands slid under his arms and around to his strong backside so he could hold me even closer. "Everything you *love* about me?"

"Is that the only part you heard?" He smiled.

I shook off his words. "I heard it all. But . . ."

His head dipped down and he rested his face next to mine. I felt his warm breath near my ear, and before he spoke, an exciting electric energy blasted through me. "Not in a bar," he murmured.

"In a bar," I argued. "Don't break the moment."

We stayed huddled together, not wanting to move even an inch away from each other. "It's not supposed to happen in a place like this. It should be somewhere romantic. Like our bed, so I can slide into you while I whisper softly in your ear."

"That sounds . . . amazing." I wished my words weren't so breathy. To distract him from his hesitation and myself from my lusty desires, I grabbed the back of his head and forced our lips to meet in a hungry duel. He growled past my lips and pulled me onto his lap up on the bar stool. I immediately felt his desire for me under my thighs.

"Really?" I glanced down at his lap.

"As long as you're in the same room, that's just how it's gonna be."

I continued seizing his mouth with my own. His plump lips surrounded mine, and I never wanted to be kissed any other way ever again.

He pulled back and panted as he tried to catch his breath. "Damn you, woman. You never let me set the pace and do things when I want to. You attack everything, right in the moment."

Once again, these didn't sound like bad things to me, so I smirked up at him. "You *love* that about me."

"Fine!" he huffed. He tried to appear annoyed, but I could see the smile in his eyes, confirming that he *loved* this. "I love you. I can't believe you're making me tell you this for the first time in a damn bar, but I love you!"

"God, you're even hotter when you're flustered." I smiled from ear to ear as my heart floated high above us.

"Raegan . . ." he growled.

"I love you . . . so much," I whispered. "I know you didn't expect to get me when you came for Kate, but you did. You are the reason I have been able to adjust back to normal life so easily. During what should have been the most confusing time in my life, I found I could trust in you and I'll love you forever for giving that to me. Thank you for being a marvelous dad to Kate and loving her the way you do. And thank you for taking exceptional care of Braden."

"I love Braden too."

"You don't have to say that," I whispered. I knew that a relationship between a man and another man's child would take time to establish.

"I'm not just *saying* that. I *love* that little guy. The second he stood up to me at the police station to protect Kate, I loved him."

My eyes welled with tears because I'd never imagined I would find someone who could even come close to loving Braden as much as I did. I had always wanted a strong male figure in his life, but after he was born I had just accepted that I would have to play both roles for him. Lane smiled at me and swiped his thumb under my eyes.

"I love you," he said with an overabundance of emotion in his voice, which would forever be seared into my bones.

"I love you." I kissed his nose. "I love you." I moved closer to his chest and kissed his cheeks. "I love you." I wiggled seductively on him. "God, I need to have sex with you . . . *now*."

"Uh, earth to the lovebirds: Sex in public is unfortunately still illegal!" Cole's words forced themselves in between our lips, and we finally realized that we were still sitting in a bar . . . with our friends . . . and about fifty other strangers.

"It's true, guys!" Em called out, laughing. "Trust me, I've tried!"

"This is why you don't start that shit in a bar," he growled in my ear. Lane stood and pulled my hand, so I was forced to keep up with him. "We're out." As we passed everyone, he leaned over and kissed Audrey on the cheek. "We'll see you in the morning, doll, when we pick up the kids."

A round of groans ensued from my new group of friends, and I smiled to see that they were actually disappointed we were retiring. I waved to the girls. "Don't leave!" a few called out.

"My girl needs sex. I deliver," Lane said unabashedly. He looked at the guys, quirking his eyebrow in question. "What would you do?"

All three of them—Jax, Jace, and Cole—proceeded to point toward the exit. I laughed the entire drive home. But with a house free of children for one night, there would be a lot more than laughing going on.

- Eighteen -

RAEGAN -

I realized Lane's mood was deteriorating as the week moved on. He hovered over me every chance he got and grew more edgy by the day. I didn't understand what was going on at first. I wasn't going to complain that he was following me around or that he would trap me up against a wall anytime we were out of the kids' eyesight, but I began to recognize that he was feeling insecure.

When out of the blue Lane decided to take Friday off, I didn't think he had done it so he could go shopping for school clothes with us. My mind had been so caught up in getting Kate and Braden ready to start school, I had forgotten that Adam, Braden's father, was still picking me up tonight.

So when Friday morning rolled around and Lane stuck to me like glue, I finally registered his feelings of unease. He didn't want me to go tonight, plain and simple. What he probably didn't fully comprehend was that I didn't want to go either. But I also didn't want Braden's father causing any trouble, so I was willing to sit down and talk to him like an adult about my son. I didn't know why now, after all this time, he wanted to be in Braden's life, but I would at least hear him out.

I moved down the hallway looking for my handsome man and finally found him in the spare room, which was kind of Lane's catch-all room. He had gym equipment that he used when he couldn't sneak off to his boxing gym. On the opposite side, he had a large desk that he sat at and finished up any work he didn't get done at the office. He was staring at a stack of papers, and there were creases in the corners of his eyes.

I stood in the doorway taking him in until he looked up at me. "Hate to break it to you, but one day we'll have to convince them they need to have separate bedrooms." I gestured around the room. "And then we're going to have to figure out a new place for this stuff."

He smiled because he loved when I spoke about the future, *especially* when I mentioned the four of us together. I made my way around the desk and sat in his lap, snaking my hands around his neck.

"I think we should buy a house, actually."

My mouth widened in shock, because that's not something I had been expecting. He chuckled and continued, "You want to paint walls and all that girly shit, right?" I nodded but stayed quiet. "It'll be good for us in the long run to own real estate."

"You would do that?" I asked quietly.

"*We* would do that."

"But . . . I don't have anything to contribute. I'm broke, if you haven't noticed."

"Trust me, you contribute way more than I do. Just because I take care of things financially doesn't mean I don't need you just as much. You've made my house our home. I've never been so happy to come home every day. You keep this place running smoothly. I could barely handle myself, let alone Kate *and* Braden. I don't know what I would do without you."

"Oh, so that's why you keep me around. You need me to do the laundry," I said, laughing. He tickled my sides until I screamed for him to stop, because I was about two seconds away from peeing my pants.

"Are you happy staying at home? Taking care of the house?" I nodded my head, because it gave me pleasure to take care of my family and actually cook them real meals every day. "You could always get a job if you really wanted to. I'll only say this once and the rest is up to you. I love you at home. I love how you take care of us. I love that I can call you up any time of day and you're available to meet me. I love that our kids can come right after school to our home and not go to some strange day care. But that's my opinion, and I'll support whatever you decide."

The fact that he'd said "our kids" was not lost me. I think I felt my heart grow a few sizes in that moment alone.

"I just don't want to ever burden you."

He kissed my temple and smiled. "You could never be a burden. And I don't want you to worry about money. I can afford to take care of all of us and still take a family vacation each year."

I gasped playfully. "I have no idea what a vacation even is!"

"Well, then, when the kids are on Thanksgiving break this year, I'll show you."

I lay against his chest and listened to the beat of his heart. The last thing I wanted to do tonight was leave his arms and go see my douchebag of an ex-boyfriend.

"I don't want you to be worried about tonight." I tried to sound as strong as I could, because I knew how he had been feeling.

"I want you to take my cellphone. I don't know why I haven't gotten you one yet. I'm taking Braden and Kate to Jace's tonight. Call me anytime. Seriously, if he even looks at you wrong, call me."

"Why are you going to Jace's?" I asked suspiciously. I had visions of him and Jace secretly following us.

"He's my friend."

"We'll see them tomorrow, though."

"Call me for any reason." He wasn't going to answer me. "Even if you want to just tell me what you ordered for dinner. Do not, for any reason, go anywhere alone with him. I'm serious about this, Rae. You agreed to dinner, nothing else."

"We're going to the restaurant and back." I decided to pacify him. It was obvious that he was feeling out of control, but he had never—not even once—asked me not to go. "I love you, you know that, right? Like over-the-moon love you."

"Make sure you tell him that, okay?" he said with a smirk. "You know I thought when I truly fell in love that my mind would only think about that girl and there wouldn't be anything else. But that's not how it works at all. Everything around you becomes important because all of those things could potentially take you from me."

"No one can take me from you," I whispered. I slipped down to the floor and found a spot in between his legs. He looked at me with wide eyes and I grinned. With my hand, I stroked him through his gym shorts. I hadn't given him much of a heads up, but he was quickly catching on as I felt him stiffen under my palm.

"Rae . . ." he breathed out harshly. "The kids are in the next room."

"They can't see me past the desk." I blew warm air through the thin fabric of his shorts, which worked him up even more.

"They could come around."

"Well, then, I better work fast."

"No way. I learned my lesson painfully the last time Braden decided to come check on us." He scooted out of the chair, and I heard the lock of the door slip into place.

He sat back down and lifted his hips without any further resistance and helped me slide his shorts down to his ankles. I loved when he went commando. When he walked through the house, I could always see the outline of his perfect butt, but now I was really reaping the benefits. I took hold of his large length in my hand and hummed against his scorching hot skin.

"Mmm, baby," I mumbled. My breath blew across him and his head dropped backward. His hands clutched the arms of the chair tightly, and I moved my grip up and down his erection.

He looked absolutely beautiful in my hand. His strength was visible through every single mouthwatering inch of him. That made me think about the thoughts I'd had of him when I was only the nanny. I didn't let it happen often, but I couldn't stop my dreams late at night.

"You're giggling with me in your hand?" He had trouble speaking through his barely contained desire.

"I was thinking something very inappropriate," I whispered. I let my tongue slide lazily up and down the underside.

"Tell me, baby. I want to hear what you could possibly find inappropriate with my dick seconds away from your mouth." His voice was a guttural groan.

I let him slide between my lips while I spoke. "I may have fantasized about this once or twice while I was . . . working . . . for you." His body froze, and I immediately took him fully into my mouth. I was feeling self-conscious about telling him now. It had only happened a few times, and I'd woken up panting and sweating, feeling dirty. But, God, it had been so hot.

"Are you serious?" he rasped. My hair hung loose down the entire length of my back, and he reached for it to hold in his grasp. I loved when he grabbed my hair, as if he just needed to be holding me any way he could.

I nodded my head, but I didn't know if he really knew the difference between my bobbing motion up and down his length and the nod.

"God . . ." he moaned, "babe. Oh, sh—" The words were flowing past his lips without much thought, and I loved making his thoughts this jumbled. My hand squeezed the base of his cock tighter and he groaned. "You're right, that was terribly inappropriate. But God, it makes me so fucking turned on right now." I smiled and worked harder. "That's it, baby . . . so good."

I moved my mouth up and down and used my hand to cover the inches my mouth couldn't take. I felt his fingers grip my hair tighter, but he didn't force me to move any faster. He liked my rhythm, and he was close to losing all control anyway.

When I felt him begin to swell in my mouth, I whimpered at his pleasure. His hips jerked and I squeezed around him as hard as I could.

"Ahh, damn it," he growled. I could tell he was trying to stretch things out and make it last longer, but my relentless cadence consumed him, and he just couldn't hold back any longer. I reveled in his release and the look of satisfaction on his face.

His hands had moved to grip the edges of his desk, and he looked down at me in complete awe. He appeared authoritative and oh-so-sexy, yet he was looking as if I were actually the one with all the power.

"What is it about guys loving blow jobs at their desks?" I smirked up at him while licking my lips.

"Must be that whole secretary fantasy," he breathed out as he pulled his shorts back up.

"Remind me to tell Jace that you are *never* allowed to have a secretary."

When he finally caught his breath again, he pulled me up onto his lap, and I relaxed against his large chest. He let out a huge breath and held my face close to his body. Strong fingers ran over my face and down through my hair.

"He doesn't get to touch you," he whispered.

I groaned. "You weren't supposed to be thinking about him. You were supposed to be thinking about my mouth—and maybe me pretending to be your secretary next week."

"I was. Then I started thinking about some other guy getting that and I saw red for a moment." I sighed at his words and he rushed to say, "I've got it under control."

"I never doubted that you didn't." I rubbed my hand across his chest, enjoying the hard planes, followed by the tough ridges on his abdomen.

Lane was physically the strongest person I had ever met, and his self-control was even more tenacious. He didn't rile easily and he didn't allow others to egg him on. I had witnessed guys in the gym trying to coax out the beast inside of him, but he never let it escape until he was in one particular controlled environment—the boxing ring.

I'd only witnessed him in the ring the few times I decided to join his workouts. I marveled at the power each of his fists possessed and at the lithe movements he made as his feet carried him around. I had never known someone with that much muscle who could hold back the way he could. Outside of the ring, he was calm, easygoing, and gentle. But on the inside of the ring, he fully let himself go, using all of his energy and hard-earned strength. He was absolutely beautiful.

Regrettably, I still needed to take a shower and get somewhat ready for tonight. I turned in his lap and glanced at the papers he had been reading before I interrupted his work. Usually, his papers were filled with numbers and spreadsheets. It was all so confusing, and I generally tried to stay away from it.

But today the papers appeared different. The first thing that stuck out was an official-looking seven-pointed star. At a closer glance, I saw the words *Policía Federal* and then *Miguel Flores*. That stupid name. Would I ever be able to escape it? I'd hoped to never see or hear that name ever again. I thought that was behind us.

"What is this?" My voice was only a whisper.

"Charlie faxed it over."

"You're still keeping tabs on him?"

"I told you that I intended for him to pay for his crimes. I know how corrupt it is down there. My friend Mateo used to work for the police in Mexico before he quit because of the double-dealing fraudulence."

"So . . . what do these say?" I tapped the stack in front of me.

"Well, his happy ass is still sitting in prison. It could take a year until he's sentenced, but so far Charlie said it sounds like they have a pretty damn tight case against him."

"Any chance he could pay his way out?" I asked nervously.

"I'm sure there's always a chance. But for now there seems to be media attention that's persuading the judges to keep him there." His words caused me to breathe a little easier. "Don't worry."

"I'm done hearing about him, Lane. I'm going to trust that you will keep us safe, so I don't want to hear his name ever again. Even if he gets life in prison or the damn death penalty, please don't tell me." Maybe it was weak of me. Maybe I was running from my problems, but that man stole four years from me. I was done giving him any more of my thoughts.

"Deal." His quick response was finalized with another heated kiss.

Sadly, I slid from his lap and walked toward the bedroom to get ready, knowing I had to face another unfortunate part of my life I wish I could bury forever. My nerves were skyrocketing at the thought of seeing Adam. I had a bad feeling about why he was here. If he wanted more time with Braden, or even—God forbid—shared custody, I just didn't know what I would do. I didn't want to give up any of my time with Braden, and Adam didn't deserve his time. But could I keep Braden from his real father?

LANE -

I stood on the front porch with Raegan and waited for the ass-hole to arrive. Unfortunately, he pulled up at exactly 7:00 p.m. He probably understood that I would have taken her out to dinner myself if he had been at all late, and there would be no second chances. Damn him.

She started to pull away when he came to a stop in my driveway, and I noticed that he made no move to get out of the car . . . probably another good move on his part. I tugged her back into my arms and tilted her chin to look up at me.

"You got my phone?" She nodded her head and I continued, "Call Jace if you need me. I'll answer."

"You two aren't going to secretly follow us, are you?" she asked, smiling.

"Should we?" My stomach was flip-flopping, and I didn't like the idea of her being alone with him—not even for a second. But there was absolutely nothing I could do to stop it.

"No!" she laughed. "Lane, this will be over fast. I'll call you if I need anything."

"I don't like this." I had to be truthful, even if it made her uncomfortable.

"I don't either. I'd rather hang out with you guys any night." Her voice was filled with melancholy, and I pulled her tighter into my arms and kissed the top of her head.

"This is only to talk about Braden, right? You'd tell me if it were something else?"

"Of course! I love you, Lane. Please know that."

"I do. Now, show your douchebag ex how much you love me." I smirked down at her, challenging her to do as I asked.

She complied with ease as her hands wound behind my neck and her fingers threaded through my short hair. She rose up onto her tiptoes and lifted her face closer to mine. I wanted her to take me. And, yeah, I wanted Adam to see her doing it. Her lips crashed against mine, and without words, she told me everything she loved about me and everything she would let me do to her later tonight.

I pulled back before she made me so hard I would have to hold her hostage for the rest of the night. Her cheeks were flushed and I grinned from ear to ear.

"Damn, I love you. Now, hurry along." I swatted her ass and she giggled. "Come back to me as quick as you can."

She skipped down the walkway, and I noticed Adam had the windows down on his car. I leaned over to view him eye to eye through the opening. "Drive safe," is what I said. What I knew he understood I was saying was, "If you do *anything* to her, I'll hunt you down and tear you apart, limb from limb." And he knew I was damn well capable of it too.

∾

"Why are we at Uncle Jace's house?" Braden asked from the backseat.

I pushed the car into park and unbuckled my seat belt. We had hopped in the car almost the second Raegan and her ex-boyfriend turned off my street. She had asked if Jace and I were going to follow them tonight, and I couldn't say that the thought hadn't crossed my mind a time or two today. But I was really only here for one reason.

"I need to hit the punching bag in Uncle Jace and Jaxon's barn."

"Oh! I want to come too!" Braden exclaimed. I reached back behind me and helped the kids unclip their straps.

"Can I go see Auntie Audrey and the baby?" Kate asked. I knew that she would ask that. I loved how easily Braden and Kate had become part of my extended family. Everyone had been so great with them and accepted them as if they really were their niece and nephew. I nodded my head at both of them. "Yay! I hope Auntie Em is over there. She's so funny!"

At the sound of her name, Braden turned to look at Kate. "I like Aunt Em too. She's pretty." I couldn't believe it, but he actually blushed!

"Boy, you're too young for that." I chuckled. These two could help any rotten mood I was in. I came here to pretend the sandbag was Adam's face, but Kate and Braden were helping me calm down, little by little, all on their own.

"I'm gonna go with Kate, okay?" Braden requested. Guess Auntie Em was more appealing than punching a bag in the barn.

"I'll walk you guys in."

Jace and Audrey were lounging on the couch in their family room. Baby Jocelyn was perched in her dad's arms, snoozing away. Audrey was stretched out across the couch with her head on Jace's shoulder. She was so happy now, and that was all I had ever wanted for her. As Kate's and Braden's feet pattered across the hardwood, the two lovebirds looked over the back of the couch and smiled.

"Hey, guys," Jace called out.

"Come join us," Audrey invited. Kate was the first to crawl up next to her, and Braden wasn't far behind.

Jace handed Jocelyn off to Audrey, and I knew it wouldn't be long before she was in either Kate's or Braden's arms. Jace stood and walked toward me.

"Beer?" he asked.

"You have beer in your house?" I laughed, because Audrey and Jace had never been drinkers. Insane, I know.

"Audrey buys it for y'all," he said with a shrug.

"I'm good, thanks. I actually came for the bag." I pointed down the road a bit, where I knew the big red barn stood. On the inside of it, Jace had strung up different weighted punching bags. Sometimes it was nice to come here instead of the gym, especially if I had the kids with me.

"Let me change and I'll come." As he jogged up the stairs, I noticed he was still in his suit from work.

Kate and Braden had already settled in on either side of Audrey, as close as they could possible get to her. Audrey was naturally such a motherly person that children had always flocked to her. And she absolutely loved it. She was beaming and soaking in every moment. They all sat and listened to Jocelyn coo at them, while Kate and Braden giggled at her every noise.

"Damn, that's cute," Jace said as he reached the bottom step.

"Hey, little man, you coming or do you really want to stay?" I called out to Braden.

"Can I stay here?" he asked while looking over the backside of the couch.

"You sure can. Watch out for the girls for me, okay?" He nodded his head and we bumped knuckles.

Jace and I jogged down the road toward the barn so we could warm up. We had been working out together for over a year now and had our routine down pat. He was a great sparring partner in the ring because he could take and deliver the hard punches I needed. Tonight, that's exactly what I was desperate for. Otherwise, I might explode and end up hunting down Adam and pissing off Rae. I didn't need to think about those two off alone together. Jace already knew where she was, so thankfully he didn't have to ask.

By the time Jaxon strode in through the barn doors, Jace and I had already gone seven rounds. The only problem now was that I still craved more of it. And I wanted it to be Adam's face that met my fist next, not a padded-up Jace.

"What are y'all up to tonight?" I panted, as I pulled the red gloves from my hands. Jace was doing the same and tossing his headgear to the side as well, trying to catch his breath.

"Fucking absolutely nothing," Jax groaned. "Seeing as I just went to the store to buy chocolate and tampons, I should probably say absolutely no fucking."

"That blows." I chuckled at his sullen state.

"Shouldn't you be at home giving her that stuff?" Jace nodded toward the bag Jax had tossed to the ground.

"Yeah, but I'm gonna hide out here for a while. Quinn's over, and they're watching sappy movies just so they can make themselves cry." Jax made his way to a mini-fridge and pulled out a beer.

"Seriously?" I laughed. "I'll never understand chicks."

We sat and shot the shit for a long while, and I hoped the clock was ticking along at a rapid pace. I forced myself to not look at the time, but I hoped this dinner would be wrapping up soon.

Jace's phone began to chime and he pulled it from his gym shorts. "You're calling me, dude," he said, puzzled.

"Shit, it's her. Toss it," I called out. I caught it midair and had it next to my ear in a heartbeat. "Need me to come get you, baby?" I asked into the line.

"I had a cheeseburger," Raegan's voice said quietly. "It came with French fries, so I ate a few of those too." Her voice sounded sad, and I wanted to rip apart Adam's throat for doing whatever the hell he had done.

"Rae, do you need me to pick you up?" I walked outside of the barn and into the cooler summer night air. My skin was already heating up in anger again.

"No, I'm fine. You said I could call you for any reason. Even if it was to tell you what I ate."

"Well, I love hearing your voice."

"What are you doing?"

"Punching Jace."

She laughed and then asked, "Where are my babies?"

"You can't keep calling them babies; you know that, right?"

"They will always be babies to me."

"Where do you think they are? Fawning over the *actual* baby inside. I think at one point Kate was holding her and Braden was simultaneously feeding her."

"Those two! Get them away before they start begging us for one." She laughed, and I heard the stress begin to lift away.

"I'm down for practicing," I murmured directly into her ear.

"Mmm," she moaned.

"Where are you, babe? I thought you were supposed to be talking about Braden with him?"

She sighed heavily and said, "I'm sitting on a bench outside of the restaurant. He's on the phone inside on some business call. I don't really care. I'm just ready to go."

"Let me come get you."

"No. I just want to talk to you, and then hopefully he'll finish and we can leave."

"I hope you aren't falling for it."

"Falling for what?"

"He's pretending to be the successful businessman, trying to woo you with his money."

"You know I don't care about that stuff," she scoffed.

"I know you don't, and that's why I'm smiling. Because he's pulling that shit with the wrong girl." My grin was probably audible through the phone's speaker and grew even wider when she laughed in response.

"He hasn't even tried to talk about Braden tonight, Lane. He's only trying to get back together with me. What is wrong with him? He has this wonderful, beautiful, brilliant son, and he's just trying to get into my pants." Her long sigh afterword spoke volumes.

I wanted to slam my fist and demand to know exactly how he was trying to get into her pants, but her grief told me now wasn't the time.

"I'm genuinely sad for him, Rae. I'll never understand how a father wouldn't want to be in his child's life. And to miss out on a kid like Braden is truly tragic. I know it's not what you're wanting right now, but I know that I can be good enough for Braden. I can be the dad that he needs, Rae. I'll make sure he knows how loved he is every day. Besides, I know that asswipe can't teach Braden to throw a left hook like I can."

A sniffle came through the line and she said, "You're exactly what I'm wanting, right now and forever. For myself and for our children."

The wobble in her voice told me the kinds of emotions that were running rampant through her right then, and the last thing I wanted her to do was cry. If she was going to cry, I didn't want Adam the asshole to try and comfort her; that was my job.

I cleared my throat, straining to get my own damn feelings in check. "So, tell me more about the times when you were a hot little waitress in Brooklyn, back before you met the douchebag. I bet you were trouble with a capital T."

She laughed, and I felt relieved that I'd helped clear the air for the moment. There was nothing I wanted more than to talk about our future together, but I just couldn't do it with her so vulnerable around him. Any second now he would come outside and want to know where she had gone.

"I used to smoke," she confided.

"Seriously?" I laughed. "That shit's terrible for you, naughty girl."

"Yeah, when I found out I was pregnant, I had to quit cold turkey. I was a complete bitch."

For the next twenty minutes or so, we sat on the phone and told each other stories about our past that we hadn't yet divulged in one of our many late-night, under-the-covers, postsex chat sessions. I made her laugh, and in turn, she made me fall in love with her even more.

"Rae, do you realize that you left me a little over two hours ago and yet you've spent almost a quarter of that time talking to me?"

"I always want to talk to you." After a pause, she sighed and finally asked, "Okay, can you come and get me? I guess whatever he's talking about is much more important than discussing Braden. We're at that burger house on McDermott."

"Of course, babe. I'm leaving now." I grappled for my car keys and went back inside to tell the guys.

"Thanks. I'll wait out front for you."

Through the line, I heard Adam's voice growling from the background, "What the hell, Ree Ree? You didn't even finish eating."

"You were busy, and now I'm ready to go home. There isn't anything left for us to discuss," she responded.

"Like hell," he said. "Tell your guard dog I'll bring you home when I'm ready."

"Too late, your *guard dog* is already on the way, babe," I shouted through the line.

- Nineteen -

RAEGAN -

R aegan, why did you do that?" Adam looked at me with anger and confusion.

"Why are you making me do this? Why are you even here?" I raised my voice and held my hands out, indicating our location.

"Because I miss you. I've always missed you."

"Bullshit, you left! You left the second you found out I was pregnant."

"I was nineteen, Raegan. How the hell can you hold that against me?"

"Because he was your child. Because you were supposed to love me."

"He's still my child. I still love you."

"No. He could have been, but he never was." I chose to ignore his last statement. "You aren't even on the birth certificate, nor does he hold your last name." He cringed at my words, and I was shocked he actually had the balls to think he deserved any of those privileges. "I don't think you hold any claims, but I want you to sign a parental rights termination, just in case."

"Hell, no!" he growled.

"I can't have you popping in and out of our lives whenever you're feeling lonely."

"Raegan, stop it."

"I'll find a way to cover all of the legal expenses; you won't have to worry about any of that. Just sign the papers," I continued on, ignoring his protests.

Suddenly, he had my shoulders in his hands and he begged, "Please, Raegan. We can be us again."

"You want me. Not Braden. Please understand what you're saying. You don't care about Braden and you can't have me. Please don't drag him through this drama."

"I miss you, honey," he whispered. He moved in closer and all at once, I realized why he was doing it.

"*Don't you fucking dare!*" Lane's voice roared from across the parking lot. Adam's hands left my shoulders instantly, and I thanked the heavens for Lane's timing.

He came running at full speed from where his car was parked haphazardly near the curb. Jace pushed out of the passenger side, and Jaxon pulled up in his truck behind them. He had brought the cavalry. Adam's eyes widened when he saw the three of them quickly approaching. They were a magnificent sight.

"Who the hell are you hanging out with these days, Raegan?" Adam questioned harshly.

"My family." I smiled at the guys who had come to help Lane. Not that he needed any help taking care of Adam, but I knew that they were coming to prevent him from doing something stupid. I moved into Lane's large embrace and loved the comfort he exuded for only me.

"You good, babe?" he asked into my ear.

"I am now."

"What's up," Jace said as he reached us, but it wasn't really a question.

"Ready, Rae?" Jaxon asked when he reached his brother's side.

I let go of Lane and looked toward Adam. "Please, just sign the papers when they come and let us be." I threaded my fingers back through Lane's and pulled him away.

"Ree, please don't do this." Adam's desperation was bleeding through his voice. "I've been waiting years for you. Don't throw away what we once had for some guy . . . you just met."

"We didn't just meet. I've known him," I called back.

"Don't bother, love," Lane said gently down to me. "He's egging you on."

"It wasn't fucking supposed to be like this!" Adam roared.

"Ignore it, Raegan," Jaxon offered. "Let's just get back to every-one."

With Lane's hand resting on my lower back, I straightened my spine and stayed on track for the car. He guided me toward the passenger door, and I looked back one more time at Adam, who had moved forward with us.

"Good-bye."

Adam was rocking back and forth nervously with a pained expression on his face. I just wanted to get away from him. I could tell he thought that this was what he wanted, but I'm sure he'd been fine without me for years.

"Get in, babe. I want to go home," I told Lane and gently pushed him in the direction of the driver's side.

Adam groaned loudly. "We were supposed to be together again. You were going to take me back! Remember when I came to visit you again in New York?"

I did, unfortunately. He had come to see me a week before we'd been taken. He'd said he wanted to talk and I'd agreed to meet him.

I didn't know what he wanted to tell me, and I had no idea what my feelings were when it came to him. I cringed to think that more than likely I would have taken him back. At least now I knew better.

"Yeah, I do remember, but I guess fate stepped in . . . in her own cruel way."

"That wasn't supposed to fucking happen!" he roared. "They weren't supposed to take you or that little girl. It was just supposed to be the boy."

My entire body turned to ice and my head snapped up to face him. Jaxon moved to my side in an instant, and Jace barreled around the car toward Lane.

"What did you just say?" I spoke each word with a punch of rage.

"It wasn't supposed to happen like that . . ." he continued.

I moved forward, but Jaxon grabbed my upper arms to hold me off. "Cut to the chase, dude," Jaxon ground out. I looked back at Lane, who had gone as white as a ghost. Jace was barring him from moving forward, but it didn't seem as if Lane was physically capable of moving anyway.

"It was just a bet," Adam said simply. "I gambled against Flores in a fight, but I didn't have the money to pay him off. I did have something he wanted more, though."

I lunged, but my movements were pointless with Jaxon containing me. Mentally, I was clawing his eyes out. "Please, don't say what I think you're saying!" Tears rushed to my eyes and the world blurred before me.

"Don't you understand how much I love you? How much I wanted it to be just the two of us again? That's why I did it," Adam hollered back. "Flores was a powerful guy. He always bitched about his old lady wanting kids. Well, I had a kid!" His words were knives, and yet he had no fucking idea that he was killing me slowly.

"*You didn't have a kid! I did! Lane did!*" I pointed across the car. "*You had nothing!*"

Adam turned with wide eyes toward the man who could easily crush him with one blow. "That girl was yours? *You* were the police officer?"

Lane's body hurled across the hood of the car in an action that would have made the Dukes of Hazzard jealous. Jace couldn't react quickly enough to stop him, and Jaxon was too busy pulling me from his disastrous path. Lane's landing was flawless as his feet planted him inches away from Adam's frozen form.

"You gambled your son in a bet with Flores and lost?" Lane snarled.

"Flores *thinks* I lost. You don't win against a guy like that and live. I gambled something that he would think I was losing," Adam responded, trembling slightly as he spoke.

I had always known Adam was a gambler. Hell, he used to tell me all the time about his wins. I was the naïve one who thought he was in Vegas just working some blackjack tables. Not this . . . never *this* kind of gambling.

Adam's body hit the ground before any of us even realized that Lane had just punched him square in the nose. Blood poured from his nostrils, and he moaned on the ground while trying to scamper away like a petrified crab.

"You're an idiot!" I screamed down at Adam. "You *did* lose! He took both of us!"

"Yeah, that wasn't the fucking plan. His bitch had to get involved, and I guess when she met you in the park, her greedy ass wanted all of you. *You* were mine, Rae. First, that boy took you and then Flores took you."

In the blink of an eye, Lane flung himself on top of Adam and pummeled his face. I turned and tucked my head into Jaxon's chest to shield my eyes from the carnage.

"Please, stop him," I whispered to Jace, who stood directly next to us.

"The guy got his daughter kidnapped . . . I don't know if I can . . ." Jace stared with wild eyes down at the mess before us. Jaxon shoved me into Jace's arms, and I vaguely heard him tell his brother to call the police.

Jaxon grunted as he manhandled Lane with all of his strength, pulling him from Adam's limp body.

"How did they get into my apartment?" Lane barked down at Adam.

I peeked over at Adam as he groaned while writhing on the ground. I didn't want to see all the blood I knew would be covering his face and Lane's fists, but I wanted to know the answer just as much as Lane did. I watched Lane's body in my peripheral vision as it hovered over the man who I now knew had destroyed my life as I once knew it. When Lane jumped to attack again, Adam cried out.

"I took her keys!" His words were mixed with wet gurgles and I felt almost sick at the sound. "When I came to visit her, I stole her keys. I made a copy and tossed them back in her stroller when I saw her at the park."

I thought I had gone crazy when those keys disappeared. I'd turned the apartment upside down, and when I easily found them in the stroller later, I thought I had just somehow overlooked them. But he had stolen them and then allowed strangers to come in and take his son. I lunged for the flowerbed near us and threw up my entire dinner. Although it hadn't been much, it was all gone now. Jace held back my hair and supported me by my arms. How could anyone betray someone they supposedly loved so much?

I heard Adam grunt again, and I assumed Lane had landed another of his deadly blows. I prayed that he wouldn't kill him. Adam deserved to rot in prison.

"Jace, Lane can't go to jail. What about Kate?" I moaned.

"Jax has him. Adam's . . . passed out," Jace whispered in return.

"Passed out or . . ." I couldn't finish.

"He's breathing."

I sighed and slumped into Jace's arms. Slowly, I turned and saw Lane staring down at his hands, looking as if he couldn't figure out how they had become so bloody. He genuinely appeared puzzled, and his confusion tore at my heart. I pulled out of Jace's arms and stepped in front of my heartbroken man.

This wasn't fair. It answered so many questions, but if given the choice, I think I would have chosen to never know. Not this—this was too sick.

"Lane . . ." I breathed. "Oh God, I can't believe this." I reached out for his shirt and he stepped back quickly.

"No," he clipped out, "bl-blood." His hands were covered in it, his shirt had splatters, and some of it had even reached his face. I dug around in my purse quickly for a tissue. When I reached up again—this time to help wipe his cheek—he turned away from me.

The sirens began to sound in the distance and Jace moved forward. "One of us should take Raegan back."

"No—" I started to protest, but then stared at the pained look on Lane's face as he looked down at Adam's prone body.

"Give him a moment," Jace whispered. "He hates fighting unless it's in the ring. A guy with his strength, he knows he can't let that out and he just did. He needs some time."

"He's right, Rae." Jaxon joined us. "It's getting late, and the kids will wonder."

And they would. Especially Braden. He's a stickler about schedules and he knew I would return before bedtime. I swallowed harshly and looked back at Lane. Staying a safe distance from him, so he wouldn't feel uncomfortable, I approached.

"I'm going to give you your moment. But I'm so sorry, Lane," I whispered.

As if my words hadn't even penetrated his brain at all, he croaked, "Please, leave Kate. Once I'm cleaned off, I need to hold her." I looked at his face to try and understand what he had meant, but he moved away and continued pacing. He was in a state and I hated leaving him.

"You should take her," Jaxon suggested to Jace. "I'm pretty familiar with the cops in this town." A brief smirk crossed his face before he wiped it away.

"That's no lie. They handcuffed you enough times in high school," Jace responded drily.

"I never actually got arrested, though," Jaxon jested. I handed him my little package of tissues so he could help Lane clean up a bit. I dug around further in my purse and also found a tube of hand sanitizer he could use. Jaxon nodded in appreciation.

When we climbed up in Jaxon's truck, Jace turned the key and peeled out of the parking lot. The second my seat belt clicked in place and I looked over to see Lane's hunched form in my mirror, I lost it. Big gulping breaths seized my throat, and giant streams of tears poured from my eyes.

"What do you think I should do, Jace? What would *you* want?" I asked through my hiccupping sobs.

He cringed and said, "I have no idea. I think maybe he just needs a little time to process this."

"Oh, God, he'll never look at me the same again."

"Don't say that. He loves you," he consoled.

"No, think about it. He just found out that I was practically the reason his daughter was abducted. He'll always think about that when he looks at me. Put it this way . . . Jocelyn is practically the same age Kate was when she was abducted. What if that had happened to you?" I don't know why I said it like that, but my emotions were on overdrive. "He told me to leave Kate. Does that mean he wants me to leave?"

"Look, I've never handled emotional situations well. Hell, I once pushed Audrey away when things got tough. I'm probably not the guy to go to for this type of thing."

"He told me to leave Kate . . ." I repeated. "He doesn't plan on seeing me when he gets home."

Jace kept quiet the remainder of the drive, and I used that time to sort out my thundering emotions and calm my quiet sobs. I couldn't let Kate and Braden see me this torn up. I wiped my tears dry. With my ring fingers, I massaged around my eyes, starting from my cheeks and working them out in little circles. I couldn't go back with swollen eyes; Braden would know. Who was I kidding? Braden would know, regardless.

- TWENTY -

LANE -

Blood. It was splattered across my shirt and covered my hands. Even though I could tell it was mostly from his nose, it still made my stomach turn over. Those suckers really leaked when knocked just the right way. I'd seen it happen, and I had been covered in it just like this a time or two, except every other time, a bell would chime or a ref would call for us to separate.

The part that worried me the most is that I hadn't even fully unleashed. It had been building up to that point, though. If he hadn't passed out so quickly, I would probably still be working him over. Jaxon and Jace could have pulled me away a million times, but my fists still would have sought out his face.

I watched a trail of red liquid glide down my fingers and drip with a small splash on the ground. It hit me that I had done all of that with Raegan standing only a few feet away. She'd had to witness the rage inside of me that I tried to keep calm every single day. Ironically, boxing had helped me control my strength and harness it into something I was really good at. But I needed the restrictions. I craved the rules and the ropes that told me when to go hard and when to pull back. Not this concrete parking lot free-for-all.

I heard the sirens blaring closer, and the anger I felt toward myself reached an astronomical level. I thought I had been thinking of Kate. Of Raegan and Braden. I thought I had been avenging them somehow. But would Kate be proud of me for successfully pummeling the reason she had been taken from me for the first four years of her life if it landed me in jail for assault?

Jaxon shoved tissues and a miniature bottle of sanitizer in my hands and mumbled something about cleaning myself off. I ducked into my car and quickly scrubbed the carnage from my hands. The tissues flaked, and it took even more time for me to remove all the pieces than it did to get rid of the blood. I bathed my hands in the sanitizer until the bottle was practically empty.

"I'm fucked," I groaned when Jaxon moved to the open window.

"Nah, I think I can handle this. See that guy getting out of the cruiser? He's put me in handcuffs more times than I can count," he stated with a chuckle.

"Dude, that doesn't sound like you got this. It actually sounds like the opposite, in fact."

"I used to put some excitement in this boring town for him. He likes me."

I groaned at his less-than-reassuring words. "Where's Rae?" I managed to rasp out. I couldn't look at her earlier . . . I didn't want to see the disappointment or—God forbid—fear in her eyes.

"Probably at Jace's." He didn't sound too confident in his words, and my heart squeezed tighter than my fists. How could one single moment fuck up everything? Kate, Raegan, and Braden had become everything in my life that I didn't realize I'd wanted. They were my sunrise and sunset—every single day. It was the four of us, and I wouldn't recover if it became any less than that.

I reached behind me in the backseat, praying for a spare shirt. Thankfully, my gym bag sat on the floorboard, so I quickly tossed on an old, sweaty shirt, welcoming it if it meant I could shed the bloody one.

When I exited the car, Adam was pushing up off the ground, holding his shirt up to his nose. Looking at him only caused me more agony and fury. If he made any eye contact with me whatsoever, I'd maul him again. I proceeded to the opposite side of my car so that I couldn't even catch a glimpse of him in the corner of my eye.

"Jaxon Riley . . . boy, tell me you didn't do this mess." The sheriff casually pointed to Adam's scrawny, crumbled form.

"You know me, Mack—I can never pass up an opportunity to bring some spontaneity to your day," Jaxon responded with a cheesy-ass grin, and I was baffled by the dynamic between these two.

"Tell me what happened and why I gotta get the damn parking lot cleaned up," the sheriff's gruff voice replied.

Jaxon marched toward the older man, and I watched as his body straightened up and began to look serious. At least this wasn't a complete laughing matter to him—I really needed him to help me out here. Adam didn't move from his spot on the curb when he was caught in the questioning glare of the uniformed sheriff.

After thirty long fucking minutes, the sheriff, joined by Jaxon, paraded back to stand over Adam, who had finally gotten his nosebleed under control. I moved around the car a little closer, hoping the law enforcement presence would keep me in check.

"You do what he told me you did?" Mack barked down at him.

"Well, seeing as I don't know what the hell he told ya, I can't say. But probably." At least he wasn't going to deny it.

"That's sick," Mack replied, holding his duty belt. This whole calm, cool, and collected approach baffled me. Not once in New

York had I witnessed an officer approach a scene this casually, as if he had all day to chat.

Adam shrugged. "I've done worse." My muscles locked and I called upon every ounce of self-restraint I possessed to help me stay where I was. I spread my fingers out against my legs to keep them from clenching.

I cannot kill him. I cannot kill him. I cannot kill him.

"You ever seen Raegan? If you did, you'd understand," Adam said as he slowly stood to his feet.

"Ain't no damn girl worth my son. I don't care what she looks like or how good she can blow me," Mack growled. Adam opened his disgusting mouth, and I knew this would be the moment I would get locked away for life. Mack quickly jumped and shoved Adam face-forward against my car before pulling his handcuffs from his belt. "Do not respond to that. You've already said enough," he warned before he began reading him his rights.

Once Adam was properly secured, Mack left him leaning up against the side of my car. Shit, now I was definitely going to have to get another vehicle. I would never look at this one again without thinking of this bastard dripping his blood all over it.

"How the hell am I supposed to explain his busted face?" Mack asked Jaxon while eyeing me.

"We found him that way?" Jaxon shrugged with a smart-ass smirk.

"Boy, you've already pulled that one on me before!" He wagged his finger at Jaxon with a smile.

"Come on, give Lane some slack. The fucker just admitted to conspiring to have his daughter kidnapped," Jaxon argued.

"Hey! The girl and Raegan were not part of the plan. It was only supposed to be the boy. I'm not going down for all three," Adam called out.

"Don't you understand those rights I just told you? Keep your mouth shut, 'cause you're just diggin' a bigger hole for yourself," Mack hollered back.

"I'm fucked, regardless," he said with a dispassionate shrug.

"Not another word about *any* of them," I growled.

"I see you're married." Adam turned to Jaxon, completely ignoring me. "You're a good-looking dude, and I'll bet the Mrs. is smokin'." Jaxon nodded his head in agreement, but I could see the cautious look on his face, not knowing where this was going. "You would do anything to keep her, wouldn't you?" Adam questioned.

"If you're trying to get me to say that I would have my own son kidnapped so that I could have my wife all to myself, then you can get your fucking convoluted sense of camaraderie elsewhere, you asshole," Jaxon barked. "The day my wife tells me she's carrying my child, I'll worship her every move . . . hell, I'll be her shadow. When that day comes, I'll be fucking thankful for the honor that I created another human being with her. And every day from that day forward will be about *them* and how I will make them happy—both of them."

"Damn, you have grown up," Mack said with a smile. "I almost teared up."

"Just take him in," Jaxon said, shaking his head.

"You gonna press assault charges on this guy?" Mack asked Adam, pointing with his thumb at me.

"Will it lessen my charges?" Adam asked arrogantly.

"Not even by a day."

"Then no. I don't care for all that extra bullshit. He hits like a fucking bitch anyway." Oh, *now* the big, tough guy is going to come out and play. His pride will get him killed one day, and I won't be sad about that at all. What did Rae ever see in this guy?

Mack shoved Adam's body into his beat-up old cruiser and sauntered back our way.

"How's your mom doing?" he asked, looking at Jaxon.

"Please tell me you aren't interested in her too. If one more guy asks me if my mom is single, I'm gonna start throwing punches," Jaxon threatened. That got a small laugh out of me.

Mack shrugged his shoulders coyly. "I'll see her around." When Jaxon groaned, Mack turned his attention toward me. "How's your daughter doing?"

"She's perfect."

He nodded his head. "Good . . . good to hear. That was some tough news, son. Hug 'em all tight tonight." His words sounded exactly like something my dad would tell me right now, and I reached out to shake his hand in appreciation. "You'll need questioning, so don't go headin' outta town."

"He used to be a cop; I'm sure he knows the drill, Mack," Jaxon added.

"Yeah?" Mack's eyebrows perked up. "Need a job?"

I chuckled and shook my head. "No thanks. After the last four years I've had, I look forward to my boring desk job."

Mack nodded his head as if he understood and then lifted his chin toward Jaxon before walking away. Jaxon feigned a jab at me. "There isn't anything boring about working at the Riley Group, you ungrateful bastard," he smirked while rounding the side of my car.

"Thanks, man . . ." I started. "You really saved my ass. I could easily be sitting in the back of that patrol car right now, so I appreciate it."

"That fucker deserved it, and I would have been honored to bail your ass out of jail," he said with a shrug. We both sat down in the car, and I reached out to shake hands with him.

"Let's head out . . . I want to get back to my family."

~

With a new set of clothes on and a small bag packed for Kate, I stormed out of the house and ripped open my passenger door. Jaxon had taken over the driver's seat, claiming I wasn't in the right state of mind to handle the roads. My chest was squeezing in on itself, and I couldn't get my hands to stop shaking.

"Where the hell did she go?" I barked.

"Dude, calm down . . ." Jaxon tried to placate me.

"No, fuck that. If this were Emerson, you'd be blowing up! Braden's terrarium is gone."

"Oh . . . okay . . ." I knew he didn't understand my words.

"His favorite thing in the world. If that's gone, then something's up. What the fuck is up, man?"

"Okay, I don't really know yet. I know that Raegan was upset. Jace and I told her to give you a moment to cool down. Let's just get back to their house and I'm sure we can figure this all out."

"You told her to give me a moment?" I was incredulous.

"Yeah . . ."

"And she listened?"

"Well, when you weren't responding to her . . ." he trailed off. Raegan never left anything alone. She always pounced on me to fix problems, right there and then. What was going through her mind? I had been in a state of shock after I beat Adam down, so I don't remember hearing anybody saying anything to me. I guess Rae could have been trying to talk to me . . . but I just didn't hear it. There had been blood everywhere, and I just couldn't forgive myself for erupting like that in front of her.

"God, I freaked her out, didn't I? I was so angry . . ." I tried to focus and remember what exactly had happened after Adam passed out. I didn't think I'd said anything to upset her . . . hell, I didn't remember saying anything at all. "She wouldn't take Kate . . ." I wasn't sure why I said that out loud. Raegan would never do anything like that to me.

"No, she wouldn't," Jax confirmed.

"I can't stand the other option either."

"What's that?" he asked, turning onto the dirt driveway.

"Her *leaving* Kate. Leaving me."

Before he could push the gear into park, I went flying up the porch steps and shoved inside Audrey and Jace's door. Just as I stomped into the foyer, a little blur flew past me. I looked down and watched Kate, in stocking feet, using the wood floor as her personal skating rink. She ran past me again and then stopped before quickly scurrying back in front of me.

"I'm skating, Dad!"

"I see that," I said, chuckling.

The instant I saw her brilliant blue eyes, a large piece of my heart unclenched and I scooped her up. Her arms wrapped around my neck and we squeezed each other as though we hadn't just been eating dinner together only a few hours ago. This is how she greeted me every time I went away, either to work or just to the gym. How could I ever live without out this again? How had I not suffocated, living without it for so long? No matter what happened with Rae, she would be my constant, and I swore I would be hers.

But I didn't plan on letting her mom and brother go anywhere either.

"Daddy," she began quickly, "we get to have special Daddy-and-Kate time. Mommy is having special time with Braden. I really miss Bubba. But I got to play with the baby. I even helped Auntie Audrey give her a bath and she really liked it. She kicked her feet really hard! Do you know when they're coming back?"

A small part of me had hoped that Rae and Braden were in the house somewhere—that they hadn't actually gone anywhere. But her words confirmed what Braden's missing terrarium had already told me. They weren't here.

I looked up and noticed everyone was sitting in the family room, watching us. The whole crew was there, minus two of the most important ones.

"How about you take this bag to Aunt Em and have her help you get into your swimsuit. We're going to have special Daddy-and-Kate time."

Her face lit up and she squirmed out of my arms, bouncing on her toes when they reached the floor. "We can swim when it's dark?" she shrieked excitedly. "Can we eat ice cream too?"

With a laugh, I asked, "Does that sound like fun to you?"

"So much fun!"

"Well, then, of course we'll swim at night and eat ice cream too! Go on, get your suit on and meet me out back."

She skipped away, half sliding and half hopping across the wood floor, straight toward Em and Quinn. I pointed to Audrey and Jace and nodded my head toward the backyard. Jace flipped on the pool lights as we headed out, which cast a black glow across the darkened concrete. Their pool had a black bottom, which at nighttime made it appear like glass on the ground.

I tugged my shirt over my shoulders and decided my gym shorts would have to do for swimming tonight. When Audrey returned from lighting candles, I approached them both.

"Where is she?"

"At a hotel," Jace responded.

My fingers moved raggedly through my hair and I looked to Audrey with clear stress in my eyes. "I freaked her out, right?"

"You?" she questioned. "I only got the scene secondhand, but I think she believes you'll never be able to look at her the same."

"Why the fuck would she think that?"

"Dude, that guy just admitted that Raegan was the reason your daughter was kidnapped." Leave it to Jace to cut to the chase.

"That disgusting asshole was the reason. Not Rae," I spat out.

Audrey dashed toward me, slamming into my chest and throwing her arms around my neck. I instinctively squeezed her tightly.

"You could've been hurt. You could've gone to jail, you idiot," she babbled.

"I know, I know. It was bad."

"I think you should really think hard before you go chasing after her," she said, completely shocking me.

"What the hell do I have to think about?"

"The situation." She gestured toward the house. "Your daughter was kidnapped, Lane. Raegan's boyfriend was the one who made that happen. Think hard about your feelings toward that. When you look at Jocelyn when she's a year old and she's just starting to walk, you'll think about what Kate looked like when she was that age. Will you look at Raegan and wonder, if she hadn't been your nanny, would you have lost all those years?"

"So Raegan should be punished for her scumbag ex? Which, by the way, punishes all four of us?"

"No, I don't think that all. But I do know how resentment can build over time. Even irrational, nonsensical resentment. I just want you to know your true feelings now, so they don't surprise you later."

"Take the night to process everything you were told tonight, man. Let Raegan process it as well. I know she feels terrible," Jace added.

I began pacing the length of the black pool. How could they tell me she was feeling terrible and expect me to sleep on it tonight?

"You paid for her hotel?" I asked. He didn't answer so I helped him out. "I know she didn't. I found her wallet on the floorboard of my car. She must have left it there earlier today, and she didn't even have it with her at dinner."

"Yeah, I paid for it." He sighed.

"You're sending me that bill." Before he could protest, I said, "That's my family. I take care of them. Now which hotel is she at?"

"Lane, you already promised Kate you would be with her tonight," Audrey warned.

"And that's exactly where I'll be until she exhausts herself from all the fun. After that, I'm going to get Raegan and Braden. Now please, what hotel is she at?"

"She's at the NYLO Dallas, but I don't know her room number," Jace responded.

"That's fine. I'll just call her."

"She left your phone here," Audrey said, cringing.

"You guys really aren't making this easy on me tonight," I groaned.

A few beats later, my little ball of energy came flying out the patio doors with a bright pink swimsuit on. It was difficult, but I managed to put the majority of my thoughts aside so I could enjoy our Daddy/daughter night. Worries about Raegan and Braden were still in the back of my mind, though, relentlessly taunting me, reminding me that I needed to go get them.

- TWENTY-ONE -

RAEGAN -

The hotel where Jace and Audrey had made reservations for us was a really interesting place. The rooms were set up as if they were downtown New York City lofts, complete with exposed brick walls and modern furnishings. The walls that weren't covered in light red brick were industrial concrete. The bedroom area held a king-size, all-white bed, and there were deep purple curtains adorning the windows. The living room had a modern couch, which pulled out into a full-size bed that faced a huge flat-screen television.

It was almost one in the morning, and I was still lounging on the pullout bed with Braden, because the king-size only reminded me of strong arms that should have been holding me from behind. Braden had fallen asleep a few hours earlier. Once I knew he was out for the night, I finally let the tears fall.

I always understood that I might not have known Adam as well as I thought I had, but never would I have expected this from him. I mean, I never pressured him to tell me where he was heading off to or even how he got the money he seemed to always have. I had just never thought to ask, honestly. Money had never been a big player in my life. My aunt made enough to keep the apartment and buy food. We never had cable, and she tried to use the electricity as little as possible. So I'd never cared whether or not Adam had money.

How could I have misjudged him so poorly, though? He bet our child in a game with Flores. He bet our child, knowing he would lose . . . *hoping* he would lose. All so he could have me to himself. My only consolation in all of this was that Flores's wife was greedy and took me too. Not only would I have been lost without Braden, but she did me a favor by getting me away from Adam. This terrible kidnapping didn't seem so terrible for me and Braden anymore, but I couldn't help thinking about Lane and the fact that he should have never lost his daughter, and then ultimately . . . his wife.

But if the kidnapping hadn't happened, I never would have been thrown into a situation that allowed Lane and me to fall in love with each other. I was shown just how wonderful a man could truly be. How deeply a man could love his children—and his woman. But now I was going to have to look him in the eyes, knowing I was the reason for the years he had to endure without his daughter.

A fresh round of silent sobs rattled through me, and I tried to mop up the tears with the sleeves of Lane's shirt. When Jace took us by the house to grab some clothes, I couldn't help myself when I saw the shirt that Lane had worn yesterday tossed across our bed. It still smelled like him, and I was almost able to imagine his big arms wrapped around me and his soft whispers in my ear telling me all the ways he loved me.

I hated giving him this moment to himself. It went against everything inside of me to step back and let him come to terms with what he had learned. But maybe Jace, Jaxon, and Audrey were right. I just needed to give him time.

A soft tapping sound jolted me upright, and I paused to see if I was actually hearing something or if it had been noises from the city outside. Right around the time I had convinced myself that the sound was coming from the streets, I heard it again. *Tap, tap, tap.* With a speed I didn't know I possessed, I raced for the door and gazed through the peephole. The most gorgeous sight stood there with his eyes glaring at the door between us.

I swiped my fingers underneath my eyes and tried to scrub any running mascara away. I flipped the deadbolt and quickly pulled the chain free. As I was pulling the door open, Lane pushed his way in. He took a long, hard look at me, and I gulped at his intense gaze. His hair was wet and he was breathing heavily, and I couldn't help noticing that he didn't look too happy to see me.

With a cold politeness, he moved me to the side and scrutinized the little living room. He tapped Braden's terrarium on the dining table as he passed it. Braden had insisted that he wouldn't be able to sleep without it tonight. I watched as Lane quickly made his way across the living area and then lowered his body softly onto the pullout next to Braden.

I knew that Kate and Braden hadn't really understood the reason for us spending time away from each other tonight, but they took it in stride when we were saying good-bye. I had tried to explain it away as a fun night of one-on-one time, and with Braden it had worked for about the first hour. While I made a true effort to have a good time with him at the hotel, he still asked about Kate and Lane until the moment he fell asleep. Even worse, I missed Kate something terrible. I didn't know how I would ever be able to *not* live with her.

Lane pulled Braden's sleeping body out from under the covers and into his embrace. His massive arms surrounded my little boy's body like a giant, warm cocoon. He pressed Braden's head to his chest, and there was a deep sadness written across his face as he hugged my son tightly. I watched from the doorway as he rocked Braden back and forth in his arms.

Braden's hand materialized from its entrapment in Lane's arms and patted his scruffy face.

"Daddy?" Braden croaked with a sleepy voice. I gasped at the word, and Lane's eyes shot wide. He squeezed him tighter and buried his face in Braden's shoulder.

I could barely hear Lane's voice, but I was able to make out that he responded, "I'm here." He looked as if he were breathing Braden in. "I'm here, I'm here," he repeated.

Braden had never—not ever—called anyone *Daddy*. We had never spoken of a father for him, and for him to say that word all on his own, broke me—especially in light of this evening. I had to hold a hand out to brace myself against the wall as my whole body shook from my heaving breaths.

I must have stood there for at least a good ten minutes before Lane finally lowered Braden's sleeping form back underneath the covers and meticulously tucked him back in. He tried to quietly remove himself from the bed without any of the springs squeaking. When he was free, he strode purposefully back toward me.

"Lane . . ."

"Don't."

My legs were in the air in one swift movement and my arms shot out to grab hold of his neck to balance myself. Without a word or even much emotion on his face, he carried me to the bedroom, closing and locking the door behind us. I shoved my face into the crook of his neck, and eventually my legs made their way around his waist. I was only wearing his T-shirt and my panties, so I shivered when his warm hands cupped my ass in support.

The bed dipped as he climbed on top with me securely wrapped around him. He pulled back the sheets and then laid us down on our sides, facing each other.

"Did you hear what he called me?" His hoarse whisper brushed across my cheeks. I nodded against his chest and held my arms tightly around him. I could hear the awe in his voice, as if he didn't believe what he had actually heard. "Don't ever do that again. Don't ever leave me. Don't ever take him from me. He's mine just as much as you are mine." His hand clutched the back of my head as though he didn't want to let me go. It wasn't necessary, though, because I never wanted to be anywhere else. "Please, just don't ever do that again."

"I wasn't leaving. I was just giving you time to process everything."

"You *never* give me time to process. It's one of the things about you that I love so much," he whispered. "Just don't do that. I don't ever want to come back and find you guys gone. I can't handle that."

"Oh, Lane." I sighed.

"His terrarium was gone. That's how I knew."

I squeezed in as close as I possibly could, still trying to let my haywire nerves get the memo that he was here and in my arms.

"You told me to leave Kate . . . I just thought . . . you didn't want to see me when you got back."

He groaned painfully and said, "Babe, I'm sorry. I was speaking nonsense. All I could think about was that asshole causing my daughter to be taken from me. I just wanted to hold her and never let anyone touch her again. I didn't know if you would go back home, and I knew I needed to go by Audrey's. I'm sorry; I shouldn't have said that. But I would never—and I mean never—not want to see you."

I kissed his lips and let his words filter in, erasing any doubts I had been having about us.

"I'm sorry I scared you tonight. I was furious at him for everything, and his mouth just kept spewing more and more shit and I snapped. I never snap, I swear." His eyes were pained, and I couldn't believe he felt any ounce of remorse for what he had done to Adam.

"Adam deserved worse, Lane."

"Yeah, but you shouldn't have had to witness it. I don't like that side of me," he mumbled.

"The side that is fiercely protective of your family? The side that would risk jail time in order to right a wrong? I love all your sides, Lane. *All* of them. But please, don't ever risk getting locked up again. I'd rather Adam go to jail all in one piece than you guys becoming cellmates. We need you here." I ran my hands through his now-drying strands.

"I promise I won't take that risk ever again. I want to be wherever you guys are."

"Lane, I need to apologize. I was the reason—"

"Don't you dare."

"Lane, if I hadn't been in your life, you would have seen Kate grow up. You would have seen her laugh, her first words, her first tooth . . ." I sighed heavily as I let the information finally sink in for myself. "Ash would still be alive."

"Look, babe, we can sit here and 'shoulda,' 'woulda,' 'coulda' all night, but that's not going to change anything. Don't let that sick bastard let you believe for one second that any of this was because of you."

"I'm not saying it's my fault . . ." I whispered.

"Not in so many words. But you are placing some blame on yourself. This is how life worked out for us. It sucked really bad for a while. It was awful. I'm sure you and I both have cried ourselves to sleep more nights than most people cry in their whole lives. But now . . . now it's incredible. Can you honestly tell me you had one day while you were with Adam that was better than any of the days we've shared together so far?" He pushed me back only a few inches so we could look each other in the eyes.

"*Today* was better than any day I ever had with him."

"Damn . . ." he laughed. "I'll admit, I was a cocky bastard and knew you would tell me that you hadn't, but man . . . I wasn't expecting that." His grin melted me.

"It's the truth," I offered.

"I know our friends try and help, but please promise me in the future you'll go with your gut. The girl I love so much wouldn't have run off to this place."

"I didn't want to."

"And I knew that. I panicked for a little bit before realizing you would never do that to me." He moved in closer and gently kissed my lips.

"Thank you for coming after us, though. How did you find our room anyway? Jace didn't stick around for check-in."

"There's a girl working the front desk." He shrugged as if seducing a receptionist was an everyday occurrence for him. "Oh, here." He reached in between us and dug deep into his pocket. He pulled out a slip of paper and handed it to me. "I don't actually need this."

I glanced at the little yellow page and snapped my eyes back up to him. "Oh, God, what did you do to the poor girl? She even kissed it with bright red lipstick and everything." My hands wadded up the page with her number and lips.

"I didn't do anything," he said, laughing. "I merely asked for your room number. I thought she was writing it down for me, but then she handed me that. Do you really think I was going to argue with her? I would use all of my charms if it meant finding you."

"Hmm . . . that sounds pretty possessive of you. And it sounds like something Jaxon and Jace would do."

"Well, maybe I should start taking some pointers, because they're in their own beds with their women tonight. I had to chase mine down." He began to run his lips up the side of my neck, and I tilted my head to give him more room to work. "Don't be mistaken, Rae. Just because I let some douches at a bar have their fun flirting with you, that doesn't mean I won't come out swinging when I think things have gone too far. You're mine. You sleeping in a bed that I'm not in, it's just not happening, baby."

"I love you," I breathed out.

"I have a son." His awed tone made me smile.

"I'm glad *someone* understands the significance of having him in their life." For as long as I live, I would never be able to understand why a father would not want his child.

"I do, baby. Trust me: I will treasure him every day. I would never let anything happen to him. I *promise* that I will always love and protect you guys. No more holding back because I'm afraid of someone forcing me to break my word. I promise the three of you that you have me forever."

"I believe you, Lane. And I promise we'll do the same for you."

"You've already done everything for me," he responded, while placing more of those delicious little nips across my collarbone. His eyes met mine again, and he said, "I love you. I love you so much that sometimes I feel as if it's never enough. I'll always want more of you. Every day I wish that I had found you sooner so I could love you longer."

My mouth moved against his, trying to show him the words I could not articulate. His warm hands caused a fire to spread across my skin, and I thanked all the powers in the universe for aligning our paths.

"I like you in my shirt, babe," he said, as he began pulling it over my head.

"It smelled like you." My hands found the hem of the shirt he was wearing and brought it up over his head.

The second we were both topless, we stared at each other, just drinking each other in. I looked at his hard, chiseled chest that he worked so meticulously on every day. Each curve was finely tuned, and I still couldn't believe he was all mine.

He was the first to move, and his warm hands cupped my breasts roughly. I moaned in complete satisfaction. His body moved down mine, slowly kissing a lazy trail down my chest.

"This is gonna have to be quick, babe, if we're gonna get any sleep tonight," he murmured against my stomach. His hands moved down my sides until he hooked his fingers under my panties and pulled them down my legs.

"Why?" I whimpered.

"Because I'm waking you guys up at the crack of dawn. I want to get back before Kate wakes up."

That sobered me a fraction. "Oh . . . we could leave now." A part of me wanted to, while another part of me was screaming at me to keep my mouth shut.

"We already paid for this huge bed. I had to hunt you down after this god-awful night. We aren't leaving until I've made sure you understand how much I love you—how much I never want you to run from me again, and that I'd do anything to keep the three of you safe and happy." His body moved down mine until he looked up at me from between my legs.

I let my head fall back and enjoyed whatever this man had to give. And God, did I enjoy it. With his mouth, his hands, and his heart, he helped ease the pain caused by the horrible events of our past. Together, we had come to terms with the hand we'd been dealt and maybe even become thankful for fate—as twisted as that bitch could be. But we had both finally been given a hand worth fighting to possess, and how could anyone not be grateful for that?

- EPILOGUE-

LANE, *Ten Months Later* -

"Christ, Raegan, finish it up already," I complained while hunched over.

"It has to be perfect," she mumbled.

"It's six letters, baby. Write them, so we can finish this."

"Lane, this is permanent. Let me get it exactly right." I didn't think her cold hands would be warming up anytime soon. I would never understand how she could have iceberg hands when it was ninety damn degrees out.

"B-R-A-D-E-N, that's it. It shouldn't take you an hour," I continued.

"No, Mama, fix that 'R.' It doesn't look right," Braden added.

"Oh, you're right, sweetie," Raegan cooed.

"Can we let the man do his job now?"

"Almost . . ." I felt her dragging the pen across my skin. "There! It's perfect." She clapped her hands and moved to sit directly in front of me.

I was straddling the chair and leaning over the back. Raegan smiled brightly when we finally sat face-to-face. Kate sat on her right, looking both worried and uncomfortable. It was Braden that made me chuckle, though, because I had never seen him smile so much in the entire year I had known him.

"Smile, Kit Kat." I grinned at her.

"Will it hurt, Daddy?" her little voice asked.

"Dad is strong; he won't cry!" Braden chimed in, while flexing his muscles.

"I can handle it, Kate. Besides, it's time for Braden to join you, right?"

She nodded her head but still looked concerned. Braden was bouncing in his seat, and Raegan mouthed "Thank you" to me. As if she had to thank me—these three were my whole entire world.

I tried not to think about my life a year ago and how lost I'd been without them. I hadn't known if Kate was alive or dead, and I had no idea that Raegan and Braden would one day be such a huge part of my life. Now I loved them so much it hurt—literally.

I almost cringed when the needle touched the back of my neck, but I was able to maintain a stoic yet relaxed face in front of my anxious crew. After a few minutes of the buzzing sound across my skin, Kate finally let out a deep breath. I watched as she realized I wasn't being tortured and that this was something it was time to do for her brother.

Ash had once written Kate's name across the back of my neck. I wanted a piece of both of her parents to show my love for her. It was only right to do the same for my son. And Raegan needed to be the one to write his name.

My son. Those words still blew my mind.

The formal adoption papers had finally come in the mail this past week. Raegan had officially adopted Kate, and I had done the same with Braden. I wasn't surprised when Adam had readily terminated his parental rights, even though Rae had been worried we'd have to fight him. It wasn't hard to convince him, though. I put a little extra on his prison commissary tab and, just like that, he signed over his son. *Disgusting bastard.*

Our family was now legal. Raegan and I had gone to the court-house and said our vows not long after the whole Adam debacle. I'd protested and said that we should have a big affair because she deserved to be spoiled, but she swore up and down that wasn't what she wanted. All she wanted was to work on the adoptions, and we had to be married for that to happen.

My mom kicked my ass from New York to Texas when she found out I was married in a courthouse. She even traveled the fifteen hundred miles just so she could frown at me while she made me help her unpack. She and my dad bought a little house in the same town where we lived, after he retired from the force and joined the county sheriff's office to work alongside Mack. Mom would never let him putter around the house in retirement; they would drive each other nuts. I loved that they lived so close to us, and the kids loved having their grandparents nearby, who did everything in their power to spoil them rotten.

"You done back there?" I asked over my shoulder.

"Lane!" Rae hissed. "Do *not* rush him!"

"I'm antsy, babe."

"The plane doesn't even leave for another six hours. We can't get there any faster." She laughed.

"Maybe we could ask them if they have any flights going out sooner?" I asked, grasping at straws. She mouthed "No" to me, and I lowered my head back down to my chest in defeat.

"Dude, I can't believe you're getting a tattoo right before you head to the beach," Jace's voice called from behind me.

"Uhh . . . I have to advise against that," James, the tattoo artist, said between the buzzing sounds of his machine.

"I'll be fine." I shrugged it off without actually moving my shoulders.

"Yeah, my dad is strong!" Braden cried out. I reached out my fist and bumped knuckles with the little dude.

My front door opened and closed a few more times, and I knew the whole gang was here now. I paid the tattoo artist extra to come to the house. I didn't feel right about taking Kate and Braden to a tattoo shop. There was no telling what the other artists would be tattooing or piercing on their clients. The kids weren't old enough for that stuff yet.

"Hey!" Audrey called out. She walked into my view and held out her arms for Braden. "It's the big day, huh?"

"Yeah! That's my name, Aunt Audrey. It's gonna be there for-ev-er!" I loved how he had enunciated that last word.

"That's right, you're stuck with me for the rest of your life, bud," I said.

"Hey, doll, guess what?" Braden asked. The whole room burst into laughter. Braden had taken to using my nickname for her a few months ago, and it still made us all laugh.

"What, love?" Audrey responded.

"Mama and I get new last names now! I get to be Braden Parker!" he cried.

Braden really had opened up and was becoming quite outgoing, just like his sister. Who, by the way, was currently cuddled up in Jaxon's arms. Those two had built a pretty solid bond, and anytime they were both in the same room, she suckered him into holding her until I would finally have to go steal my daughter back.

"That's right, buddy, your mom is finally admitting who she belongs to." I eyed Raegan playfully and tried to tamp down my libido. When Raegan and I had said our vows, she decided not to take my last name until Braden could officially have it as well. I couldn't argue with the idea of not leaving Braden behind, but I also couldn't help the caveman inside of me that wanted his woman to be branded with his last name. When I thought about her being

Raegan Parker, I needed to rip her clothes off and christen the marriage all over again.

"I think the tattoo around her ring finger pretty much covered that for you," Audrey said, laughing.

I looked down at the ink around my own ring finger and smiled. I'd proposed to Raegan less than a week after we left the hotel, but I didn't have a ring ready because I wanted her to pick it out.

She hadn't had any freedom to make choices for herself during the years that she was gone. So every chance I got, I wanted her to be able to have the option to choose things for herself. I remember frowning when she told me she didn't want a ring because she would more than likely lose it.

What she did ask for made me smile like crazy, though. She wanted to be branded. I jumped at the opportunity to do the same for her. Wrapped around our left ring fingers were the words, *I Promise.*

She didn't have enough skin on her body for me to mark all of the promises I had made to her. All the promises I would keep. And if for some reason someone forced me to break those promises, Raegan knew that I would fight like hell—I would take on the world, if need be—to keep my family safe and happy. They were my everything.

". . . build sand castles, and go swimming, and eat cake, and go sporkeling." I heard Kate chatting Jaxon's ear off.

"You mean snorkeling?" he said with a laugh. She nodded her head and he said, "I can't wait!"

James patted my back and mumbled, "Finished." He turned toward his black bag and began efficiently packing everything away. "Keep it covered from the sun, out of the water, away from sand, blah, blah, blah. I doubt you'll listen to anything I'm telling you, so more than likely I'll see you in a month for a redo." He shrugged. I had a feeling he didn't care because that was more money for him.

"Thanks, man." I laughed.

"Is everyone packed?" Raegan asked the group.

"Oh, keep rubbing it my face!" Quinn's annoyed voice called out. I found her leaning against Cole's chest, and he chuckled at her discomfort. His hands reached forward and rubbed her bulging belly. "Y'all really should have told me eight months ago you were planning on going on an awesome trip together . . . before I had unprotected sex with this guy." She pointed back to her husband.

"Hey, this is my son you're complaining about," Cole scolded, kneeling down to kiss her belly. "She doesn't mean it, buddy," he whispered.

Every once in a while, I thought about what Raegan would look like with a belly like that. I couldn't even imagine knowing that I had filled her with that growing life, but then I got worried because I already had a daughter and a son. How would I love another one as much as I loved those two? Surprisingly, Raegan had been putting these ideas in my head of maybe having a baby someday. I think Kate and Braden were breaking her down for a little brother or sister. I wanted whatever Raegan wanted, but that didn't mean it scared me any less. For now, I'd enjoy the perfection that is my family.

"Hey, this is *our* family vacation," Raegan chided. "Everyone else is just tagging along."

She might try to act cool in front of me and everyone else, but she was just as excited for this trip as I was. We had also invited our friends to join along. More babysitters meant more alone time with Raegan. We had been waiting a long time for this trip. The legal costs for Kate's and Braden's adoptions were pretty outrageous, and therefore we hadn't been able to take a family trip like I'd originally planned last fall.

Now, summer was in full swing, we had a resort booked in the middle of the Caribbean, and for six whole days we would be carefree and living the island life. No work. No school. No responsibilities. I could play with the kids all day and then play with Raegan all night. My kind of heaven.

"Babe," I heard Rae call out from down the hall.

"Yeah?" I asked, while crouching down so Braden could get a closer inspection of my new ink.

"I need your help for a second," she hollered back.

"You like it, buddy?" I asked Braden before standing fully upright.

"It's awesome, Dad."

"It's all for you, bud. You know I love you, right?" He nodded his head and repeated the sentiment back to me before he ran off to play with Kate.

I padded on bare feet down the hallway and found Rae in the laundry room, tossing some extra clothes into our suitcases. Her back was to the door, so I walked up behind her and slipped my hands around her waist.

"I can't wait to see you sprawled out on a beach chair with the sun kissing your gorgeous skin," I whispered into her neck.

"Lane . . ." she moaned. "I think you're more excited than the kids."

"That's probably true," I chuckled. "Come on! It's our first family vacation . . . this is epic!"

"You're adorable," she said, giggling. "Okay, let me have my turn to look at it. Turn around, please."

I spun around and once again crouched, so she could see the back of my neck. Her finger danced around the tattooed skin, not touching the new ink but getting close enough that I could feel her appreciation.

"I love it," she whispered.

"Baby, I love you guys so much."

"Hey, guess what?" Her tone changed so quickly that my eyebrow automatically cocked in question. "I accidently overheard Jaxon and Em talking earlier."

"You were eavesdropping?" I laughed.

"I didn't mean to! But guess what? He asked her if she packed her birth control for the trip." I had an idea where this was going. "And she said no!" she whisper-shouted in excitement. Raegan had recently jumped on the get-Em-pregnant train with Audrey and Quinn. Girls were funny creatures.

"We knew it was coming, babe." I smiled at her excitement, even though I'd known it wouldn't be too much longer. Ever since Jaxon had laid into Adam that day in the parking lot about how he would worship the ground Em walked on if she were carrying his child, he had become more and more open to the idea of kids. I actually wondered if he wasn't the one now trying to convince Em they were ready, but I wouldn't tell Raegan that.

I dipped down to take her lips against mine. The soft plump of her lower lip pushed in and I gently grazed my teeth across it. She whimpered as my hands pulled her in closer to my body.

I pulled back and said, "This past year, babe—it's been the best year of my life."

"It's been a pretty good one," she replied casually. I tickled her for that and she shrieked, but I didn't let up until she breathlessly said, "Okay, okay! Best . . . year . . . ever!"

"Damn straight." I gently nipped at her lip. "Can we please leave now and try to catch an early flight?"

"No, Lane!" she laughed. "Do you have any idea how hard it would be to change tickets for eight adults and three kids? Impossible. You'll just have to be patient," she chided.

"We can meet everyone else there. I mean, just the four of us go early."

"You're as bad as a little kid waiting to go to Disney World."

I smirked. "You in a bikini for six glorious days *is* my Disney World, babe."

"Get out of here and let me finish our packing." She shoved me toward the door with a grin on her face. As I was heading down the hall, she poked her head out and shouted, "Oh, and put your shirt back on! I don't need Em ogling your body anymore."

I laughed and Em shouted, "You can't keep him clothed this entire trip, my dear friend. I'll get my eye candy, don't you worry." She winked at me and Jaxon rolled his eyes.

I slipped a gray tank over my head, one that dipped down enough around the neck not to rub my tattoo. I plopped down on my couch and watched my front door open again as Charlie walked in with Jace's secretary, Josephine. Raegan and I apparently had an open-door policy in this house, since no one seemed to bother knocking anymore.

"Charlie!" Kate shouted. "You're going to the beach too?"

"Sure am, babe." He lifted his suitcase to show her the evidence.

Charlie still worked for the force up in New York, but he seemed to be venturing down south more and more these days. I invited him and Mateo along on our vacation because I wanted to thank both of them. Those two guys were crucial, not only in my mission to find Kate, but in helping me maintain my sanity. Charlie was on the case every second he could be, always keeping me up-to-date when he received new information. He became my eyes and ears, and I would never be able to thank him enough.

Mateo had helped me navigate the underground fight clubs, and he played a critical role in helping me keeping tabs on Flores. Even though I wasn't able to bring Kate back on my own—I had Rae to thank for that—Mateo had been there every step of the way, willing to assist me at the drop of a hat.

Unfortunately, he had to decline our invite since he was already on another case, helping to try and bring another family back together. The guy was good to the core. He did, however, accept my gift of a pricey bottle of whiskey and said that maybe he would be able to catch us on our next trip.

Recently, Charlie had taken a liking to Jace's secretary, whom he met a few months ago when he came down to see us. Josephine was tagging along on the trip as well. Charlie said it was just so he wouldn't be the odd man out in a group of couples, but the way they were holding hands and giving each other lovey-dovey eyes told me it was probably a little more than that.

"Yeah, Kate, Charlie's gonna babysit you and Braden every night so I can take Mama out," I bellowed.

Charlie shot me a glare and quickly turned his charming smile back to my daughter. "I'd never pass up an opportunity to hang out with you, little lady."

Raegan finally made her way back into the living room and sat down on the couch next to me. Her head rested on my chest, and I brushed my fingers through her long, silky hair. Everyone else eventually wandered into the living room, finding a spot wherever they could. Braden sat down on my leg, and Kate crawled up onto Raegan's lap.

This was my family. Everyone in this room I happily called my family. We didn't have the same blood running through our veins, but that didn't mean we loved one another any less. Every one of us would go to the ends of the earth for one another. This was the life I had always wanted for my new family. I never knew it was possible for a group of people to mesh together in the most randomly wonderful way, but I loved them all.

Especially the three squeezed in around me. The little boy in my lap who exuded the same fierce sense of protectiveness for his family that I did. The little girl who could bring us all to tears with laughter on a daily basis. And the beautiful woman next to me, who radiated strength, determination, and the deepest love I had ever felt. They were the ones I would fight for every day.

A little over a year ago, I was wallowing in my own misery. I was convinced it was time to finally move on, and that what I wanted just may not be obtainable anymore. But life was a funny bastard. Sometimes it gave you what you always wanted, and then it liked to throw in a little extra you never knew you needed. Call me greedy, but I wanted it all. And I'd be damned if it was going to be taken from me again.

ACKNOWLEDGMENTS

From the bottom of my heart, a huge thank-you goes out to my proofreader, S. G. Thomas. You answer my late night e-mails, you are so dang picky, and you keep me on my toes. You clean up my grammar and make sure I don't switch to some weird tense. You are definitely a ball-buster. It should go on your business card! You are one of a kind, and I'm so glad we found each other through *Beautiful Broken Rules*. You make my story stronger, and you understand my characters almost as much as I do. Please don't ever leave me!

To my writing group, AS101, I am extremely grateful for your endless help. Especially Brooke Cumberland, who without a doubt is the nicest person I have come across in this writing world. You never stop helping, and I just hope that we can all return the favor in some way.

To all the bloggers who send messages and support my books, a million thank-yous would never be enough.

And, of course, to my husband. You do it all and then some. Every girl deserves a guy like you in her life.

ABOUT THE AUTHOR

Photo © 2014 Zachery Parr

USA Today best-selling author Kimberly Lauren started out life as an avid reader. Inspired to challenge the more traditional relationship roles she came across while reading romances, she decided to write the scintillating and celebrated new-adult series Broken. She currently resides in Texas with her husband, their son, and their three dogs.